MILTON PARK

RUSSELL COOPER

RED BALLOON PRESS

For mum and dad

If You're Going Through Hell, Keep Going

— WINSTON CHURCHILL

A NOTE TO MY DEAR READERS

Dear Reader,

On a warm summer's evening in Somerset, I listened to Joy Lofthouse tell her wartime story to a small village gathering over tea and jam sponge. The passion and enthusiasm had not abated from the nimble eighty-something-year-old Spitfire pilot from the 1940s.

Joy relived her exploits with a dry wit and a sparkle in her eye, and it made me think, how would I have coped? She flew every aircraft from RAF's bomber and fighter command while battling her emotional grief. Her husband was a POW in Stalag Luft III and was part of the Great Escape.

I wrote Milton Park to celebrate the untold stories of brave women in World War Two before this extraordinary generation begins to slip, sadly from our lives.

For history boffins and military experts I will admit, I fictionalised the plot, but not the heroism. Maybe Britain didn't have the stomach to hear such stories about female bravery and sacrifice in the '40s. But we do now.

Thank you for picking up this book and following the stories and witty interchange of Florence, Alice, Mandy,

Rosie and Lizzie, and in some small way, I hope my characters represented the few, from our finest hour.

Happy reading,

Russell

<><><>

Once you've finished Milton Park I would appreciate if you left me a review on Amazon.

Get new release updates, and author news by signing up to my newsletter:

RussellCooperBooks.com/subscribe

CHAPTER 1

Berlin: New Year's Day 1940

The second-floor room was sparsely furnished with an old wooden desk and a narrow bed. Otto Flack perched on the edge of the lumpy mattress and received his final communiqué. Above the rat-a-tat hammer of the ticker tape printer, he heard his father's voice reverberate through the message from England.

He re-read the last three words and a few unwelcome, salty tears wound their way beneath the bandages and pooled under his chin. His father told him at the outset of the war that one of them, or both of them, wouldn't survive their duty.

Otto struck a match and lit the tail of the message. The paper curled inwardly and the words, *Good luck, son,* were barely visible as the slow-moving flame reduced the paper to ashes. There was no turning back, not now; not that Otto wanted to turn back from executing his father's plan.

Acrid smoke hung in the air. The only warm thing about the room was Otto's breath. He packed his brown leather suitcase. His time had come. He stepped outside into Berlin's cold winter and climbed into a compact black car parked behind the building. He pressed the starter button and a chorus of resistant mechanical coughs echoed through the alley. The battery, with hardly enough juice to start the car, succeeded on the third attempt and a black plume of exhaust belched into the night air, and the over-laboured engine burst into life.

The pretty hedgerows of the narrow country lanes were laden with snow. Otto didn't care for the hedgerows; he didn't care for much at all other than his father's plans. And for that, he had an unwavering dedication. There was no marching band or assembly of officials to accompany his send-off, just a cold car and a leather suitcase. Nobody witnessed his departure or recorded his intent to deliver a decisive victory for the Fatherland. He drove with one hand on the wheel while the other pulled his bandages apart just enough to see where he was going in the falling snow.

God knows he had a job to do.

The drive to the deserted airfield took on the form of a man on his way to the gallows. It was a silent, one-way ticket for a spy intent on ending the war with a single, knockout blow. The unlit airfield was as unwelcoming as the snow plains of Siberia. Otto eased his car through the gateway and drove towards an aircraft standing on the apron of the runway. A ladder leaned against the aircraft door. He grabbed his leather case and climbed into the belly of the aircraft. Inside, he ensured the black security blanket was securely pinned between his bench and the cockpit.

Through the small, steamed-up window, he could see the dispersal hut where the flight crew waited his signal. He flashed three bursts of light from his torch and the pilot and navigator appeared. They stamped their feet and blew into their cupped hands in a losing battle to keep out the cold. They tucked their chins deep into their flying jackets and walked, bent double, across the airfield to the aircraft.

The orders given to the Luftwaffe by Otto's father gave meticulous instructions not to engage in conversation with the single passenger on the only flight leaving Berlin for England on New Year's Day.

The crew climbed into the cockpit, and through the curtain, Otto heard the pilot switch on the radio and request permission for take-off.

The chatter to the tower was brief.

He heard gauges being tapped and switches being flicked in preparation of the night flight. He made himself as comfortable as possible on the bench and overheard the crew.

'What are you doing on your forty-eight-hour pass?'

'When we get back tonight, I'm taking my girl to a little guest house, so we can keep each other warm. How about you?'

'My mother hasn't been well, so I'll visit her. There's no girlfriend to keep me warm.'

Otto's concentration faded from the crew's chatter as he unravelled the blood-stained bandages from his face and held up a mirror to study what he saw looking back at him. It was a face he knew well, but it wasn't his.

His face had gone long ago.

He took a syringe from his suitcase and jabbed himself in the leg with a shot of morphine; enough to remove the pain from the surgery, but not enough to muddle his thoughts. He rubbed his chin and re-bandaged his face.

The propellers chopped through the bitter wind, and the cold metal aircraft struts vibrated and rattled every nut, bolt and rivet. A high-pitched squeal from the brakes was shortly followed by the first turn of the wheels. The aircraft picked up speed along the pitted runway until the wheels lifted off the frozen ground into the night sky.

Otto Flack's mission had begun.

This was his turn. This was his time. He'd spent the past twelve weeks undergoing extensive, facial surgery in readiness to serve Germany. He took a deep breath and closed his eyes, not to sleep, but to dream of what lay ahead.

The aircraft flew in the silent darkness above the clouds; only the tiniest sliver of moonlight lit the night sky. Three more hours of his old life remained, then a new beginning. And one which would alter the course of the war, and the fate of the world. Otto took a wooden box from his suitcase and laid the contents on the bench.

He sat and waited for the red light to indicate they were twenty-minutes from England's coastline. The all-important green light was his jump-light.

The low glow of the red light flashed on.

Otto changed into his insulated, alpine suit and buckled up his parachute.

He waited.

The aircraft dropped below the clouds and reduced speed. Otto looked out of his small window, England's coastline was featureless and unlit. The blackout was total. He attached the parachute's ripcord to the rail above his head and gave it a reassuring tug to check it was secure. He opened the hatch in the floor, and a blizzard of snow blew inside and swirled around the aircraft.

He pulled his goggles over his eyes and gripped his suitcase under his arm and sat braced on the lip of the hatch.

The green light flashed on and without hesitation, he fell into the dark abyss. The freezing wind cut into his face and bit into his raw flesh; his yells went unheard and his screams were lost in the turbulence. Otto's parachute twisted in the buffeting wind until it ballooned open, and he descended into England's emptiness.

He lived alone, worked alone, and predicted he'd die alone. Otto watched the shadow of the aircraft slip from view and he reached his mental count of thirty.

He waited.

The explosion ripped the aircraft from wing to tail. Otto had set the timer on the bomb to trigger when the aircraft climbed back into the clouds. The orange inferno bled through the darkness and illuminated Otto's alpine suit as he parachuted towards England. The fireball lit up the snow-covered hilly village of Friston which nestled neatly in the Sussex valley near the sea.

He watched the burning debris fall through the night sky to a watery grave in the English Channel and felt nothing; a vital trait for a wartime spy. Soft emotions of pity would only get you killed.

Friston village appeared to be draped in white sheets, thanks to the recent heavy snowfall. The only recognisable landmarks were the church tower and the snow-topped tombstones in the graveyard.

Otto guided his parachute beyond the church and out of view of the village. Twenty feet from the ground, he threw his suitcase into a snowdrift and readied himself. He thudded onto the snow and rolled sideways; he lay still listening for sounds, footsteps, shouts or anything.

Nothing—all was quiet.

He waited a further minute for torchlights to bounce off the trees.

Nothing. No barking dogs. Friston was deathly silent.

He dug with his hands. He buried his parachute and alpine suit in a snow hole. Otto would be in and out of

England before the snow melted.

The last time he visited Friston village was twenty-five years ago, and yet, everything looked the same. He picked up his suitcase and made his way along Church Road, and stopped outside 19b. He lifted the latch on the wooden gate, cursed the squeak and followed the path around the back of the cottage.

Otto removed a small cardboard box from his suitcase and hung it around his neck. He climbed into the woodshed and buried his case under a pile of logs. He stood next to the back door, and with his ear pressed firmly against the glass; he listened for movement inside.

All was quiet.

And, not uncommon for a cottage in a valley, the door was unlocked. Otto stepped inside and removed his shoes. The kitchen was tidy; fastidiously tidy. The evening's meal of fried bacon and potato clawed at the air. Two dinner plates, two knives, two forks and two teacups were stacked in the rack, and a pile of white towels was neatly folded on the kitchen table.

Otto took the spanner from the hook above the cooker and unbolted the gas cylinder. He filled the sink with cold water and soaked the towels, then opened the cardboard box around his neck and put his gas mask on. He placed the gas cylinder over his shoulder, grabbed the dripping towels and headed to the bottom of the stairs.

He positioned his feet at the far edge of each wooden stair to reduce the sound of creaking and climbed the staircase. Otto stood on the small landing and opened the bedroom door at the front of the house.

An old couple lay sound asleep like cosy fur animals, curled up together under a thick blanket. A raggedy overcoat lay on top of the covers, and still, their noses were red from the cold.

Otto liked the sleeping couple, Arthur and Doris Feathers, but they had to die, that decision had been made earlier by his father, and that was that. No going back, they had to die.

Otto wedged the wet towels under the door and at the base of the window. The bedroom was sealed up like a tomb. He sat on a wooden chair in the corner of the room, turned the gas cylinder on, and breathed through his mask.

And waited.

The sour gas was a quiet killer. Arthur and Doris didn't move, and they didn't choke or fight for air. They died silently, side by side. Otto checked for a pulse; there wasn't one. Their skin was cold. Their lives were over within a few minutes.

Otto took the gas cylinder and towels downstairs to the kitchen and loosely reconnected the gas line to the cylinder. Shoddy police work, from an overstretched and diminished police force, would ascertain that the old couple had died from an accidental gas leak. He hung the wet towels over the oven door.

Otto stepped outside and collected his leather case from the woodshed, went back upstairs and entered the second bedroom. He opened the windows, and a fresh breeze filled the room. All lurking remnants of gas had gone. He took off his gas mask and breathed in lungfuls of crisp, cold air.

The bedroom belonged to the old couple's son, Malcolm Feathers. The time-trapped room clung heavily to the past, unchanged since Malcolm was a young man living at home. A layer of undisturbed dust offered evidence that nobody had been in there for some time.

A photograph sat on Malcolm's dresser of four inseparable fellows from Oxford University with the world at their feet. The snap was taken from outside the Latin classroom on a warm summer's day; a different time, a different war.

Two of the students were dead, lost to the muddy carnage of the trenches during the First World War.

Otto lay on Malcolm's bed; his body ached and tingled as the adrenaline subsided. The throb and pulse of pain returned to his face. He unravelled the bandages and found only small spots of blood dotted on the white material. His surgery was healing. He injected a shot of morphine into his leg, enough of a hit to make him drowsy. His world slowed down as sleep pulled and tugged at him. Stretched out, he knew he would not be disturbed for the rest of the night. His final lucid thoughts were of his father. Not warm father-son moments, those had gone—instead he mentally ticked off the first entry of his father's mission list.

Kill Mr and Mrs Feathers: done.

Otto's fragmented thoughts were disjointed through the haze of morphine. The photograph on the dresser of the four students featured Florence. Seeing her face brought her, and her beauty to the fore. He'd denied his love for her back at university, by suppressing and shutting down his emotions. Otto's only wish was that his father hadn't ordered she must be killed. Outside the cottage, snow fell silently in the dark and covered his footsteps.

CHAPTER 2

Florence Fairweather pulled her fur-lined hood tightly around her face to shield herself from the bitter cold. A through-to-the-bone cold. The worst kind. She stood at the entrance to the airfield; it was a desolate, dark place located a few miles outside Paris. She was ready to fly home, back to England, and back to Henry.

Her Spitfire was covered in a fresh fall of snow. She clambered onto the wing and pushed the snow off with her bare hands. Her fingers burned like they did when she was a young girl playing in the snow. That was fun; this was not.

Florence fumbled with the clasp on the glass canopy and heaved it back. She climbed into the cockpit, and with a breathy sigh, strapped herself in the harness.

The blizzard swirled around the airfield and snowflakes stuck to the metal wings like white feathers to hot tar. Her take-off would be blind, and her navigation home would be on blind-faith.

Luck is what she needed. Luck; a lot of it.

Her fingers hovered over the starter button. She'd only

get one chance to start the engine; the conditions would see to it that she wouldn't get another.

Best not bugger it up.

Florence pushed the button and the engine coughed, staccato fashion. The exhaust barked a rich baritone roar, the only sound among the silent snowfall. The propeller stuttered once, then twice, then caught hold and cut through the cold thin air. Florence's spinning propeller was a comforting sight. She was going home. Her years of training kicked in which pushed aside her weather impeded indecision.

Come on, what's next?

Radio on, yes.

The blue glow from the dials lit up her face.

'Henry?'

A long moment passed before his voice crackled through.

'Florence, is that you? I can just about hear you.'

'Yes, it's me. I'm going to scram for home. Conditions here are getting worse.'

'Did you deliver the package?'

'Yes, safe and sound.'

'Our customer happy?'

'Yes, and so they bloody should be.' Florence steered her Spitfire into position for take-off.

'I'll be waiting at the airfield.'

'Thank you. We ought to drive to Oxford tonight.'

'Tonight! Are you crazy? You'll be lucky to land in this weather, let alone drive to Oxford.'

'We have a debrief with Winston at ten o'clock tomorrow morning. You know Winston, he hates to be kept waiting.'

'He'll wait for you.'

Florence reached inside her flight jacket and pulled out Henry's white silk scarf and lifted it to her face and breathed him in. Where she went, his scarf went. She accelerated across the frost-hard runway and climbed into the night sky.

'I can't see a damn thing in this storm,' she said.

'I suppose there's no point in telling you to slow down, is there?'

'No, none.' She used the back of her hand to clear the condensation from the windshield.

'Just get back in one piece.'

Florence pushed her Spitfire across the Channel.

She said, 'Henry, I need a piping hot cup of tea and a long bath.'

'I'll see to it.'

'And, one more thing?'

'Yes?'

'Let's drive to Oxford in the morning; I'm too tired to tackle any more snow tonight.'

'Splendid idea,' he said.

The early morning brought more cold.

'We need to get a move on,' said Florence. 'It will take us at least five hours to get to Oxford in this weather.'

Sir Henry blew cigarette smoke towards the ceiling. 'Is it still snowing?'

She peered through the bedroom curtains.

'No, but the roads look slippery. Let's grab an early breakfast before we shoot off.'

Sir Henry stubbed out his cigarette. He opened the bedroom door and they headed downstairs.

The Grand Hotel was quiet.

Eastbourne, a seaside town, didn't get too many visitors during the winter months; fewer when it snowed, fewer still since the outbreak of war. Florence and Sir Henry were the only guests in the restaurant.

A waiter, wearing a starched white jacket, an ankle-length

apron, and a scowl permanently stamped on his face, limped over to them.

On arrival, he blurted out,' We don't have eggs, bacon, jam or sugar.'

'I see,' said Florence. 'Do you have bread and tea?'

'Yes, but no butter, and the milk hasn't arrived, and what with the state of this weather, it won't.'

'Well, then, dry toast and black tea it is,' she said.

His scowl unchanged, the waiter turned and walked away, his limp more pronounced.

'I doubt if he was always miserable,' whispered Sir Henry.

'Why do you say that?'

'I see it all the time.' He lit another cigarette. 'The country is full of men his age, injured during the First War, unfit for this war, and now suffering from remorse as they're unable to do their bit for king and country.'

'He might just be miserable.'

'No, trust me, his life was ripped apart as a young man in some God-awful muddy trench in France twenty-five years ago during the last war.'

'My guess is that he's a miserable man with a limp,' she said. 'I'll ask him.'

'You're so competitive. Leave the poor man alone.'

'You started it.'

The waiter returned with a tray of tea and toast and placed it on the table. He spoke like a spy revealing a state secret, 'I found a small jug of milk and two lumps of sugar.'

'Marvellous,' said Sir Henry.

The waiter shifted his weight from one leg to the other, unable to stand still, the eternal problem of having only one good leg.

He said, 'I spooned a little of my wife's homemade blackberry jam onto your plate. It's delicious.' His faint smile was a testament to the tastiness of his wife's jam.

'You are a marvel,' said Florence.

He turned to leave, 'I'm sorry if I was short with you earlier.'

'That's quite alright,' said Sir Henry. 'We fully understand.'

'I fell off a ladder a couple of years ago and broke my hip, entirely my silly fault, but it plays up something rotten in this cold weather. My wife says I'm a grumpy old bugger in winter. Anyway, enjoy your breakfast.'

'What terrible luck,' said Florence. Her smile was far from hidden. 'Your wife's jam looks and smells fabulous. Please thank her for us.'

The waiter added, 'Would you like me to ask the valet to warm up your car in the garage?'

'Splendid idea,' she said.

The waiter limped away.

Sir Henry turned to her, 'You're going to be insufferable today, aren't you?'

'Probably—no; definitely.' She smiled at him until he smiled back. She spooned a dollop of jam onto a slice of toast, spread it to the corners and handed it to him.

Florence finished her breakfast first. 'If you grab our bags from the room, I'll bring the car to the front of the hotel and drive us to Oxford.'

Sir Henry stared at the ceiling for a moment. 'You know what Florence? Your flight back from France last night was dangerous enough.'

'Yes, and?'

'Well, blasting up to Oxford, with you behind the wheel of my new Bentley, will be far more treacherous.'

'Oh, nonsense, I hardly ever crash!'

'That's like saying the Titanic had a mostly successful maiden voyage.'

In the garage, Florence sat in the pale blue and silver

Bentley; it reminded her of Henry with its abundance of style and classic gracefulness.

She drove up the ramp and out onto the forecourt of the white-washed seafront hotel. Sir Henry waited for her with an overnight bag in his hand.

The daylight replaced the winter gloom and the first shoots of brightness pierced through the darkness to reveal the countryside's prettiness.

The Bentley's blacked-out headlamps offered only a meagre supply of light.

Florence drove at high speed.

Sir Henry knew she would. She always did.

'Why do you drive so fast?'

'It's hard to say.'

'We won't get there any quicker, you know.'

'Of course we'll get there quicker—twice as fast in fact.' Florence used her motor-racing skills to keep the Bentley moving on the ice. Anyone else would have lost control and mounted a wall.

'I've no idea what Winston wants to talk to us about,' said Sir Henry.

She fell silent for a few moments.

She said, 'I'm rather pleased he asked us to Oxford.'

Sir Henry reached out and touched her hand. 'I'm aware of the date.'

'Thank you for remembering what this day means to me.'

Florence raced the Bentley out of Sussex, through Surrey and picked up the route to Oxford.

She said, 'It was twenty-three years ago today; what a stupid bloody waste.' Florence only mentioned the loss of her husband, Douglas, on the anniversary of his death.

Sir Henry didn't interrupt.

She said, 'I struggle to remember how desperately sad I must have been back then.'

Florence took her time to let the words tumble out. Douglas, her late husband, had been a dashing Oxford graduate. He was fashionable and witty, and was suitably matched by Florence's adventurous soul.

They were Oxford's golden couple and were married for only six weeks when Douglas was machine-gunned down in no man's land on the second day of 1917.

Douglas died that bleak morning alongside Oliver Barrington, his closest friend from Oxford and fellow rower: two dead, from the four inseparable fellows.

Douglas and Oliver spent their university mornings rowing on the Thames at Oxford. They dreamt of Olympic gold, and the Oxford blues were certain of glory.

Florence fell hopelessly in love with Douglas, and in a small Oxfordshire church, Florence became Mrs Fairweather. Oliver Barrington, his rowing partner, naturally, was the groom's best man.

Six weeks later, the grim awfulness of the war had claimed the lives of her husband and Oliver Barrington. Their bodies lost to the mud of the sodden, bloody battlefield.

And then Florence met Sir Henry Pensworthy.

She held herself back from loving him for several years. He didn't push or pry. He gave her time to rebuild emotionally. And, it was his gentleness which gradually dissolved her grief-ridden bitterness towards the world.

Florence pulled the Bentley onto the gravel driveway in front of her former university. They stepped out of the car, and their breath spiralled into the chilly morning. The ornamental fountain had frozen over; the water caught mid-flow as if a still from a photograph album. The buildings were frosted white, and the neat green lawns lay hidden beneath a fresh dusting of snow.

Florence led the way into the hallowed hallways. The mid-morning lectures were in session for those students who remained over the festive term break.

She stood in front of a board lit by an overhead brass lamp and stared at the names of two rowers; her husband, Douglas Fairweather and his best friend, Oliver Barrington. Her finger traced over Douglas's name, knowing that somewhere in France his body had been interred in a blood-soaked, muddy grave. Momentarily, she felt connected to the past, and connected to Douglas.

A crisp, clear voice came from behind her, 'Good morning, Florence.'

She turned around and embraced the tall, smartly dressed man.

'How are you?' he asked.

'Cold, otherwise very well.'

Christopher Barrington was also in Oxford to meet Churchill. His dark suit, crisp white shirt and neat, unfussy silk blue tie matched his confident air.

He said, 'It means a lot to see you standing in front of our boys. Twenty-three years, where has the time gone?' Barrington didn't take his eyes from the gold-lettered names. 'I think about my boy, Oliver, every day. He would have been forty-four this year. Oliver and Douglas were such wonderful young men, and how they both adored you.'

Florence and Sir Henry followed him through the polished corridors. Barrington knocked on the Principal's door.

'Come in!' A voice bellowed out of the room into the hallway.

Barrington opened the door to the private chamber and thick aromatic cigar smoke filled the room.

Churchill stooped in front of an open fireplace and stabbed at the logs with a poker, and in response, the wood sparked and spat up the chimney.

Without turning, Winston said, 'Ah, Barrington, good of you to come.'

'Morning, Churchill.'

There was no tangible trace of friendship, but there was mutual respect between the two political heavyweights, not unusual in high-level Government circles.

Churchill replaced the poker in the basket and turned to face his arrivals.

'My dearest Florence, how are you? Henry, stand aside and let me take a look at the loveliest of all my friends.'

Florence ran over and gave him a warm hug. Churchill was a good hugger. He paced about for a few minutes, and finished his diluted whisky.

He said, 'I'm addressing the lunch assembly today in the main hall. I fear this war will rage on long enough to tear the lives of those young boys apart. Half of Britain's cream will be lost to another war, what an awful waste.'

A lady with a broad smile entered the room and handed Sir Henry a tray of tea and biscuits.

'Put it over there, Henry,' said Winston. 'Let me begin; we have limited time.' Churchill stood, his back to the fireplace with his hands clasped behind him.

Barrington, Florence and Sir Henry took their teacups together with a few biscuits and sat in well-worn chairs, arranged in a semi-circle.

Florence handed Winston a cup of tea and one of his favourite biscuits.

He said, 'It's no secret; the Germans are about to invade deeper into Europe. They have the means and desire.' He bit into the biscuit.

'That's not news, Churchill,' said Barrington.

Winston ignored the barb and continued. 'I'm hoping the French can hold out for a year, but I fear they'll surrender in the face of Germany's punishing assault. We know the French haven't the stomach for it.'

'That's a little harsh,' said Barrington.

Churchill spoke over Barrington, 'Once the Battle of France is over, we must brace ourselves for the Battle of Britain.'

'You really do say things which are so very wide of the mark. Germany wants Europe, not us.' Barrington spoke in a slow, ponderous way.

Churchill didn't react.

Winston said, 'We'll face a different proposition from the French offensive.' He picked up the poker again and waved it in the air as he made each point. He was conducting his mini-orchestra. 'The war in France will be on land, army to army, face to face. Nasty business. But our war, the Battle of Britain, will be in the air, airforce to airforce; our young fresh-faced RAF boys versus their Luftwaffe battle-hardened pilots.'

Barrington shifted in his chair. 'I would imagine the Prime Minister would hatch some sort of peace treaty with Germany by the time the war gets that entrenched, Winston. There is no need for you to worry about it all.'

Churchill snapped, 'Over my dead body. The cabinet is split, half of them side with the Prime Minister while the other half agree with me that we cannot do deals with Berlin. Not while Hitler is at the helm.'

'Half? It's not anything like half who agree with you. Nobody wants this blasted war. Only you!' said Barrington.

'There's only one thing for it, Winston,' said Florence. 'You'll need to become prime minister. A deal with Berlin is never going to end well for us, not ever.'

'Quite so,' said Sir Henry.

'Whether I'm the next prime minister or not, France will fall by June. Therefore, we must prepare for an air invasion.'

'So why the urgency to see us today? You're talking about being ready half a year from now,' said Barrington.

Churchill held the poker like a baton. 'Let me ask you, Barrington, what is the one thing the Germans don't have, that we have, that they want?' He crunched on another biscuit and the crumbs wedged in the folds of his waistcoat.

Barrington said nothing.

Florence raised her hand, 'Our Spitfire.'

'And the Nazis have a nasty habit of taking whatever they want,' said Winston. 'If we lose the Spitfire, we'll lose the Battle of Britain. If we lose the Battle of Britain, we'll lose the war, and if we lose the war, well, quite simply, we lose the world.'

'A little overdramatic, don't you think, even for you, Churchill?' said Barrington.

Winston stood and faced the fire. 'I can assure you, Germany want our Spitfire. Our job is to ensure they never get it.'

Barrington put his cup and saucer on the tray. 'What sort of evidence do you have?'

'Oh, absolutely none at all,' said Churchill. 'I heard a whisper, and I have a gut feeling. But, I've learned to listen to what my gut tells me.'

Barrington stood. 'You mean to tell me you've dragged me to Oxford, in these wretched conditions, because you have a gut feeling?'

'Well, yes, why ever not?' said Winston.

'Surely this could have waited until you returned to Westminster,' Barrington was openly unimpressed.

'I was wrong once before,' said Churchill. 'But that was a long time ago.'

'You've been wrong plenty of times, on many things, over

many years,' said Barrington. 'I need to get back to London.' He turned to Florence. 'I'm sorry for my outburst. I have enough to do in parliament without listening to Churchill's unsubstantiated overreactions.'

'It was lovely to see you. Have a safe journey back to London.' She hugged Barrington goodbye.

He stood at the Principal's door, and barked, 'Churchill, don't go peddling your drama-soaked stories around Westminster. We don't need you stirring the war pot. Stick to admiralty matters, where you belong.'

He pulled the door shut behind him.

'Gosh,' said Florence. 'I don't think I've seen him so agitated. The man was positively fizzing. What you said Winston, about Hitler wanting our Spits, was there any truth in it?'

He said, 'Absolutely, because it's what I would do if I were Hitler. I need you both to be on your guard.'

'Naturally,' she said. 'What about the whisper you heard?'

'The whisper was real enough.'

'Have you spoken to Prime Minister, Chamberlain, about this?' asked Sir Henry.

'The Prime Minister will step down from office soon; he'll have no choice. And the moment Barrington knows the PM is leaving office; he'll put his hat in the ring for the top job. And we can't have that, can we?'

'No, we can't,' said Florence. She refilled their teacups and handed out the last of the biscuits. They gathered around the fireplace with their heads close together. 'So, Winston, what do you want us to do?'

CHAPTER 3

London resembled a cheery Christmas card, and for all its splendour, it seemed impossible that Britain was at war.

And yet it was.

Malcolm Feathers picked up a photograph from his desk. Four bright Oxford university faces stared back at him. Two of them, his chums, Oliver Barrington and Douglas Fairweather, were gone, lost to the battlefields of January 1917. What might have been? Two brilliant minds. Their lives unfinished.

Malcolm's offices in Buckingham Gate were cold; unpleasantly so. Once his mother heard about the chilly conditions, she knitted him a long, blue woollen scarf and matching fingerless gloves. He made a fuss initially about wearing such an ensemble; his mother, as mothers do, won through, and he wore the scarf.

The shelves at Buckingham Gate buckled under the weight of books on aircraft design and the cupboards were crammed with blueprints and drawings. It was an odd mixture of tidy and messy, order and disorder. But it worked. Malcolm could put his hand on anything in an instant. The Spitfire, and all that it stood for, had become Malcolm's world: it consumed him, it was his war.

And he loved it.

A man born for routine, Malcolm walked the same way to work every day, he wore his black suit on Monday, Wednesday and Friday and his blue suit Tuesday, Thursday and Saturday. Routine for Malcolm was mathematical purity and no further thought was required.

The other two offices on the sixth floor of Buckingham Gate housed a group of engineers. Their complex work was responsible for repelling the Nazis from invading Britain.

The engineers were talented and hardworking who enjoyed a drink at the Old Star pub after work. Brenda, the barmaid, always had their pints of beer ready on the bar—just like clockwork—just how engineers liked it. The Old Star was a popular haunt of senior staff from Whitehall. If the German High Command knew how many heads of department from the war office frequented the pub, they could bomb half the war ministry in one go.

In the security of their offices, the engineers were comfortable huddled over a blueprint, and could talk long into the night about drag coefficients and power ratios, measurements and outputs.

Socially, they were awkward, painfully so, except one: Owen Black.

He was the polar opposite. A creative thinker, good looking, witty and a snappy dresser. An American from Charlotte, North Carolina, Owen Black had a Degree in Engineering. Malcolm Feathers and Owen became close friends from day one. They took long walks in Hyde Park, and would often call in to see Florence and Sir Henry at Horse Guards Parade.

Malcolm invited Owen Black to join his engineering

team at Buckingham Gate. Owen was enthusiastic about the work and was confident Britain would be safe from a Nazi invasion, as long as they were able to keep up aircraft production. Owen moved into Malcolm's spare bedroom in his apartment on Victoria Embankment. And, from there, each morning, they walked to work through St James's Park.

They grew close. And in secret they grew closer, inseparably so. Those few months of togetherness with Owen were Malcolm's happiest. To the outside world, they were a couple of fellow engineers who enjoyed a beer and a lively chat about how to beef up the Spitfire's performance. Behind closed doors, they were two people who cared deeply for each other and would spend late nights carving out their future together in a world without hostility.

The news of Owen Black's death hit Malcolm hard. He was utterly heartbroken. Malcolm had lost his closest, dearest friend, and since Owen's death, the love in his heart had drained away, leaving him alone in the darkness.

Owen's car had been hit by a fuel truck. Onlookers said the inferno was horrific. Malcolm needed time to recover, he didn't have time. He had a job to do, because Britain was at war. And yet, in an odd way, he didn't want to recover. For Malcolm to remain in a state of heartbreak meant he would be locked in an eternal cycle of grief with Owen. And a state of constant sadness was alright by him, but for the sake of the war effort, he had to bury his emotions and soldier through.

Overcoming his grief would have to wait. Owen's death changed everything; time surely would change nothing.

The knock on Malcolm's office door broke into his thoughts about Owen. Still clutching the photograph of the four Oxford fellows, he put it back on the desk.

'Cup of tea my lovely?' The rosy-cheeked tea lady said.

'Yes, please, thank you, Gladys.'

'I've saved you a biscuit. Those lads of yours next door would've eaten the lot if I'd turned my back on them.' She handed him a steaming cup of tea.

He took a sip, 'Oh, that's lovely.'

'You look like you've got the troubles of the world on your shoulders, Mr Feathers. A cup of tea will put everything right, just you see.'

'Thank you, Gladys, I hope so.'

'I'll come back in a few minutes and top you up.' She closed the door and pushed her rattling trolley along the hallway.

Malcolm stepped next door and asked the engineers to assemble in his office. A minute later they ambled through. Gladys brought the teapot back and topped up everybody's cup and handed out the last of the biscuits.

Without preamble, Malcolm said, 'It's vital we create more of an efficient assembly line, we need specialised hand-made parts in fewer locations spread out around the country.'

The engineers nodded and lit their pipes.

Malcolm rubbed his hands together to generate warmth.

He said, 'For example, the wiring loom is based eighty-two miles away from the main assembly plant. However, it's needed before the fuselage can be riveted. We can reduce build-time by tightening up those pitfalls. We'll need to rehouse some of the skilled workers or retrain a new team. I've identified the assembly bottlenecks we need to fix. Some of the machinery cannot be moved due to its size so we'll have to consider building new tooling machines from the ground up.'

The nodding continued as did the pipe smoking.

'We have to do this work without halting production by a single aircraft.'

Malcolm looked at his chief engineer, Fletcher.

'Fletch,' he said. 'Can you take charge of looking into these trouble spots?'

'Yes, of course,' said Fletcher.

'Good, come and see me Monday morning and we can go over your findings.'

'I'll get right on it.'

A police officer stood in the office door and tapped lightly on the glass. He cleared his throat. 'I'm looking for a Mr Malcolm Feathers.'

'I'm Feathers, how can I help you?'

The policeman stepped into the office. 'Is there somewhere I can talk to you in private, Mr Feathers?'

The engineers picked up their teacups and trouped back to their adjoining offices. The policeman closed Malcolm's office door.

'There is no easy way to say this, Mr Feathers and I'm sorry to be the bearer of this awful news. I'm afraid your parents have been found dead in their cottage in Friston.'

Malcolm stood in silence, and put his hands on his desk to support himself.

'Dead? How?'

'It would appear, from what the local police have told me, there was a gas leak, and your parents died in their sleep. I know it's of little comfort right now Mr Feathers, but your parents didn't suffer.' The policeman let a moment pass. 'Is there anybody I can contact for you?'

Malcolm thought about Owen Black, he needed Owen to console him. Tears welled up in his eyes, and an uncontrollable wave of sadness washed through him. The emotion was as much for Owen as it was for his parents.

He wanted Owen. But Owen was gone.

Malcolm's voice croaked, 'I have a close friend nearby—I can visit her.'

'That's good,' said the officer.

Malcolm, numb with shock, said, 'I'll take the train to Friston in the morning. I can be there by lunchtime. It's funny, my father was most particular about the gas cylinder.'

Malcolm's father would lean over the cooker in the kitchen, giving him precise instructions on the importance of nut and bolt tightening procedures. His mother would stand behind them with a fresh pot of tea.

She'd say, 'Our boy builds Spitfires for the RAF, dear, I think he can change a gas cylinder.'

The officer cut through Malcolm's thoughts, 'I regret my visit has brought such sad news to you.'

'I appreciate you coming to tell me.' He showed the policeman to the door and Malcolm took a second to look out across St James's Park, and the unchanged world.

Snow covered the grass, the lake was frozen over, children threw snowballs at each other, and soldiers guarded Buckingham Palace.

Malcolm's world had changed again.

He called Fletcher into his office and told him about his parents, and his plan to visit Friston in the morning.

'I'm going to see Florence at Horse Guards Parade, but let's still get together Monday morning and sort out these assembly logjams. We've so much to do and I'm counting on you, Fletch.'

Fletcher touched Malcolm's arm.

Malcolm grabbed his overcoat and scarf from the hook behind the door.

'Go and take care of your dear old mum and dad,' said Fletcher. 'I'll keep things ship-shape here.'

Malcolm wandered out into the hallway, locked his office door and put the key in his pocket. He stepped out of the building and made his way along Birdcage Walk and across the gravel yard at Horse Guards Parade. He climbed the staircase to Military Intelligence.

Alice Jones walked past the door at the top of the stairs. 'Hello, Malcolm, lovely to see you.'

'Good afternoon Alice, I was hoping to catch Florence, is she about?'

'She is, I'll tell her you're here.' Alice Jones wore comfortable tweed suits and sturdy brown brogues like a military uniform. She stepped into Florence's office.

'Malcolm is in reception. He wants to see you, and I think he's been crying. Maybe I should make him a cup of tea.'

'Come on through, Malcolm,' called Florence.

The biting wind had roughed up his cheeks, and his eyes welled-up to the point they overflowed.

'It's my parents; they're dead. It was some sort of gas leak the police think.'

Florence put her arms around his frame and held him tightly. He looked defeated and consumed by grief and was no more than an empty vessel. Maybe grief hadn't reached him yet, maybe it was shock before the grief. She hugged him some more.

'Malcolm.'

She whispered his name over and over.

'They died in their sleep,' he said. 'A policeman came to see me at my Buckingham Gate office a few minutes ago.'

She let him continue.

Malcolm gained a little composure. 'I'm going to take the train to Friston in the morning. I wanted to see you before I go.'

Florence looped her arm through his.

She said, 'Listen, you've had a tough couple of months; firstly, Owen, and now your mum and dad. If there's anything Henry and I can do, we'll be there for you. Let's grab a bit of air outside, I know it's freezing, but I have something to run by you. I'll grab my coat and get Henry.'

Rags, Sir Henry's golden retriever, barked with excitement at the prospect of going to the park again.

Alice walked in with a cup of tea, 'Drink this before you go, it will keep out the chills.' She put a slice of cake in Malcolm's pocket. She gave him a firm, yet reassuring pat on his arm.

In the park, they walked along a cleared pathway where the snow had been shovelled to one side. Rags jumped from deep drift to deep drift.

Florence picked her moment. 'Henry and I were with Winston yesterday. We planned to visit you to explain Winston's thoughts. Are you up to talking a bit of shop?'

He nodded.

'Winston feels the Germans are somehow planning to steal the Spitfire.'

'There's absolutely no need to worry about that; they don't need to steal one.'

'Why not?' asked Florence.

'Because they already have one.'

'They do?' said Sir Henry.

'Yes, they've shot down a few Spits that didn't explode on impact. So, I wouldn't be surprised if they've already reverse-engineered it. They could call it the Fritzfire!'

'Oh I say, that's very good,' said Sir Henry.

Malcolm stopped walking and faced them both.

He said, 'They couldn't mass-produce it without the Spitfire's sheet of code. It's a highly sophisticated aircraft, and they would need the code to mass-produce.'

Florence said, 'Winston believes they want to mass-produce it, and this is the big one; he believes they want to destroy our capability to build more of our own.'

'Britain not having the Spit puts a whole new slant on it,' said Malcolm.

Florence said, 'If we enter the Battle of Britain without it, we'll lose the war.'

'We wouldn't last a week,' said Malcolm.

She said, 'Listen, I want you to tighten security, and keep the locations of where the Spitfire parts are made top-secret. And hide that code! It's the one thing that will keep us from losing the war.'

'I'll see to it, Florence.'

'France will be in the thick of it any day, and we'll be next. The Bosch have every bugger on the run.'

Malcolm wrapped his scarf tighter around his neck.

He said, 'After the funeral on Sunday, I'll return to London Monday morning.'

She hugged him, 'Everything's going to be alright.'

He nodded.

'That Spitfire code is all that's stopping Germany from crushing us out of the war,' she said.

'I'll go straight back to the office and hide it. Nobody will get their hands on it, that's one thing I am certain about.'

Sir Henry looked up at the darkening sky, 'Let's go back to the office. Rags, come on boy, we are going in for some of Alice's fruit cake.'

CHAPTER 4

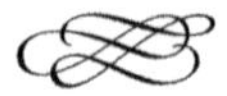

Malcolm Feathers stared through the frosted train window at the blurred white countryside rushing past. He pulled the slice of cake from his coat pocket, he wasn't hungry, and couldn't remember if he ate the day before. The cake brought a smile to his face as he remembered Alice Jones.

Malcolm adored her.

Alice was legendary within Military Intelligence for her wild inventions, but what he loved most was her no-nonsense fruit cake. Alice made things tick. His thoughts were a mild distraction from the pain that awaited him at Friston.

And then he thought about Owen Black.

Malcolm had fought in vain not to love Owen and to keep his emotional heart under control, but failed; he loved him wholeheartedly, and that was that.

Malcolm sat in a trance and surrendered to the memories of Owen Black. He gripped his slice of cake as heart-stabbing pains rode rough-shod over him.

Looking further back, Malcolm had attempted not to fall

in love once before. He failed then too.

At Oxford, he felt the same unstoppable urges towards one of the 'four'; Oliver Barrington. Malcolm's animal instinct was raw and unrestrained. He didn't know how to repel or contain his feelings, so he worked. Working was better than admitting his love for Oliver.

He took daily cold showers as if in some way his attraction towards Oliver Barrington could be scrubbed away. When Oliver died in the trenches in the 1914-1918 war, Malcolm's emotions spiralled downwards into a dark pit of loneliness. And now, openly, he could cry for the loss of two men, Oliver and Owen. Everyone would assume his tears were for the loss of his parents. And they were.

His train rattled towards Eastbourne, and the crumbs from Alice's cake gathered in his lap. Tears dripped off his face into the crumbs.

At Eastbourne station he waited for his connecting train to the village of Friston and watched the snow settle on the tracks. Malcolm welcomed the cold as if there was a chance the bleakness might remove the dull ache from his soul. The train arrived, and he stepped into the carriage.

After he left Florence and Sir Henry in St James's Park the day before, he ran back to his Buckingham Gate office and hid a code of significant value. A single page of numbers, dots and dashes: codenamed 12g295. Without this page of complex code, the Spitfire couldn't fly. Malcolm felt a sense of calm, his duty completed. The 12g295 code, and the Spitfire, were safe. His duty was fulfilled, and no matter the effort the Luftwaffe made they would not be able to mass-produce the Spitfire without the code.

The train made its couple of stops and Malcolm exited Friston station. He wore heavy boots in preparation for the trek across the snow-covered fields. He trudged through the drifts and headed towards the church spire which lay just beyond his parents' home. He was emotionally empty and had cried himself out of tears. The freshening air rouged his cheeks. He climbed over the fence in the churchyard into Church Road.

Malcolm stood outside 19b and breathed in a history of memories. There was only silence, no chatting neighbours, no barking dogs, no cars, and no children playing outdoors.

He put his hand on the gate latch. The squeak of the spring was as reliable as night follows day. He walked up the pathway, opened the door, and stepped inside to the familiarity of home, the smells, the worn paint on the door. He was home.

Otto Flack watched Malcolm Feathers standing outside the cottage through the curtains from Doris and Arthur Feathers' bedroom. The gate spring squeaked, the key turned in the lock, followed by feet stamping off the snow from heavy boots. The front door closed and Otto heard Malcolm sigh as he hung up his scarf and overcoat.

Otto had eaten bread and a tin of salmon from the pantry. The alarm was raised when Arthur hadn't shown up for work at Denton's, the local hardware store in Friston village. Doris was the treasurer of the Women's Institute, and when she didn't appear in the morning at the church hall, the police investigated. Otto spent two uncomfortable days in the woodshed and watched the fumblings of the local police. He couldn't have made it easier for them. He left enough clues.

Otto could hear Malcolm downstairs in the kitchen, making a cup of tea. The wooden staircase creaked as Malcolm stood on the first step. Otto counted the footsteps as Malcolm climbed the stairs, crossed the landing, and stood outside the front bedroom door.

. . .

On the landing at the top of the stairs, Malcolm put his hand on the bedroom door handle and hesitated for a moment. His parents had died in their bed and a part of him didn't want to go in to say his final goodbye. Another goodbye.

He entered. The crack on the back of his head caused him to instantly black out. He lay, spreadeagled on the bed, his hands and feet tied to the four corners of the bed frame. His senses, one by one, began to register. He opened his eyes and the pain thumped through his head. His mouth was gagged tightly, and metallic traces of blood hit the back of his throat.

Malcolm stared up at the ceiling, and thoughts bombarded his consciousness and cluttered his ability to think coherently. The throbbing pain pulsed over him as he fought back rising nausea. The curtains were closed. The room was dark and there was nothing to see. He strained his ears, but there was nothing to hear.

How long had he been unconscious? Was it night or day? He couldn't tell.

The bedroom door opened.

A man with a bandaged face stood in the doorway. Malcolm's eyes followed him as he stepped into the room and sat on the bed.

The man spoke, 'Hello, Malcolm, my old friend.'

Malcolm didn't move.

'It is good to see you again, although I didn't want it to be like this. But, there's no other way.'

Malcolm didn't move. He couldn't move.

The man reached out and removed Malcolm's gag.

Malcolm opened his dry mouth. A hundred questions filled his head, but he failed to ask any.

The man started to slowly unravel his bandages.

He said, 'My name is Otto Flack, and I need something of

yours.' He continued to remove the bandages and winced as a piece of skin caught in the dressing. 'Malcolm, You can't imagine the pain I've been through to change my face. The surgery was a little primitive, but the results, I think you'll agree are most effective.'

Malcolm watched him remove the last of the bandages. He looked at the man's face. Malcolm's chest and throat constricted; he couldn't breathe deeply enough, such were the restrictions—the weight of a mountain crushed him. Malcolm snatched shallow mouthfuls of air. He grew light-headed and fainted.

Malcolm felt his face being slapped, and his eyes blinked open.

'You haven't guessed yet, have you? Can't you see who I am?'

Malcolm stared at the man's features in utter bewilderment. His mouth formed dry words.

He said, 'You . . . you look like me.' He snatched at another breath. 'You look exactly like me.' Malcolm's eyes traced across Otto's face and his voice sank to barely an audible level, 'Why would you do that?'

Otto imitated Malcolm's voice, 'I've been close to you for a long time, long enough to get everything I want from you, and from this moment on, I am Malcolm Feathers.'

Malcolm stared back, his lips moved, but he was unable to produce sound.

Otto sat up straight as if to play the piano, 'This should help. Maybe, if I spoke with an American accent, you might understand better.' Otto switched his voice to a North Carolina accent. 'Do you recognise me now? Do you know who I am when I speak like this?'

Malcolm mouthed the name, 'Owen Black.'

'A bit louder, Malcolm, say my name louder.'

'You sound like my friend, Owen Black.'

Otto shook his head slowly, 'You just aren't getting this are you?' Otto pointed at his face, 'I was Owen Black, and now I'm you.'

'No, no, no, this isn't happening.' Malcolm looked away to shut out the confusion.

'Malcolm, I lived with you in your apartment in London, as Owen Black. I studied you, right under your nose. I staged Owen's death. The fuel truck was a nice touch because there was no body to identify.'

Malcolm roared and tugged at the ropes.

Otto said, 'I slipped back into Germany the day after Owen's funeral and underwent the first of many facial surgeries to become you. And look at me now, I'm you, I'm Malcolm Feathers, Head of Production for the RAF's Spitfire.'

Malcolm couldn't form a cohesive thought.

Otto said, 'I spent all those months as Owen Black, getting close to you. I let you do those things to me, despicable things that repulsed me.'

Malcolm's tears rolled down his face.

Otto said, 'Do you know why?'

Malcolm shook his head.

'I had to get into your office at Buckingham Gate to steal the Spitfire codes and blueprints. And what better way of doing that, than for you to invite me in. I walked right through the front door as Owen Black virtually hand in hand with you.'

Malcolm sobbed, and his chest heaved.

'I was close to getting everything I needed. Berlin needed one more thing to win the war, the 12g295 Spitfire code, but I couldn't get my hands on it, so eventually, I had to become you to get what I needed for Germany.'

Malcolm's fight left him.

Everything he knew had no meaning.

His memories swirled around in foggy circles. Images flooded his mind of him and Owen overlooking the Thames from his balcony, walking in the park, and working side by side. All sodding lies, bloody sodding lies.

Malcolm watched Otto open a cardboard box and put a gas mask over his face, then reach beside the bed where a gas cylinder stood.

The hissing sound sharpened his senses.

He watched Otto place wet towels under the windows and at the foot of the door. It dawned on him that the bedroom had been turned into a gas chamber. Did his parents face the same evil? His wrists started to bleed as he yanked and tugged hard against the ropes.

Otto moved close to his face, 'I'll walk into your office and take what I want, and nobody will suspect a thing.'

Malcolm's eyes darted from left to right. He whispered, 'There's not a chance in hell you'll get away with it.'

Otto snarled, 'I'll walk out of your office with the code in my pocket.'

The sour gas filled Malcolm's lungs and he began to cough and choke. His eyes bulged and streamed and his mouth opened and closed.

Otto held up the photograph from Malcolm's bedroom of Oxford's inseparable four. 'Can you see this?'

Malcolm's head flopped and his eyes closed.

'Look at the photo! You still don't see it, do you? At your parents' funeral on Sunday, I'll be standing next to the lovely Florence Fairweather, she'll console me, and I'll wrap my arms around her as your dear mum and dad are lowered into the ground.'

Malcolm's whispers grew fainter, 'You'll never find it.' He smiled up at Otto, 'You're already too late.'

Otto yelled through his gas mask. 'What do you mean, I'm already too late? What do you mean?'

Malcolm didn't speak again.

His tears stopped. His thoughts stopped. His rasping breaths stopped. His pulse stopped. His world stopped. His heart stopped.

Malcolm Feathers was dead.

And Malcolm Feathers was alive.

Otto turned off the gas and opened the windows and removed his gas mask. The cold air refreshed the bedroom. He untied Malcolm and stripped him naked and dressed in the dead man's clothes. He took a pair of scissors from his pocket and cut his hair to match Malcolm's. He looked in the mirror and admired his work.

Otto worked efficiently.

He ripped up the carpet from the landing and carried Malcolm from the bed and rolled his body in the dense weave. He tied rope around each end of the carpet roll and dragged it downstairs, then propped it up against the back door. He wrapped Malcolm's blue scarf around his neck and put on Malcolm's heavy coat.

It was four-thirty on Thursday afternoon, and Friston was quiet. The midwinter sunshine was losing the last of its light, and the evening was drawing in. It would be dark in an hour.

Otto needed a vehicle, he had a body to hide.

He walked into the village and stopped outside Denton's hardware store and took a deep breath. This would be his first test at being Malcolm Feathers.

He pushed the door open and walked in.

'Oh Malcolm, my dear boy.' Mr Denton walked out from behind the shop counter, 'What a terribly sad day. Your parents were such a popular couple in Friston. I'll miss them. We're all in a state of shock.'

'Thank you, Mr Denton. I arrived a little early so that I could spend some time in the cottage. I wanted to come in and thank you for alerting the police when my father didn't show up for work.'

There was not a flicker of doubt on Denton's face.

Malcolm's father had worked at the store for over thirty years, and Mr Denton had known Malcolm since he was a young boy.

'May I ask a favour, Mr Denton?'

'Of course.'

'Would it be an inconvenience to borrow your delivery van for a few hours this evening?'

'Is there anything I can do to help you?'

'Oh that's most kind, but really, there's no need. I'll bring the van back after you've closed this evening. I'll pop the keys through the letterbox.'

'Take all the time you need, son. I'm not going anywhere in this weather. Make sure you drive carefully, the roads are slippery. And if I don't see you before, then I'll see you at the funeral on Sunday. And remember, anything you need Malcolm, just come and ask.' Denton shook Otto's hand, 'I still can't quite believe your parents have gone.'

Otto didn't concern himself with Denton's flush of condolence, it meant nothing. His only concern was to deceive the old man.

Otto drove the small delivery van to the rear of 19b Church Road. He went inside the cottage and pulled the carpet out through the back door. A quick check that nobody was looking, then Otto shifted the carpet towards the vehicle. He heaved the roll into the back of the van, shut the rear doors and climbed behind the wheel.

The conditions were worsening, and the roads glistened with black ice. He drove the few miles to the coast and selected a quiet spot at the pebble beach.

In the fading light, Otto spotted a rowing boat at the water's edge. He opened the rear doors of the van and lifted Malcolm's body onto his shoulders and marched across the wet pebbles.

Otto had trained hard, for years, in all weather conditions. The German Military pushed him, starved him, hunted him, and put him under intense pressure so he could survive behind enemy lines, far beyond human limits. In him, they'd created a ruthless killing machine, and a survivor. They drilled into him to bury his emotions deep into his soul when taking a life.

Otto reached the rowing boat and pushed it into the cold water with his foot. The body slumped into the middle of the boat and Otto grabbed the oars. Half a dozen hard pulls and the rowing boat began to move through the dark sea. The frozen air found its way through Malcolm's blue scarf and into Otto's lungs. His hands grew raw from the unforgiving salty spray, and his coat turned white from the snow.

Otto rowed beyond the headland and pulled the oars into the boat. The waves sprayed over him as the boat, in danger of capsizing, tossed about in the turbulent swell. He grabbed Malcolm's body and balanced the carpet roll on the side of the boat. He leaned backwards and rammed his heels into the carpet; he pushed with his feet and kicked it overboard.

And with a splash, Malcolm was gone.

Otto was Malcolm.

He rowed back to shore. His arms burned and ached from the cold. He clambered up the pebble beach to the van, started the engine and headed back to Friston.

Otto had a funeral to prepare, and Florence would be there. She was next on his father's list.

<><><>

CHAPTER 5

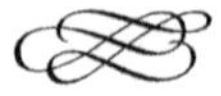

Florence stood between Sir Henry and Churchill at Ten Downing Street.

'You should be Prime Minister,' whispered Florence. 'I would vote for you.'

'I doubt I'll even be considered,' Churchill said. He puffed on his cigar and the smoke circled above his head.

Sir Henry, nudged Florence, 'Try not to provoke anyone this evening. This room is full of people who are desperate to broker a peace deal with Germany.'

'What utter poppycock,' she said. 'Any deal is worthless, and the sooner this room of dusty, old buffoons know it, the better.'

'Quite so, Florence,' said Churchill. 'Hitler didn't spend the last ten years, building up his military muscle to spread peace. No, he wants domination, and we need to defend ourselves. However, Henry is right, don't provoke anyone tonight.'

'Why not?'

'Because that's my job!'

Christopher Barrington, the war minister, entered the

room, 'Gentlemen, good evening.'

Winston cleared his throat and caught the attention of Barrington and pointed his cigar at Florence.

Barrington corrected himself, 'Good evening gentlemen and good evening, Miss Fairweather. Please, everyone be seated wherever you can.'

The floor above the cabinet room housed an eighteen-seater oval table, and a century of beeswax polishing gave it a flawless reflection. The barricaded windows provided wisps of light and the air was smoke-stale.

Thirty-six people crammed themselves into the seats. Military leaders, cabinet ministers, strategists and civil servants wedged in together.

'This is how I like it,' said Churchill.

Florence lifted an eyebrow, 'Like what?'

'Uncomfortable as buggery.'

'Why?'

'It'll be easier to raise the temperature in those pinstriped corpses sat around the table.'

The hubbub subsided.

At the head of the table, Barrington shuffled his papers. He began, 'I'm preparing a statement for Berlin.' He waited for the members to concentrate on his next eight, vital words. 'I'm extending Britain's hand of peace to Germany.'

Churchill drew heavily on his cigar and looked at the assembled men. He noted a common denominator, one of lost hope.

They, in turn, viewed Churchill as a warmonger.

Churchill stood in response to Barrington's opening comments, and the room fell silent. He cleared his throat and held his lapels. 'I know what you are thinking. You assume I want war. Well, I don't, I want peace, but not the peace Hitler offers. We would merely be a puppet state dancing to his demented tune. Any peace deal would be at the convenience of Berlin.' He paused and drew once more on his cigar. 'And, while we spend time idly brokering a futile peace plea, we waste precious time arming ourselves to protect this island.'

Whispers of discontent reverberated around the room.

Churchill continued. 'As we dither, Germany will continue to crush Europe, and while we prepare pointless peace documents, Germany grows more powerful. We must build our forces in the air, on land and at sea. We must transform Britain into an impregnable, iron fortress. Because, if Britain falls, then Europe will fall. And if Europe falls, the rest of the world will fall under a Nazi regime. Germany believes the Third Reich will last a thousand years, I say we kill it now, in its infancy.' Churchill studied the tired faces. 'Gentlemen, you look defeated. If you don't have the appetite to fight, you must make way for those who do. But, be under no illusion, we face a long, brutal, bloody war. But a long, brutal, bloody war is infinitely better than a millennium of Nazi rule under the warped pretence that we are at peace.'

The murmuring grew louder.

Barrington looked at Winston and waited for silence. 'You are whipping up an unnecessary storm, Churchill. We are going to courier a document to Berlin, via Italy, outlining our demands for a peaceful resolution. We can't have you running around Parliament, frightening everyone into thinking England is about to be invaded by German paratroopers.'

Churchill interrupted.

'Barrington, my words are not without merit. France will fall. And remember, we are not the aggressors, we are the defenders; this is not theory: we are already at war. We must never surrender. If we do, history will define us in a most unkindly fashion. This is not the time to seek peace. When this war grips the world, and it will, we will be viewed as spineless men who threw in the towel without a fight.

Britain needs robust moral strength, and must, at all cost, face up to the impending, darkening terror.' Churchill drew heavily on his cigar, and silence filled the room. 'Now is not the time to raise the white flag. We must not succumb to Nazism and its evil experiments. We must not fail our future generations. We must not slump in defeat without raising our fists to fight.'

Christopher Barrington made a gesture to suggest Winston had been drinking. 'Save us the amateur dramatics, Churchill. Look around you, the cameras aren't rolling, and the wireless sets are not broadcasting your babbling rhetoric. Our responsibility is to save Britain from falling into a ten-year war. You are a single voice, lost in the wind, begging for war in a room full of peace seekers, you are out of touch and out of time. We've had a war to end all wars.'

Churchill punched the desk and barked back.

'Yes, but nobody has told Hitler! And when the Nazis goose-step up Whitehall to take their seats in Parliament, maybe then you'll realise you've been taken for a simple fool. Step outside and ask the man in the street what he thinks. Tell the bus driver your ideas about peace in our time. He'll laugh in your face, for it is you who is out of touch and out of time.'

Barrington straightened his polka dot tie. He stood, his voice steady and calm, 'If I suspect Berlin is not serious about negotiating a favourable peace deal, then I'll step down from this office and you can have your war.'

Churchill took one final puff of his cigar, rested it on the side of an ashtray and walked to the door.

All eyes were on him.

He said, 'Beware of the man who promises you peace, for it is often he who wishes to rule the world.'

And with the final word, Churchill left the room.

. . .

Outside Number Ten, Florence spoke first. 'Did you change any minds in there, Winston?'

'Maybe a few,' he said. 'Henry, let's go to your house, we need to remain active while those men up there, remain inactive. '

Florence looked up at the sky. 'This snow has brought London to a standstill, if I were a German spy, this is when I'd strike.'

'I agree,' said Sir Henry. 'These conditions are perfect.'

'What do you think Barrington's game is?' Asked Florence.

'I can't be sure,' said Winston. 'He's a clever politician with a glittering career, far more successful than mine.'

'That's true,' said Sir Henry.

'Thank you, Henry. It's so comforting to know you are on my side. Plus, Barrington has the Prime Minister's ear, both ears, and the support of the King.'

'You have support,' said Florence.

'Yes, but not from the King, nor the Prime Minister, they both think I'm unfit for duty.'

'You have us,' she said.

'Yes, I do.' Churchill thought a moment, 'Barrington lost his son, Oliver, during the Great War, and that makes him untouchable.'

'We all lost someone,' snapped Florence.

'Yes, sadly we did. But Barrington played his bereavement card cleverly after Oliver perished. He used his loss to bludgeon others to his way of thinking.'

Florence drove them from Downing Street and pulled the Bentley into the driveway of Sir Henry's home in Belgrave Square. 'Come on, let's go inside and have a nightcap. I have a plan,' she said.

'That's more like it,' said Churchill, 'I love Florence's plans.'

Inside, Florence said, 'I'm going to take the key people from the Spitfire programme away and keep them safe. I need Malcolm and his engineers under one roof, my roof.'

'Why?'

'It's a gut feel.'

'I thought you might say that,' said Churchill.

'Also, I'll forge a team of female spies and turn them into a fighting force.'

'Why women?' said Winston.

'You have to ask?'

'Well, no, not now.' Winston looked at Sir Henry.

'Don't look at me,' said Sir Henry.

Florence handed them both a large glass of brandy.

'I'll work out the details and come and see you before we disappear,' she said.

'Do what you have to do; it's in your hands.'

'Nibbles anyone?' Asked Sir Henry, 'I've got some cheese and biscuits.'

'Lovely,' said Winston. 'Evenings with you two are the ones I enjoy most.'

'I managed to get a decent wedge of stilton from a little shop in Piccadilly.'

'Does anything in this boiling world of trouble, bother you, Henry?' Asked Churchill.

Sir Henry thought for a moment. 'Yes, it bothers me when Florence rides my Norton, flat out with me on the back, and when she drives my new Bentley too fast.'

Florence reached out and grabbed both men by the arm. 'Look, we can run Military Intelligence from a remote location,' she said. 'Alice Jones will come with us; we can't win the war without her and we need the Spitfire engineers safe and sound away from the action.'

'Alice Jones bothers the life out of the Germans,' said Sir Henry.

'Out of me, too,' laughed Winston. 'That idea—right there—about taking the show on the road is why you run Military Intelligence.'

'I thought I ran it,' said Sir Henry.

'Not when Florence has a plan,' said Winston.

'That's true,' said Sir Henry.

Florence smiled at her two favourite men. 'Henry and I are going to the funeral of Malcolm Feather's parents on Sunday. He needs our support.'

Otto left the delivery van outside Denton's store. He posted the keys through the letterbox and walked back to the cottage in Church Road. He carried an armful of dry logs from the woodshed into the front room and lit a fire.

For the first time in two days, Otto felt warm. He went into the kitchen and cooked an egg and bacon sandwich. He sat in the front room with a mug of tea and allowed himself a moment to feel a sense of accomplishment after successfully carrying out the first part of his mission.

He was alone.

From now on he was Malcolm Feathers, Head of the Spitfire programme. He had to think and act like an Englishman once again, and Otto knew all there was to know about that particular breed.

The orange warmth from the fire filled the cottage, and he felt his aching body unwind. Otto's mind filled with a certainty that he would succeed. He injected the last shot of morphine into his leg and made up a bed in front of the fireplace. He took a bottle of beer from the pantry and drank it as he stared into the flames.

Becoming Malcolm Feathers was a work of art. Otto planned to walk into Malcolm's Buckingham Gate office and help himself to the information he needed. His first task would be to discover the multiple Spitfire assembly locations. His second task would be to find the secret 12g295 Spitfire code, tuck it in his pocket and walk out of the building.

Nobody would suspect a thing. Why would Malcolm Feathers steal something he already owned?

Otto would do anything to win the war. He changed the way he looked, he killed, and he faked love for a man. He was a patriot, a soldier and a servant of Germany.

The flames lit up his eyes.

Serving the Fatherland, summoned within him a warmth a log fire could not match. Above his own life, he treasured the Fuhrer's life. The British would never understand such loyalty.

His hands were raw from rowing in the icy sea. He stoked the fire, added a few more logs and settled on the mattress. Tiredness brought thoughts of his mother.

Otto had called at her home, on the outskirts of Berlin when he had the face of Owen Black; she didn't recognise him. He talked to her on the doorstep while collecting money for the Nazi party. He wanted to reach out and tell her it was him when she bragged about her son.

Otto lapped up his mother's loving pride. It was all he could do that day to stay in character. He knew if he could convince his mother that he was somebody else, then he could convince anyone.

The embers glowed in the grate and Otto rested his head on the pillow to let the combination of beer and morphine take effect. The thoughts of his mother drifted from his mind and his eyes closed.

CHAPTER 6

Florence and Sir Henry lived in two magnificent houses next door to one another on Belgrave Square, London SW1. On each of the four floors, they fitted adjoining doors.

They lived alone, yet lived together.

In the middle of Belgrave Square, a communal walled wildflower garden sported two grass tennis courts, and in the summer, Florence, Sir Henry and Rags sat under the giant oak with a bottle of wine and some cheese and read and chatted long into the evening.

Florence popped her head through the adjoining bedroom door.

'I'm going to Horse Guards Parade this morning and then, let's drive down in Eastbourne in the afternoon and stay in the Grand Hotel. In the morning we can shoot over to Friston for the funeral.'

'What are you thinking?' asked Sir Henry as he walked through to her bedroom.

'If we're to win this war, then we need Winston to become Prime Minister. And, if this threat is real, which we must assume is the case, then we must be on the highest of red alerts.'

'I know that face of yours all too well, Miss Fairweather, you're scheming and plotting and planning. What do you have in mind?'

'Henry, who would you say is your best operator at Bletchley? I don't want just a codebreaker. No, what I need is a thinker. You know the sort I mean: Oxford, Eton, sharp, quick, witty. They'll need to speak German, be athletic, and have a strong bent towards coding and engineering. We need to be ready for everything.'

'I have one who stands out above all others.'

'Good, who?'

'Butterworth, Percival Butterworth. He's a smashing chap, and as clever as they come, with a first from Oxford. He's an excellent amateur fencer and enjoys a spot of poetry.'

'Perfect, I'll take him.'

'You can't just take him.'

'Why ever not?'

'There are procedures.'

'Sounds great, can you proceed promptly with the procedures?'

Sir Henry knew, when Florence's mind was made up, it wasn't worth the energy to try to un-make it. She gazed out of the bedroom window across the communal garden. There were no wildflowers swaying in the breeze, no tennis matches, and no lovers sat on blankets reading and chatting under the oak. There were only grim realities. Her mind raced with complex possibilities, each one unfinished and with it the possibility of losing Britain the war.

'I'll fix it for you to have him,' he said.

'Marvellous, and one more thing, can I have him by Monday afternoon? Tell him nothing, of course.'

'How can I? I don't know anything.'

'That's how spying works, Henry.'

'Yes, but, we're on the same side-' he stopped speaking and looked at Florence who busied herself with her suitcase; she was already in a world of her own.

'I want to bring Mandy into the team.'

'Mandy Miller?' he asked.

'Yes.'

'Do you think she's ready?'

'She's ready, but I'll need to cash in a favour.'

'A favour?'

'I haven't told you, have I?'

'Told me what?'

'Mandy's in prison.'

Florence drove from Belgrave Square to Horse Guards Parade and ran up the stairs to Military Intelligence. Alice Jones was already making a cup of tea and eating a slice of toast.

'Morning Alice, tell me, how's Rosie getting on in Berlin?'

'She's doing well. I heard from her on Christmas Day. She managed to sneak into a radio room during a staff lunch break to tap out a coded message to me.'

'Your daughter is a girl after my own heart.'

'She reminds me so much of you.'

'She should; we raised her together.'

'What do you have in mind?'

'Do you think Rosie is ready for a spot of real action? I don't have details yet, so if you think she needs more time then-'

Alice cut in. 'Rosie's been undercover in Berlin for two years now, and she's chomping at the bit to get stuck in. She's been training since she was a child.'

'She was always going to be a spy.'

'And, she's far better prepared than you and I were in the last war. Do you remember, we used to slip behind enemy lines with nothing but a pocket knife and a spare pair of knickers in our pocket,' said Alice.

'You had a spare pair of knickers?'

'Florence, I taught you everything you know, but I didn't teach you everything I know.'

'One more thing, we're going to relocate Military Intelligence and take Malcolm and his engineers from the offices at Buckingham Gate with us.'

'When?'

'As soon as we are packed.'

'Where are we going?'

'Milton Park.'

'Fantastic, I'll start to pack up our equipment. Does Sir Henry know?'

'Not yet, why?'

'Well, I thought with Milton Park being his country estate. . .'

'Henry will love the idea. Can you ride his Norton motorbike up there?'

'No problem, the Cotswolds in January are perfect for a Military Intelligence set up,' said Alice.

'We're going to leave for the funeral in about an hour. Are you coming with us?'

'I'd love to, but I should make a start on the packing. Give Malcolm a firm handshake from me.'

Florence walked towards the front door. 'We'll be back late on Sunday evening. Do you think we'll be ready to head out early Tuesday morning?'

'If I start now, yes!'

'Oh Alice, one more thing, leave an hour free on Monday morning.'

'What for?'

'To get Mandy out of prison.'

Otto Flack spent Saturday morning at church making funeral arrangements with the vicar of Friston.

Otto practised Malcolm's walk and handshake. They weren't unusual in any way. However, common behaviours stick out if they are a little off. He needed to be on top form when he faced Florence and Sir Henry. His father had warned him they would pick up on the slightest difference. Otto had to keep out of their way at the funeral and become a ghost in London. He intended to complete his mission in solitude, then slip, unnoticed, out of Britain and back to Berlin with the Spitfire code.

The temperature continued to drop as the afternoon wore on. Otto returned to the cottage and went into the woodshed and took off his shirt. He spat into his hands and grabbed the axe and wielded it at a ferocious rate to split logs. The winter wind blew off the sea and chilled the sweat on his back.

'Hello, Malcolm.'

Otto turned round.

A pretty young girl in her late teens stood in the doorway of the woodshed. She had blond hair with gentle curls and welcoming eyes.

He'd been surprised by her, 'Hello,' he said.

'You don't recognise me, do you?'

'Well, I wouldn't say that.'

'It's been ten years since you last saw me. I'm Lizzie Denton. Your dad worked with my grandad.'

'Yes, of course, Lizzie Denton from the store, how are you?'

'I've grown since you last saw me, don't you think.'

'I think you have.'

'I was sorry to hear about your mum and dad, they were such lovely people. I came over to see if I could help you with anything.'

'What did you have in mind?'

Lizzie stared at the sweat glistening on his muscular chest, and an image of him pushing her against the woodshed flooded into her mind. She did her best to shut the image out and pull herself together.

She said, 'Maybe I could cook something for you?'

Otto stepped closer to her.

She breathed in his heat and her head filled once more with images of him kissing her. The fantasy played out in her mind as she held on to the door frame.

Otto used his shirt to wipe his chest.

'Cook, you say, good idea, I'm starving.' He pushed through the narrow doorway of the woodshed. She didn't attempt to move out of the way. Their bodies, for the briefest moment, were wedged together.

'You've grown up,' he said.

The most Lizzie had done with a boy was to let him touch her. She didn't feel much that afternoon on a haystack. The boy took more pleasure from the fumbling than she did. That was in the summer, and nothing else happened. She decided she wanted to go with a man, but didn't know who. Then Malcolm appeared in the store last evening, and her mind was made up.

Lizzie followed him into the front room and sat on his makeshift bed. She watched him add a few split logs on top of the embers and sparks crackled up the chimney.

'I saw you when you came over to the store to borrow the van yesterday evening.'

'I didn't see you.'

'I was peeking through the rear door from the back room. I heard you talking to my grandad.'

Otto closed the curtains in the front room.

She said, 'You looked so sad, and yet somehow, not. You looked different from how I remembered you. I couldn't quite put my finger on it.'

Otto stared into the flames, listening to the young girl.

'Then I realised what it was.'

Otto reached for the poker and took a firm grip of the cold steel. A swift blow to the head would kill her outright. He could row out to sea and drop her body into a watery grave, next to Malcolm's.

'I was looking at you for the first time as a woman. I was only a young girl when I saw you last.'

Otto let go of the poker. The silly girl knew nothing. To her, he was Malcolm.

'I had to come over to the cottage and see you.'

'I'm glad you did.'

'Nothing ever happens in Friston.' She shifted herself on the bed to sit in the middle of the mattress. 'I watched you chopping logs in the woodshed. I stood there for a long time, and you didn't see me.' She looked up at him with doe eyes and her voice tapered away to the faintest whisper.

Lizzie's uncontrollable sensations built up quickly inside her. She felt no shame. She pushed against him and ran her hands over his chest. He undid his belt and rolled her skirt up beyond her waist.

The moment of lust was fleeting: too fleeting.

Lizzie heard sounds reappear one by one; the crackling logs, the wind beating against the window and Malcolm's rapid breathing.

Her previous boldness now deserted her, and with the onset of embarrassment, she pulled her skirt over her naked legs and drew her knees up under her chin.

Otto reached out and stroked her cheek, 'Let's keep this to ourselves.'

Lizzie said nothing, focused on nothing. She got what she came for.

He said, 'I'll be going back to London after the funeral, but I'll be in Friston again in a week. We can meet up if you like?'

She nodded.

Silence followed until she lost her coyness, 'I'm famished, how about you?'

'Starving.'

'Good, then I'll make us something to eat.'

Florence returned to Belgrave Square from Military Intelligence and called up the staircase. 'Are you ready, Henry?'

'Yes, you?'

'Pretty much.'

'Shall I drive?' he asked without conviction.

'Henry, darling, I want you to read a pile of papers—so best that I drive, and you read.'

'Sounds like a good plan.'

'How do you fancy fish and chips tonight at Henderson's, on the seafront?' she said.

Sir Henry's eyes lit up. 'That's a fabulous idea, Henderson's serve the best fish.'

They loaded the back seat with a small suitcase, and Florence pulled the Bentley out of Belgrave Square, along Chester Street and drove around Buckingham Palace on Hyde Park Corner.

'I will never tire of looking at the Palace,' she said.

Florence and Sir Henry spent long evenings with the King at Buckingham Palace in the years leading up to the war. The King loved her World War One stories, notably how she evaded capture by pretending to be dead or when she threw herself into a muddy ditch. The King was fascinated with her ability to outsmart the enemy in plain sight and her strength to remain calm when faced with adversity. He didn't doubt she could persuade anyone to do anything.

'I hope your war hero is at the hotel this weekend,' she said.

'War hero?' asked Henry.

'Yes, the waiter with the limp and jam; you remember.'

'You love to win, don't you?'

'Yes, at everything!' Florence drove effortlessly. 'Do you think I'm right to take Malcolm's Spitfire crew out of London and hide them at Milton Park?'

'Milton Park?'

'Oh yes, I thought it would make a fabulous base for us, what do you think?'

'Yes, I suppose it does,' he said.

'But is it a good idea to hide them away?'

'Trust your gut, Florence. Your sixth sense has never let you down. Besides, the Cotswold air will do us good. It might inspire the engineers to come up with some clever ideas.'

Florence drove over Chelsea Bridge and across Clapham Common. She didn't slow down in the snowy conditions as she sped towards Eastbourne. He pulled his white silk scarf from his neck and wrapped it neatly around her. His scarf smelled so unmistakably of him.

Florence touched the back of his hand. Her feet danced across the pedals as she changed gears and accelerated south towards the coast.

Henderson's fish and chips were as enjoyable and as delicious as always.

'Henry, why don't you go and check us into the hotel? I'm

going to stroll on the beach for a bit, I need to get my thoughts in line.'

'Don't get too cold. I'll have a glass of something waiting for you up in the room.' He wandered off towards the hotel.

Florence stepped onto the beach.

There were drifts of snow dotted about, and her steamy breath trailed behind her as she walked along the seafront.

Relocating to Milton Park was the right thing to do, and if an attack was coming—which she was certain it was—then she needed a fort to defend them.

Her thoughts turned to her team.

Florence needed Mandy Miller's bluster and confidence. And with the indispensable Alice Jones and her daughter, Rosie, they were capable of achieving anything. Together, they were fearless. The four of them made quite a team. Henry would clear the way for her to collect Percy Butterworth, the codebreaker from Bletchley Park.

She stepped off the beach and headed towards the graceful Grand Hotel, and to Henry.

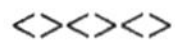

CHAPTER 7

The morning of the funeral opened with a winter burst of yellow sunshine, like the first act of a play. Otto made a pot of tea, he hated tea, but Malcolm drank it, endlessly. He spent the remainder of the previous evening cursing himself. Would Lizzie Denton keep their exploits to herself? After she left, he fell asleep thinking about her. Was that his first mistake? Should he have killed her and rowed her body out to sea?

Otto thought about her young firm body. He was her first. The German girls hadn't thrown themselves at him the way Lizzie had done. She was lustful, and he was unable to hold himself back, and in truth, he didn't want to stop. He was a lone spy living in perpetual danger so he convinced himself he deserved her.

He dressed in one of Malcolm's suits and polished his shoes, bringing them up to a perfect Sunday-best shine. He wrapped the knitted blue scarf around his neck and put on Malcolm's overcoat, then took a few deep breaths to clear his head. Otto stepped out of the front door and walked up the hill to the church. He'd mastered Malcolm's walk, Malcolm's mannerisms, his soft Sussex accent and the way he listened with his head tilted slightly to the left.

Malcolm was a good listener. Otto had to remember that and never cut across when someone was speaking.

Malcolm was gentle and gracious.

Otto was not.

No church bells rang out for the Sunday funeral, nor on any other Sunday morning. The war had seen to that. There was no traffic in the village, the snow had seen to that. The vicar, despite the war and traffic, stood at the church door ready to welcome Malcolm.

He said, 'A most beautiful day, Malcolm. How lucky we are with the weather, and to think, we've had snow, snow and more snow; the good Lord is looking down on us today.'

'Yes, Vicar, it's a perfect day, Mum and Dad would approve.'

'Everything is ready for you inside.'

'Thank you for all you have done.'

The vicar put his hand on Otto's arm, and with a look of genuine concern, he said, 'Mrs Pritchard is warming up the organ, quite vigorously, I'm afraid. And I ought to warn you, she's rather ham-fisted but plays with a lot of enthusiasm, although never in time, and always out of tune. However, nobody seems to mind.' The vicar guided Otto into the church.

The church was candlelit, and Otto took his seat in the front left-hand pew and knelt to pray.

Otto didn't pray, Malcolm did.

He intended to prepare for the day ahead, instead, in the quietness of the church, he thought about Lizzie Denton. Last night was unexpected. She had groaned loudly with pleasure. He hadn't heard a woman cry out before. Otto needed to focus. He held on to Malcolm's leather-bound Bible and closed his eyes.

'Good morning, Malcolm,' the voice came from behind him. It was Lizzie. Her hair curled around the collar of her black coat, and she looked as gorgeous in the morning as the night before.

'Good morning, Lizzie, oh, and good morning Mr Denton.' Otto stood and shook hands with Lizzie's grandfather. 'Thank you both for coming.'

'Dear chap, this is the saddest day I can remember in quite a while. I'll be back in a moment. I need to catch up with the vicar; he wants to talk about his lawnmower, of all things on all days.'

Lizzie remained with Otto. She'd dabbed French cologne on her neck before she dressed.

She glowed.

'You look fabulous,' he said: a Malcolm word.

She stepped closer to him and whispered. 'Today is a sad day, but yesterday, was the happiest day of my life. I can't stop thinking about you. I couldn't sleep, and I've been useless all morning.'

Otto stared at her. He wanted to tell her he thought about her last night too. 'I'm leaving first thing in the morning,' his manner was short, he didn't mean it to be. Her eyes dropped, and he reached out and touched her hand.

She said, 'My grandad takes the dogs for a walk on the beach at five o'clock. I can come over and see you if you like?' Lizzie's cheeks reddened. She wanted to experience the feelings of ecstasy again.

The church began to fill with villagers and friends. Otto knew not one of them, but they all knew him. However, he did know the next two who walked through the arched doors, Florence Fairweather and Sir Henry Pensworthy.

Otto looked beyond Lizzie. 'We'll talk about it later.'

. . .

Florence and Sir Henry walked towards him.

Otto made his move. 'Florence, I'm so pleased you came, and Sir Henry, lovely to see you.' He'd carefully rehearsed his first encounter.

Florence hugged him tightly. 'Malcolm, how terribly sad we are for you.' She held him for a while longer, 'let's talk after the service.'

Sir Henry offered his support with a firm pat on Otto's shoulder. 'Anything we can do to help, we're here for you.'

'Thank you. You are both so wonderful.'

The church pews swelled with sombre faces. The deaths of Malcolm's parents had affected everybody in the village. Friston had witnessed significant losses during the first war, and now, a gas leak had brought the grip of grief back to the small Sussex village. Malcolm's parents didn't die in combat, yet Friston mourned their passing as if they'd died at the hands of the enemy—which they had, and were Friston's first casualties of war.

The funeral service began.

The vicar spoke kindly about Malcolm's mother and father, he'd known them for many years, they had been an integral part of the church and a vibrant, busy couple in the village. Two coffins rested side by side near the altar. A photograph of the couple, taken at the pebble beach, was placed on a table between the coffins. Mr Denton stood at the front of the church and summed up the thoughts of the villagers. He brought many of them to tears.

After the service, the congregation gathered outside and circled a freshly dug, double grave. Otto felt nothing. The funeral meant nothing. He willed some tears to fall. None came. He opened his eyes to the chilly wind until they watered in time for the coffins to be lowered inch by inch into the grave.

As Otto's tears fell, Lizzie reached out and brushed his hand.

The vicar ended the burial with a passage from the Bible. Otto blanked out his surroundings. He wanted to get to London and complete his mission. Berlin was waiting for him, and his father was expecting a speedy resolution.

An invitation was extended to everyone for drinks and sandwiches at the Tiger Inn, on Friston green.

'Moving service, Malcolm,' said Sir Henry. 'I say, why don't you come back to London with us later this afternoon? Florence thought it would be much better for you than getting a cold train in the morning.'

Otto thought through the advantage of being back in London earlier than expected, 'Thank you. I'll be ready and waiting for you at the cottage.'

On the way to the Tiger Inn, Lizzie caught up with him and tried to catch his eye.

Without a quantum of grace, he said, 'My plans have changed, I'm leaving for London this afternoon.' He walked off, and she chased after him.

Lizzie tugged at his arm, 'When will I see you again?' Can I visit you in London?'

'No, I'll be too busy. Listen, when I come back to Friston, I'll come over and see you.' Otto had snapped into mission mode.

He had a job to do.

'You weren't too busy last night, were you?' She waited for an answer. She didn't get one.

Otto walked across the village green and entered the Tiger Inn pub. The villagers gathered in groups and told stories about Malcolm's parents. The voices became a single, incomprehensible blur. Otto stood with a pint of beer in his hand and thought about his father, and was certain he would never see him again, for no other reason than he would willingly give his life for Germany.

Florence came and stood next to him, 'Penny for your thoughts.'

'Penny for what?'

'What are you thinking about?'

'Oh, you know, mum and dad, that sort of thing. How have you been, Florence?'

'Busy, what with Churchill, Barrington, and Military Intelligence. Everything is beginning to stack up at the moment.'

'Christopher Barrington?' He asked.

'Yes, him, and he's a royal pain in the arse, but let's not drag that into today.' She sipped her beer. 'Step outside with me a minute, Malcolm. I've something to tell you.'

Otto took a knife from the buffet table and slipped it into his coat pocket and followed her outside.

Florence stood with her hands behind her back and her hair caught the breeze and it twirled above her head. She began to speak before he reached her.

'Malcolm, I've been watching you closely today.'

Otto stamped his feet and blew warm air into his hands and wrapped the blue scarf tighter around his neck. He slipped his hand into his coat pocket and gripped the handle of the knife in a single, smooth movement. He calmed his breathing and steadied his heartbeat. He tilted his head slightly to the left, as Malcolm would. Yet inside he was Otto, a warrior, a killer. Prepared to kill Florence.

She said, 'Yesterday evening, I decided to pull you off the Spitfire team, and you know me, I rarely change my mind.'

'You can't do that,' he demanded.

'You need a break, Malcolm.'

'No, Florence, I'm fine, really I am.'

'You were a wreck when I saw you in St James's Park.

However, from what I see today you've pulled it together, and I've decided I want you to stay in charge of the programme. We can't lose you at this vital stage. Germany will turn on us once they've cut France to bits.'

Otto released the knife handle and blew warm breath into his cupped hands once more.

'Thank you, Florence. I won't let you down. You know that. You and Sir Henry have always put a lot of faith in me, and now it's my turn to repay you. Come on, let's go back in and have a drink to my dear old mum and dad, they always liked you.'

'Owen would be proud of you. I think you were at your happiest when you were with him. You must still miss him terribly.'

Otto followed her back into the Tiger Inn and ordered two beers and stood by the fireplace.

Florence said, 'Malcolm, you seem to have a secret admirer. The young, pretty girl standing by the doorway can't take her eyes off you.'

'Ah yes, that's Lizzie Denton, she came over last evening to the cottage and cooked for me. She lost her mother and father when she was young and now lives with her grandad in the hardware store. I've not seen her for ten years. She's a real sweetie but hasn't put two and two together yet that I prefer barmen to barmaids.'

'Be nice, Malcolm, and go over and speak to her, then I'll pick you up later from the cottage and run you back to London.'

Otto walked over to Lizzie and put his arm around her in a brotherly fashion. 'Come over to the cottage at four o'clock.'

'You mean it?'

'Of course, I mean it. Look, I'm sorry I was unkind

earlier, the whole day became a bit too much for me. I want to make it up to you.'

Lizzie smiled at him. 'I should have been more understanding. I'll sneak out and come over.'

She curled her fingers around his.

While others toasted Malcolm's parents, Otto looked over at Florence who stood with Sir Henry. He raised his glass towards them; they, in turn, raised theirs back at him. If she got in his way, he wouldn't hesitate to kill her.

One by one, the villagers left the pub, Otto was the last to leave. He walked across the green, up Friston Hill and turned into Church Road and entered the cottage. He stoked the fire to warm up the front room and went upstairs to pack Malcolm's clothes.

In Malcolm's bedroom, Otto picked up the photo taken at Oxford of the inseparable four. He looked at Florence and ran his fingers over her face. She hadn't changed since University, forever young. He put the photograph in his suitcase and carried it downstairs.

Lizzie was standing in the front room.

'Hello, you,' he said.

'I haven't got long. I told grandad I would take the dogs for a walk on the beach with him in an hour.' She looked down at her shoes.

Her sexual fearlessness from yesterday had gone, replaced instead with a youthful, coy vulnerability.

'Take your coat off,' he said softly.

Lizzie didn't move.

He steadied her with one arm and peeled her clothes from her slender frame. She tried to cover her nakedness with her hands. Lizzie felt his soft kisses on her neck and with each kiss, the sensations grew more intense. Her eyes closed as she began to experience waves of unstoppable pleasure. She moved her body against his and discovered new heights of passion. Lizzie wanted their time together to stand still, it was how she had dreamed it would be like to be with a man.

A car horn sounded in the road outside, and in an instant the spell was broken.

Otto ran to the window and looked through the curtains. A pale blue and silver Bentley pulled up outside, with Florence at the wheel.

She sounded the horn again.

'Lizzie, I've got to go.'

She knew the moment was over.

Otto dressed and grabbed his suitcase, 'I'll see you again.' He smiled at her, then walked out the front door.

Lizzie Denton pulled the blanket up to her chin. She heard the car door shut, and drive away from Friston, away from her. She continued to listen until there was nothing more to hear other than her heartbeat.

Lizzie and her grandad put the dogs in the back of the van and drove to the beach.

'You like Malcolm, don't you?' He asked.

'I do. I know he's twice my age, but I want to see him when he returns to Friston. He said he was going to be busy in London. When he's back, can we invite him over for dinner?'

'That sounds like a lovely idea.'

Mr Denton drove through the winding lanes towards the beach. As they neared the seafront, the dogs barked with excitement. Mr Denton parked the van and opened the doors, and the dogs bounded out and chased one another across the pebble beach.

'Let me do your coat up, Grandad,' she said. 'I don't want

you to catch a cold. We have a lot of work to do in the store now that Malcolm's father is no longer with us.'

'I'll miss my old friend. I still can't quite believe he left the bolts undone on the gas cylinder. It doesn't make any sense. He was meticulous to a fault. Of course, a bit of old age creeps up on all of us.'

He stopped talking and squinted his eyes.

'What's wrong, Grandad? What are the dogs barking at?'

'I'm not sure. They've found something over there. Let's go and see, come on, Lizzie.'

They ran over to where the dogs barked at a bulky shape covered in seaweed at the water's edge.

'What is it?' asked Lizzie.

'I don't know, stay here, my love, I'll go and take a closer look.' Mr Denton walked over to the discoloured lump on the beach. The dimming light made it difficult to make it out. And then he saw it.

'Can you see anything, Grandad?'

'Stay there, Lizzie, stay back.' He prodded the lump with his walking stick.

It was a bloated, disfigured, naked body.

Lizzie went over and stood next to him. She put her hand to her mouth, fell to her knees and screamed.

'Malcolm!'

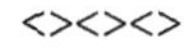

CHAPTER 8

Florence's cheeks burned rouge from the whip of the wind. She'd set off early from Belgrave Square at a quick pace, and her boots beat out a rhythmic march on the road, and when Florence walked with purpose, her thoughts became orderly and decisive.

Churchill had spelt it out to her: lose the Spitfire and we lose the war. He phrased it more poetically as if he'd practised his lines all week, and she knew he had. Lose the Spitfire, lose the war. His message was clear, and Florence understood what she had to do. She walked across Horse Guards Parade and up the stairs into Military Intelligence. Alice Jones was pottering about.

'Morning Alice, it's fresh out there.'

'I love a crisp morning. I ran a couple of laps around Hyde Park before I came in. I'm going to finish packing up the offices today; I've most of the important bits done already.'

'You didn't waste any time.'

'Nor will the enemy. I've ordered an unmarked military truck to collect everything at three o'clock, and then I'll lock down our offices. Administration and signals departments can stay operational. We can leave unnoticed.'

'I'll have my office packed and ready,' said Florence.

'Good, I'll lead the advanced party on Sir Henry's Norton and set up Milton Park ready for your arrival tomorrow.'

'You're a day ahead of schedule.'

'No point in hanging about is there? As I always say, the Bosch won't be taking a day off, so neither can we.'

Alice had an unusual amount of energy for her age, she shared the same date of birth with Churchill, yet nobody ever believed her. She was driven by pure impatience and patriotism to win the war, revenge too, but she never spoke about it, not even to Florence.

Sir Henry and Rags appeared at the top of the stairs. 'My goodness, Alice, you must have been here all night.' He stood among the boxes. 'I need the file on Percy Butterworth, the Bletchley chap, can you put your hands on it?'

'On your desk, third pile,' she said.

Florence said, 'Henry, can you tell Percy to be ready for collection at eight o'clock this evening?'

He nodded.

Florence looked out of her window across Horse Guards Parade. Churchill's words echoed in her head; *Lose the Spit, lose the war.* The formation of Military Intelligence was for precisely this purpose. To protect King and country.

'I'm popping out with Alice for an hour,' she said.

He fished about in his pockets and patted the outside of his clothing in search of his car keys.

'Left side, jacket pocket,' said Florence.

He handed her the keys, 'Going somewhere nice?'

'Prison!'

'Ah yes, our very own jailbird, Miss Mandy Miller.'

'Do you want to come with us?'

'No, I think I'll wait here. There's no need for all of us to go charging about.'

Outside on the gravel parade ground, Florence and Alice stepped into the Bentley. Florence started the engine.

She asked, 'Have you heard from Rosie?'

'No, not yet, but I've only sent one message; she's a smart girl and won't take unnecessary risks. The Germans have radio trackers all over Berlin.'

Florence pulled out of Horse Guards Parade, headed over Westminster Bridge and turned right towards Wandsworth.

Alice came to the point. 'What's the real reason you want to relocate to Milton Park?'

'Because I know what I would do if I were the German spy assigned to stealing the Spitfire.'

Alice thought for a moment, 'We can't hide the Spitfire, there are hundreds of them.'

'We can't hide them, and we won't.'

'I'm glad you cleared that up then,' said Alice.

'If you wanted the tallest tower in town, what would you do?'

'I'd knock everyone else's tower down and prevent them from ever building one again, then build mine as tall as possible.'

'Precisely, that's exactly what I would do. It's a classic empire-building strategy. If I were the German spy recruited to steal the Spit, I wouldn't worry about the ones Britain have already built. I would go after the codes, blueprints, and assembly plants. I would make sure Germany could mass-produce tens of thousands of Spitfires while Britain couldn't put any more back in the air.'

'I see, so we're not going to hide the Spitfire; we're going to hide how to mass-produce them.' She slapped the dashboard of the Bentley. 'You're a clever girl, very clever! And at Milton Park, we can keep a tight lid on everything. Neat and tidy under one roof.'

Florence drove through Battersea and into a parking space outside Wandsworth prison. She turned the engine off and turned to Alice. 'We can't mess this up.'

'Let's make sure we jolly well don't then.'

The guard at the prison gate took their names. 'Go through the middle door and follow the red line; it will take you to the East Wing. The officer on duty will show you where to go.'

They walked through the middle door and found the red line. 'You would think crime would stop during the war, wouldn't you?' Alice said.

'Criminals take advantage of situations. The police are stretched, which makes breaking into places pretty easy.' Florence led the way to the East Wing.

'Name?' Asked the guard at the entrance.

'Fairweather, Florence, and Jones, Alice.'

'Prisoner's name?'

'Miller, Mandy.'

'Ninth door on the right, you have ten minutes.'

Florence and Alice walked along the gangway of cells.

From inside cell nine, Mandy Miller shouted. 'If you touch me again sunshine, I'll slap you so hard, when you wake up the war will be over.' Mandy stood in the middle of her cell squaring up to a heavy-set prison guard.

He barked, 'You'll do three years in here, and I'll see to it you have a really shitty time of it.' He grabbed Mandy and pushed her against the bunk bed. She used the bed to push herself back at him and slapped his face with an open hand.

'You little slut,' he snarled and threw a punch.

Mandy ducked. She bobbed back up and hit him on the other cheek with a stinging slap, and then rabbit punched him hard in the lower gut. The guard bent double and reached for his truncheon attached to his belt.

'Stop right there,' Florence ordered. 'Step back.'

He spun around. 'Who the hell do you think you are?'

'If you touch her once more, you'll be dealing with me.'

'And, me,' said Alice.

'And who the hell might you couple of busy-bodies be then? Shouldn't you be at home washing-up or something?'

'You need to leave this cell, or I'll assign you to the Atlantic fleet dodging U-boats for the rest of the war. Do you understand me?' said Florence.

Alice rolled her tweed sleeves up. 'I'll deal with this clown.'

'No need,' said Florence.

The red-faced guard barged past the two women and stormed out of the cell.

'Florence, Alice,' yelled Mandy. 'That fat-arsed fool has been pushing me about from the moment I arrived.'

'How are you?' asked Florence.

Mandy threw her arms around her and Alice. 'Am I glad to see you, it's been rotten in here.' Mandy stood back and looked at them. 'Tell me you've come to get me out.'

'What are you in for this time?' asked Florence.

'It wasn't my fault.'

'It never is,' said Alice.

Mandy sighed and put her hands on her hips. 'My commanding officer at the training base in Croydon couldn't keep his creepy hands to himself.'

'Ah, one of those, is he?' said Alice.

'I warned him and told him straight, if you touch me again I'll give you a slap.'

'He didn't take you seriously?' said Florence.

'He thought I was joking. He touched me once too often, so I clumped him. The silly old bugger fell over backwards and cracked his head on the edge of a table. He pressed assault charges, and I got sent down.'

'That's all that happened?' asked Florence.

'Yes, apart from when I kicked him in the you-know-whats when he was on the ground. You should have heard him cry like a baby.'

Alice winced, 'You sound innocent enough to me.'

'Agreed, you're innocent, case closed,' said Florence.

'Can you get me out?'

'How long have you been in here?' asked Alice.

'Three days, but it seems forever.'

Florence lowered her voice, 'I need you for something big. Your training is officially over, and you'll be working with Alice and me. How do you fancy that?'

Mandy picked up her hairbrush and put it in her pocket. 'I'm packed.'

Born in Battersea, Mandy Miller never met her father. He left before she was born. Her mum, Betty, was loved by everybody. She was a tea lady during the day, and an office cleaner at night. It was not unusual for her to work sixteen hours a day, though Mandy never heard her mother complain; not about anything. Betty was a smiler who had a cheeky word for everyone, and she made Mandy laugh about the silliest things.

One Tuesday morning at work, Betty felt a sharp pain in her chest as she waited for a pot of tea to brew. It was a heart attack, and she died instantly.

Mandy was fourteen, and left school the same day.

The village hall in Battersea held friendship meetings for mothers on Wednesday evenings. Betty would take Mandy with her to serve tea and cake after the get-togethers. Wednesday was Mandy's favourite day of the week.

She went to the village hall the day after her mother died, she knew that tea and cake would still need serving. She stood at the back of the village hall holding back her tears. That November night, Mandy's life changed forever. Florence was the speaker.

Alice noticed Mandy's interest in Florence's speech and introduced herself. Mandy had lost her mother, but that night, she found a new family, and she adored Florence and Alice from the start.

Florence and Alice kept in close contact with her over the following ten years and sent her on endless training courses.

Mandy was an impressive learner. She learned how to drive cars and ride motorbikes at high speed, how to fight dirty, how to stand out and how to blend in. She learned languages and excelled at the intricacies of spy work.

As a student, she passed her tests with flying colours, helped by the discovery that Mandy had a photographic memory. She had thought everybody's memory was the same, she had no idea her skill was perfect for spycraft.

Mandy stayed with Florence in Belgrave Square. She'd never known such a lifestyle. Florence never tried to change Mandy's coarse Battersea accent or tame her short fuse. Mandy was a live wire, and that was how Florence wanted her.

Until Mandy met Sir Henry, she didn't have a respectable male role model in her life. Sir Henry didn't have children, so Mandy became like a daughter. He took care of her welfare with a generous weekly allowance and was always there for her with guidance and intelligent advice. Naturally, he fussed too much, yet to Mandy, he was the kindest, most wonderful man in the world.

. . .

In the governor's office, at Wandsworth prison, the three women sat in front of Frank Mckenzie.

Florence began, 'Mr Mckenzie, I need a huge favour. Can you release Mandy Miller into my custody?'

'That's not going to happen.' said the governor.

Mandy took a deep breath in readiness to speak.

Alice tapped her knee and whispered, 'Not now, dear.'

Florence played her one card, 'I've come directly from Winston's house, in Morpeth Terrace.'

'Mr Churchill?'

'Yes, and here's the thing you see; Winston has assigned Mandy Miller to me for a secret mission. Although, I'd prefer to see her rot in here a little more.'

'A lot more rotting,' added Alice.

'However, I'm sure you'll understand when Winston wants his man,' she tailed off her words, then added. 'He told me you were the indisputable backbone of our prison system.'

Frank Mckenzie was a short, old fashioned man in his sixties. He disliked women offenders and hated having them clutter his prison, especially when they were as brash as Mandy Miller. But wartime meant sacrifices, even to the prison system. He sat back in his leather chair and soaked up the praise from Churchill. He looked at Miller and thought for a ponderous minute. A summons of help from Churchill was welcoming, but recognition from Churchill was an honour.

'Get her out of my sight, and be sure to tell Churchill he owes me one.'

The three women left the prison without another word. Alice said, 'I didn't know Winston knew the governor.'

'He doesn't, he's never heard of him.'

The Bentley filled with laughter as it sped back over Wandsworth bridge.

. . .

Otto Flack opened the doors to the balcony of Malcolm's London apartment and stepped outside. He breathed in a gulp of London morning air.

It tasted good.

Otto wanted to be in Malcolm's office in Buckingham Gate before the engineers arrived. He needed two items to complete his task: the Spitfire secret code and the locations around Britain where they made the component parts. He knew his time would be limited, so he planned to get in, get out, and get back to Berlin, with his mission completed within two days. Otto's facial surgery, and the killings in Friston, were merely a precursor for the coming forty-eight hours.

The night before, when he was in the back of the car, Florence and Sir Henry talked about dinner parties, the changing seasons, and the disruption to the train service between the Cotswolds and London. All of it of no value to him.

Otto put on Malcolm's overcoat and scarf and walked out the front door. He'd walked from the apartment to the Buckingham Gate offices countless times with Malcolm, as Owen Black.

This morning was different.

Nothing could have prepared him for the weight of anticipation. He was in the centre of London and was about to rip the heart out of England's war.

He walked along the Thames to Westminster Bridge, he looked up at the silenced Big Ben and marched across Parliament Square. The whole German army would follow in his footsteps soon enough.

At the entrance to the Buckingham Gate offices, he tucked his chin into his scarf and pulled Malcolm's identity card from his coat pocket, something he'd seen Malcolm do each morning.

'Morning Albert,' Otto said to the doorman.

'My dear chap, how was the funeral?'

'Everyone seemed to think it went well.'

'I thought you might have taken a few days off.'

'Oh, you know how it is, better to be busy than sit about feeling sorry for myself.'

'That's the spirit, lad.'

Albert didn't look at Malcolm's identity card, he never did. Malcolm always showed it just the same.

'And how's the good lady wife?' It was a question Malcolm had asked Albert every day.

And the answer, every day, was the same.

'If the bloody Germans ever march up Whitehall, they'll be in for one bloody big surprise when they set eyes on her. They'll turn on their heels and run.'

Otto took the stairs to the top floor, unlocked the office door, and for the first time, he was alone in Malcolm's office. The shelves were crammed with folders, and in contrast to Malcolm's eccentric untidy life, each folder had a neatly written, colour-coded spine.

There was a knock at the door.

'Come in.'

Fletcher poked his head through the door. 'Morning, old boy, how was the funeral?'

'Emotionally tough, but it was comforting to have so many kind people attend from Friston.'

'I should have gone with you, moral support and all that.'

'That's alright, Fletch.'

'Do you still want to go ahead with our meeting?'

'Meeting?'

'This morning, our meeting? If it's too much for you, I can come back later.'

'Don't be daft, sit down Fletch, and I'll make some tea. My brain's a bit fuzzy, what with the travelling, the snow—you know how it is.'

Fletcher took a seat and lifted his voice above the rattle of the boiling kettle, 'I worked through the weekend on our little project. And I have to say, you were spot on with our logjams.'

'Go on, Fletch.' Otto handed him a mug of tea.

Fletcher had a genuine look of worry on his face. 'We need to get to work immediately, or we won't have a Spitfire in the air in a few months. Our system is a disaster.'

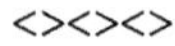

CHAPTER 9

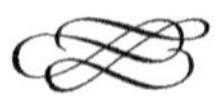

Friston village was too small to have a dedicated police station or a resident police officer. Inspector Giles came from the Eastbourne Constabulary. He dealt with serious crime and was a specialist in murder cases. His retirement loomed, and after forty years of service, this was to be his last case. He was tired of crime and tired of criminals. Forty years of seeing the worst in people would do that to you.

The body in the morgue was formally identified as Malcolm Feathers by Mr Denton and his granddaughter, Lizzie Denton. Giles walked around the body on the marble slab and studied its cuts and abrasions. And the body; while swollen and battered, showed no apparent signs of a struggle: no bruising, no knife marks, no defence wounds.

Did this man simply walk naked into the sea, on a cold January afternoon immediately following his parents' funeral? And if so, why no pile of clothes, why no abandoned vehicle, and why no note? Nobody had noticed any peculiarities in the dead man's behaviour during the funeral. Even so, his body would not be in this state.

Nothing added up.

Giles had a nose for murder, and something didn't smell right. A distressed girl—Lizzie Denton, stood opposite him in the morgue with the body between them; she appeared fragile.

Inspector Giles used the softest tone he could manage, a voice he saved for moments like this. He asked, 'What do you mean you think you made a mistake?'

Lizzie Denton shifted from one foot to the other. She lifted her head and looked the Inspector dead in the eye. 'I'm saying, this is not Malcolm Feathers.'

'But only yesterday, young lady, both you and your grandfather confirmed it was him.'

'Well, it's not.'

'And you're quite certain.'

'Completely.'

'So what's changed since yesterday?'

'When I saw the body on the beach last night covered in seaweed, it was dark, and I couldn't see properly.' She bit her lip, 'Whoever this is, could be Malcolm's twin brother.' Lizzie looked at the body on the slab. The wintry saltwater had caused the body to bloat and the skin to split.

'Did Feathers have a twin brother?' Again, his voice soft and steady.

'Not that I know.' Lizzie turned away from the grotesque body.

'What makes you so sure this is not him?'

Lizzie blushed and looked down at her shoes.

'Miss Denton, whatever you say stays between us.'

She took a deep breath. 'I was with Malcolm over the weekend. And whoever this is, is most certainly not him.'

The Inspector needed to be sure he understood. 'I need you to be a little more precise.'

She cleared her throat, 'Malcolm's shoulders, arms, and

chest are muscular; his whole body is muscular, like a movie-star. Whereas this man's body is soft and shapeless as if he'd never-' her voice tailed off.

'You've been most helpful, Miss Denton. I'll have one of my officers run you back to Friston.'

'There's no need. I drove here in the delivery van.' Lizzie walked towards the door of the morgue.

Inspector Giles said, 'Miss Denton, when was the last time you saw Malcolm Feathers, before this weekend?'

'Ten years ago, why?'

Giles pulled the sheet back over the body. 'No reason, drive home safely.'

Mandy Miller ran on ahead of Florence and Alice, across Horse Guards Parade and up the stairs, and burst in through the office door of Military Intelligence. The offices echoed with an emptiness like a house on moving day.

Rags barked with excitement.

'Sir Henry,' she yelled and ran over to him.

'Mandy, my sweet, lovely girl,' he wrapped his arms around her, then kissed her on both cheeks.

'I've missed you,' she said.

'And I've missed you. So, tell me, what have you been up to since I saw you last? I've not seen your little face for more than a month.'

'Oh, you know, the usual. I've been busy with training courses at the base in Croydon. At long, long last I broke up with Stanley-bloody-Blagdon, I spent the last few days in prison, and oh yes, I cut my hair, do you like it?' She spun around and flicked her blond hair.

'Hold on, go back, what did you just say?'

'I cut my hair.'

'Back further.'

'I broke up with Stanley. He turned out to be a total arse.'

'Tell me about the prison bit.'

Mandy looked at him with sorrowful blue eyes.

Florence arrived at the top of the stairs. 'It's been sorted out, Henry.'

'I don't doubt that for a second.' He looked at Florence and Alice standing together. 'You two can be pretty persuasive.'

'Mandy had to defend herself against a creepy officer at her base,' said Alice. 'She's completely innocent, well, nearly completely.'

'I warned him plenty,' cut in Mandy. 'He wouldn't stop grabbing me, so I slapped him a few times, and in court the judge played the old school-tie routine and sent me to prison.'

Sir Henry gave Mandy another reassuring hug. 'Let me have the name of the officer on the base at Croydon. I'll make sure he won't bother anyone else again. I'll reassign him somewhere dangerously unpleasant for the rest of the war.'

Mandy spun around and put her hands on her hips, 'Good, that's that then, thank you, Uncle Henry.' She skipped off into the kitchen.

'You cheeky monkey,' said Sir Henry.

Alice walked over and asked, 'How's your Norton running, Sir Henry?'

'Like a charm. Those adjustments you made turned it into a flying machine. It's fuelled and ready.' He handed Alice the keys to his garage in Belgrave Square.

Mandy returned with a pot of tea and a plateful of buttered toast. She set the tray on Florence's desk. 'What is it you need me to do then?'

Florence bit into a slice of toast, 'I want you to drive

Henry's Bentley to Bletchley Park and collect Percy Butterworth at eight o'clock this evening. He's a codebreaker.'

'I can do that.'

'Then drop him at Henry's house.'

'A codebreaker boffin called Butterfingers,' said Mandy. 'He sounds like a barrel of laughs.'

'Butterworth,' said Sir Henry. 'Butterworth!'

'And then you can stay with me tonight,' said Florence. 'We'll pick Henry and Percy up in the morning at five.'

'Where are we going?'

'Milton Park.'

'Fantastic, I've always wanted to go there, this day is getting better and better.'

'Make sure you take care of my Bentley,' said Sir Henry. 'It's still new.'

Mandy rolled her eyes.

Florence stood. 'Henry, drink up, we need to visit Malcolm at Buckingham Gate.' She handed Mandy the car keys. 'They're expecting you at Bletchley at eight, so you best be going.'

Mandy looked at the three dearest people in her life. 'It's so good to be back.'

'You've been in prison for a couple of days,' laughed Alice. 'Hardly a stretch, is it?'

'I've served my time,' she said. 'I'm going to my house in Battersea to pack a few things, then off to get Mr Polly Butterfingers.'

'Percy Butterworth, his name is Butterworth,' said Sir Henry.

'Yeah, I got it. Goodbye.' Her voice trailed off as she bounded down the stairs and ran outside into the freshness of Horse Guards Parade.

Sir Henry opened the window and shouted, 'Drive my

Bentley carefully.' The screeching tyres and spitting gravel drowned out his words. 'That girl.'

'You love that girl,' said Florence.

'She is quite something.'

Alice said, 'I'll set up base in the room overlooking the lake at Milton Park. It will make a great ops room.'

Florence put her coat on and took a final look around her office. She knew she wouldn't be back anytime soon.

Outside, she looped her arm through Henry's. He took his scarf out of his pocket and wrapped it around her neck.

Florence's thoughts were, at best, jumbled. She had an abundance of ideas, but the core of her plan was still in its infancy.

'Do me a favour, will you tell Malcolm we're relocating?' she dipped her chin into the warm silk scarf.

'Yes, if you want me to.'

'No explanation though, and if he asks anything, keep the information to a minimum.'

'I can do that. Why don't you want to tell him?'

'He responds well to you. I'm too close to him at the moment.'

'Then leave it to me.'

'Tell him to pack up Buckingham Gate completely and be ready to leave by five in the morning. His engineers will need to work through the night.' She fell silent for a moment as they walked through St James's Park.

'What's going on in that head of yours?'

'We have to seal off Military Intelligence; nobody in, nobody out. From now on, we can't make a mistake. It is time to circle the wagons.'

Sir Henry nodded, and said, 'Let's see Winston tonight and fill him in on everything. He needs to know what we're doing.'

'Good idea, and I suppose we ought to invite Christopher Barrington, he should be kept in the loop.'

They walked up to the office block at Buckingham Gate.

'Hello Albert,' they said. Albert was an old serviceman, part of the old guard.

He gave a crisp salute.

Florence stepped closer and lowered her voice. 'We're evacuating Buckingham Gate for a while, security reasons, we can't say more than that. However, we need you to look after the building as if nothing has changed. Can you make this place look busy?'

'I'll make it look like Piccadilly Circus around here, don't you worry about a thing, Miss Fairweather.'

He saluted again and whispered, 'Is this part of the big push? Are we going to stick one on the Bosch at last? I wish I was forty years younger.'

Florence covered her mouth to hide her words. 'Yes, Albert, but you can't tell anyone.' She put her hand on Albert's shoulder. 'Only you, me and Churchill know the score. So keep it that way.'

He stood to attention and gripped his service rifle.

They walked into Buckingham Gate and made their way to the sixth floor. Malcolm's office door was open. Sir Henry could see Malcolm talking to Fletcher.

'Good morning, Sir Henry,' said Otto. 'Did we have a meeting planned for this morning?'

'No, no meeting planned, but I do need to talk to you and the engineers. Can you get them assembled?'

'Absolutely,' Otto jumped up and went into the other office.

Sir Henry followed him into the engineers' office to begin the briefing. Florence listened from the hallway.

Sir Henry began, 'As a security measure we are moving out of here. I want these offices stripped bare. Pack up the blueprints, maps, diagrams, charts, codes, and leave absolutely nothing behind, and be ready to move out at 0500hrs.'

'Why the sudden rush?' asked Fletcher.

'Orders from above,' said Sir Henry. 'When we get to our new location, you'll have to set up a new base.' He looked around at the shelves and drawers stacked with papers and folders. 'This will take you most of the night.' He took out his wallet and handed Malcolm a handful of crisp banknotes.

'Thank you very much,' said Otto. He tucked the money in his pocket.

The engineers laughed.

'Malcolm, take the boys to dinner at the Old Star pub behind Birdcage Walk, tonight. Invite Albert, from downstairs, and his wife. But gentlemen, you must be ready to leave at five in the morning, and pack for a long, cold trip.'

The engineers collectively murmured their acknowledgement while getting back to their desks, and Otto walked towards his office.

Florence grabbed his arm in the hallway, 'Malcolm, a quick word.' Otto followed Florence through into his office.

He said, 'Do you think this is a good idea moving out of here? I mean, shouldn't we get on with our work?'

'I have to tell you something, Malcolm, something I've just learned. Winston Churchill is going to become Prime Minister,' she said.

'Oh, really?'

'He must become Prime Minister if we are to stand any chance of winning this war.'

'But why are we relocating?'

'Because Winston suspects an attempt to steal the codes for the Spitfire is a genuine threat. But in my opinion, a German spy doesn't have a chance in hell, they simply don't have the imagination to pull it off.'

'I agree, not a chance in hell.'

'You've got your work cut out here. I would stay and help, but I have to get over to see Winston and Christopher Barrington.'

Florence picked up Malcolm's photo of the inseparable four and smiled at the fresh faces staring back at her. She put the photograph in an empty cardboard box. 'There, now you can't say I didn't help you pack.'

Otto gave Florence a Malcolm smile.

'I'll see you and your boys in the morning. Have fun at the pub tonight with Sir Henry's money. He isn't expecting any change, so spend it all.'

Once out on the street, Florence looped her arm through Sir Henry's. 'Nice touch giving them money for dinner.'

'We are taking them into the unknown, and we don't know for how long, so the least they should get is fish and chips and a few glasses of beer.'

Mandy carried her army kitbag and an old leather suitcase down the narrow staircase at her mum's Victorian terrace house on Queenstown Road, in Battersea.

'You bleeders,' she yelled out. 'If you scratch that car you'll get a slap, do you hear me?'

A gang of boys leaned against Sir Henry's Bentley.

'Who the hell do you think you are, the bleedin Queen?' A pale, skinny boy of sixteen stepped out in front of the others. 'What did you say you'd do if we scratched your stupid car?'

'I said you'd get a slap.'

'You and whose bloody army?'

'I am the bloody army, you cheeky bugger! Now scarper, the lot of you.' Mandy put her suitcase and kitbag in the boot of the car.

The skinny boy stood in front of the driver's door, blocking Mandy's way.

'You want to watch yourself, sunshine,' she said.

'Or what?' Skinny boy didn't see the combination of slaps coming. His hands involuntary went to his stinging cheeks. Mandy spun him around, pulled his shorts down to his ankles and gave his backside a hard smack.

The other boys pointed and laughed at Skinny as he struggled to pull his shorts back up. Mandy slapped him again, this time around the top of his head.

'There's a bloody war on you silly boys. We haven't got time to keep you lot in order.'

'We're bored. There's nothing to do,' said Skinny.

'Go and help out, do something useful down at the village hall. They always need things doing down there. Tell them Mandy Miller sent you. They'll give you a job.'

She reached into her pocket and pulled out a few coins and handed them to the boys. 'Get a cup of tea and a slice of bread and jam at the van in the park.'

'Thanks, Miss,' said Skinny.

She smiled at the gang of boys.

Skinny spoke up. 'You're alright, you are, Miss. So how come you drive a flash motor like this then?'

'Because I catch Jerry spies and shoot them dead.'

The boys stood in a semi-circle with gaping mouths.

'You got a boyfriend then?' Skinny asked.

'Bugger off you cheeky blighters.'

The boys cheered and ran after the Bentley as it sped off. Mandy looked in her rearview mirror, she knew if the war raged on for a few more years, those boys would be in the thick of it and not all of them would see Battersea again. She raced over Chelsea Bridge and into Sloane Square. The Bentley responded to her light touch, and the engine roared around Hyde Park corner, up Park Lane and through Marble Arch.

She lit a cigarette, checked her lipstick and straightened

her blond hair in the mirror, then headed out of north London towards Bletchley Park.

She'd heard stories from Florence and Sir Henry about Bletchley Park. They referred to it as Station X. A top-secret location, tucked away in the countryside for boffin code-breakers to crack Nazi codes. The most gifted people in Britain were funnelled into Bletchley to decipher messages and crack the uncrackable enemy codes. Mandy had met some of the codebreakers at Florence's house before the war. They were thin, pale, greasy-haired bores.

Mandy fancied brave, rugged, handsome army types.

Stanley Blagdon was a rugged, handsome army type, and she hated him; that's why she broke off their engagement.

Bastard.

Mandy and Stanley grew up together in Battersea, and to the others in Queenstown Road, it was a forgone conclusion they'd be married and have lots of noisy kids.

But that wasn't what Mandy wanted.

After Mandy's mother died, she drifted towards Stanley, and when she turned sixteen, they got engaged.

Mandy fought against the constraints of Stanley's jealous control and ignored his demands for her to quit her army training with Florence. He would say that spy work was for the stuck-up, work-shy snobs who minced about with no bloody backbone.

But Mandy knew better. She wanted better.

She decided to be alone for a while. She didn't need a boyfriend; brave, handsome or otherwise.

Stanley Blagdon had not taken the break up well.

Mandy pulled the Bentley through the front gates of Bletchley Park a few minutes before eight o'clock and stopped at the barrier.

'Papers?' The guard held out his hand.

Mandy handed over her documents.

He studied them. 'Park your car to the left of the building.'

She parked and walked into the building. At the reception desk, a uniformed soldier was filing cards in cardboard boxes.

Mandy tapped politely on the desk with her knuckle, 'I'm here to pick up Percy Butterworth.'

'Wait over there.' Without looking up he pointed to a wooden bench in the corner of the entrance hall.

Mandy didn't move. She pulled her warm army coat around her body, 'Will he be very long? I need to get going as we have a long way to go.'

'He'll be down when he's ready, driver. Sit and wait over there,' he pointed once more at the bench.

Mandy walked straight outside into the dark and lit a cigarette. The smoke curled away into the night. Before she finished, a well dressed, dark-haired man in a black suit and white open-necked shirt exited the building. He walked up to the Bentley and stood by the back door.

'Are you Butterfingers?'

'I'm Butterworth, Percy Butterworth,' he said politely.

'Jump in then, sunshine. I'm not your bloody chauffeur. You can open your own door.'

Percy opened the rear door.

'Not in the back,' she said.

He looked at her unsure what to do next.

'Come and sit in the front with me.' She patted the front passenger seat.

Percy opened the door and climbed in. 'I'm Percy. I'm sorry, I thought you were my driver.'

'I am your driver. My name is Mandy Miller.'

'I hope this car has a good heater, I'm freezing. I swear,

Bletchley Park is the coldest place on earth.' Percy's accent was precise and unmistakably upper class Eton.

Mandy reached behind her and handed him a flask. 'Have this. A cup of hot soup will see you right.'

'You might have just saved my life, Miss Miller.' Percy looked at her for more than a glance, 'I'm a scatterbrain, I've left my matches behind, do you have a light?'

She beamed a smile directly at him and handed him a box of matches. Her fingers brushed against his hand. It was the slightest, lightest of touches. But she felt it, and was certain Percy felt it too. Mandy knew the feeling all too well. The dashboard dials illuminated their faces with a soft, blueish glow as Mandy steered the Bentley out through the gates of Bletchley Park and headed for London.

CHAPTER 10

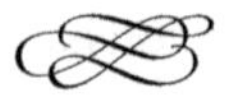

Raised voices echoed from inside Winston Churchill's graceful London residence on Morpeth Terrace.

Florence knocked.

Churchill's housekeeper, Ivy Amos, opened the door and invited them inside.

'Sounds lively in there,' said Florence.

'I've heard worse,' said Mrs Amos. 'Mr Churchill has been most boisterous tonight, but seeing you, Florence, might just calm him down a bit.'

Ivy Amos, according to Winston, was officially the nicest person in the world. And, everybody who met her agreed.

Ivy had been Winston's housekeeper for thirty years. She could brush Winston's foulest moods aside with ease, and every head of state had enjoyed her fruit cake. Without Ivy, Churchill's homes in London and Kent would fall apart at the seams. Churchill's world could not function without the indispensable Ivy Amos.

He often joked: Take away my Generals, if you must, but not my Ivy.

'Winston,' Florence called out. 'It's me. I'm with Henry.'

The raised voices fell silent.

Winston popped his head out of his study door, and a smile spread across his face when he saw her.

'Don't just stand there, come on through.'

Sir Henry hung up their coats.

Churchill nursed a brandy in one hand and held a thick cigar in the other. 'I was discussing a few things with Barrington; he arrived a little early.'

A log fire glowed orange in the grate, and the full-length red velvet curtains created a cosy snug. Christopher Barrington stood with his back to the fireplace. He was, as always, smartly dressed in a grey pinstriped suit and a pink silk tie and looked comfortably like a statesman and every bit a future Prime Minister.

Barrington nodded at the new arrivals. 'I'm afraid I can't stay long, I have to get back to Downing Street.'

'Then let's get to it,' said Florence.

Churchill sat next to Sir Henry.

Florence remained standing, eye-to-eye with Barrington. She was not one to shrug away. 'We're going into hiding,' she said. 'We've packed up our office at Military Intelligence. We'll be uncontactable until this threat is over. And one more thing, we are taking the boys from Buckingham Gate with us.'

'Into hiding? Uncontactable, and what threat?' jabbed Barrington.

Florence looked directly at him. 'Winston heard a rumour-'

Barrington cut her short and waved her away. He addressed Churchill. 'Are you still peddling that preposterous notion that Germany wants our aircraft? I've never heard such foolish nonsense.'

'I'm sure you probably have,' said Winston.

'The German airforce have plenty, perfectly good aircraft

of their own.'

'It's not about stealing our aircraft,' said Florence.

'What's it about then?' Barrington snapped.

'It's about stealing our icon, our war hero. Britain believes the Spitfire is invincible. If we were to lose it to the Germans, it would be a catastrophic disaster. We'd lose the war.'

Barrington didn't hide his smirk. 'So you plan to run away like scared little children?'

'That's only part of it,' said Sir Henry.

'You don't win wars by hiding.' Barrington let out a long irritated sigh. 'This is your meddling, Churchill.'

'I think it's a clever idea, and I back the plan,' said Winston.

'What's so clever about running and hiding?'

Churchill peeped over his gold-rimmed spectacles. 'Barrington, if your enemy can't see you, they can't defeat you. In conflict, if you cannot win, then it becomes critical you do not lose.' He drained his glass in one gulp. 'And, if hiding gives us a slight edge, then that, I can tell you, is how we'll eventually win the war, with a slight edge.' He puffed heavily and poured himself another generous brandy from his crystal decanter.

'It's completely unworkable and is poorly thought out. There must be a better option. Please tell me this is not the only plan Intelligence has come up with.'

'What would you suggest we do instead?' asked Sir Henry.

'I wouldn't run scared and hide in a hole.'

'Naturally,' said Winston. 'There is a time to hide and a time to fight. Right now is the time for us to be cunning. Not all Germans will wear tin hats and run at us with guns. The clever ones will find a way to get among us and destroy Britain from within, so Military Intelligence must fight a very different war.'

Barrington let out a breathy whistle. 'I suppose if you must run and hide, then you must. Where are you going?'

'I'm afraid I can't tell you.' said Florence.

'Saints preserve us! I must know, I'm head of Military Defence.'

'I know that, and I still can't tell you.'

'And keep it that way, Florence,' said Winston. 'Tell nobody. Fight the way you want to fight.'

'You old fool, Churchill,' said Barrington. 'We can't lose contact with Military Intelligence.'

'You aren't losing contact,' said Sir Henry. 'You just won't be able to make contact directly with us. We'll be contacting you.'

Barrington didn't hide his displeasure. 'So when does the hiding start?'

'It starts when we leave here this evening,' said Florence. 'There is too much at stake to stay in full view. You won't see us again. Not until the threat is over.'

Barrington thumped his fist hard down on his leg. 'There's no threat! If we lose this war, it will be because of idiotic blunders like this. It's on your head, Churchill. You encourage this loose-cannon behaviour.' He stood and paced around. 'You are predicting the Germans are going to invade us. We have plenty of time to make peace. We don't have to sacrifice Britain, and we can still avoid war. What we need is time to talk to Berlin. If we talk, they'll listen.'

Florence stood in front of Barrington. 'There is nothing to be gained from peace with Berlin. They want war. They're already at war, and they won't stop now. If, and only if, there was a genuine chance of total European peace then naturally, we must take it. We cannot under any circumstances, sit this one out. We can't let the rest of Europe be under Nazi rule. We must demolish their dark ideas and defend our island, whatever the cost, and stop Hitler's march upon our way of life.'

'Good God, Florence,' barked Barrington. 'You even sound like Churchill now. What possible hope do we have if you are just a bunch of nodding dogs?'

Winston stood and stretched his back, 'Where on earth are my manners? Look at the time, Barrington. You must be going, let me show you out. Downing Street awaits you.' Churchill ushered him to the study door. 'Mrs Amos will see you out.'

Barrington shot a glance at Florence. 'I expected more from you.' He looked at Churchill, 'I expected nothing less from you. While you stand here and plan for war, I'll prepare for peace.' He slammed the door behind him.

Winston put his finger to his lips and listened for the front door to shut. Barrington's car roared to life and sped away from Morpeth Terrace.

'So, where are we going, Florence?' asked Winston.

'Milton Park.'

'Oh, smashing idea, it's a beautiful place. I spent my school summer holidays there with Henry.' He looked up towards the ceiling to recall a more peaceful time.

'I'm afraid you aren't coming, Winston.'

'I'm not?'

'No, you're too valuable to be stuck out in the countryside waiting for something to happen. You're needed here, in the heart of Government.'

'I thought you might say that.'

'Alice has already gone, she left this afternoon, we're heading out first thing tomorrow morning with Malcolm Feathers and his team.'

'Barrington is no fool,' said Winston. 'He knows more than he lets on, and he has eyes and ears everywhere. He wants to become the next Prime Minister even though he spends his time denying it. I will be up against him at some point, and the trouble is, he has the vast majority of the party behind him.'

Florence hugged Winston. 'We'll set up a line of communication and keep you in the loop.'

Churchill looked at them both. 'Set the traps, spin the wheels, use smoke mirrors, and skulduggery, but at all costs, don't bugger it up.'

'You can count on it,' she said.

'And Henry, do try and keep her out of trouble.'

They left Winston standing in a haze of cigar smoke warming another brandy in the palm of his hand. His thoughts and attention most likely already focused on something else.

Mandy pushed Sir Henry's Bentley fast from Bletchley Park to the outskirts of London. Percy sat quietly and drank Mandy's soup to warm himself.

He was unlike the other codebreakers she'd met before, 'How do you know Florence?'

'I don't. I mean, I know Florence through Sir Henry when he placed me at Bletchley a couple of years ago.'

'Are you some kind of genius?'

'Oh gosh no, nothing as sophisticated as that. I'm into boring numbers, lots of tedious calculations.'

'Like what?'

'I work out how many bricks are required to build a hangar, that sort of thing. It's all very dull I'm afraid.' He replaced the cap on the flask. 'I seem to have finished all your soup.'

'You're a useless liar.'

'No, really I've finished it.' He shook the flask.

'Not about the soup, you're lying about your job at Bletchley.'

Percy stared straight ahead through the windscreen.

'Do you think Florence is going to send me to Bletchley Park in this snow to pick up a handsome bloke who is good at counting bricks? I wasn't born yesterday.'

'Well, as I said Miss Miller, I don't know Florence.'

Mandy let silence fill the car, then she spoke. 'When my mum died ten years ago, Florence took me under her wing. I don't know where I'd be if it weren't for her. She recruited me into the army, and well, here I am picking you up.'

Percy took his eyes from the winding roads and looked at her.

'What you looking at?' she said.

'You. Sir Henry surrounds himself with the best of the best, so tell me, Miss Miller, what's best about you?'

'I'm a great driver.'

'And what else?'

'If we ever get into a fight, stand behind me because I can punch my way out of a bar full of drunks.'

'I'll remember that . . . so you drive and bar fight?'

Mandy smiled at him.

He smiled back and blushed.

She steered the Bentley around Belgrave Square and pulled up. 'I'm dropping you here, at Sir Henry's house. I'll pick you up a few minutes before five in the morning. Don't oversleep.'

Percy stepped out of the Bentley and grabbed his bags. 'It was charming to meet you, Miss Miller, I look forward to seeing you in the morning.'

'One thing before you go,' she said.

Percy held the car door open. 'What's that, Miss Miller?'

'Call me, Mandy.'

Percy smiled, 'Mandy it is, goodnight.'

'Goodnight, Percy.'

She drove the Bentley six yards to the house next door and turned the engine off. She stepped out of the car, and walked up to the front door.

He looked across at her and smiled again, 'Where are you going?'

'I stay with Florence, she lives next door.'

'How convenient,' he slowed to a standstill. 'Well, goodnight again, Mandy.'

Without taking her eyes off Percy, she attempted to put her front door key in the lock. Florence opened the door as Mandy stood on the doorstep, stabbing her key aimlessly in mid-air. Florence pulled her inside.

Mandy said, 'I'm going to make you a cup of tea, Florence, and then you're going to tell me everything you know about Percy Butterworth.'

'That won't take long,' said Florence.

'Why?'

'I've just laid eyes on him for the first time. But I can see you are in lovey-dovey land.'

'Don't be daft. We hardly chatted on the way down.'

Next door, Percy began to unpack, he could only think about one thing, the rather lovely Mandy had called him, handsome.

Otto walked with Fletcher from Buckingham Gate, along Birdcage Walk towards the pub. The others had gone on ahead.

'I need to tell you something,' said Otto.

'What's that?'

'I've mislaid something, Fletch, something essential.'

'Not the money Sir Henry gave you?'

'Oh God no, that's safe,' Otto tapped his coat pocket. 'I

can't seem to put my hands on the Spitfire code. I'm sure it will turn up at some point.'

'Bloody hell, Malcolm, we can't build a single Spitfire without the 12g295 code.'

'Any suggestions?'

Fletcher stopped, 'I'm joking, Malcolm. In all honesty, we don't need it.'

'We don't?'

'Come on Malcolm, you know it's not needed. Not unless we lose all our aircraft assembly factories and have to start from scratch. But I shouldn't worry, it will turn up when we unpack at our new location.'

'I must be getting absent-minded these days.'

'You've had a tough time, old boy. Everything will work itself out, you'll see.'

Otto had seen the 12g295 code only once: when he was Owen Black. An innocent-looking, and somewhat unimpressive series of numbers and symbols. A single sheet of paper which could win the war for Germany. And simultaneously, lose the war for Britain. But for all the searching through Malcolm's office, he couldn't find it.

Fletcher and Otto walked into the noisy, smokey pub. Albert played the piano, and his wife belted out music hall songs with full gusto.

Otto took off his coat and scarf.

Brenda, the barmaid, called out, 'Evening Malcolm, evening Fletch, a couple of beers?'

'Perfect, yes please,' said Fletcher.

Otto never acquired a taste for warm, flat, stagnant-hop tasting English beer. He took a long sip, 'Lovely, just what I needed.'

Fletcher walked off, pipe in mouth, towards the piano and joined in with the raucous singing.

Brenda attracted Otto's attention. 'How are you, my lover

boy? You look a bit different tonight, more handsome than usual, perkier I'd say.'

'Perkier?'

'Yes, perkier, maybe you have a secret girlfriend stashed away?' she gave him a flirtatious wink.

'I'm afraid there's no secret girlfriend.'

Otto enjoyed Brenda's flirtatious behaviour when he was Owen Black. He couldn't act on his desires back then, and he couldn't now. A friendly hug and a pat on her back were as far as Otto could go. He looked over at the engineers who gathered around the piano and listened to Albert and his wife. He took out the money Sir Henry had given him. 'This should cover the drinks and fish and chips for everyone.'

Brenda took the money, 'I'll keep a tally.'

'If there's any left over, keep it and buy yourself something nice.'

'Thank you, Malcolm, you are adorable.' She leaned over the bar and kissed him on the cheek.

The evening wore on and after too many beers, and platefuls of fish and chips, and more singing, the engineers started to leave. Albert and his wife played one last song and left the pub unsteady on their feet. Otto and Fletcher finished their beer, left the pub and walked through the gates into St James's Park.

'Oh bugger,' said Otto. 'I've left my scarf in the pub. I'm bound to need it where we're going in the morning. I'll pop back and get it. Don't wait for me Fletch. I'll see you at Buckingham Gate at five in the morning.'

'Goodnight, Malcolm.'

Otto walked back to the pub and could see Brenda stacking chairs. He banged on the side door.

'Hello my love, what are you doing back here?'

'I left my scarf behind.'

'Come on in.'

'I'd forget my head if it wasn't screwed on.'

'Fancy another beer?'

'I'd prefer a cheeky whisky if you have one.'

'There was more than enough money left over for you to have whatever you want.'

Otto picked up his scarf and wrapped it loosely around his neck.

'I think I'll join you. It's been a long day.' She poured a couple of whiskies. 'Malcolm, when are you going to tell me about this girl of yours?'

'What girl?' No loose ends. Only dead ends.

She sat on a barstool next to his. 'I know the way someone looks at me if they fancy me or not. You had that look in your eye when you came in tonight. I've been working behind the bar long enough to know a thing or two.'

'I suppose a pub is a good place to learn about people.'

'I didn't know you fancied me like that. Maybe I was wrong about you.'

'Maybe you were.' He clasped his hand on her leg.

Brenda winced.

He put his arm around her and pulled her closer to him.

'What are you doing? That hurts, stop!' She pulled away. 'All these years you've been as shy as a goose. Now you've turned into some kind of sex maniac.'

Otto pulled at her skirt, and it ripped at the back. She tried to push him away, but he was too strong. 'What do you think you're doing? I was being friendly to you, that's all. It doesn't mean you can rip my clothes off.'

He grabbed her blouse and a button pinged off and skidded across the floor.

She slapped him across the face.

He didn't flinch. His eyes narrowed, and without warning, he slapped her face with the back of his hand and in an instant blood bubbled at the side of her mouth.

'What the hell has got into you?' she put her hand to her mouth.

'You hit me, so I hit you back,' his voice was cold. Germanic cold.

'Who the hell are you?'

Otto took off his scarf and towered over her. 'You shouldn't have said I looked different. I can't let that go. I like you, but you should have kept your filthy mouth shut.'

He wrapped his scarf around her neck and yanked it tight. Her fingers clawed at the wool, but his force was too much, and she began to choke. Otto rammed his knee into her back and kicked her feet away. She fell with a thud to the ground, and he pulled tighter on each end of the scarf. The struggling was soon over and Brenda's arms flopped by her side, and her feet stopped twitching.

Otto pulled his scarf from her neck and walked over to the bar, he poured himself a large whisky and gulped it down, then stepped into the kitchen. He used a sharp knife to slice through the rubber pipeline that ran from the gas cylinder to the cooker.

Gas hissed from the severed tubing. Otto lit a candle and placed it on the bar. He turned off the lights and walked out of the back door.

Brenda's body lay in the darkness among the stacked chairs. The explosion echoed around St James's Park, and Otto watched the fireball climb into the night sky. He pulled his collar up around his neck and walked towards Malcolm's flat on Victoria Embankment.

Tomorrow was going to be a long day, and he still needed the code.

<><><>

CHAPTER 11

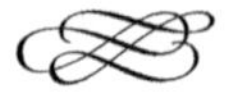

Alice was awake at five o'clock, and Milton Park was perfectly silent. She'd worked until after midnight to set up the new ops room, as she'd suggested, overlooking the lake.

Alice spent her life protecting Britain and knew it to be true the Germans would not stop at England's front gate now that they were blitzing their way through Europe at a frightening pace.

Her trust in Florence and Sir Henry had been generated over years of saving and protecting each other. They'd experienced their fair share of crouching in hell-holes under intense gunfire on battlefields.

They'd been through everything together.

Sir Henry's role was like that of a chairman: a safe pair of hands holding the many moving parts of Military Intelligence together. He could manage up and down the chain of command. His experience in spying was complete, and he'd been there from the outset. Sir Henry was Military Intelligence; he was England's master spy. He ought to be, he was the original man in the shadows. Alice, Florence and Sir

Henry fitted neatly together, like a three-piece jigsaw puzzle.

Florence was a sharp blade which cut straight to the bone with her precision strategies. Her vision was clear, and her certainty was unwavering. Florence was a leader of unequalled measure when it came to completing a mission. The three of them formed a lethal fighting force, and Churchill placed his faith in the trio to overcome the darkest, and most unsavoury of Germany's offensives.

Alice made herself a large pot of tea and stood outside to breathe in the chilly Cotswold air. She had despatched the military truck back to London late in the evening after they'd unloaded the boxes and the new HQ at Milton Park had begun to take shape. She watched the morning mist peel off the lake, and saw the faintest spears of light reach down to touch the water. Alice messaged Rosie before she went to bed but hadn't heard back from Berlin. They devised a secret code using their favourite Rudyard Kipling novel: The Jungle Book, a book Alice had read to her daughter when she was a little girl.

Rosie was posted to Berlin before the war and served in the German civil service as a clerk. Nothing risky, and nothing which required a high-level security clearance. Like all good spies, Rosie moved around unnoticed and remained unremarkable. She hadn't returned to Britain for more than eight months and continued to be another pair of trusted eyes and ears for Military Intelligence in Berlin.

Albert stood to attention outside the Buckingham Gate offices. He said the same line to anyone who would stop and listen.

'I can't believe Brenda's dead, such a sweet girl. I've known her since the day she started down the pub. The poor lass couldn't pull a decent pint, but she was a lovely, lovely girl.'

The engineers arrived before five o'clock, each with a small suitcase and a big hangover. The talk was not of relocation but of the pub explosion. Otto stood by the coach door and checked off their names on a clipboard. Malcolm loved clipboards.

Sir Henry's Bentley pulled up. Florence stepped out of the car and climbed into the coach. She said, 'Good morning, chaps, are you ready for the off?'

'Where are we going?' asked Fletcher. He puffed on his pipe. 'And why all the secrecy?'

'Think of it more a surprise than a secret.'

'Ooh, I like surprises,' said Fletcher. 'Nasty business at the pub last night, did you hear about it?'

'You boys didn't get into a brawl, did you?' She couldn't help but smile at the thought of the most unlikely group getting into a bar fight.

'No, it was the pub, it blew to smithereens a few minutes after we left.'

'Anyone hurt?'

'Albert told us that they found Brenda's body burned to pieces. It's a right old mess down there,' Fletcher said.

'That's dreadful,' Florence said no more. She stepped off the coach and stood next to Otto and looked at his clipboard. 'Everyone here and ready, Malcolm?'

'The only thing left on the sixth floor is paint on the wall and dust on the shelves.'

'I bet you're wondering where we're going?'

'It crossed my mind, but I trust you, Florence, you know that. I was thinking more about Brenda. We were in there drinking and eating just a bit earlier, makes you think doesn't it?'

Florence caught the attention of the coach driver. 'Follow me. We'll take it steady because the roads are icy.'

He gave a meaty thumbs-up sign and started the engine. Otto closed the coach door and took his seat next to Fletcher.

Florence walked over to Albert, who still looked shaken.

He saluted, but it lacked its usual crispness, 'Morning, Florence.'

'Morning Albert, what do you know about the pub explosion?'

'Don't know much, one minute the pub was there, the next minute, the gas explosion ripped it to shreds, and it was gone with the poor kid inside. Brenda was a sweet girl, she couldn't pull a pint but-'

Florence cut him short. 'How do you know it was a gas explosion?'

'The fireman told me on my way in this morning.'

Florence took a step closer to him. 'I need you to do something essential, Albert.'

'Of course, anything.'

'If anyone comes looking for us, anyone at all, Churchill or even His Majesty the King himself, it is imperative you don't tell them we're going to the Highlands of Scotland. And under no account tell them we are going off the grid. Have you got that? No mention of Scotland, understood?'

'Message received and understood.' Albert took a step back and stamped to attention. He was a proud veteran from the trenches of the First World War. A survivor, not a hero, as he corrected people who labelled him so. He stamped his feet to generate some heat, and the crisp echoes from his boots bounced inside the courtyard. Left-right, left-right, he marched on the spot, left-right, left-right.

Florence walked over to the Bentley and sat behind the wheel and explained what she had said to Albert.

'He'll have told half of London by lunchtime he thinks we're going to Scotland. And once his wife knows we're heading over the border, then the other half of London will know by tonight.'

'We're going to Scotland?' said Percy.

'Don't be daft,' said Mandy.

'But Florence just said. . .'

Mandy nudged him in the ribs. 'And you're supposed to be the best at Bletchley Park, God bloomin help us.'

'So, we're not going to Scotland?'

'Nobody is going to Scotland.'

'Come on, wagons roll,' said Sir Henry. He looked at his watch. 'It's exactly five o'clock, let's go, Flo.' He laughed at his rhyme. Rags sat in the front seat with Sir Henry and barked with excitement as the convoy pulled out. Florence steered around the coach and headed west, out of London.

She said, 'Mandy, I'll drive the first stint then we can make a breakfast stop, then you can drive from there and take us on to Milton Park.'

'Deal,' said Mandy. She grabbed a plump, white pillow and placed it against Percy's shoulder. She wriggled until she was comfortable and then closed her eyes. Percy continued reading. He had a book of poetry in one hand and a ream of coded papers in the other; he was attracted to both, and since the night before, he was also attracted to Mandy.

After an hour of treacherous driving, they parked, and Florence stepped onto the coach of sleepy engineers.

'Breakfast?' They nodded.

She returned to the vehicle and Mandy stepped out of the car and stretched her shapely limbs in a tightly fitted, black combat suit.

'Sleep well?' Asked Florence.

'I did, I've no idea why but I've not felt this good for years.'

'You looked comfortable all cuddled up with Percy.'

'I wasn't cuddled up with anyone.'

'You're probably right,' said Florence.

Rags bounded out of the car and started sniffing the grass. Florence picked up a large box and handed it to Mandy. 'You did a first-class job last night making these sandwiches, go and hand them out to the engineers.'

Pairs of dreary eyes peered through the steamy coach windows and focused on Mandy swaying towards them.

'Wakey-wakey, anyone fancy a bacon and egg sandwich? I made these with my own fair hands in the middle of the night for you lot, so you better enjoy them.'

Sir Henry watched the proceedings on the coach from the warmth of the car. He looked at Florence. 'Is there no end to your genius?'

'Not that I know of.' Florence handed Sir Henry and Percy a sandwich and a mug of tea.

'Mandy certainly has a unique skill for getting attention,' said Percy.

'You haven't seen anything yet,' said Sir Henry. 'That girl is quite something.'

Mandy walked back to the Bentley, leaned against the bonnet and bit into her sandwich. She looked into the car at three faces looking out, 'What are you lot gawping at?'

After breakfast, Mandy took the wheel, and Percy sat next to her. Sir Henry and Florence made themselves cosy in the back seat with a warm blanket over their laps. Rags spread out across them in a deep sleep as they discussed operations.

Percy said, 'Excellent egg and bacon sandwich.' It was the first thing he'd managed to say without being tongue-tied.

'My mum was a tea lady. Her cheese and onion sandwiches were the best in the world. I can still taste them.'

'You were lucky to have a mum who taught you well. I

can't even boil an egg. That's pretty pathetic, don't you think?'

'Very pathetic, but you probably did well at school.'

'I did quite well.'

'I'm guessing, Eton, then Oxford?' she said.

'You're right. And you?'

'Battersea.'

'I'm not sure I've heard of it.'

'You wouldn't have, it was a dump.'

'Did you go on to university?'

'Percy, let me clue you in, it will save us a lot of time. I left school the day my mum died. I was fourteen. I met Florence and Alice a few days later, and they taught me about life, well, they taught me everything. I can speak French and German, and I can memorise the correct order of four decks of shuffled playing cards in under a minute. I never met my dad, and by all accounts, I didn't miss much, but my mum was the kindest person in the world. And, university you ask? I didn't get that chance.'

Percy let all the new information sink in. 'I would pick you above anyone I met at Eton, or Oxford, or Bletchley Park.'

'Pick me for what?'

'Driving, pub fighting, of course, and definitely sandwich making, memory card tricks and everything else in between.' He blushed.

Mandy smiled directly at him. 'You are sort of lovely, Mr Percy Butterworth.'

He blushed again. She got his name right.

Florence poked her head between the two front seats. 'Are you keeping an eye on the coach?'

Mandy glanced in the rearview mirror. 'Oh shit, shit. Where the bloody hell is it?'

She pulled the Bentley over to the side of the road and

looked at Percy. He looked back at her, and they burst out laughing.

He said, 'I'll jump out and have a look.' Percy stepped out into the icy wind. 'I can see it, here it comes, chugging up the hill.'

'Mandy, try not to lose the one thing we intend to protect,' said Sir Henry.

Mandy looked at Percy through the side window.

'You listening?' Sir Henry's words pierced Mandy's thoughts.

'Yes, I'm all ears, don't lose the coach.'

Florence tapped Mandy's shoulder. 'I want you to drive the coach into Milton Park. We can leave the driver on the side of the road while we go and unpack. I don't want civilians to know our new location.'

Mandy spent the next hour with one eye on the coach watching it struggle up and down the Cotswold Hills. A couple of miles from Milton Park, she pulled the Bentley off the road. A minute later, she was behind the wheel of the coach and left the bemused driver on the roadside.

Two miles of twisty lanes later, Florence nosed the Bentley through a concealed, stone gateway. Mandy followed her, expertly negotiating the coach into Milton Park.

Mandy hadn't seen anything like it before. The Cotswold-stone stately home sprawled across the horizon. Its four imposing pillars rose from the ground to the roof which covered the front entrance. The morning sun contained a little warmth and glazed the surface of the lake with a yellow glow. Alice waved with enthusiasm from the front door and ran out to meet the vehicles. Florence parked the Bentley next to the garage block and directed Mandy to park the coach close to the front door. Mandy turned off the engine and looked over her shoulder.

'This is our stop.'

Florence stepped onto the coach, 'Look lively, grab a couple of boxes each and follow Alice.' The engineers ambled off the coach with a box under each arm.

Florence introduced Otto to Mandy.

Mandy said, 'I've heard so much about you from Florence and Sir Henry. It's always Malcolm-this-and-Malcolm-that.' She paused a moment. 'I was so sorry to hear about your mum and dad. I know how that feels.'

Otto smiled back, 'Thank you, Mandy.'

Florence picked up a couple of boxes, 'Malcolm and I were at Oxford together; he's more like family. And Mandy, well, she is family.'

Otto said, 'Mandy, you make a great sandwich, and you drive better than the coach driver, we were all getting a bit queasy.' He picked up two boxes and put them under his arms and stepped off the coach and joined the engineers inside the house.

Florence turned to Mandy. 'I need you to do something for me. No questions asked.'

'Ooh good, I love a mystery.'

'Not this one, you won't.'

'Is this Buckingham Gate office?' asked a man in a black coat and matching hat.

'Identify yourself, sir.' Albert faced the man, his rifle at the ready.

'Inspector Giles, Eastbourne police station.' He showed Albert his badge and credentials.

'What's your business at Buckingham Gate, Inspector Giles?'

'I'm here to see Mr Malcolm Feathers. Has he arrived yet, or am I too early?'

'Too early? I'm afraid you're too late, sir.'

'Too late?' Giles took off his hat and scratched his head. 'Too late, you say.'

'Their coach pulled out ten minutes ago.'

'Coach? What time will he be back?'

'Inspector, they aren't coming back.'

'Oh I see, have they gone far?'

'Well, yes.'

'So what are you doing here then?' asked Giles.

'I'm guarding the building until they get back.'

'Oh, so they are coming back.'

'I think I've said too much already,' Albert looked flustered.

Giles waited a beat, 'I'd say you've kept tight-lipped. After all, I still know nothing.'

Albert lifted his chin, 'I do my best, Inspector.'

Giles turned away from the front of Buckingham Gate and stood on the bottom step. 'There was one thing.'

'What's that, sir?'

'You probably see everything, and I doubt much gets past you.'

'I'm on the ball if that's what you mean.'

'Has Malcolm Feathers seemed a little off since his parents' funeral?'

'I would say, considering the near miss we all had last night, I've never seen Malcolm be, well, more like Malcolm.'

'Near miss, last night?'

'Yes, the pub, the one behind Birdcage Walk, it blew up in the middle of the night. We were all in there, moments before, singing and drinking, we must be the luckiest people in the world, apart from Brenda.'

'Brenda?'

'The barmaid, she died in the gas explosion.'

'What makes you think it was gas?'

'I stopped and talked to the fire-crew on my way to work

this morning. That's what they told me. The whole bloody lot went up. Poor Brenda, a lovely girl, couldn't pull a decent pint though.'

Giles turned to leave, 'I hear there's a facility in Wales, maybe I'll find them there.'

'I think you mean the Highlands of Scotland.'

'Ah yes, the Highlands, that's right. Well, I'll be off, have a good day and thank you again, you've been most helpful.'

Albert waved him off.

CHAPTER 12

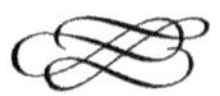

Florence stood by the bay window overlooking the lake. It had been a long day, and there was more to come. Her mind flooded with a conflicting mixture of half-finished plans for the shifting landscape which lay ahead. And that's the way she loved to work.

Alice had divided the ops room into three sections using bookcases and boxes. In the centre, there was a section containing a double-sided desk for Florence and Sir Henry. Alongside it, Alice set up her workbench packed with oddments and prototype contraptions. There was a quiet area in front of the bay windows with two soft leather chesterfields facing each other and a pile of comfortable blankets. The third area was a briefing section along the back wall with maps, charts, a blackboard and a dozen folding wooden chairs facing a white screen.

Later in the evening, the whole team gathered in the new ops room. Mandy sat in the front row between Percy and Otto with Rags curled up by her feet. Alice sat next to Sir Henry and the engineers assembled in the rows behind.

Florence stood at the back of the room and waited for the room to fall silent, then turned off the lights.

She said, 'We are under attack.'

Florence's words punctured the air, 'The battle we face is an invisible one. German Intelligence has put a plan in motion to steal our Spitfire.'

Murmurings filtered through the briefing area.

Then silence once more.

'If German Intelligence succeeds, Britain will fall, and Europe would be in Nazi hands.' Florence paused. 'America is undecided whether to join the fight, so Berlin, essentially, would control half the world with Hitler, its supreme commander.'

She switched the lights back on, and the murmuring started as Florence walked to the front of the briefing area. 'We've never been more vulnerable than we are right at this moment.'

'Why's that?' asked Fletcher.

'Because our security is stretched and dislocated across the country. The Spitfire production locations are unprotected, and worse still, we don't know from where the threat is coming. We're blind and gaping wide open for an attack. Our soft underbelly is exposed. If the Germans knew our position, they'd arrive tonight and be standing outside this room.'

'Bloody hell, can it get any worse?' asked Fletcher.

'Yes, much worse, the Government is split. Some seek peace with Berlin while others are fighting to protect Britain by arming up.' She put her hands on her hips. 'We are at war with Germany, and worse, at war with ourselves.'

Fletcher raised his hand.

Florence pointed at him, 'Yes?'

'Is that why we're here, tucked away, out of sight?'

'Precisely, we've sealed ourselves off. From now on it's nobody in and nobody out.'

'What do you want us to do?' asked Fletcher. 'The Germans aren't planning to steal every single Spit in one go, are they?'

'We don't have a clue what they plan to do.'

A bearded engineer from the back row asked. 'Do the Bosch know that we know that they want to take our kite?'

'We don't know.'

'What do they know?' Asked the engineer.

'We don't know,' said Florence.

Otto raised his hand. 'How do we know the blasted Bosch are planning to do this?'

'Churchill heard a whisper in Parliament. And, one thing is for sure, when it comes to whispers, he's never wrong.'

Alice reached up with a hooked stick and unrolled a wall-sized map of Britain. Coloured flags were pinned in locations from the south coast, to the north of England. The group gathered around the map. For the next two and half hours, they listened to suggestions to tighten up fighter command's operations.

'Let's take a break, then press on later,' said Florence.

The engineers lit their pipes and milled about the ops room by the leather sofas overlooking the lake.

Alice and Mandy walked through to the kitchen, and Rags ran after them. They returned with huge pots of tea and platefuls of thickly sliced bread and jam.

'There are fifty jars in the pantry,' said Alice. 'So, damson jam it will be, while we're here at Milton Park.'

The engineers swarmed around the tray like chickens pecking at corn seed from a spilt bucket.

Sir Henry bit into a slice of bread and jam, 'You can't beat a cup of tea to lift your spirits, especially after a long day.'

Alice nodded.

Rags ran under the table to pick up breadcrumbs.

Otto walked over and stood next to Florence. 'How much longer do you need us for tonight?'

'Thirty minutes should do it; your boys look jaded.'

'They do a bit.'

'You look tired too, Malcolm.'

'It's been a superb evening, very enlightening.'

Florence shouted above the din. 'Take your seats!'

The chatter faded, and Florence dabbed her stick on the twenty-one coloured flags dotted around the country.

She said, 'This is it. These are the disjointed, secret manufacturing sites for the Spitfire where they make windshields, wheels, wiring looms, and electric components. These parts are collected and sent to Supermarine's factory at Woolston in Southampton for assembly.'

Mandy stood, 'If I was a snotty Bosch spy, I'd hand that map to the Luftwaffe so they could send over a wave of bombers. Game over, and good night Britain.'

Otto stared at the map. And God knows he tried not to stare. But there it was in front of him, laid out in multicolour, Germany's victory. He forced himself not to smile. The English were nothing but amateurs.

He raised his hand.

'Malcolm?' said Florence.

'How do we stop the threat?'

'That's why we're here,' she said and rolled up the map. 'It's been a long first day, let's call it a night.'

Alice coughed to attract the group's attention. 'We'll take a brisk, refreshing walk around Milton Park at six in the morning, then enjoy a hearty breakfast.'

Mandy stood and stretched. Several pairs of eyes watched the material of her combat suit stretch tightly over her body.

She nudged Percy, 'Have you got a light?' He handed her a box of matches. She rolled her eyes and immediately gave them back. 'Don't be silly, come outside and light my cigarette.'

He jumped up and followed her through the double doors onto the terrace.

Mandy swivelled her head to take in the house, 'I've never seen anything as amazing as this. It's more like a palace. I bet your family home looks just like this.'

He lit their cigarettes. 'Not at all, this is a Cotswold-stone stately home, ours is Tudor; completely different era.'

Mandy shivered, and he took off his jacket and wrapped it around her shoulders.

She kissed him on his cheek. 'Thank you.'

'For what?'

'For noticing I was cold.'

He smiled.

She said, 'I doubt you have any idea how the rest of us live. Our house in Battersea didn't have an inside loo or running water. Me and mum shared one bedroom, and in the winter we went to bed wearing our coats, it was so bloody cold.'

'I bet you were happy though.'

'I was, but not because we had nothing, but because we had each other.'

'Then, Mandy Miller, you had everything.'

'Everything but money,' she said.

Percy watched her lips as she spoke. Her lips looked as if they were preparing a kiss with each word. He imagined what it would be like to hold her, to kiss her, his thoughts spiralled until he imagined a full kissing embrace.

'Percy!'

'Yes, what?' he snapped out of his trance.

'Are you listening?'

'I'm right here, of course I'm listening, what do you think I was doing?'

Rags pushed the back door open and ran out on the terrace. He sniffed at the cold air and chased around in circles, then ran off to find a tree.

'Let's go inside,' Percy said.

He watched her slink her way through the chairs and pick up teacups and plates. He couldn't take his eyes off her. Nor did he want to.

Mandy's bedroom was next to Percy's.

The adjoining door was locked, and the key was not in the lock. Mandy looked for it without success. She pressed her ear to the door and listened to Percy shuffling about in his room. It sounded like he was getting undressed, hopping from one foot to the other. She heard him light a cigarette. She followed the creaks from the floorboards and heard his balcony door open.

Mandy opened her door and stepped out onto her balcony. 'I thought you would be asleep by now.'

'No, not yet, I'm wide-awake and far too excited. My head is full of, well, full of all this.'

'Do you have a spare one of those?' she asked.

'It's my last, take it.' He reached across the balcony and handed her his cigarette. The moon lit up one half of her face with a silver shine, and the other was cast in dark shadow.

He stared at her.

'You're gawping at me again.'

'I know.'

She leant over the balcony, and he mirrored her movement, they met halfway and kissed; slowly at first, then slower. They held onto the railings with their fingertips to make their kiss linger a little longer.

She whispered as they kissed, 'In the ops room, my elbow brushed your elbow, and I felt a shock.'

'Me too,' he said.

A knock on Mandy's door pierced the moment.

Their lips parted.

She shot Percy a glance. 'Don't move.'

'Hurry up. It's freezing out here. I brought a bottle of brandy with me, do you fancy a glass?.'

'Love one,' she said, then ran through the bedroom and opened her door. Florence walked in.

'You're working late,' said Mandy.

'Lots to do. And what I'm going to ask you to do is best done in private.'

'Is this the mystery mission you mentioned on the coach?'

Florence didn't preamble, 'I need you to collect someone in the morning. Take one of Sir Henry's cars from the garage—not the Bentley—something small and discreet; I don't want you to draw any attention. There's a military exercise taking place tomorrow, and I've arranged for one of the soldiers to be discharged from duty and handed over to us for security. I need someone I can trust to guard Milton Park.'

'That makes sense, where do I need to go?'

'The other side of Oxford, there's a military base with a deep water tank where they test submarine parts. The person you'll be collecting will be waiting in the guardhouse.'

'Sounds easy enough, so why all the cloak and dagger charade?'

'Because the person you're picking up is Stanley Blagdon.'

'Florence, no! Of all the soldiers in the British army, why did you have to pick the biggest wanker?'

'There's more, the girl who died in the pub explosion was Brenda Blagdon, Stanley's sister.'

'Oh my God, that's awful, that's so sad.' said Mandy. 'I can't believe it, poor Brenda. Does Stanley know?'

'No, he doesn't. And I don't want you to tell him.'

'I won't say anything. You know he took our break up badly. He came after me and got into a right old rage.'

'He'll get over it,' said Florence. 'I need him here. I can trust him. And, all said and done, he is a good soldier.'

'Yes, I suppose he is. But Florence! Stanley bloody Blagdon! You want me to pick him up and bring him back here to babysit us. Just like that, as if nothing has happened.'

'Sounds like you've grasped the gist of it.'

'Why don't you want me to tell him about Brenda?'

'I'll tell him soon, but right now, I need him to focus on security.'

'That's harsh, but I'll take care of it.'

'I'll say goodnight then, and I'll leave you and Percy to finish your last cigarette and enjoy a glass of brandy. And whatever else you were doing.' Florence smiled at her. 'Get some sleep. It's been a long day, and tomorrow will be longer.'

'How do you know about the cigarette. . . and whatever else we were doing?'

Florence put her finger to her lips and looked around the room. 'I'm a spy.'

'I wish you would stop saying that.' Mandy shut her bedroom door and ran back onto the balcony.

Percy stood in the dark. 'Everything alright?'

'Yes, I suppose.'

He reached over and handed her a glass of brandy.

She took a sip. What she wanted was to kiss him again, but the moment had gone. Usually, she was the one in control around men, but not around Percy. She felt her heart pound when they kissed.

'Put your glass down,' she said, and stepped onto the ledge and jumped into his arms.

Percy wrapped his coat around them both, and they took turns sipping brandy from his glass.

'That was Florence at the door,' she said.

'Did she come to tuck you in?'

'No, silly, she came to give me a job for the morning.'

'A driving, fighting job?'

'Both! I have to collect Stanley bloody Blagdon.' Mandy turned around in Percy's arms and rested the back of her head against his chest.

German spies were coming, Stanley Blagdon was coming, yet Mandy was happier than ever.

'Who is Stanley bloody Blagdon?'

'My ex-fiancé, we broke up before I went to prison.'

'Ex-fiancé? No, wait, you went to prison? What did you do?'

'It was nothing really, I slapped an officer in the face and kicked him in the you-know-whats. But he had it coming.'

'That's generally true about officers.'

'I warned him. Touch me again, and I'll wallop you. He didn't listen; he grabbed my arris once too often. So I flattened him.'

'That raises another question, what's an arris?'

'You're a posh boy, Percy Butterworth. Your arris is your arse.' She pushed her backside into him.

He kissed the top of her head. 'They sent you to prison?'

'Yeah, Wandsworth prison has a military wing for naughty soldiers. I was only there for a couple of days until Florence and Alice whisked me away. The same day I drove to Bletchley Park to pick up some codebreaker clown. And here we are.'

'Clown?'

'You're not a clown, you're lovely.'

'What happened to the officer?'

'Sir Henry instructed him to report for duty in some very shitty hell-hole for the rest of the war.'

'And what about Blagdon?'

'We grew up together in Battersea. We were more like brother and sister, and it was never going to be more than that, but then my mum died, and we became a couple. He took our break up badly. And tomorrow I pick him up.'

'That doesn't sound too bad.'

'He'll hate you.'

After Midnight, Milton Park was quiet. The engineers made their final bathroom visits, put out their pipes and settled down for the night.

Otto Flack lay awake.

Luck was running his way. He'd walked straight into Military Intelligence under the protective gaze of Florence and Sir Henry, and on the ops room wall was a map displaying the twenty-one locations he needed to bomb Britain out of the war.

Otto stared up at the ceiling. He knew that without the 12g295 code, he still had nothing. Had Malcolm hidden the code, burnt it, or maybe he handed it to someone for safe-keeping? Otto's thoughts drifted away from codes to think about Lizzie Denton and vowed not to let his emotions get the better of him again.

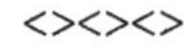

CHAPTER 13

Nobody could escape Alice's morning march.

Mandy and Florence stopped by an oak tree on top of the ridge. Mandy gazed back at the sandy-coloured country estate which stretched from the lake to the woods. The house was set over four floors, and each window had a balcony with a view of the Cotswolds.

It was breathtaking.

'Is Sir Henry, the richest man in the world?'

'Don't be silly,' said Florence. 'I think he's the thirty-ninth.'

Mandy put her hands on her hips and whistled through her teeth. 'He should try a bit harder then.' She ran ahead to find Percy.

The engineers, who were unaccustomed to the great outdoors, coughed and spluttered, and their pipes left tumbling trails of aromatic smoke behind them. Florence looped arms with Sir Henry while Otto picked up the rear and chatted with an out of breath, Fletcher.

Rags ran non-stop around the grounds of Milton Park

following the scent of rabbits. He barked and chased the birds who flew away when he bounded towards them.

Sir Henry and Florence caught up with Mandy who was walking with Percy. The four of them walked along the ridge together. Mandy never held back a question when she had a thought bursting to come out.

'Sir Henry, you know King George, why does he always look so serious.'

'Being King is a serious business. I can assure you, he's a decent man.'

Florence added, 'Henry begged the King to take the Royal Family away from London to take refuge somewhere safer, but the King refused to budge.'

'Is he an honourable king, would you say?' asked Percy.

'Oh, very much so, he's witty too. Although, there was this time before the king became king when we used to play golf together. I had a course built here at Milton Park to host a Royal tournament. The greens and fairways looked magnificent, and the groundsmen worked for months, making it absolutely perfect. It was 1927, a bone-dry July and a beautiful sunny day. Thousands of spectators turned up and lined the course to watch Bobby Jones play Walter Hagen. The confident, sure-footed amateur up against the mighty, unbeatable Hagen. Winston was here; he loved the whole day.'

'Is Mr Churchill much of a golfer?' asked Percy.

'Good gracious no, he refers to golf as a most hateful game. Winston likes the cameras though, and there were hundreds of press photographers who snapped away at the two great golfers. Winston seemed to be in every photograph.'

'What was the prize?' asked Mandy.

'A stunning cream and blue Rolls Royce with red leather seats. I can remember it as if it was yesterday.' Sir Henry pointed to the left of the lake. 'The eighteenth green was down there. Bobby Jones sunk a perfect thirty yarder to win the match. All the money raised was sent to a wounded soldiers' fund.'

Florence added, 'When the King presented the Rolls Royce to Bobby Jones, he drove Walter Hagen, Winston and the King around the course. They drank champagne and waved to the crowds.'

'Happier times,' said Percy.

'But not as exciting,' said Sir Henry with a wink. 'After the match, when everyone had left Milton Park, the King—who was Prince Albert before he was king—challenged me to a game of golf. The loser was to pay for lunch at the Dorchester Hotel in Mayfair, so the stakes were high. On the last hole, Prince Albert sent his shot into the long grass, and if he couldn't find his ball, he would have to forfeit the shot, lose the match, and pay for lunch. I watched him hack away with his golf club searching for his ball. He spent more than twenty minutes looking everywhere for it. Then, he suddenly found his ball. And so, here was my quandary.' Sir Henry looked at Percy and Mandy. 'You asked me if the King was an honourable King? Well, I have to tell you, I knew he'd cheated that day. He couldn't possibly have found his golf ball.'

'Why not?' they asked.

'Because I had it in my pocket the whole time.'

The group headed for the kitchen. Mandy cooked scrambled eggs on toast for everyone.

Otto walked over to Florence. 'I have an idea, but it's probably a bit silly.'

'Spit it out, then we'll know.'

'Why don't you put a dozen burly guards at each of the sites and protect the Spitfire that way?'

Florence put her teacup down, 'That would work if we knew what we were guarding against. I don't think for a minute a Jerry will march up to the front door wearing a red swastika armband. Extra guards will just make everyone jittery, and besides, we don't have the manpower. I feel a low key approach is what's needed.'

'That makes perfect sense,' he said.

Mandy stepped outside and sat on the edge of the terrace. The lake's black mirror-surface reflected the low slung morning sun. Rags was behind her sniffing at a tuft of grass. She hugged him, and Rags kissed her face and rested his head into her lap.

'Time to make your collection,' said Florence.

'Rags, you old lump, off you get, I have to go.'

'I'll come over to the garage block with you and see you off,' Florence pulled Mandy to her feet.

Mandy looked into the kitchen and saw Percy chatting with Alice, or rather, Alice was talking at him while he listened. Percy nodded in all the right places. And, at that moment he looked up and smiled at Mandy.

Percy was genuinely lovely.

He waved, she waved back.

'Hey, concentrate,' said Florence.

'Yes, right, I'm all yours.'

'Take the Austin this morning, it's small, slow, the heater doesn't work, and for some reason, it smells of wet grass, and it is definitely low key.' They walked to the garage block, and Florence opened the garage doors to reveal a line up of exotic racing cars.

'Wow,' said Mandy. 'Look at these beauties. Sir Henry certainly has taste.'

'He does, that's true, but these beauties are mine. Henry

prefers the sedate Bentley and his Norton motorbike, although not when I ride it with him on the back.'

There were six trophies bunched up on the shelf and a set of racing overalls hanging on the wall.

Mandy picked up the trophies, 'Yours?'

'Yes, from Brooklands. I still hold the track record.'

'I'll pop down and beat it when I have nothing else to do.' She took the racing overalls off the wall. 'You must have looked a proper racer wearing these.'

'You have a job to do, no more delaying tactics.'

Mandy took the car key off the hook and opened the driver's door of the little black Austin. She started the engine and swung the car out of the garage in one smooth movement. She slid the side window open an inch, 'You're right, it smells of wet grass.'

Mandy had banked on never seeing Stanley again. But for Florence, she would do anything. She sped the Austin along the sweeping gravel driveway and out through the pillared gateway.

Sir Henry walked out onto the driveway and put his arm around Florence. 'You alright?'

'You know, I couldn't love her more if she were my own daughter. You should have seen her face when I asked her to pick up the Blagdon boy.'

'Somehow, you manage to get people to do the very thing they least want to do, and that includes me.'

'She'll get over it, she's tough.' She held his arm. 'Let's go and get started in the ops room.'

Mandy drove as fast as the little, underpowered car would go, just like Florence. She took the racing line and clipped every corner with a screech of squealing tyres. She arrived at the military base several minutes early and was directed to park her car in a bay.

Through the guardhouse window, Mandy saw two soldiers and the unmistakable silhouette of Stanley Blagdon. He sat on a wooden bench next to his kitbag.

During one of her training exercises, Mandy had to swim underwater through a pipe filled with thick, gluey mud. The lesson was not about swimming in mud; it was how to overcome the rising panic. At the sight of Stanley, Mandy put her shoulders back, her chin up, lit a cigarette and walked into the guardhouse.

'Mandy! what the hell are you doing here?'

The two other soldiers looked Mandy up and down. The taller one said, 'What's a pretty little thing like you doing for the war effort, missy?'

Mandy ignored him.

'I know what I want you to do.' The shorter soldier grabbed his crotch while the other soldier laughed.

Mandy said, 'Calm down sunshine, or I'll have to tell your sobbing mothers why I had to beat you both to death.'

'Who the hell do you think you are, threatening me like that? You want to watch yourself,' said the short one.

'I'm here to collect that,' she pointed at Blagdon.

'You need to calm down and keep your bloody hair on,' said the taller soldier. 'We're only having a bit of fun.'

'Would your wife find it fun?' said Mandy.

'My wife?' The guard turned ashen.

'I think she'd cut your little bits off and put them in a jar.' Mandy stared at the two men until they fell silent. 'Blagdon, get your kitbag soldier, and look lively, you're coming with me.' Without another word, they walked to the car and Mandy drove the Austin out of the military base and headed towards Milton Park.

'It smells of wet grass in here,' said Blagdon.

'Don't speak! Sit there and shut up.' Mandy didn't look at him, and he didn't look at her.

'We need to replicate our Buckingham Gate offices in here,' Otto looked at the splendour of the room, 'Whatever this is?'

'It's the ballroom,' said Fletcher.

The engineers rolled up their sleeves and took the boxes off the stack one at a time.

'Fletch, I need you to help me with the crates from my office.'

Fletcher lit his pipe.

Otto picked up three heavy boxes and marched to the middle of the room. Fletcher struggled with one.

'Have you been doing push-ups?' said Fletcher. 'Look at you humping three boxes at a time. You're normally work-shy when it comes to a bit of graft.'

Otto put the boxes down, 'I'm doing my bit to get stronger and stay in shape.'

'You've done a bit of running but you've never been *in* shape, I suppose it's about time you did a bit of real exercise.'

'Fletch, I must find that code. It has to be in these boxes somewhere. It can't have just walked out of my office.'

'Don't panic, Malcolm. You've probably put it somewhere safe. It will turn up.'

'If you find it, give it straight to me, I don't want anyone else knowing I've mislaid it. Imagine what Florence and Sir Henry would say if they knew I'd lost the one code I've been assigned to keep safe.'

Fletcher gave Otto the thumbs-up sign and carried on moving the crates. Four hours of sweating and sorting, and they had recreated the offices from Buckingham Gate in the palatial ballroom.

'Time for lunch, I think,' said Otto. The engineers

followed him and Fletcher into the kitchen. Alice was talking with a uniformed soldier.

'Gentlemen, meet Stanley Blagdon,' she said. 'He is going to be the security presence during our stay at Milton Park. He wants to meet you all personally to find out your movements and show you the protocols for coming and going.'

Stanley introduced himself to each of the engineers.

'I hear you once dated the charming Mandy Miller,' said Fletcher.

'Who told you that?'

'This is Military Intelligence, old sport,' said Fletcher. 'Secrets fly about all over this place.'

'I'm Malcolm Feathers,' said Otto. 'I appreciate you guarding us here. I think a bit of security is an excellent idea.'

Alice walked from the kitchen into the ops room. Florence was studying a wall map with Sir Henry.

'How are the engineers?' asked Sir Henry. 'Are they settling in and getting their office set up in the ballroom?'

'They've set up. Now they're eating, drinking tea and meeting with Stanley Blagdon.'

'Did Fletch ask him if he used to date Mandy?' asked Florence.

'Yes, he did, and Blagdon blew up. Did you put Fletch up to it?'

'It's what I do best,' said Florence.

'I can't argue with that,' said Alice.

Sir Henry looked at the wall map and pointed at a blue flag. 'These chaps make fuel tanks for the Spitfire, a company called Hodges. It's a non-military site. I think we should visit them first thing in the morning. We should let Mr Hodges know there is a security threat.'

'Good idea,' said Florence. 'Let's take Mandy and Malcolm. Alice, will you look after the engineers tomorrow morning and keep them out of trouble?'

Alice nodded.

Mandy came into the ops room and sat next to Percy on the chesterfield. Rags bounded over and rested his head in Mandy's lap.

She ruffled his fur, 'If everyone could be as lovely as you, nobody would ever feel miserable.'

'How did it go with the boyfriend collection operation?' asked Percy.

'Old boyfriend. It's very much dead and in the past. I'll tell you what's so bloody annoying.'

'What's that?'

'The stupid comments I get from soldiers, I feel like punching the next culprit?'

'Maybe you should.'

'Florence never has to deal with it, and she is more glamorous than anyone,' said Mandy. 'Why do I get all the stick, is it because I'm blonde and have these?' She looked down at her chest.

'I imagine the only difference is that Florence sends out an early non-verbal warning signal.'

'What do you mean?'

'Florence exudes presence, and she commands respect when she enters a room.'

'How does she do it?'

'I don't know, but I met her for the first time the other morning in the car and felt it right away. Before she spoke, I knew she was in charge.'

'Do you think I could ever be like that?'

'You're already like that. You just don't know it.'

'I am?'

'Yes! You've spent so long around her; you two are like peas in a pod. You've become her while remaining very much you. Does that make sense?'

'Sort of.'

'I think you expect men to pass comment, so you're coiled up ready to cut them down before they speak.'

'You're clever, Percy Butterworth.'

Rags looked up at Mandy, and she patted his head. 'You're clever, too.'

Rags let out a sigh and rested his head on her leg.

Percy turned towards Mandy, 'When I look at you I see far more than what's visible. You are effortlessly beautiful, and you turn heads wherever you go—I see how men react when they look at you. You have a magical aura.'

Mandy blushed.

'I didn't think Battersea girls blushed,' he said.

'We don't.' She leaned against him.

'By the way, last night, we smoked my last cigarette.'

'That reminds me, I stopped in the village on the way over to pick up soldier boy.' She reached into her bag and took out four packets of cigarettes.

Percy laughed, 'Why did you get so many?'

She blushed again, 'I don't want our balcony rendezvous to end.'

'You've got yourself a date, Mandy Miller.' He kissed the top of her head.

Florence leaned in between them, 'When you two have quite finished, we have a war to win. Briefing area, two minutes.'

Otto, Mandy, Percy and the engineers took their seats in front of the roll-up wall map. Rags sat at Mandy's feet.

Sir Henry walked into the ops room. 'I just finished a telephone call with Winston Churchill. He wanted me to tell you, well done on a speedy relocation. He urged us to carry on the good work and get our plan in place. Florence, it's all yours.'

She stood in front of the wall map and took a deep breath. 'What I'm about to tell you is top secret: the

Germans need two things. Firstly, the twenty-one manufacturing locations, and secondly, they need a code called 12g295. When Reginald Mitchell designed the Spitfire, he formulated a complex code, and the Spit won't fly without it.'

'Damn genius, old Mitchell,' said Fletcher. 'The bird is a thing of beauty.' A soft murmur of agreement emanated from the engineers.

Otto raised his hand and asked, 'Florence, apart from me, who else has the code? I mean, whoever has it, do they know they need to protect it?'

Fletcher leaned close to Otto's ear, 'Very smooth dear boy.'

'Only one other person has it, apart from you Malcolm, and that is-'

The ops room door swung wide open, and Stanley Blagdon burst in, 'There's a delivery van at the gate. The driver says he has some boxes for Alice Jones.'

Alice jumped up, 'Oh, good, I've been waiting for it, Percy, would you give me a hand?' Percy followed Alice through the entrance hall and out onto the driveway.

'I'm Percy Butterworth,' he said to Stanley and offered his hand.

'I've seen you sniffing around Mandy. You keep away from her, do you hear me?'

Percy ignored him, and turned to Alice, 'What's on the truck?'

'Extremely vital stuff.'

'Like what?'

'Stilton and biscuits. You can't win a war without good cheese and crackers.'

'You bloody stupid toffs,' said Blagdon. 'You've got no idea about war. You hide away in your posh country house and play war games on maps, and order cheese and sodding biscuits. You'd shit yourself if Jerry walked in here with a gun.'

Alice spun around and faced Stanley, 'You still have pimples on your face, my boy. There are many ways of fighting a war. Florence brought you here for a reason, respect it, and get on with your job. You'll see what we're capable of soon enough.' Alice's clinical words snapped him shut.

Blagdon's face reddened. He picked up a box from the back of the van and walked off towards the kitchen, muttering under his breath.

Percy grabbed a box and nudged Alice, 'You, and Florence, and Mandy are cut from the same cloth. I've never known anyone like you three.'

'Quite so, dear boy,' she opened the box and broke off a piece of stilton and popped into her mouth. 'Delicious, it's more than good enough to win the war.'

CHAPTER 14

Night descended on Milton Park as effortlessly as the daylight crept away, and with it, a heavy dusting of snow fell across the estate.

Florence stood in the kitchen and put her arms around Sir Henry. She rested her head on his shoulder, 'Tell me everything is going to work out.'

'Very well, everything is going to work out. Feel better?'

'Not really. I don't know how this is going to end. So much depends on so little.'

'What do you mean?'

'We could lose the war in a heartbeat because of the smallest mistake, and we'd not be able to fight back.'

'Do you fancy a stroll around the lake before bedtime? We have an early start tomorrow.'

'Yes, I do, my head is full, I can't think straight. I'll give Rags a shout. Rags, Rags, come on, boy.'

Rags came bounding into the kitchen and dashed out of the back door. Sir Henry and Florence walked towards the lake. She stopped and put her hand to her ear.

'Listen, can you hear them? Spitfires, they're coming this way, low and fast.'

Three Spitfires roared over Milton Park at low-level. Their engines thundered at a staggering speed. And then they were gone, but their sound reverberated around the trees.

'I can feel it in my chest,' said Florence.

Sir Henry looked towards the spot in the sky where the aircraft had vanished into the darkness. He said, 'If ever we needed a reminder, then that was it. My pulse is racing. No wonder the Germans want to get their hands on it, I would if I was running their Intelligence.'

'Henry, you're not running their Intelligence, thank the Lord, and they're not getting their thieving Nazi hands on our Spits. I'll jolly well see to it they don't.'

'Absolutely, Florence.'

They ambled off around the lake, and Rags ran in small circles sniffing at the grass tufts sticking up through the snow. The night sky, lit by a soft half-moon, overflowed with a blanket of twinkling stars.

'I love this, Henry. The planning for victory, even the fear of losing. I want to feel alive like this forever.'

'You'll feel alive whatever you do, you are quite remarkable. After the war, we can travel the world, climb mountains, sail the seas, and do anything we want. But, your purpose right now is to snub out any chance of the Germans getting the Spitfire.' Florence gripped Henry's arm and thought through what he said.

'Thank you, Henry. You make it sound clear.'

'One more thing,' he said. 'On my phone call earlier with Winston, he told me he had given the green light to set up the Special Operations Executive. But it won't stand a chance if our mission fails. The SOE will be able to execute missions similar to what we did in the first war. Lot's of behind enemy lines sort of thing, and get at the enemy with blistering pace and disruption. It will be a new culture of warfare, but only if we stop this threat first.'

Florence knew if the SOE were to be a success, it would require dozens of qualified special agents; mostly female. Each one highly trained and prepared to go without medals and praise: Britain's silent heroes and our secret weapon of mass destruction.

She shivered, 'We should go inside.' She called out to Rags, and he followed them into the kitchen.

Fletcher sat at the table with a cup of tea and some cheese and biscuits.

He said, 'Is it cold out there?'

'Fresh,' said Sir Henry. He took off his boots. 'Has your first day been productive?'

'I think so, yes.'

'How's, Malcolm?' asked Florence.

'Malcolm, strangely, is on top form,' he said. 'You both know him well; he takes time to adapt to change. But Malcolm has a new super-human level of energy. He's adapted to the new environment quicker than any of us.' Fletcher pushed a fresh ball of tobacco down into his pipe with his thumb and lit a match. 'Malcolm has new powers of concentration too. He works all day, then all night, he doesn't stop. He's become a machine.'

Sir Henry scratched his head. 'Let's not forget; he has a lot of pressure on his shoulders at the moment.'

Fletcher said, 'Malcolm no longer has that quirky sense of humour, and gone too are his little touches of kindness, he's changed.'

Florence moved closer to Fletcher, 'Would you keep an eye on him for me? The last thing we need is for Malcolm to crash and burn. We can't afford for him to nose dive, not at this stage.'

'No problem, I'll look after him.'

'Get some rest, Fletch,' said Florence. 'We need your expertise in the coming days because Malcolm can't operate without you. We're counting on you.'

Fletcher said his goodnights and sauntered out of the kitchen and up the stairs.

On his exit, Alice breezed into the kitchen and walked over to Florence. She looked around and whispered, 'Are we alone?'

'Yes, it's only us,' said Florence.

'Rosie sent me a reversed, double-layered, coded message in a descending format. Damn thing took me two hours to decipher. Rosie was asked to type up a document about a new, super-sized, underground factory outside Berlin. The factory had been specifically designed to produce ten thousand Spuckenfeuer a month.'

Florence looked at Alice, 'Spuckenfeuer?'

'Spuckenfeuer. It's German for Spitfire!'

Fletcher walked up the east wing's staircase and stood outside Malcolm's bedroom. His knuckles were an inch from knocking on the door when he stopped himself. Fletcher pressed his ear against the door and heard loud grunting and heavy panting.

He pushed the door wide open and barged in.

Fletcher stared at Otto.

Otto stood in the middle of his bedroom, stripped to the waist, and his torso coated in a shiny film of sweat. His fists blurred at high-speed as he shadowboxed. He ducked, and bobbed, weaved and punched, as he landed punches on an invisible foe. Fletcher noticed dozens of scars on Otto's body, some new, some old, and marks that looked like sealed bullet holes.

'Malcolm, what the hell happened to you? Your body has been cut to bits.' Fletcher narrowed his gaze to focus on Otto's lean, muscular physique.

'Shut the door, Fletch. I'm building up a sweat for an experiment. All rather dull I'm afraid, let me get a towel, and get dressed.'

'Where did all those cuts and scars come from? And are those bullet holes in your back?'

'Oh, it's nothing,' Otto laughed it off. 'I had an accident with a piece of machinery years ago, and the healing process has taken ages. Nothing to worry about.'

'But your body Malcolm, you look like an Olympian, a gold one at that. What's your secret?'

'After Owen died, my mornings were hell, so I started my day with a hundred pushups, lots of sit-ups, and I ran, and ran, and ran.'

'It worked!' said Fletcher.

Otto dressed and buttoned up his jacket. 'Do you fancy a nightcap? Alice must have a secret stash in the kitchen. Let's have a snifter before bedtime.'

They walked towards the staircase.

'Do you think Alice will notice a few shots of brandy missing?' asked Fletcher.

Otto stopped at the top of the stairs, 'Hold on, Fletch. I forgot something, wait here, I'll pop back and get it.' Otto ran back to the bedroom and grabbed Malcolm's blue scarf from the brass hook on the back of the door. The two men walked into the kitchen.

'Did you hear the trio of Spits an hour ago?' asked Fletcher.

'They sounded perfect.' Otto found a bottle of brandy tucked between two cookery books. He took two glasses from the cupboard above the sink and poured a double measure for both of them.

'Cheers, Malcolm. Here's to winning the war.'

'Absolutely, Fletch. Here's to winning the war.'

They chinked their glasses.

'I've been thinking,' said Fletcher. 'Florence and Sir Henry are decent chaps, why not tell them you can't lay your hands on the 12g295 code. I'm certain they'll be totally fine. Florence even said there was another person who has the code. What do you think?'

'It's a smashing idea.'

'That's great. I was hoping you'd go for it.'

Otto put his glass down on the table. 'Drink up Fletch. We have a long day tomorrow.'

'Malcolm, I can't believe how much you've changed, what with your new-found energy, body scars and bullet holes. I can't put my finger on it old boy, but you're not quite you.' Fletcher walked to the kitchen window and looked outside. 'It's a beautiful night.' He looked up at the sky. 'Those three Spits reminded me what this is all about. I'm glad we came to Milton Park, maybe tomorrow-'

Otto yanked the scarf so quickly around Fletcher's neck he couldn't speak. His arms flayed, and his eyes bulged. His face reddened, and he gasped for gulps of air. Otto rammed his knee into Fletcher's back and kicked his legs out from under him, then slammed him face-first onto the cold stone kitchen floor.

The struggle was brief and one-sided.

Fletcher's death was swift.

Otto removed the scarf and wrapped it back around his neck. He rinsed the brandy glasses and replaced them in the cupboard above the sink. He listened for movement in the house. There was none. Milton Park was silent.

He peered out through the kitchen window and waited

for a cloud to cover the half-moon. Darkness followed. He heaved Fletcher over his shoulder and stepped out onto the terrace. He ran with the body over his shoulder until he was out of sight from the house.

He dumped Fetcher's body behind a tree, and began to tug at roots to clear away the soil, then rolled the body into the shallow grave and covered it with soil and snow. Fletcher's disappearance would be a mystery for a day or two, and Otto would be gone with the code by the time the body was discovered.

Snow began to fall and cover Otto's footsteps. He ran back to the house and bounded up the stairs to his bedroom. He stripped naked, and under the hot shower, he watched the muddy water run away. His heart pounded from the kill. It would soon pass, it always did.

He felt nothing emotionally, no sadness, no guilt, and no elation. Killing Fletcher was a functional and vital kill to pursue his mission. Otto wrapped a towel around himself, and his body steamed in the cold darkness of his bedroom. He put on a pair of Malcolm's pyjamas and climbed into bed. The only sounds were the creaks and groans that came from a living, breathing stately home. He was too wired to sleep. Otto stared at the ceiling.

Mandy cupped her hands around her mouth and whispered through their adjoining bedroom door.

'Percy, I can't sleep. Percy. Percy!' she tapped on the door. 'Percy, are you awake?'

She heard footsteps.

She raised her voice a little. 'Percy, I can't sleep. How about you, can you sleep?'

'Not now, no,' his voice was croaky.

'Do you have any brandy?' she asked.

'Would you like some?'

'Open your balcony door. I'm coming over.' She jumped onto his balcony and opened the door to his bedroom.

'That was quick,' said Percy.

She was barefoot and wore an over-sized white shirt.

He handed her a glass of brandy.

'I don't want it.'

'But you said-'

She put a finger to his lips, 'I want you, Percy.'

He put the glass on the dresser and kissed her.

It was a kiss she hadn't expected.

On the balcony, the night before, Percy kissed her tenderly. This kiss was passionate and urgent.

He undid Mandy's buttons, and her shirt fell open. Her shapely form, and her pale skin, craved his touch. He peeled the shirt from her shoulders, and it fell to the floor. Mandy stood naked, on tiptoe, to receive his kisses to her neck. Each kiss sent a sensation surging through her. Mandy wrapped her arms around his body and let the waves of pleasure roll over her. She watched as he removed his shirt, and her fingertips traced the outline of his muscular chest and broad shoulders.

Percy laid her on the bed.

Mandy's blonde curls cascaded over the pillow. She pulled the blanket over them and shut out the world.

Each of Percy's seductive touches lit a furnace inside her, 'I want to stay here, like this, with you,' her voice was breathy.

'And I want you to stay here, like this, with me.' He tucked the blanket around them and could feel every contour of her warm body. Their bodies fitted together like two pieces of a jigsaw puzzle.

Mandy fell into a deep sleep. She didn't feel coy or embarrassed about her need for sexual fulfilment. Percy let her be her intimate self, and for her, it was a new experience.

A crashing sound from downstairs woke them.

'Did you hear that?' she said. 'It came from the ballroom, let's go downstairs and see.' She jumped out of bed, 'I need some clothes, I can't go like this.'

'Take my dressing gown from the back of the door.'

Mandy wrapped his gown around her.

She opened the bedroom door, ran down the stairs, through the ops room and into the ballroom.

Percy was right behind her.

Mandy snapped the lights on.

Otto was in the middle of his office space and looked up at the startled new arrivals.

'Mandy, Percy, did I wake you up? I'm sorry, I dropped a few boxes and made a bit of noise. I couldn't sleep, so I thought I'd make an early start.'

The double-doors to the ballroom crashed open again, and Stanley Blagdon burst through, brandishing a pistol.

'What the bloody hell is going on in here?'

'It was Malcolm, he dropped a few boxes,' said Mandy.

'And what are you doing here, Butterworth?'

'I came to investigate the noise.'

'That's a bit bloody convenient,' said Stanley.

'What is?' said Percy.

'You turn up with Mandy in the middle of the night, half-naked. Anyway, you can bugger off now, mate. I've got this.' Blagdon put his pistol back in its holster.

Percy turned to leave.

Mandy did too. 'I'm going back to bed.'

'Oh, very cosy,' said Stanley. 'You two arrived together, and now you're leaving together. Go on, bugger off.'

Percy and Mandy climbed the stairs. He opened his bedroom door, and she opened hers. Mandy ran through her room, jumped over the balcony, and climbed back into his bed.

Percy smiled at her. 'I thought you were going to bed.'

'This *is* my bed.'

CHAPTER 15

Florence was awake by five-thirty. She rarely slept late once in mission mode. However, an extra hour in a warm bed with Henry was tempting.

She dressed and went downstairs. Rags followed.

The snow had continued to fall during the night, and the grounds of Milton Park looked pristine. The morning handover between moonlight and sunlight cast a crystal blue glow across the landscape.

She put her wellington boots on and set off with an excited Rags towards the top of the ridge. It was the purest way to clear her mind. In the same way, a dip in the sea is refreshing once your shoulders are under the water.

Florence first visited Milton Park in the spring of 1919, shortly after the end of the first war. Henry had been her salvation during her time of grief. During her visit, he invited her to join him in Military Intelligence. He said there are two important days in your life: the day you're born, and the day you discover why.'

Florence remembered agreeing with him, but it was Henry's next few words that changed her life.

'Join me, and let's develop Military Intelligence together.'

She said yes on the spot.

He promised her excitement, danger, travel, fast cars, good food, good wine, and a life full of genuine purpose. He'd not been wrong; that's why she adored him.

Lord only knows where I'd be if not with him.

Approaching footsteps crunched the snow.

'I brought you a flask of tea, fancy a cup?'

'You're a mindreader, Henry, I'd love one. I thought you'd sleep ages.'

He pushed the snow off a fallen tree trunk, unrolled a green blanket, and there they sat, drinking tea, looking across the Cotswolds.

'Are your thoughts falling into place?' he asked.

After a moment she said, 'I need to be one step ahead just to stay in the game, two steps ahead not to lose, and three steps ahead if we are to beat the enemy. And that is what we have to do, Henry, destroy them.'

'And where are you at the moment?'

'I'm five steps behind, and I don't like it. I can't plot my course of action yet.'

'Don't overthink it, Flo, you do best when you act on instinct.'

She sipped her tea. 'You're probably right, Henry.'

'Probably?'

She nudged him, 'Anyone else awake yet?'

'The engineers are, but they were getting under Alice's feet, so she pushed them outside.'

'Good old Alice, I've no idea what I would do without her.' They jumped off the tree trunk and headed for the house. 'I'm going to tell Stanley about his sister, Brenda. Poor lad, he'll be devastated.'

. . .

'Has anyone seen Fletch this morning?' asked Alice.

'I bet he's still sleeping,' said one of the engineers. 'He's not used to all this fresh air.'

Otto said, 'I'm leaving soon with Sir Henry to see Hodges, the fuel tank manufacturer. After I've gone, could one of you go and find Fletch, he's probably sleeping off all the box humping from yesterday.'

In a quiet corner of the kitchen, Alice caught Mandy's attention, 'I hear Malcolm was making a lot of noise downstairs last night.'

'We heard a few crashes and went downstairs to investigate. Malcolm was rummaging for something because there were boxes open everywhere. He stopped when he saw us.'

'Us, we?' asked Alice.

'I meant me.'

'But you said, us.'

'Percy must've heard noises and also came down to investigate.'

Alice could convey more with an eyebrow shrug than a politician could say in a two-hour speech.

Mandy ignored the eyebrow. 'When Stanley saw us together, he was like an angry bee looking to sting someone, so I left and went back to bed.'

'And Percy?'

'Alice, you already know too much.'

Alice put her hand in her tweed jacket pocket. 'Here, take this, I think you'll find it safer.'

Mandy looked at the key, 'The adjoining door?'

Alice shot another eyebrow shrug, 'Do you think you can leap from balcony to balcony in the middle of the night without being seen? Florence told me to give you the key because she didn't want you to fall and break your silly neck.'

Mandy smiled and put it in her pocket, 'I hate spies.'

. . .

Florence walked in and stood in the middle of the kitchen with her hands on her hips. 'Good morning, everyone. Mandy and Malcolm, can you be ready to leave in five minutes? Sir Henry is outside in the Bentley.' She looked at the engineers. 'Whatever you need today, ask Alice.'

In unison, they looked at Alice and nodded.

Mandy walked past Percy, and his gaze didn't leave her. The back of her hand brushed against the back of his hand; it was the slightest touch. Percy experienced the same sensation as the night she picked him up from Bletchley Park.

Stanley stood outside by the front door.

His eyes were red.

Mandy had only seen him cry twice; once when she told him her mum had died, and the night she broke up with him.

'Brenda's dead,' he said. There was no trace of his bullish bluster. 'Getting blown up in a gas leak in a pub, when there's a war on, is bloody ridiculous.'

Mandy put her hand on his arm, 'Stanley, we'll talk later, I've got to go.'

He grabbed her arm, 'Mandy, don't go making a bloody fool of yourself with that Butterworth idiot. You don't belong with a toff like him. He's having a bit of wartime fun with his army tart.'

Mandy pulled her arm away and marched over to Sir Henry's car and slumped heavily in the back with Florence. Otto sat in the front next to Sir Henry.

'How was Stanley?' asked Florence.

'Same as always, a massive horses arse. I could bloody hit that boy into the middle of next week. He's a bloody liability. But this once, I'll cut him some slack, he just found out Brenda is dead.'

Sir Henry drove out of the gate and along the twisty lanes towards the fuel tank factory.

'Step on it, Henry,' said Florence. 'The war will be over by the time we get there.'

'We won't get there any quicker,' he said.

'Yes, we will!' shouted Florence and Mandy together.

Stanley marched off towards the rear of the house. He pushed the kitchen door open and found Percy sitting at the table, reading his notes.

'Leave Mandy alone, do you hear me, Butterworth? Keep your bloody toff hands off her, or else.'

'Or else, what?'

'You don't want to tangle with me, pal. I don't make idle threats, so keep away from her.'

'Which is it to be, keep away from her, or keep my hands off her?'

'You posh git. You lot are all the same with your stuck-up schools and your fancy lah-de-dah uniforms. You think you own the place. I won't warn you again, Butterworth, keep away from her.'

'That won't be happening; I like Mandy, and I think she likes me. Look, I know you were childhood sweethearts, but that was in the past.' Percy went back to reading his notes.

'Outside Butterworth! We'll sort this out now.'

'Are you challenging me to a duel of some sort?'

'Get up, get out!'

'Pushing me about like a bully isn't going to change anything.'

'It will put you in your place for starters. Get outside and fight like a man. I'm going to teach you a lesson.'

'What lesson's that?' Percy followed Blagdon to the terrace. On the way past the sink, he picked up a long-handled wooden spoon.

Stanley took off his army jacket, rolled up his sleeves and put his fists in the air.

Percy stood still, arms by his side, and waited.

Stanley threw the first punch.

Percy swayed, and the moment the redundant punch sailed harmlessly by, Percy slapped the wooden spoon around Stanley's face.

Enraged, Stanley jabbed more punches. Harder and faster and more frantic. Percy side-stepped them, then struck the spoon on Stanley's other cheek and the back of his head. Percy countered each punch with a duck, a bob, a weave or sway, and then followed up with an accurate spoon-slap around Stanley's face.

Stanley's rage grew. He bull-charged, head-on at Percy and grappled him to the floor. They rolled around the terrace and landed heavy body punches.

They crawled apart and stood, their fists raised and they drew in lungfuls of icy morning air. Their breath steamed.

Blagdon jabbed three quick punches.

All three missed.

They squared up again and circled one another. Dots of blood smudged on their faces and shirt collars.

'You fight tough, Butterworth. You're tougher than you look, I'll give you that,' Stanley ran the back of his hand over his mouth to wipe the blood away.

Percy said, 'You London boys think you are the only ones who can fight. Growing up on the streets is not the only way to toughen up,' Percy wiped the blood from his nose. 'I bet you think Eton is all butterfly nets and wine tasting.'

'Yeah, I do, along with your silly top hats and girly gowns. Your problem is that you lot have no backbone. You should try living in Battersea; it's a hard growing up there.'

'You should try a term at Eton, the older boys bully and

beat you to do things for them. I had to survive, so I took up fencing and boxing.'

They continued circling, although both men knew no more punches would be thrown; to stand down would be to surrender.

'You're a good fighter, Blagdon. But understand, I will not cease my interest in Mandy, you need to know that.'

Blagdon sniffed. 'Mandy broke my heart, and now the pair of you are rubbing my nose in it.'

'We aren't doing it to spite you.'

'Keep away from her, Butterworth.'

'I'm not going to, and that's that.'

Stanley stopped moving and lowered his fists and opened his mouth. No words came out. Stanley looked to the sky as if to seek inspirational help. 'I was hurt when she dumped me. Then I get pulled in here and see her with you, all lovey-dovey. On top of that, I just heard my sister died in an explosion.' Stanley stepped closer to him. 'I saw how happy Mandy was with you, and that made me bloody mad.' Stanley held out his hand.

Percy took it, and they shook hands.

The kitchen door burst open. Alice ran out with a bucket of cold water and threw it over the two men. 'Stop fighting! Stop it now!'

'Alice,' yelled Percy. 'We've stopped.'

'I saw you were fighting, but the water pressure was a bit slow, and it took forever to fill the bucket. Anyway, no harm done.'

The two men stood dripping wet.

'Fencing, you say,' said Stanley. 'My uncle Fred was a fencer.'

'Oh excellent, which club did he go to?'

'Not a fencer like your posh sort,' he snorted. 'My uncle made garden fences.'

They walked into the kitchen together.

Percy said, 'I was sorry to hear about your sister.'

'Poor kid, everyone loved her, and she was a great sister, I can't believe she's gone.'

Percy put a hand on his shoulder, 'It's going to be tough for a while.'

'Mandy's a great girl with a heart of gold. When her mum died I suppose we became too much like brother and sister.'

'Listen, you haven't lost Mandy, she cares for you.'

'I thought she hated me.'

'Oh God, she really does hate you. You make her as mad as hell. You need to give her a bit of time. She knows she broke your heart. She's a bit defensive and a bit fiery.'

'A bit?'

'Well, a lot fiery.'

Stanley rubbed his face. 'You'll have to show me some of those fencing moves, my face stings like hell.'

'Mr Hodges, may we have a private word with you?' asked Sir Henry.

Mr Hodges was an old-fashioned man in an ever-increasing modern world. His craftsmen and newly welcomed craftswomen, used precision tools, a steady hand, and a trained eye to produce components that would be unseen. And it was that level of pride which made Hodges Engineering a trusted supplier.

Florence, Sir Henry and Otto followed Mr Hodges into his office. Mandy remained on the factory floor.

'Sorry for the mess; we took a larger than usual delivery yesterday, and we're still upside down. When the head of Military Intelligence strides into your place, you know something is going on, so how can I assist you, Sir Henry?'

Florence put a map on the desk. 'These twenty-one red

dots represent the locations where the components for the Spitfire are manufactured.'

Hodges studied the map, 'I see.'

'Mr Hodges, the Germans are coming, and they want our Spits and to destroy our manufacturing plants.'

'What do you need me to do?'

'Make sure you vet all your staff thoroughly and don't employ anyone you don't already know.'

Hodges took off his spectacles, 'Young lady, I've been making fuel tanks for thirty-seven years, and my father before that made feeding troughs for farms, and his father made nails for ships. I'm not going to let the Nazis in here. You can count on it.'

'I was hoping that's the line you'd take,' said Florence. 'This is Malcolm Feathers. He runs the Spitfire programme, have you two met before?'

Otto's mouth went dry, and his heart quickened. The feelings were familiar, but he knew how to overcome them. More importantly, he knew how to hide them. He waited for Hodges to make the first sign of recognition. If any.

'Nice to see you again, Feathers. It was early last year. I think you came down with the new dimensions for a larger fuel tank.'

'Good to see you again, Hodges.' Otto's movements were slow and gentle and very Malcolm.

'Your calculations were perfect,' said Hodges. 'Any more changes coming down the line?'

'No, not at the moment,' said Otto. The office had a window overlooking the factory floor. Otto looked at the benches and the engaged workforce. 'How many women work here?'

'Seventy-four and four shift supervisors. It's funny; my wife can't hang a picture on the wall, and yet, the women here are as skilled as any man. I don't know what I'm going to do after the war when the men want their jobs back.' Hodges took off his cloth cap and ran his handkerchief over his balding head.

Florence gave Hodges a reassuring tap on the arm. 'You're doing a first-rate job, Mr Hodges. Thank you for today, I think we've seen enough.' Mr Hodges smiled like a schoolboy getting top marks for his homework.

'Malcolm, have you seen enough?' asked Sir Henry.

'Oh, yes, plenty.'

'Good job, Hodges,' said Sir Henry. 'We'll leave you to get on.'

They walked out to find Mandy amongst a group of women learning how to solder the inside of a fuel tank.

'Mandy,' said Florence. 'Let's go.'

Otto stepped into the car and watched the factory slip from view. He was going to devote the rest of the day to search through Malcolm's files, then leave with the code once it was dark, and head to Friston. Fletcher's body was a ticking time-bomb; he had to accept that. For the rest of the journey, he thought about Lizzie Denton and warmed to the thought of her firm young body. One more night with her, and then back to Berlin.

Florence said, 'Tomorrow, Malcolm, we'll visit three sites. The propeller factory, the wing plant and the wheel assembly locations. They are within a hundred miles.'

'Sounds like an excellent plan.' Otto's tiredness caught up with him. He drifted off in the back of the Bentley with thoughts of Lizzie Denton, and his escape from Milton Park.

CHAPTER 16

Florence stood in the doorway of the ballroom and watched Otto rummage through some boxes. 'Need a hand?'

'No, no, I'm looking for some papers, that's all. They'll be useful for our site visits tomorrow.' Otto sighed like Malcolm and rummaged like Malcolm, but he was losing patience being Malcolm. 'I must be losing my mind. I'm sure I put them in here somewhere, they'll turn up soon enough.' He whistled through his teeth but didn't once look up at Florence.

'Good, I'll leave you to it then.' She walked off and entered the ops room. Sir Henry stood in front of the wall map and looked up when he heard Florence walk in.

He said, 'Percy and the Blagdon boy had a bit of a punch up. It seems like honours were pretty even. Blagdon used his fists, and Percy used a wooden spoon. They've sorted out their beef over whatever young men fight about these days.'

Alice stood behind Sir Henry and mouthed to Florence. 'I'll tell you later.'

Florence nodded, 'Well, that's good. I've made a slight

change to our plan for tomorrow. Henry, will you take Malcolm on the site visits?'

'Yes, of course, not a problem, and perhaps I won't have anyone in the back of the car telling me to drive faster. What are you going to do?'

'I'm going to shoot to London and visit Winston and Barrington to give them a quick update. We said we would keep them informed. I'll take Mandy with me. I have a special job for her to do on the way. Tell me honestly, Henry, just how good a coder is Percy?'

'They don't come any better.'

'Excellent, that's exactly what I hoped you'd say. Any idea where he is?'

'Last I saw he was in the kitchen with Mandy and Blagdon. The three of them had a few things to talk about, so I left them to it.'

Florence slipped away to the kitchen. She saw the three of them chatting around the table.

'Percy,' said Florence. 'I have a job for you. Let's go out onto the terrace. The fresh air will do our brains some good.'

'Technically, that's not true,' he said.

Mandy giggled.

Percy stepped out into the chilly evening air. Florence took a piece of paper out of her pocket, 'Do you know what this is?'

He looked at the sheet of paper. 'Yes, I believe I do.'

'Good. Without seeing it ever again, could you reproduce it, accurately, mistake-free?'

'No, it's far too complex, you'd need the original in front of you to run a double layer, simultaneous, reverse checking system.'

'Sir Henry tells me you're the best coder at Bletchley.'

'That's nice of him.'

'If you're so smart, why can't you reproduce it?'

'Let me put it this way, imagine if you wrote this code in Latin, then asked me to reproduce it at a later date, from memory. But, I didn't speak Latin. I wouldn't even know the mistakes I made.'

She looked at him with a puzzled look. 'So, is it possible or not?'

He looked at the sheet, 'Florence, the coding is highly complicated, and there are too many areas where I could make a mistake. I can tell you without any doubt; it would be impossible to reproduce this from memory without making mistakes.'

She put her arm around his shoulder and walked him towards the lake. They walked in slow, measured steps deep in conversation. Florence was still talking, and Percy was still listening, when they completed their lap of the water.

'And you want me to do this by the morning?' he asked.

'Yes.'

'It will take a week of nights.'

'Are you saying you can't do it by the morning?'

'No, I'm saying it will be hard,' he said.

'Then you'd best get on with it.' She patted him on the arm. It was a firm pat, more a push for him go to his room and get started.

She called through the kitchen door. 'Stanley, I need to have a word with you out here.' He walked outside to her, trying not to look like a lamb going to slaughter. Tricky for a soldier who'd just been humiliated by a wooden spoon.

He blurted, 'I started it. It was my fault, not Percy's.'

She ignored him. 'I have a job for you.'

'I thought you were going to give me a grilling.'

'Why, because you and Percy threw a couple of lame punches at each other? And anyway, you'll never beat Percy in a straight fight.'

'Why not?'

'He's a purist. You're a brawler, a great brawler, and I'd back you in a street fight, and I would want you in a trench next to me when the bullets start to fly. But the purist will always beat the brawler in a face-to-face standoff. You fight with your heart, and you punch on instinct, while he fights with his head. You need emotion to fight. He doesn't, that's why he slapped you with a spoon. Did you feel stupid?'

Stanley snorted through his nose, 'Yeah, bloody stupid. I landed a few good ones on him, though, I felt better after that.'

'Let's face it. You've had a tough week. But I'm not out here in the cold to talk about that. I need you to be on duty all night.'

'What do you want me to do?'

'I've given Percy an assignment. It's a job where he must not be disturbed. He'll be in his bedroom all night. Your job is to guard him. Nobody in, and nobody out. Neither of you can leave the room, and nobody can come in. Not Mandy, Sir Henry, Malcolm, Alice, Fletch, nobody, not even me, do you understand?'

'Yeah, I get it.'

'No, I doubt you do get it. What I've asked Percy to do is of the highest seriousness. If he gets it wrong, we'll be facing our final days of a war we cannot win. He knows what he has to do, and your job is to make sure he's safe. Here, take this, and take these.' Florence handed him a pistol, a combat knife and a grenade.

'Are you expecting some sort of raid on the Toff's bedroom?'

Florence didn't show any hint of laughter. She said, 'Once you enter Percy's bedroom, neither of you must leave until I knock on the door in the morning. Have you got that, soldier?'

'Loud and clear. What time does the shift start?'

'In fifteen minutes.'

'One more thing,' she said.

'What's that?'

'You can never breathe a word of this to anyone. Even after the war, not down the pub, and not to your mum or dad. Nobody, not ever, I'm counting on you, Stanley. I didn't need someone to guard Milton Park, that was a ploy to get you here. What I wanted was someone who would give their life defending England, defending the King. You'll understand the magnitude of this job in years to come. Until then, you'll have to trust me, Stanley. Because what I'm asking you to do is the most important thing you'll ever do.'

He lifted his chin and pulled his shoulders back: a soldiers response. 'You can count on me, Florence.'

'I know, that's why you're here.'

He put the pistol in his holster, slipped the knife into his pocket and hooked the grenade onto his belt.

Florence didn't say anything for a full minute. 'Mandy will somehow, someway, always be in your life, you have to be strong and let her go. You have to let it settle. I know a thing or two about lost love.'

He looked at her, 'I think I get it, it just bloody hurts knowing she left me.'

'The pain will pass.'

'I guess so.' Stanley kicked the snow, 'I won't let you down, and I'll keep that Eton toff working hard all night.'

'I'm counting on it. I'm going to London tomorrow with Mandy, so I want you to babysit Percy until I return.'

Stanley nodded. They walked back into the kitchen, and Alice handed a hamper to them both.

She said, 'Dinner for two, and a flask of coffee. Now boys, no fighting!'

'Thank you, Alice,' they said.

Stanley peeked inside the box. 'Are you ready, Eton-boy?'

'What feast lies ahead?' asked Percy.

'Cheese and pickle sandwiches, my favourite.'

'Mine too,' said Percy.

They walked out of the kitchen, up the stairs and into Percy's bedroom. Stanley locked the door.

The cold darkness drew in early.

Florence and Mandy sat on the chesterfields in the ops room. The open log fire crackled and popped.

'There's a chance Fletch is dead,' whispered Florence.

'Shit what, hold on, what! What do you mean, dead?'

'Keep your voice down. I told Malcolm and the engineers that Fletch's brother lives nearby, and maybe he'd popped out to visit him. I let them know I was angry that he hadn't told me before he disappeared. That's why they're keeping themselves to themselves.'

'Well, maybe he did go and visit his brother.'

'That isn't possible.'

'Why?'

'His brother died nine years ago.'

'It doesn't mean Fletcher has been murdered.'

'I know, but I have this feeling.'

'That's never good. But who would want to murder Fletch? He is so lovely, like a favourite uncle. And why haven't you told anyone yet?'

'It's only a feeling. I have to put the pieces together first, so I need you to keep this under your hat. Say nothing, not a word. Do you understand?'

Mandy nodded.

Florence said, 'You and I leave for London first thing in the morning, we'll take my racing Jaguar, so wrap up warmly.'

Mandy said, 'Murdering Fletch makes no sense, none at all.'

'Stay in your room tonight. Stanley is working with Percy on a special assignment, so you can't use your new key.' Florence raised an eyebrow.

Mandy raised her eyebrow back at her, 'What time do you want to leave in the morning?'

'Five-thirty, sharp. Let's go out to the garage now and get the Jag ready. And one more thing, is your memory up to speed?'

'My memory? It's good. Why?'

'I need your absolute tip-top best, and I'm not talking about memorising a few packs of cards.'

They walked across the gravel to the garage block, opened the door and flicked on the light.

Florence took the key from the box on the wall and threw it to Mandy, 'Jump in and fire it up.'

Mandy slid into the Jaguar's cream leather seat which was stiff-cold and turned the ignition key. The engine coughed and spluttered, and after two more misfires, the Jag roared to life. Florence put her ear to the engine's exhaust, then lifted the bonnet to make a small adjustment to a screw on the twin carburettors. The engine settled into a soft, melodic purr.

'What do you need me to memorise?' Mandy asked.

'A single sheet of code.'

'That's simples, pimples.'

'Not quite! I'm undecided if I should tell you how vital it is. Would your memory be impaired if you knew you had to get it right? The freedom of the world depends on you memorising it exactly right. If you make one single mistake, we will lose the war.'

'It doesn't make a difference.'

'That's a relief. Why?'

'Because you've already told me if I mess this up then the end of the world will be down to me. Is it that serious?'

'Yes, I'm afraid it is.'

'That's when you should have lied, and said no.'

'No then, it's not that serious.'

'It's too late now,' snorted Mandy.

'When we drive the Jag out of Milton Park tomorrow morning, I need you to do your best flawless work.'

Mandy nodded, 'Can I drive back?'

'Of course, we'll make it a race, fastest time wins.'

'Wins what?' Mandy revved the engine.

'What does it matter? You won't beat my time, whatever the prize.'

Mandy smiled and turned the engine off. They locked the garage doors and ran back to the house, out of the cold.

Mandy gazed at the marble entrance hall, and whistled, 'How the other half live?' She nudged Florence. 'When did you first come here?'

'A year after the first war, I was young—about your age. Winston was a budding politician and had definite views on what should happen across Europe. Nobody paid much attention to him. He told Parliament that Germany would rise up again, and he was right. It was Winston who put Henry and me together. He thought we'd make an interesting team. I lived at Milton Park with Henry for the next ten years. It became my home.'

'You're lucky, you've only known a life of country houses and posh schools.'

'You're right. But what matters is not what you have, but what you do with what you have.'

'Easy to say when you have everything.'

'I know plenty of people who have everything, but they don't have any of the good stuff that you have.' Florence hugged Mandy, 'You can't change the past, your upbringing, your start in life, but you can change what happens. Just like you did.'

'Yes, but people like me are never going to live in a place like this.'

'I know you, Mandy Miller. You'll end up with everything you want.'

Mandy looked up to the ceiling as if pondering Florence's philosophy. 'Let's go and see if Alice has any cake left.'

Upstairs in Percy's bedroom, Stanley stood by the balcony door. He watched Percy write numbers, dots, dashes and squiggles on a sheet of paper.

'What's all that then, Toff?'

'Something Florence asked me to do; it feels like some sort of test.' Percy put his pencil in his mouth like he was smoking a cigarette.

'It ain't no test.'

'How do you know?' asked Percy.

'Florence ordered me to shoot anyone who tries to break in, and I'm not to let you out, not on any account.' Stanley showed Percy his weapons. 'Whatever it is you're doing, Posh-boy, it's bloody important.'

Stanley flopped on the bed with a thump. He put his head against the pillow and swung his feet up onto the mattress and lit a cigarette. 'You know, Toff, when I was a kid we used to steal fruit from the market stalls and sell it, door to door in the big houses in Chelsea.'

'Battersea-boy, that sounds like a lovely story, but for another time.'

'What I mean is, we used to show the punters a lovely piece of fruit, then fill the box underneath with rotten stuff. They never said anything, because they were too embarrassed, or frightened that they'd look stupid or something. We used to-'

Percy put his hand up. 'Shh! Don't say another word. Stanley, dear boy, your charming fruit-selling story may have helped us not to lose the war.'

'What the bloody hell are you on about?'

'The fruit, dear boy, the fruit, your thieving grubby antics could quite possibly have saved the day.' Percy jumped up and grabbed Stanley and hugged him.

'I'll punch you if you don't stop hugging me.'

'This is the breakthrough I needed.'

'But what's fruit got to do with it.'

'I'll tell you one day. This is going to take all night, so you had better open the flask of coffee, we are going to need it.'

Percy was up against the clock, and it was nearly midnight. He had five hours. He needed five days, a coding machine from Bletchley Park and a team of fellow coders to check his work.

All Percy had was a pencil and the seedlings of a cracking idea.

Stanley opened the hamper, 'Good news toff, Alice packed us a slice of fruit cake each, you carry on with your schoolwork, and I'll keep you awake. And another thing, if you hug me again, I will stab you.' He took out his cigarettes and offered one to Percy.

'Thank you, barrow boy.' Percy got to work, and with his mind clear, his pencil flowed.

Stanley ate his sandwich. 'Bloody toff, you ain't all that bad, for a toff that is.' He handed Percy a slice of fruit cake. 'Get your chops around that.'

Otto returned, frustrated, to his bedroom in the early hours of the morning. He skulked around.

Killers skulk. Broodiness is unavoidable.

He didn't find the code, and he'd exhausted his options. Otto would have to catch Florence on her own, choose his words carefully and ask her who else had the code. Then steal it, and slip back to Berlin. Florence and Sir Henry made his mission easy by putting the map on the wall with the locations marked with coloured flags. He copied it meticulously onto a square of white silk, taking care to record the grid references.

But he still needed the code.

He skulked again.

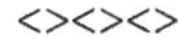

CHAPTER 17

A few minutes before five in the morning, a van pulled up in front of Milton Park. Nigel, the Ansty's Bakery delivery lad, jumped out and rang the doorbell.

'Perfect timing,' said Sir Henry as he opened the door.

Nigel tugged the side of his flat cap, 'Nice to see you, we were beginning to think you were staying in London for the duration.'

'Not possible young Nigel, we couldn't survive without your marvellous bread. Florence insisted we stock up.'

'Shall I take the trays through to the kitchen?'

Sir Henry stood aside and waved the boy through.

Nigel walked through the front entrance. Hundreds of wonderful childhood memories began with the whiff of freshly baked bread.

Alice greeted Nigel in the kitchen, 'Dear boy, put the trays on the table. Do you have time for a cup of tea, I've just made a fresh pot?'

'Not today, Miss, we're short-staffed, so I best be off.'

He smiled at Florence as he passed her in the hallway. She walked into the kitchen from the ops room.

'Morning Alice.'

Alice lifted a warm loaf out of the tray, 'Ansty's just delivered your favourite.'

'Yum,' Florence tore off a hunk of bread. 'Alice, would you go with Sir Henry and Malcolm today? I need your eyes-on.'

'Eyes-on, no problem.'

Alice and Florence were in many ways, telepathic. A nod, a word, a look, or a raised eyebrow; especially a raised eyebrow, or a combination, was enough to transmit a message. It confused Sir Henry, and that was half the fun.

Alice said, 'Tea and toast?'

'Yes, please. I'll take a tray up to Percy and Stanley, assuming they haven't killed each other during the night.'

Tray in hand, Florence climbed the stairs then banged on Percy's bedroom door with her foot.

'Who is it?' called out Stanley.

'Florence.'

'Password?'

'We didn't discuss one, open the door you blithering idiot.'

Stanley opened the door, 'No password? I thought you were the best spy in the world.'

'Who told you that?'

'Sir Henry did.'

'I wholeheartedly deny it.'

'But you are a spy,' said Stanley.

'I deny it.'

'But not wholeheartedly,' added Percy. The two men laughed at their comedy timing.

'Do you want this tea and toast, or are you going to witter on with your cabaret act?'

'Tea and toast, please. We're famished,' said Percy.

Stanley took the tray and shut the door.

'Open the door, you fool. I'm coming in. Time is up.' Stanley opened the door, and Florence walked in.

She said, 'Percy, come onto the balcony with me.' He picked up a piece of buttered toast and followed her out.

She stood close to him; the sort of close where a whisper would be loud enough. 'How did you get on, did you finish?'

Percy nodded, too tired to give a detailed answer.

'Does Stanley have any idea what you were doing?'

'No.'

Florence put her hand out, 'I need both copies. I leave in twenty minutes. You can't say anything about your work from last night; not to Mandy, not to anybody.' She looked directly into his eyes and grasped his arm, 'Got it?'

He nodded, 'Got it.'

'Last night, you pulled off the impossible.'

He handed her the copies, 'Will this work?'

'I've absolutely no idea! If we win the war, then yes, if we lose, then no.'

In the garage, Mandy and Florence sat in the red Jaguar wearing leather gloves and warm blankets across their legs.

Percy and Sir Henry came out to see them off. Stanley, true to his word, didn't let Percy out of his sight and stood behind him.

Mandy opened the window, 'Percy, get some sleep, you look like a ghost.'

He leaned in and gave Mandy a soft kiss on the cheek, 'I'm going to sleep the whole day.'

Mandy gave an impish wink, 'I'll be back late, and I'll need warming up.'

Sir Henry wrapped his white silk scarf around Florence's neck and kissed her, 'Drive safely, darling.'

'Are you kidding, I race to win.' Florence revved the

engine and reversed out of the garage in a smooth arc. She looked at Mandy. 'Ready?'

'Ready, steady, go!' Mandy pressed the stopwatch. Florence spun the wheels, and the Jaguar snaked along the driveway and out through the stone pillared gates in a cloud of spitting gravel and snow.

The second hand ticked.

Sir Henry looked at Percy, 'Those two together are reckless, they have a bet to see who drives the fastest between Milton Park and the Houses of Parliament.'

'Who will win?'

'Florence never loses, and she won't let anyone else win, especially Mandy.' Sir Henry opened the front door, and the men walked indoors out of the cold.

'Why?'

'It's her way of keeping everyone safe. She says when you win, you celebrate, but when you lose, you contemplate and try harder. Those who celebrate ultimately lose. And in times of war, we must not lose.'

'So for the good of mankind, Florence has to win every race?' said Percy.

'Yes, you've got it.'

Florence drove the Jaguar through the narrow country lanes and took the corners at high speed, as if on a race circuit. She pushed the Jag to its absolute limits.

Mandy chirped up, 'When did you know Sir Henry was the one?'

Florence collected her thoughts, 'It wasn't when I fell in love with him; it was why I fell in love with him. When Douglas, my husband died, I stopped caring about living. My heart hurt so much. I couldn't get beyond the pain. I was angry with life, and my heart pounded uncontrollably at the slightest memory.'

'What changed?'

'I met Henry.'

'And?'

'And, he sensed my loss, and handled my heart with such softness, and such care, that I melted. Henry gave me the time to heal because he knew how much I loved my husband, and yet, there he was, waiting for me. Henry didn't say a word; he didn't need to. He showed me how much he loved me by not pushing me. I fell in love with him before I kissed him.'

'How romantic; tell me more.'

'I know what you are doing, Mandy Miller. I won't fall for your little tricks.'

'What tricks?'

'You think with all this romantic, sad reminiscing I'll drive slowly and post a poor time. Not a chance!' Florence changed gear and rammed her foot to the floor. The Jaguar responded with a growl and the miles peeled away.

Mandy said, 'Malcolm's a funny old sausage, isn't he?'

'Why's that?'

'One minute he's like a commando, the next he's a brainy boffin who has forgotten to button up his coat on a cold day. And that grotty blue scarf of his, it needs a damn good wash.'

'I've known Malcolm forever, and although he never stops surprising me, he has been extraordinarily odd at times since the funeral. Now, about this memory work, are you ready?'

'I'm as ready as I'll ever be.'

'In my bag, you'll see my hairbrush,'

'You look lovely as you are, Florence.'

'I know. Take it out and reverse twist the handle, you'll hear a click, then pull the handle away from the brush head.'

Mandy reached into the bag and grabbed the hairbrush.

She twisted, clicked and pulled. 'Oh, that's clever. I want one. Who thought of that?'

'It's one of Alice's ideas. She can turn lipstick into a stick of dynamite, a hairpin into a garrotting wire and a coat button into a radio receiver. Alice is the sneakiest spy I've ever known. She wears tweed and brogues and goes unnoticed behind enemy lines. She's the reason we win wars.'

Mandy unrolled the two pieces of paper from the hairbrush.

Florence said, 'Take the top copy, and memorise it, not one error, or else.'

'Yes, yes,' said Mandy. 'Lose the war and all that.'

'Can you do it?'

'Of course, I can, but I need you to slow down.'

'Hardly!' Florence took a sweeping left-handed bend at full throttle and held the wheel with the lightest touch. The Jaguar was under her spell.

All the while, Mandy's eyes darted from line to line. 'Done.'

'Already? You've only read it once.'

'I haven't read it at all, that's not how it works.'

'How does it work then?'

'I don't know.'

Florence grabbed the coded paper from Mandy's hand. 'Line seven, ninth word, the third character, what is it?'

Mandy closed her eyes. 'V,' she looked at Florence, not for approval, but to prove a point.

'Line twenty, third word, sixth character?'

'X, followed by b-7c, it is preceded with q9z over 65.9.'

'It's unbelievable, if I spent a month memorising it, I'd still get it wrong. Percy said it's impossible to memorise it.'

'It's good he believes that; I don't want him to think I'm a freak.'

'Freak? The boy is besotted with you. And you should have paused the stopwatch when I slowed down to test you.'

'Hardly!' said Mandy.

'That day I met you in the village hall in Battersea, I knew you were special. When your mum died, your only thought was to serve tea at the village hall. Alice spotted your potential and pulled strings to get you into the army.'

'I was lucky. I owe you everything.'

'It was not luck, and you owe us nothing.'

'So why didn't you and Sir Henry get married?'

'You don't hold back, do you? We discussed getting married; we even set the date, and then Germany invaded Poland, so we decided to wait, and we're still waiting. After the war, we'll get married, and you'll get an invite.'

'Too right, I will. You and Sir Henry go together like fish and chips.'

The Jaguar didn't miss a beat as Florence sped across Parliament Square.

Mandy pressed the stopwatch, 'That's a slow time. I can beat that.'

Florence parked up, and they clambered out the car and walked towards the grand entrance of Parliament.

The guards stood, stiff-backed, as guards do, and saluted. 'Good morning, Miss Fairweather, it's good to see you again. Follow the red carpet and take a left at the end of the hallway.' The guard looked at his watch. 'You'll find Mr Churchill having tea in the lounge.'

Florence and Mandy followed the carpeted hallway through to the lounge. They found Winston brushing crumbs off his tie.

'Morning Winston,' said Florence.

'Ah, my spy-girls, how are you? How could my day get any better?' Churchill spread his arms and gathered both women into a warm embrace, 'Tea?'

'Love some,' they said.

'Sit, sit,' said Winston. 'Now tell me, how was your journey?'

'Painfully slow,' said Mandy. 'I could have timed it with an abacus.'

'Oh, I know that face. You girls are racing: Milton Park to Parliament Square.' He pointed his cigar at them. 'You won't beat the time set by Henry. That man can fly on his Norton motorbike. We set off, with me on the back, clinging on with all my might, and thundered around every bend. He was a daring rider back then. These days he drives slower than Ivy Amos, my housekeeper.'

The tea tray arrived, 'What time is Barrington due?' asked Florence. And as if scripted, he walked up to the table.

Florence stood and hugged him.

Mid hug, Barrington looked at Mandy. Men did. 'And you must be?'

'I must be, Miller, Mandy Miller, it's nice to meet you, Mr Barrington.'

Churchill pulled a chair out.

Barrington pushed it back in. 'Let's go through to my chambers. Mandy, bring the tea tray with you, that's a good girl.'

Mandy poked her tongue out behind his back and curtsied. 'Horses arse.'

'I heard that,' said Winston. 'And it happens to be true.' He held the door open for Florence and Mandy, but it was Barrington, dressed in his grey pinstripe morning suit, who marched through first.

In his chamber, Barrington sat behind a dark oakwood desk. 'This belonged to my father. A carpenter made it from wood from a captured German ship during the Great War. He passed it on to me. It's rather splendid, don't you think?'

'Has it been checked?' asked Mandy.

'Checked for what?'

'For listening devices, you can't trust those shifty Nazis.'

There was no trace of a smile. Barrington was unaccustomed to young women being unimpressed with his seat of power. He looked at Florence, 'I need an update. This whole hiding away plan is simply unworkable.'

'Oh, I rather like it,' said Winston. 'It adds a touch of mystery to what, after all, is a mysterious division within our war machine.'

'Oh, do be sensible, Churchill,' Barrington stood and leaned against his desk as Florence gave him details of site visits and security changes.

'This farcical, and unnecessary cloak and dagger performance over nothing but a Parliamentary rumour, is an utter waste of money.'

'Waste of money?' said Florence.

'Yes, a colossal waste of war funds.'

'Sir Henry funded our move, and I can assure you, it's not a waste of his money.'

Mandy stood, served the tea and glanced in the mirror to check her hair.

'That reminds me,' said Florence. 'I have something of national security, and I believe it should be in your Parliamentary safe, Christopher.'

Barrington nodded his approval.

Florence said, 'Germany is desperate to seize the 12g295 code.' She walked over to the window. 'There are only two copies of the code. One is with Malcolm Feathers, and the other should be under your security, Christopher. If anything happens to me, or Malcolm, you must be the one who guarantees our continued production.' Florence opened her bag and took out her hairbrush.

'Why can't I have the code?' asked Churchill.

'Oh Winston, you say the funniest things sometimes.' She

pulled and twisted the head of the hairbrush to reveal the secret compartment and took out the code. 'Christopher, winning the war, or indeed losing the war, is now in your hands.'

Barrington looked at the dots and dashes, letters numbers and equations, his eyes darted from line to line. The code would mean nothing to him. He bristled with self-importance none the less, 'What are you planning to do now?'

'To go for lunch,' piped up Mandy. 'Do you fancy a nibble, Mr Barrington?'

'No, I need to press on, I have a frantic day ahead and a committee meeting in ten minutes.' He folded the sheet of coded paper and locked it in his safe.

Florence said, 'Mandy, let's take Winston out for lunch.'

Outside in the draughty hallway, Churchill was in a buoyant mood. 'Where would you two like to go for lunch?'

'I know the best fish and chip shop in Trafalgar Square,' said Mandy.

They stepped outside into a cold midday wind. Florence and Mandy walked either side of Winston with their arms looped through his.

Whitehall was quiet.

'Tell me, Florence, how is it going at Milton Park?'

'Not great, and it's about to get messy. Nothing unusual about that.'

Winston looked at Mandy. 'Tell me, this restaurant of yours, is the fish fresh?'

'Fresh, Mr Churchill? The last time I was there, the fish ate half my chips.'

The three of them laughed all the way to Trafalgar Square.

<><><>

CHAPTER 18

The smell of fish and chips, and the relentless stream of red buses edging slowly around Trafalgar Square, were wonderfully London.

Churchill sat snugly between Mandy and Florence. 'What time do you have to leave for Milton Park?'

'We're in no desperate hurry,' said Florence.

'Nonsense, Mr Churchill, we're gonna be in a right old hurry, trust me,' said Mandy.

'Oh, I sense a land speed contender to your crown, Florence.'

'Fiddlesticks, the girl is deluded. Besides, these biblical portions of fish and chips should slow us down a beat.'

'And Mandy, you were right, this is the best fish in town,' said Churchill.

The three of them sat on a narrow bench looking out through the steamy window across the bustling Trafalgar Square.

Mandy ate her last chip. 'Are we going to win this war, Mr Churchill? I mean, Hitler is doing a right old job of ripping Europe to bits.' Churchill leaned forward. Florence and Mandy leaned with him.

'Yes,' he said.

'Well, I'm glad you cleared that up,' said Mandy.

He looked over his beady spectacles, 'I sense you want a longer answer than my succinct, yes.'

'I was expecting a speech.'

'In Parliament, I give long speeches about how, why, and when we will execute a destructive blow to Nazi Germany. But here in this fish and chip emporium, you get the benefit of seeing me close enough to tell if I'm speaking the truth, or fudging a story.'

Mandy, unsatisfied, asked, 'I'm feeling a bit of fudge, Mr Churchill.'

Winston smiled and glanced around, 'Yes, we will win, but I don't know how, and I don't know when. But I do know Britain, and I know its people.' He took Mandy's and Florence's hands and held them tightly. He spoke in a soft tone. 'Remember, I'm Britain's elected lion, and I have you, and you have Sir Henry and Alice. So how on Earth can Hitler, and his twisted menace, win?'

'Winston, I could listen to you speak all day,' said Florence. 'This is your war to win, and we need you at the helm, as Prime Minister. So if you don't mind hurrying up a bit and taking over as leader, then Britain can sleep better at night.'

Mandy nudged Florence, 'There are a couple of dishy young sailors looking at us.'

Churchill butted in, 'You'll find they are looking at me.' He beckoned the boys over. 'Are you on a spot of leave?'

'Yes, Mr Churchill, twenty-four hours, we wanted to say, well, we thought . . . we, well you know—'

Churchill stood and shook their hands.

He said, 'How very kind of you to come over and say hello. Have you boys eaten yet?'

'No sir, we only popped in because we saw you sat in the window with your two smashing daughters.'

Churchill put his hands in his coat pockets, rifled through his trouser pockets, then patted his jacket. 'Florence, may I have some of your money?'

Churchill gave the sailors Florence's money. 'Buy yourselves some fish and chips, and have a few beers, and catch a show in Drury Lane.'

'Thank you, Mr Churchill. We joined up because of you, our dads were in the Navy in the first bash, and they said you were the top-dog.'

'Do your dads proud.'

The young boys stood nervously, 'We'll win this thing, Mr Churchill, and give them Nazis a right good hiding.'

'I know it, and you know it, now we must let Mr Hitler know it.' Winston shook hands with the sailors and bid them a good day.

Florence and Mandy stood and looped their arms into Winston's, and said, 'Come on, dad, let's go.'

They strolled down Whitehall and across Parliament Square to their Jaguar. On the way, Florence told Churchill about her thoughts for the days that lay ahead.

Mandy jumped in the driver's seat and fired up the engine. The roar burbled and echoed around the architectural splendour of Parliament.

Churchill hugged Florence. 'Spin the stories, move the goalposts, use smoke and mirrors, and change the rules. I trust you with all that I have.'

'Winston, I'm going to throw a huge spanner in the Nazi machine, they'll be picking up the pieces of a broken Germany for the next fifty years.'

'That's why I picked you. When this mission is over, and

after you manage the impossible and defeat the undefeatable, you and Henry must bring your team to Chartwell for afternoon tea. Promise me you will.'

'I promise, Henry would never miss one of Mrs Amos's special cream teas.'

'As I thought,' said Winston.

Mandy stepped out of the burbling Jaguar. 'Goodbye, Mr Churchill,' she hugged him.

'Mandy, my girl, now that we have eaten fish and chips together, and you think my opponent, Christopher Barrington, is a horse's arse, you can call me, Winston.'

Mandy gave him an extra hug.

Winston looked up to the sky and gave Mandy a wink, 'The conditions look favourable to set a record time, so don't squander this opportunity.'

Mandy and Florence jumped in the car.

'Drive carefully back to Milton Park, and Florence, let Mandy win.'

'Never, never, never, never!' shouted Florence. She started the stopwatch. Mandy spun the wheels.

The seconds ticked.

Alice Jones, drove identically to Florence: quick, precise and far beyond the edge of comfort. Sir Henry closed his eyes during the fast corners.

He said, 'This is our last site visit for the day. These chaps manufacturer Spitfire wings.' He checked the map, 'Alice, take a left at the junction, then second right.'

She glided the Bentley through the gates onto a patch of nondescript scrubland.

Otto pointed at the building. 'It doesn't look much. It looks more like an old abandoned warehouse than a factory.'

'That's the idea,' said Alice. 'Often, the best disguise is to make something important look decidedly unimportant. Nobody will pay much attention to this scruffy green hangar. Especially the Luftwaffe. Why orchestrate a bombing raid on a building that already looks derelict?'

'Clever stuff,' said Otto. 'Military Intelligence works in clever, corkscrew ways.'

Sir Henry added, 'Entirely different from Germany's brash, plumb-straight philosophy to continuously display a visual demonstration of power.'

Alice said, 'We must never underestimate them, though. It's not their army of a million foot-soldiers we fear. It's their army of one. That one slippery spy you can't see.'

Otto listened. They fear me.

Sir Henry said, 'Let's go in and take a look around, and ensure they are securely locked down.'

Inside the hangar, Otto looked in awe at the rows of beautifully hand-crafted Spitfire wings. Each wing enabled Britain's fighter aircraft to turn, climb and dive faster than anything Germany offered. He would take great pleasure sending the Luftwaffe on a bombing raid to flatten this old hangar to the ground. A single bomb load would destroy five-hundred finished wings.

Otto had Britain at his mercy.

Sir Henry visited the site manager and spoke at length, discussing staff security while Alice strode around the plant with Otto.

'You've known Florence, forever.' said Otto.

'Yes; her whole life. I taught her the basics of spycraft, and from an early age she could persuade others to do things they didn't see themselves doing. She developed her skill of deduction to such a degree that Florence could have become a top police detective. Nothing escapes her.'

Otto said, 'At Oxford, she took me under her wing. I was a bit of a day-dreamer, and she protected me from day one.'

'She thinks the world of you, Malcolm.'

Alice put her hands behind her back and sauntered through the hangar. Otto followed.

'Alice, may I ask you something?'

'Certainly, fire away, dear boy.'

'Florence mentioned there were two copies of the 12g295 code. Maybe I ought to know who has the other copy, for security reasons.'

Alice stopped walking and faced him. 'You're right. I hadn't thought about it that way. Well, there's your copy of course, that you keep tucked behind your inseparable four photograph, and Florence is handing her copy over to Christopher Barrington today.'

Sir Henry stepped out of the office and walked over to where Alice and Otto stood.

He said, 'They are doing an excellent job of security here. What do you say to pie and chips and a beer? The Jumping Fox is a lovely old pub near Milton Park, and I've not been there since before the war. It's Florence's favourite pub.'

Otto's thoughts drifted away from the chatter about pie and chips. Momentarily he was struck dumb: the inseparable four photo. He could have kicked himself. Sir Henry, carefully steered the Bentley out of the hangar gates and headed towards the pub.

Stanley poked Percy with his finger. 'Hey, Eton boy, my duty here is nearly done.'

'What do you mean?'

'You're alive, aren't you? I've prevented you from getting your silly-self killed. Let's take Rags for a walk.'

'Great idea.'

'Shake a leg then, Toff.'

They descended the stairs and entered the kitchen.

Rags bounded up to them.

'Come on old boy,' said Percy. 'Let's go and chase some rabbits.'

'And more great news, Rags,' said Stanley. 'Percy is going to bring his butterfly net.'

'You know what?' Percy said. 'If things were different, and we'd met in a pub or at a football match, I know one thing for sure . . . I still wouldn't like you.'

Their laughter echoed through the kitchen as they ran out on to the terrace.

'Come on, Toff, I'll race you.' They reached the top of the ridge together. They puffed and panted, and filled their lungs with misty cold air.

'You're a fast runner, for a toff,' said Stanley.

'I thought you grubby street urchins could outrun anyone, with nothing but a cheeky smile on your face.'

'I reckon you're alright, Percy bloody Butterworth, for a toff that is.'

Dusk descended like a dark veil covering the world.

Percy pointed. 'What's going on down there? Rags is barking like a lunatic.' They ran from the top of the ridge into the forested area. Rags was frantically digging, spraying mud and snow between his hind legs.

Stanley was the first on the scene.

'Christ, I can see a person's hand sticking up out of the ground. Rags, get away, boy!'

Percy arrived. Together they pushed the snow away and scooped the loose mud from the shallow grave.

A dead-eyed, blue-grey face stared back at them.

Mandy drove the Jaguar to its limits.

She shouted above the roar, 'At this speed, I should beat you by two minutes.'

'Nonsense,' said Florence. 'You'll miss out on becoming world champion by about thirty-seconds. It's the silver medal for you tonight. I'd say it was a spirited attempt, but alas, no winning cigar.'

'It's not over yet.'

'Oh, it is, and you know it,' said Florence.

'Have you always been this competitive?'

'Have you?'

'I asked first,' said Mandy.

The engine drowned out their laughter.

'Winning is the only option,' said Florence. 'Coming second is not a reason to celebrate. It's win, or don't win.'

'I wish I didn't care so much,' said Mandy. 'It must be peaceful not to give a damn. I wonder what it's like to be a loser.'

'I wouldn't know. But tonight, Mandy Miller, of Battersea, you can tell the world what it feels like.'

Mandy gripped the wheel and squealed the Jag's tyres around a tight bend.

Florence glanced at the stopwatch. 'Milton Park is three miles away, and our times are neck and neck. I know you'll find a way to snatch defeat from the jaws of victory.'

Mandy changed gear and rammed her foot hard on the accelerator pedal. The Jaguar's bonnet lifted with the new rush of power.

'Come on old girl,' Mandy shouted at the sports car. The gates to Milton Park were in sight. 'How much time left?'

Florence checked the stopwatch, 'Twenty-seconds, I don't believe it, I think you're going to beat me.'

Sir Henry turned into the lane a few yards in front of the Jaguar. Mandy stood on the brake pedal and brought the racing car to a juddering halt. Sir Henry looked through the side window of his Bentley and lifted his hat at the two startled girls, then steered sedately through the gates of Milton Park.

'That's simply not fair,' said Mandy.

'You're right. It most certainly is not.'

'So do I win?'

'Most certainly not.'

Percy and Stanley ran out to meet the cars. Sir Henry, Alice and Otto stepped out of the Bentley. Mandy and Florence jumped out of the Jag to meet the men who were shouting and waving their arms.

'We found Fletch,' said Stanley. 'In the woods, over on the far side of the ridge, out of sight from the house. The poor bugger is in a shallow grave.'

'Show me,' said Florence. She turned to face Alice. 'Code-red, lockdown!'

Alice called out to Sir Henry, Mandy, and Malcolm to get inside.'

Florence ran behind Stanley and Percy over the top of the ridge and down into the forest. Their torches danced off the darkening shadows.

And there it was.

Fletcher's stiff body lay beside the shallow grave.

Florence circled the corpse. Her footsteps were slow, but her thoughts were quick. 'What did you notice? Don't think, just blurt it out.'

Percy spoke first, 'There's no sign of facial bruising and no sign of a knife or bullet attack. I'd say, Fletch was attacked from behind.'

Stanley added, 'We saw the body in the last knockings of daylight, and from the colouring around poor Fletch's neck we think he was strangled. He was surprised alright; his pipe is tucked away in his top pocket, filled and ready to light.'

Florence had seen enough. 'Put Fletch's body in the garden shed, and I'll call the police.'

Alice gathered everybody in the kitchen. 'We need to stay here until Florence gets back.'

Otto raised his hand. 'Alice, I drank one too many beers at the Jumping Fox, and I need to pop to the loo. I'll only be a minute.'

'Go, but come right back here.'

Otto dashed straight to the ballroom. He snatched the photograph from the shelf and unclipped the backplate from the glass. A single sheet of white paper fell into his hands.

Otto held it as if cradling a newborn.

He uttered softly, 'Malcolm, you old sneak. I should've known you would hide it in plain sight.'

'But you didn't know, did you?' said Florence.

Otto spun around.

Florence stood in a dark corner of the ballroom; her hands and boots were plastered in mud.

She said, 'I saw Fletch's body, where you buried him, in a cold, shallow grave in the woods.'

Otto's mission had been reduced to a single scene. His senses were raw, coiled and prickled on full alert. He folded the sheet of code in half and put it in his pocket.

He let out a sigh, 'What gave me away?'

'I won't give you the whole list; just some of the highlights?'

Otto nodded.

'Since Oxford, I've never known Malcolm to clean his shoes. Also, you can change your face, you can change your voice, you can even act the part, but you can't hide lean muscle. When you hugged me at the funeral, I knew you weren't Malcolm. He had a body of a wet sponge.'

Otto drew his pistol and walked over to Florence and aimed it at her face. 'I'm getting out of here-'

Stanley barged through the ballroom doors and saw Malcolm's pistol aimed at Florence's face.

He said, 'What's going on in here?'

Florence raised her hands to signal her surrender.

She whispered, 'Stanley, stand down, let Malcolm go. Let him out.'

Stanley rooted himself to the floor; his eyes remained focused on the pistol.

Otto side-stepped Stanley, and slipped out through the ballroom doors, and ran along the hallway towards the entrance hall. Mandy came out of the kitchen and clattered into him.

'Malcolm, you clumsy chump,' she yelled.

Otto grabbed her around the neck and pulled her to him. His grip was vice-tight, and he rammed his pistol against the side of her head.

Percy ran into the entrance hall. 'Malcolm, what the hell are you doing? For goodness sake man, let Mandy go. Take me instead.' He edged closer.

Otto barked, 'Get back, or I'll shoot her.'

Otto's voice no longer mimicked Malcolm's, as harsh Germanic tones filled the entrance hall.

Percy froze.

Mandy froze.

The barrel of Otto's pistol indented a red ring on her temple.

Stanley came running from the ballroom.

Mandy saw him, 'Keep back, Stanley.'

Stanley continued full tilt.

Otto fired twice, and Stanley clattered to the ground in a tangle of limbs.

Otto pushed Mandy towards Percy and pointed the pistol at the assembly.

Sir Henry said, 'Careful everyone, let Malcolm go. Let him go.' The palms of his hands faced the floor: another ancient signal of surrender.

Otto barged out of the front door and jumped into Florence's Jaguar. He roared the engine to life and sped away.

Mandy knelt at Stanley's side. Thick blood pooled out from under his body onto the white marble tiles. His breathing came in short laboured gasps.

Stanley reached out with his muddy hand. Blood bubbled in his mouth. 'Mandy, that toff, Percy . . . he's alright, he's alright.'

'Take it easy, Stanley. Don't speak. You'll be fine, you'll see, we'll patch you up as good as new.' She looked up at Percy. 'Don't let him die, not like this. Do something, anything.'

Percy clamped his hand over the bullet wounds and checked for a pulse. There wasn't one.

Stanley Blagdon was dead.

Sir Henry, Alice and Florence stood in silence. Mandy laid her head on Stanley's body.

Percy gently laid his hand on Mandy's head. 'He's gone.'

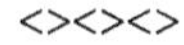

CHAPTER 19

The gunshot fashioned its final echo around the marble entrance hall. Dead silence followed. Nobody moved; movement would make Stanley's death a reality.

Sir Henry's hushed tone punctured the stillness.

He said, 'Florence, go and do what you do best. I'll take care of business here.'

Mandy snapped, 'Stanley isn't business!'

Florence whispered at Percy, 'You're coming with me.'

'What about me?' asked Mandy.

'Stay here with Stanley. I'll contact you later.'

'No! I'm going with you and Percy. If you're going after Malcolm, I'm going too. You can't stop me.'

'You are not. . .'

Florence's words were cut short.

'I'm going with you, and that's that.' Mandy looked down at Stanley's body. 'Florence, you have to put me on the team.'

'Mandy is right,' said Alice.

Florence gave a nod of agreement, 'Mandy, you're in, go with Percy and pack, and be back here ready to leave in five minutes.'

Mandy was already halfway to the staircase as Florence finished her sentence.

Sir Henry put his arms around Florence, 'You're doing the right thing by taking her. But, keep an extra eye on her and Percy. They're not like you and Alice.'

'What's that supposed to mean?'

'You two are indestructible. I've seen bullets and grenades bounce off you, then you spring back up and keep going.'

'Mandy is made from the same fibre as us,' said Alice.

Sir Henry knew when to abandon his point of view. 'When you leave, I'll contact Stanley's parents. They've lost both their children within a week.' He wandered off towards the staircase and collected Florence's bag.

Florence said, 'Alice, did you put the radio tracker in my Jaguar?'

'This isn't my first day as a spy, you know. You'll be able to pick up the signal from up to fifty miles away.'

'I think I know where he's going.'

'Friston?' said Alice.

'Yes, Friston, he'll go to what he knows. A spy needs familiarity. If it were me, I would have hidden my radio, clothes and documents there.'

They walked into the ops room. Alice stared at a flashing green dot in the centre of a monitor. She said, 'There he is, about twenty miles away heading towards London.'

'He will have a rendezvous with a boat somewhere along the south coast. I'll head towards London then contact you for an update.'

Alice touched Florence's arm, 'Before you rush off, I want to show you something I've been working on. It's at the prototype stage, but it's worth taking with you.' She took three small metal boxes out of a drawer. Each one was the size of a cigarette packet with a hook protruding from the top.

'What are they?'

'It's a . . . well, I don't have a name for it yet. In non-technical terms, it's a portable telephone.'

'Where's the cable and receiver, and where's the dial phone bit? Alice, is this one of your crazy ideas?'

'Yes, it is, but you should pay attention because it's completely brilliant.'

'How does it work?'

Alice picked one up and opened the front cover to reveal ten, round black buttons numbered zero through nine.

'Watch, you take this hook, like this, and attach it to a telegraph line, like that.' Alice hooked it over her finger. 'You put your ear close to this front panel and wait for a dialling tone. Then you punch in the telephone number. When the person answers, you speak into this bit here.'

'Have you tested it yet?'

'Define test?'

'Alice, does it work?'

'I don't know. But the good news is, you get to be the first to find out.'

Florence opened and closed the front panel. She pressed the buttons and put it against her ear. 'It's dead! Are you sure about this?'

'Hook it over the telegraph line, and it should pop into life. And like all new things, it takes time to work out all the niggles.'

'I think it's a clever idea,' said Florence.

'Yes, I know it is.'

Florence hugged her, even though Alice was not a hugger. She was ready to leave, but she didn't make a move.

She said, 'It's completely my fault Fletch and Stanley are dead. I played a dangerous game, and it cost the lives of two good men.'

'War is dangerous,' Alice's voice was sharp. 'Now, go and

wash your face in cold water, and pull yourself together. We need you wide-eyed and switched on. There's no need to worry about anything back here; I'll look after Sir Henry, Rags, and those pipe-puffers. Get going, go on, go.' Alice shooed her out of the ops room.

Death remained in the hallway.

Sir Henry stood with Florence's bag, 'Which car do you want to take?'

Florence snapped into mission-mode, 'We need speed. Put Mandy and Percy on your Norton, and I'll take the single-seater racer, the one I use at Brooklands race track.'

'I'll get them warmed up,' he said.

Florence walked outside into the cold air with him.

He put his arm around her.

'I'm doubting myself,' she said.

'Doubting, how so?'

'If what I'm about to do goes horribly wrong, Britain will face the gravest peril it's ever faced. And it will be entirely down to me. We'll lose the war because of me.'

'And, if it goes right, you'll be responsible for giving Britain a slight edge to stay in the war, and all we need right now is a slight edge.' He pulled his silk scarf from his pocket and wrapped it around her neck. 'You can't go without this.'

Florence breathed in the silk.

Lord knows it was comforting.

Sir Henry was right; she couldn't go anywhere without it. She took Alice's metal box telephone invention out of her pocket and explained it to Sir Henry.

With a look of puzzlement, she said, 'I'll call you before bedtime.'

'You don't think for one minute that contraption is going to work, do you?'

'Alice's weird stuff works eventually.'

'Why don't you go back inside while I warm up the engines, the temperature has dropped.'

Florence met Mandy and Percy in the entrance hall.

'Percy, go and give your bags to Sir Henry,' said Florence.

Mandy couldn't take her eyes from the soaked blood stains on the blanket covering Stanley's body. 'I was so horrible to him.' Tears rolled down her cheeks. 'I'm the worst person in the world. I pushed him away. And now he's dead.'

'You were not horrible; you ended it with him. You and Percy take the Norton, and I'll drive the track car.'

Mandy said, 'I'd better ride, I doubt if Percy has even been on a motorbike.'

Florence and Mandy went outside to the garage where Sir Henry had the engines purring like a basket of kittens. He lit a cigarette, stood back, and listened. And with a small screwdriver, he tinkered again.

Florence climbed into the cockpit of the track car and switched on the makeshift headlight. She wrapped the silk scarf around her neck and pulled on her leather driving gloves. Sir Henry helped button up her fur-lined flying jacket.

He leaned in and kissed her goodbye. 'We seem to be saying a lot of goodbyes. Darling, be safe, and I mean it, the man you are chasing is a cold-blooded killer who will stop at nothing. Don't play with him.'

'You know me,' she said.

'Yes, I do, hence the warning.' He kissed her again.

Mandy and Percy strapped their bags on to the back seat of the Norton.

Alice said to them, 'Ride safely, this thing is a flying machine. I tuned it so you'll have no trouble keeping up with Florence in her racer.' She gave Percy a firm handshake, then glanced at Mandy's red, tear-stained face. 'Take care of my girl.'

Percy leaned close to Mandy and said, 'My uncle had a Norton just like this one. I used to ride it to Bletchley Park every day from my digs in town. Why don't I ride, and you hold on tightly to me?'

Without argument, Mandy slid backwards along the saddle and pressed herself against their bags.

Percy put on his gloves and pulled up his collar. He turned around to offer a comforting word or two, but Mandy had already buried her face into his back and wrapped her arms tightly around him.

Florence beckoned Alice over, 'It's time to activate Rosie in Berlin.'

'I'll send a message right away.'

'And one more thing,' said Florence. 'If Percy is captured and taken prisoner, I'm prepared to shoot him dead. If I'm captured as well, then you must find him, and kill him. He won't be able to hold out for long under Gestapo interrogation, and his time at Bletchley Park would put Military Intelligence at great risk.'

'Got it.'

Florence drove out of the driveway and through the gates. Percy and Mandy followed on the Norton. Sir Henry and Alice watched and waved until they could no longer hear the engines or see their lights flitting through the trees.

'Tea?' asked Alice.

'That would be lovely,' said Sir Henry.

Florence's front lamp barely lit the way, especially at the speed she drove. Percy and Mandy leaned, as one, into and out of, each bend. He was an accomplished rider and kept in close contact with Florence.

They pressed on for an hour then stopped on the side of

the road, Percy pulled up behind Florence. They were stiff with cold.

'I'm going up there,' said Florence, and pointed to a telegraph pole.

'What for?' asked Mandy.

'To make a phone call with Alice's new contraption.' She showed them the box.

Percy laughed, 'You can't be serious.'

'Deadly, I'll be back in a few minutes.'

She put her foot on the first peg, then pulled herself up onto the next one. She climbed to the top of the pole and held on with one hand, then reached into her pocket and took out the metal box. She hooked it over the telegraph wire and opened the flap. Florence listened for a tone, then dialled Milton Park, and pushed her ear against the cold box.

Crackles and pops followed, and then a ringing tone.

Alice's voice sounded tinny, 'Milton Park, four, seven, two, how may I help you?'

'Alice, it's me, I can hear you, I can't believe it, it works.'

'Well, of course, it works, and, you don't need to shout quite so loudly.'

Florence looked down at two eager faces looking up, 'It works, I'm talking to Alice.'

'It's a miracle,' said Percy.

Mandy said, 'Alice might look like a country vicar's wife with her tweed, brown brogues and apple crumble, but trust me, she's smarter than most of your lot from Eton, Oxford and Bletchley.'

Percy conceded, 'I don't doubt it, she's an absolute marvel.'

Florence pushed her ear tightly against the cold box. 'Yes, I see, I got it, yes, yes.' She looked down, 'Alice says, Malcolm in the Jaguar is approaching Friston, and his estimated time of arrival is one hour.' She spoke into the box again, 'Kiss Rags for me. Is Henry there?'

She waited.

'Henry, it's me.'

'Where-Are-You?' He overemphasised each word.

'Up a pole,' she said.

'Sounds unpleasant.'

'I told you I would telephone to say goodnight.'

'You did. Goodnight, and take care my love, goodnight.'

Florence climbed down and handed Percy and Mandy a metal box each, 'These are for you. For military purposes, not for late-night love chatter.'

'My very own chatterbox,' said Mandy.

'Chatterbox is a great name,' said Percy.

Otto memorised the route to Friston; the village where his mission began. Road signs and mileage markers had been removed and stored away until after the war. Otto thought it a futile gesture; a few missing signposts wouldn't stop the German army marching across England's fields.

The Jaguar's fuel gauge read low, and would not get Otto to Friston. He spotted a tractor behind a hedge. He parked the car on a grass verge and pinched a bucket and a rubber hose from a nearby barn. He syphoned off a bucket of fuel and filled the Jaguar's tank.

Thinking about Friston, brought thoughts about Lizzie Denton's lithe body, and her eagerness to please him. He could be outside her house within an hour. He set off with a renewed vigour, but the long days and endless nights were catching up with him, and he was making silly mistakes: clipping corners and overshooting junctions.

He cursed his errors, and later than planned, he drove into Friston village in the middle of the night.

The thick blanket of snow deadened every sound.

He parked in front of Malcolm's cottage and walked into the village and stood outside Denton's store. He picked up a few small stones and threw them at Lizzie's bedroom window. Three direct hits on the glass and a small light pinged on to light up the narrow gap in the curtains.

Lizzie opened her bedroom window.

'Malcolm?' she looked again at the man standing in the road. 'Malcolm?' she put her hand to her mouth. 'How? I mean, wait, I'm coming down.'

Lizzie opened the side door and wrapped her arms around him. 'Malcolm, I thought you were dead.'

'Why would you think that? Lizzie, come to the cottage with me, I don't have long, this is a flying visit.'

'I have a better idea; my grandad is away in London for two days buying supplies, so come upstairs with me. I bet your place will be freezing, and I have a log fire in my bedroom.' Otto checked up and down the road, then followed her upstairs to her warm room.

He said, 'I've been travelling all night, and I'm exhausted. I've thought about you, Lizzie Denton.'

'I love the way you say my name.' She turned to face him. Lizzie sniffed, and faint tears welled in the corners of her eyes, 'Malcolm, I saw your body on the beach. Later I realised it couldn't possibly be you, but for that brief moment, I thought you were dead.'

Otto said nothing. He didn't want to kill her.

He gathered her up in his arms and kissed her; it was an urgent kiss, not tender. She unbuttoned her dressing-gown; it slipped to the ground, and she climbed naked into the bed and held the covers open for him. Otto joined her.

Killing Stanley Blagdon, and escaping from Milton Park used the last of his energy reserves, and no matter how much he wanted her, his eyes began to close.

Lizzie pulled the bed covers over them as she cuddled into him, then took his cold hands and placed them on her body. She craved him, but Otto didn't move. His breathing slowed to a soft rhythm, and he slipped into a deep sleep.

CHAPTER 20

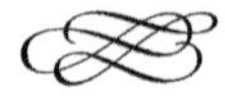

Florence smiled to herself; how dull life would be without Alice. And how dull life would be without Mandy. Poor thing, crying over Stanley's body in the entrance hall. Florence's thoughts turned and twisted around in her head like the winding road stretching out in front of her. She blamed herself for everything.

Florence held the steering wheel with a racing driver's touch and applied the slightest dab on the brakes going into a corner, and then full speed coming out of the bend. Her feet danced and flitted across the pedals like a ballerina, and her eyes were alert to the road ahead. Instincts flowed through her, like a natural racing driver.

Percy had impressed her with his complex coding, and equally, his kindness towards Mandy. His handling of Stanley had impressed her, too. Not surprisingly, Henry had been right about him.

Henry usually was.

Florence buried her chin instinctively into his scarf. To anybody else, the silk scarf would smell of tobacco, engine oil and wood polish, but to Florence, it smelled of a lifetime of memories with a man who captivated her heart.

She breathed him in.

Mandy wrapped her arms around Percy and rested her head on his back, she felt him grip the motorbike each time they took a corner. She pulled herself closer to him, partly for shelter from the biting cold, but mostly for intimacy. She didn't know how he'd reached into her soul and stirred her emotions, but she liked that he did.

Florence slowed down and pulled over on to the side of the road. Percy parked the Norton alongside her car.

'Everything alright?' he asked.

'Yes, I want to use the chatterbox-phone-thing and check-in with Alice.' She climbed up the pole and attached the hook to the telegraph wire, and diallcd.

Alice's voice piped up, 'Milton P-'

'Alice, it's me. Check the green dot on your screen and see if our man has reached Friston.'

'He's parked your Jaguar outside Malcolm's cottage.'

Mandy shouted from the bottom of the pole, 'Have you found the murdering little shit?'

Florence climbed down, 'He's parked outside Malcolm's cottage.'

'Malcolm's cottage? Why are you saying it like that?'

'It's time to tell you what's going on,' said Florence. 'But first, let's get out of the cold and find somewhere warmer.' She stepped over the snow-covered verge and spotted a farm building.

They pushed the barn doors open and sat on warm, dry hay bales. Percy found a lantern and the orange flame glowed between them in the dark.

'Come on, Florence, who the bloody hell is Malcolm?' asked Mandy. Her tone was harsher than she'd intended.

'Sorry, Florence, I didn't mean to snap, it's the whole Stanley and Fletch thing.'

Florence released a long breath.

'Germany's top spy, Otto Flack, had reconstructive surgery to look identical to Malcolm Feathers. The likeness was incredible, and he fooled nearly everyone. Otto killed Malcolm's parents, and waited for Malcolm to arrive for the funeral, then killed him, and became Malcolm.'

'When did you figure all that out?' asked Percy.

'The instant I met him at the funeral.'

'What gave him away?' asked Mandy.

'Clean shoes and muscles.'

'Did Sir Henry figure it out as well?' asked Mandy.

'No, not right away. After the funeral, we took Otto to London. I went to see Alice at Horse Guards Parade. I knew she would spot Malcolm, was not Malcolm. She doesn't miss a trick. We hatched a plan to take Military Intelligence to Milton Park, and that meant taking Otto Flack impersonating Malcolm, with us to keep him in our orbit.'

'This Otto chap didn't know that you'd rumbled him?' said Mandy.

'He had no idea. I fed him juicy bits of information as if he was Malcolm, all of it useless but he wouldn't have known that.'

'Why didn't you tell me?' asked Mandy.

'I didn't tell anyone,' said Florence.

'Did you tell Sir Henry?' asked Percy.

Florence cleared her throat. 'Henry is from a different era. A time of gentlemen spies. And like Winston, he's a terrible actor. I wanted Henry to be as normal as possible around Malcolm. Only Alice and I knew what was going on. But once Henry cottoned on, I had to make sure he didn't over-ham it like an old thespian.'

'What do you know about Otto Flack?' said Mandy.

'I've known about him for a long time. He's a ruthless, stone-cold killer, and I never thought I would have him under my roof, yet there he was. We caught word about a German spy who regularly went under the knife to change his appearance so that his mother no longer recognised him. You've got to be a deranged psychopathic individual to put yourself through that sort of treatment. We thought Berlin's propaganda machine was embellishing the Otto Flack legend, but when I met him in the church, parading as Malcolm, I nearly lost control. It was a brilliant plan, and he was close to pulling it off.'

'And his mission was what exactly?' asked Mandy.

'To steal the Spitfire code and identify the twenty-one sites where the components are made. The Luftwaffe would then bomb them to pieces.'

Mandy whistled through her teeth. 'Those sods could build thousands of Spits and use them against us, while we're scrabbling around trying to stick the bloody wings back on.'

'Correct.'

'The bastards!' Mandy whistled through her teeth again.

'The next part of the plan is the tricky bit. Otto has the code and the locations, and our job is to make sure he gets back to Berlin and succeed with his mission.'

'That makes no sense, we should go and stick a knife in the pig,' said Mandy. 'I'll happily do it.'

'I think I know why we can't,' said Percy. 'Florence has a deeper plan that's more destructive than the assassination of a spy, even if he is Germany's best.'

'I still want to stab him,' said Mandy.

'You'll get your chance,' said Florence. 'But first, Otto must complete his mission. Germany must haemorrhage money, and commit labour, plus vital resources to build tens of thousands of Spitfires.'

'Why do we want them to do that?' said Mandy.

'Because they'll never fly,' said Percy. 'My code will see to that. They'll be building fat pigs, not Spits. Fat pigs that will never fly.'

Mandy said, 'So everything was staged?'

'Yes,' said Florence. 'Milton Park was rigged up with the incorrect locations on the wall map. The site visits were elaborate charades with actors and local women who thought we were making a film for the war effort. The whole thing from top to bottom was a hoax to string Otto along into believing he'd found the Spitfire code and the twenty-one manufacturing locations. We were on standby from the beginning of the war for such a plan. We must make sure Otto gets back to Berlin, thinking he has stolen the code and locations. His daring escape and bravado about fooling Military Intelligence should be enough to convince Germany's High Command that he has the originals.'

'That's brilliant,' said Mandy.

'Yes, I thought so too, right up to when Fletch and Stanley were murdered.' Florence dabbed her eyes with Sir Henry's scarf. 'I got those lads killed.'

Mandy went over to Florence and put her arm around her. She said, 'Listen, I know Stanley better than anyone, and he would have done the same thing even if he knew he would end up getting killed. If he knew he was part of some elaborate secret plan to beat the Bosch, he would have gone for it just the same.'

Florence shifted on the hay bale, 'There's only one genuine copy of the code, and it's in a safe, under lock and key.'

'You only have one copy?' Percy said. 'Is that a good idea?'

Mandy said, 'There are two copies because I have one as well.'

'Where's your copy?'

Mandy tapped the side of her temple. 'In here.'

Percy scoffed, 'What do you mean it's in there?'

'I've memorised it.'

'Don't joke. You couldn't possibly have memorised it, the code was written in triple-backs with interchanged underlays, and a double reversed overwrite. You would need to photograph it to be certain of total accuracy. Even then, it would be a two-man job.'

'Or a one-girl job,' said Mandy.

Florence said, 'It's best if we show you what Mandy can do.' She looked around the barn, and found an old newspaper, 'Select a page and give it to Mandy.'

Percy thumbed the newspaper and selected a page, then handed it to Mandy. She looked at it and gave it back to him.

'Ask me anything,' she said.

He looked confused.

Florence grabbed the paper, 'What's the word, third column along, fourth paragraph down, eighth line, the second word from the left?'

Mandy's eyeballs darted from left to right under her eyelids. Her eyes pinged open, 'Changes.'

'Correct,' said Florence.

'You two are pulling my leg. This is simply too fantastic for words.'

Florence handed him the newspaper.

He looked at the page and then at Mandy, she already had her eyes closed. He checked Florence was not making signals.

'Second column, third paragraph, seventh line, the fifth word from the left?'

'Parliament,' she said without hesitation.

He selected another word.

'Hangar,' she said.

And then another word.

'Coventry.'

He selected word after word, and Mandy was correct on each one. Percy was speechless. The evidence was clear; Mandy had a photographic memory.

'Do you have the Spitfire code in your head like a photograph?'

'That's exactly what it's like.'

'So, why haven't you taken a degree, you could pass any exam with your memory.?'

'I have three degrees!'

'But you said you didn't go to University.'

'You're right. I didn't. Passing a degree is boring. Page after page of dull, dull, dull, then I sit in a room and write it down, trying my best to make some mistakes, so it doesn't look like I've cheated. I could pass dozens of degrees, but for what purpose?'

'With a gift like that, you could be a spy in Military Intelligence.'

'She is, you fool,' said Florence. 'What do you think she's doing here? Mandy has a unique skill, quite beyond our understanding. Her gift is the only real way of keeping a secret a top-secret. Wars have been won and lost on account of words written on pieces of paper. We can't take a single chance with the 12g295 code. So it's locked away in Mandy's head, safe and sound.'

'I've heard about things like this, but never thought it was real,' he said.

'You thought I was your driver when I picked you up from Bletchley Park. What a cheek. All you saw was blond hair and curves inside a uniform.'

'I feel silly about that, but I love you now, Mandy Miller.' He slapped his hand to his mouth. 'Did I say that out loud?'

Florence and Mandy laughed spontaneously, 'Yes, you did.'

He put his face into his hands, then ran his fingers through his hair. His face flushed red, and then he peeked at Mandy through his fingers.

She looked into his eyes and smiled a warm, red-lipped smile, 'I love you, too.'

Florence said, 'Now that we all love each other, we should press on and make sure Otto gets to Berlin. I have a contact over there who can get us travel passes and permits.'

Percy blew out the lantern, and Mandy stepped close to him in the dark. She said, 'Did you mean it when you said, you love me?' her voice was soft; the faintest whisper.

'I'll write it down for you, so you'll remember that I love you forever.'

'That's the most romantic thing anyone has ever said to me.'

They followed Florence across the snow to their vehicles. The sky, full of twinkling stars went unnoticed by Mandy as she climbed on to the back of the Norton.

The bedroom fire had long since gone out, and Otto woke up in the early hours to the smell of cold ash. Lizzie was naked in the bed next to him. He dressed, and without disturbing her, crept downstairs, and ran to the cottage. In the woodshed, Otto clambered over the logs and grabbed his suitcase. He wound the aerial wire around a nail in the woodshed roof.

His radio set crackled into life.

Red light.

Green light.

Ready.

He used the black handle to tap out his code name.

He waited, then repeated his call sign.

An acknowledgement demanded his password.

He tapped in the digits.

Otto received clearance, and he gave his coordinates and requested a nighttime sea pickup. He packed away the radio set and buried the suitcase under the logs.

Otto ran back to Denton's hardware store and climbed the stairs to Lizzie's bedroom. He stripped naked and crawled into bed next to her; she hadn't moved. He nestled against her and closed his eyes. His mission was drawing to a close, and he would soon be gone from Friston and Lizzie.

Mission completed.

Nearly.

Florence parked under a hunched willow tree on top of Friston hill, on the far side of the church. Percy and Mandy climbed off the Norton; they were stiff with cold.

Their footsteps crunched the snow beneath their boots. It was the only sound in the village.

Florence stepped out of her car and stretched.

She said, 'Malcolm's cottage is down the hill. I need to use the chatterbox first.' She shinned up the willow tree and hooked the chatterbox over the telegraph wire and dialled.

'Milton Park.' Sir Henry's voice came through as if he was sitting on the branch next to her.

'You sound tired,' she said.

'Hardly surprising, it's four in the morning. How are you, my darling?'

'I'm well.'

'Where are you?'

'I'm cold and sitting halfway up a willow in the church graveyard. Tell Alice we're in Friston.'

'Alice said she's heard from Rosie, and that she's on standby.'

'Excellent. Henry, can you go to London and stir the political pot a bit? We must keep Churchill in the running for Prime Minister.'

'I'll do what I can.'

'And, Henry, one more thing.'

'Yes?'

'I love you. I can't remember my life without you, and I can't remember ever not loving you.'

He said, 'I love you. Be safe.'

Florence pushed her ear against the cold metal box listening to his words that came through on waves of crackles, pops and pips. And then he was gone.

She jumped down from the tree and the three of them walked out of the graveyard and down the hill towards the village. They edged slowly around the last corner and peered down the lane. They saw the red Jaguar parked outside Malcolm's cottage.

Florence said, 'Let's find somewhere to hide and keep watch.'

She went through the side gate of the cottage opposite and headed around the back. She tapped on the rear door. No answer.

She knocked again. Louder.

The door opened an inch, and an old lady, in a dressing gown and hairnet, peered through the gap.

'Yes, can I help you?'

'I'm Florence Fairweather. I'm so sorry for the late hour of my visit. I work with Churchill, may I come in?'

'Churchill, you say. Winston Churchill?' said the lady.

'Yes, that's right.'

The old lady said, 'My husband met him in 1914. He said he was a horrible, rude, fat ugly man, and it turns out

Churchill was right; my husband is a horrible, rude, fat ugly man.'

Florence laughed and smiled and the lady opened the door a little wider and beckoned Florence inside.

CHAPTER 21

Mandy and Percy joined Florence in the old lady's kitchen.

At the end of the narrow hallway, the staircase creaked. Florence looked into the darkness towards the sound. A half-asleep stout man, in blue stripy pyjamas and well-worn red slippers, staggered into the kitchen. His dishevelled old man's grey hair stuck up like a crown; he seemed not to notice the new arrivals.

'He's deaf,' said the old lady. 'Eddie! Eddie!'

The man turned around.

Startled, he said, 'Who are you?'

'They've come to take you away.'

'What did you say?'

'They work with Churchill.'

'I don't like him,' he said.

'He doesn't like you either.'

'What did you say?'

The old lady turned to Florence, 'Don't worry about him, he'll go back upstairs with a cup of tea in a minute and forget about seeing you. Silly old bugger.' She changed her tone. 'Now my dear, how can I help you and your little friends?'

'We need to keep watch on the cottage opposite,' said Florence.

'You mean The Feathers' place?'

'Yes.'

'Such a shame what happened to them.' The old lady took a closer look at Florence. 'I know you. You were at their funeral.'

'I'm an old friend of Malcolm's. We were at Oxford together.'

The old lady nodded as she spoke. 'I've not seen Malcolm much since he moved to London. I saw him at the funeral, of course, then he pulled up in that posh red sports car a few hours ago. But he's not in the cottage.'

'Where is he?' asked Florence.

'He's shacked up with that Denton girl, in her grandfather's hardware store. It all happens in Friston, you know.'

Percy said, 'I would imagine nothing much happens without you knowing about it though, Mrs . . .?'

'Baker, Mrs Amy Baker,' she pointed to her husband. 'Eddie always said Malcolm was a bit of a mummy's boy. It's nice to see him with a girl at last. Lizzie Denton is feisty but lovely.'

Eddie turned around, 'He's a poof.'

'And Malcolm thinks you're a moron.'

'What d'you say?'

'I said, there's a war on.'

Eddie tutted and wandered off with his cup of tea into the passageway, and up the creaky staircase.

'He can hear when he wants to,' said the old lady.

'Did your husband suffer from shell-shock in the trenches during the First World War?' said Percy.

'Eddie never suffered, and he never went near a trench.

He was too old to fight, but he wanted to do his bit, they wouldn't let him have a rifle because he couldn't shoot straight, so they put him in the kitchen, but he was a terrible cook. I was surprised he didn't poison half the British army.'

'Mrs Baker, we're going to need to use your front room as a hideout for a few hours,' said Florence.

'You make yourselves comfortable, and I'll make a pot of tea. Malcolm's not in any sort of trouble is he?'

'Malcolm? Goodness no,' said Florence.

The front room was cold and damp and appeared to be Mrs Baker's best room; reserved for when the vicar dropped in for tea and cake.

'I'm going to walk around the village and check out the Denton's place,' said Florence. 'You two stay here, get warm and keep your eyes peeled. I'll be back in half an hour. It will be daylight in two hours.'

She slipped out of the back door.

Mrs Baker brought the tea on a tray and placed it on the table. 'It's dark in here, shall I put the light on?'

'No, we're fine in the dark,' said Mandy.

'I'll be going back to bed then. I'm glad to have been of service to Mr Churchill. I hope he becomes Prime Minister soon. That lot at the moment seem a bit wishy-washy to me.'

'We think so too. Thank you for the tea Mrs Baker, good-night,' said Mandy.

Percy sat heavily on the sofa with a tired sigh.

'I'll take the first watch,' said Mandy. 'Stay exactly where you are.' She sat squarely on his lap and looked into his eyes, 'Tell me once again, that you love me.'

Percy said, 'How do I love thee? Let me count the ways.'

Mandy put her finger to his lips.

She whispered, 'How do I love thee? Let me count the ways. I love thee to the depth and breadth and height. My soul can reach, when feeling out of sight. For the ends of being and ideal grace.'

He kissed her finger, 'How utterly beautiful you are. I didn't know you loved poetry.'

'I don't. I read it when I was studying for one of my degrees. I didn't know that I knew it until you quoted the first line. Then it just popped up.'

'You can quote poetry, what is not to love about you, Mandy Miller?'

The beginnings of morning pushed the end of the night aside to usher in a new day.

Florence stood in the shadows across the street from Denton's hardware store. She stared at the upstairs window. Even if Otto were asleep in the girl's arms, his senses would be on high alert, tuned in for out of the ordinary sounds.

Skilled spies are survivors, and she knew, Otto wouldn't make basic mistakes. He was comfortable behind enemy lines.

Alone in the shadows, Florence cursed the loss of Fletcher and Stanley. Two good men were dead due to her lack of foresight. There was no bringing them back. And nothing but peace could melt the cruelty of war. Sometime later, together with Henry, she would mourn the lost men, and let grief consume her. She owed them that.

But not now, not yet.

Florence walked back towards the willow tree in the churchyard and hooked the chatterbox over the wire. A distant ringing followed crackles and pips. Henry answered.

'Henry, it's me.'

'My darling, everything alright?'

'I just wanted to hear your voice. Where are you?'

'In bed. Rags is asleep on your side.'

'Kiss him for me.'

'Done,' he said. 'Everything going to plan?'

'I guess so. We're in a cottage opposite Malcolm's place.'

'How are Mandy and Percy?'

'They are incredible. We make a smashing team.'

'You sound tired.'

'I'll sleep later.'

'You can't keep going on fresh air.'

She sighed, 'Henry, those lads, Stanley and Fletch, I can't get them out of my mind. It's clogging up my brain.'

'Let it settle; don't force it out. When you get back to Milton Park, we'll take Rags for a long walk and talk about them. Those chaps adored you and wouldn't want you to blame yourself.'

Henry's voice had the desired effect.

It always did.

She said, 'I needed to feel you. Somehow you say the right thing, the right way.'

'I've arranged to meet up with Winston and Barrington in the morning. I'll stir the pot as you suggested. I might attempt your speed record, Milton Park to Parliament Square, what do you think?'

Florence laughed.

He said, 'Get some sleep, my lovely.'

She climbed down from the tree and walked down the hill and stood outside Malcolm's cottage. This was her best chance to search the cottage while Otto was asleep at Denton's store. She signalled her intentions to Mandy.

The gate squeaked as it opened, and Florence walked around to the back door; it was unlocked. She stepped inside the kitchen; it was stone cold and eerily quiet. Death hung in the air, as did the smell of stale food. Florence moved swiftly from room to room. Malcolm's bedroom was exactly as he'd left it from his time at Oxford. His

Quantum Physics degree, together with photographs of rowing teams adorned the walls, and engineering books filled the shelves.

An undisturbed layer of dust coated every surface. Otto hadn't left a hint of his presence.

Good spies don't leave easy clues.

Florence stepped across the small landing and opened the door to the front bedroom.

The same there—no clues.

She looked at the bed and pictured where Otto sat to watch Malcolm's parents choke to death on the gas. He was a savage killer, and she wanted him dead, but she needed him alive to return to Berlin. But how she would enjoy ending him, snapping his life away. Florence decided she would track him down. She would make an exception and enjoy his death. He was never going to get away with murdering Fletcher, Stanley, Malcolm and his parents.

The gate squeaked.

Florence peeped through the curtains and saw Otto walking down the path. She signalled to Mandy, then crept downstairs, out the back door, then dived into the woodshed. Mandy slipped out of the side door and watched Otto walk around the back of the cottage. She waited, then followed.

Otto went into the woodshed.

Mandy took off her boots and trod in Otto's footsteps in the snow. She heard him rummaging through the logs and pressed her ear against the side of the woodshed.

Otto unwound the aerial wire and hooked it around the nail near the roof. He switched on the radio set.

Red light.

Green light.

He tapped out his coded message, then packed the radio and the aerial in the suitcase, along with four red house bricks, and left the woodshed.

Otto headed out of the cottage and along Church Road towards the village.

Mandy followed thirty steps behind and watched him throw the suitcase into the middle of the duck pond.

Otto snuck back into Denton's store.

Mandy sprinted to the cottage to see Florence emerge from the woodshed.

'Where did he go?' asked Florence.

'Back to Denton's. On the way, he threw his suitcase into the duck pond. Shall I go and get it?'

'No, he won't have left anything in there of any use.'

Mandy asked, 'Why did you jump in the woodshed?'

'If I'd known he was going in there, I wouldn't have hidden there. I pulled an old sack over me, which reeked of old cabbage. Otto was so focused on sending his message that he didn't search the shed.'

Mandy tapped her temple, 'I heard the message and memorised it.'

'Nobody likes a show-off. What did it say?'

'No idea, it was a jumble of dots and dashes, but I know a man who can figure it out.'

They ran to their lookout post opposite.

'You are both crazy,' said Percy. 'You're playing with a crazed killer.'

'Don't worry about that,' said Florence. 'Grab a pencil and a sheet of paper. Mandy has a puzzle for you to solve.'

Mandy closed her eyes and pictured a sheet of paper suspended in space; it contained seven lines of dots and dashes.

Percy scribbled as Mandy recited the page of code. When he finished, he handed it to her.

'Spot on,' she said.

'Just like that?'

Mandy nodded.

He said, 'You should get some sleep, there's nothing more you can do now. Leave me to crack this message open.'

Mandy curled up on the sofa and pulled a blanket up to her chin. Her eyes started to close the moment she felt the warmth. Percy concentrated on the page of dots and dashes; he turned his head and caught her eye.

Nothing needed to be said.

She knew.

He knew.

She fell asleep.

Percy turned to Florence, 'This will take me hours. You should grab some sleep. You look more tired than Mandy.'

Florence sank into a well-worn leather chair and rested her head on a soft corduroy cushion.

'I'll rest my eyes for a moment or two. Nudge me when you're done.'

Her last thought was of Henry. And for a brief moment, the heavy crush of worry lifted.

Her eyes closed.

Percy went to work.

He studied the two-line sign-off; the last line was one digit longer. The first line could be Otto's name. How else would you sign off?

Heil Hitler, surely not.

And yet, it fitted.

Using Heil Hitler and Otto Flack's name provided Percy with four vowels. A critical break in any code-breaking exercise. The format was complex. But Percy reasoned that for Otto to use the code while on a mission, it had to be something he could remember and not risk carrying a codebook.

Percy paced about, then sat back down, then paced about again. Hours passed until a faint line of silver winter sunshine lit up the pencil-thin crack in the curtains.

There was movement upstairs.

Footsteps and chatter.

The old couple were stirring.

Percy's study of intricate codes at Bletchley Park prepared him for this precise moment. And he knew it. Cracking a code was generally not based on a hunch or an inspired thought; it was a challenging process of slogging your way through a long list of probabilities. And luck.

Percy's list of probabilities was nearing its end.

He ran his hands nervously through his hair and slapped his cheeks to inject some life into his brain.

And there it was.

Otto had used an eighth letter displacement with a double decreasing reverse spacing format. Hard to spot, but easy to unravel once you cracked it. Percy wrote the message out in full, then stepped into the kitchen. He lit the stove and made a pot of tea and walked back into the front room.

Mandy and Florence were still sleeping.

He said, 'When you are ready to start the day would you like to hear what the message says?'

Mandy rubbed her eyes, 'Did you crack the code?'

'That was the easy bit.'

'What was the hard bit?'

'Figuring out how to light the stove and make a pot of tea.'

Florence clambered from her chair and climbed in next to Mandy under the blanket.

Percy pulled a small table towards them and poured three cups of tea.

Mandy took a sip, 'Lovely, tea in bed.'

Percy said, 'I have to hand it to Otto. He is a smart spy. That coded message was encrypted with a rarely used series of double backs and displacements on the eighth letter. Beautifully intricate, but I'm certain you don't want to hear about that.'

'We're absolutely certain,' they said.

He cleared his throat.

'In the first part of the message, Otto confirmed the coordinates for his sea rendezvous tonight. Then he requests a meeting with Max Ernst Bauer at Gestapo HQ, Berlin. Saturday midday. He mentions a password: Lizzie's eyes starburst blue.'

'All those dots and dashes for that?' said Mandy.

'It's all we need,' said Florence. 'We have his rendezvous coordinates for later, and meeting details in Berlin with Max Ernst Bauer. All we do is make sure he gets there.'

'And then?' asked Percy.

'Then we scarper back to England.'

'So, what now?' asked Mandy.

'We prepare for a deadly serious game of cat and mouse. Until now, this mission has been like a gentle bike ride on a summer's afternoon.'

CHAPTER 22

On the terrace, Sir Henry briefed the engineers, and they nodded intently at the day's schedule. Pipes were lit and pointed to emphasise and agree with the essential comments. After the briefest of briefings, Sir Henry put his head around the kitchen door and called out to Alice.

He said, 'I'm taking Rags over the ridge. And afterwards, I'm heading to London.'

Alice waved him off.

He popped his head back through the door. 'By the way, your telephone contraption worked. Florence called me in the middle of the night from a willow tree. Quite marvellous, I don't know how you do it.'

She raised her eyebrows.

Rags jumped into the icy lake to retrieve his stick, and Sir Henry walked with purposeful long strides, over the ridge, and along the tree line. Later, in Parliament, he intended to promote the increasingly unpopular notion that Winston Churchill should become Britain's next Prime Minister. He would suggest that only Winston had the necessary backbone, muscular intelligence, an abundance of bluster, and the bare-faced wit to defeat the darkening menace of Nazi Germany.

And yet, the man most likely to become Prime Minister was Christopher Barrington. His reputation in politics was unrivalled and untainted, unlike Winston's, whose tattered political misgivings were under constant scrutiny.

A man not to be trusted was Westminster's populous tune.

Meanwhile, Barrington had the king's ear, and the confidence from the majority of Members of Parliament, and the blessing from Chamberlain himself. Sir Henry knew the public wanted Churchill, but they didn't get a say as to who would be their champion.

Rags ran about on the snow-topped grass tufts, barking with excitement.

'Oh to be a dog, a life of joy and love, chasing sticks and sleeping in front of log fires. Lucky boy.'

The unmistakable roar of a Spitfire boomed overhead. The Rolls Royce engine beat like a warm heart, and its roar hung in the chilly air long after it had vanished from view. Sir Henry loved the whiff of high-octane fuel left in the aircraft's wake.

Rags bounded into the kitchen and woofed back his breakfast in a few hungry mouthfuls.

'Are you ready for the off?' said Alice.

'I am, I'll stay in London with Winston tonight.' He stepped out into the entrance hall, picked up his bag, and walked across the crunchy gravel to the garage.

Rags followed.

'You'll have to stay here old boy, I won't be long,' he kissed Rags's head and rubbed his ears.

. . .

Britain was mobilising. Activity was visible. Trucks and jeeps jammed up the roads as troops moved between bases. Sir Henry arrived in Parliament Square a few minutes after midday and walked into the Houses of Parliament. He knocked on Churchill's door and entered.

Churchill leaned against his desk and barked down the telephone, 'If those fools get in your way, call me, and I'll deal with it from this end.' The receiver thudded back on its cradle.

Winston drew heavily on his cigar.

Sir Henry said, 'Good morning, Winston.'

'Lovely to see a friendly face.'

'Are you having a morning of it?'

Churchill grumbled, 'Barrington is making political moves, and his circles of influence are influential; I'll give him that. I can't compete on his terms. He has everyone in his pocket. On both sides of the house. He's as popular as a pin-up.'

'What's he been up to?'

'Absolutely nothing, and that's the maddening thing. He agrees with the Prime Minister and takes tea with the King at the Palace. The man is a saint.'

'I see, that is maddening.'

'And the King likes him. No, he loves him,' said Churchill.

Sir Henry said, 'Who wouldn't? He's intelligent, tall, good looking, and wants to make peace with Germany. He's the perfect choice to be the next PM.'

'You are here to help, aren't you, Henry?'

'Can't you tell?'

Churchill added, 'At this rate, Barrington will become Prime Minister any day. He plays his cards with precision while I'm losing ground, a lot of ground. My biggest fear is that I might not even be a contender.'

'This afternoon, let's set about creating a tactical plan of attack to garner some support from members who are against Barrington. There must be some, and we'll find them, one member at a time.'

'Have you eaten?' asked Churchill.

'I had one of Alice's ham sandwiches in the car on the way up.'

'Lunch?'

'That sounds splendid.'

Churchill opened his chamber door, 'Let's go to the main restaurant. All the Members of Parliament eat there.'

'They do, why?'

'It's free.'

'You can't beat free,' said Sir Henry.

Sir Henry followed Churchill into the restaurant. The homely smells of grilled Dover sole and mashed potato wafted out to meet them, but it was acerbic hushed tones that emanated from whispered conversations.

'I feel like a criminal slinking his way to the gallows,' said Sir Henry.

They sat at a central table.

'Can you feel judgmental eyes burning a hole in your back?' said Winston.

Sir Henry nodded, 'Barrington has been sprinkling his unsavoury rumour dust around. That shows me you are his worthy adversary. Only equals lock horns. I would be more concerned if they ignored you. So you can consider yourself an official contender. Now we need to find a way to get the majority of members back on your side.'

Barrington walked into the restaurant.

His pinstriped grey suit, yellow silk tie, gold-chained pocket watch, and regal aristocratic looks stole the attention of the room. He walked over to Churchill's table.

'Barrington,' said Winston; his tone lukewarm.

'Churchill, Sir Henry,' Barrington nodded at the two men.

His greeting was tepid and unfeeling. Easy to accomplish when you feel nothing but contempt.

'Do join us,' said Sir Henry.

'What's the Dover sole like today?' asked Barrington.

Winston smiled, 'Very fresh, so fresh in fact, it ate half my chips.'

Sir Henry couldn't stop a laugh from escaping.

'Tomfoolery has no place in Parliament,' said Barrington.

'If that were true, this place would be empty, it's full of fools,' said Churchill.

Barrington sat opposite the two men and assumed a position of power: hands flat on the table, and a bolt-upright straight back. He unfolded the starched napkin and laid it squarely on his lap.

He stared at Churchill, and said, 'Before you hand Britain a tin hat and go to war, allow me to paint a picture of what it will be like fighting the Nazis.'

'Oh, please do,' said Winston.

'Britain will be a feeble, sickly David, against Germany's undefeatable Goliath. And in your quest for personal glory, your blinkered failings will destroy this country.'

Churchill nodded, 'I would suggest that war with the Nazis will be much worse than your prediction. Britain will be an unarmed David, fighting a dozen Nazi Goliaths. However, our Empire will rise up and come together to fight the evil. Your impotent desire to sit at the peace table with Hitler will never result in the resolution you seek. Peace cannot be made with the devil.'

'Stand down, Churchill. You've missed your moment in history. Your time has come and long gone, step aside and let the younger, fitter, more able men take it from here.' Barrington stood and held onto the back of the chair. 'Listen, Winston, what do you think about retirement?'

'I would miss you very much, Barrington, but if you wish to retire, then so be it,' said Winston.

Barrington stormed off.

Sir Henry said, 'I think that was witnessed by all.'

'Perfect, are we in the game?'

'Right in it,' smiled Sir Henry.

Midday in Friston was as quiet as midnight in Friston.

Florence and Mandy kneeled, side by side, on Mrs Baker's saggy sofa, and looked out of the cottage window. Percy slept in the chair, wrapped in a blanket.

'How on earth did he crack the code?' said Mandy. 'It was a mish-mash of dots and dashes.'

'Sir Henry said he was his best chap from Bletchley Park, and he certainly proved himself last night.'

Mandy looked at Percy, 'He's lovely, isn't he?'

Florence rolled her eyes, 'I'm going to make a call from the willow tree in the churchyard.' She slipped out of the cottage and walked up Friston Hill towards the churchyard. She grabbed the branch of the tree and swung herself up to sit level with the telegraph wire.

She dialled.

Alice's voice came through crystal clear.

'Morning Alice, did Henry get off this morning on time.'

'Yes, bright and early, he'll be there by now plotting and planning with Winston.'

'Alice, I need you to do some digging on Max Ernst Bauer. We intercepted a coded message sent by Otto last night. He's going to meet Bauer on Saturday.'

'I'll make some calls, give me a couple of hours, and I'll put together a dossier for you.'

'Oh, and one more thing, call the police station in Eastbourne and ask the Detective, on the Feathers' case, to meet me at the beach this afternoon?'

'I'm on it,' said Alice.

Florence clicked off the chatterbox.

'Hello up there, everything alright?' The vicar from the church looked up from below.

'Ah, yes, good morning, vicar. I'm just checking a few things on your telegraph wire.'

She jumped out of the tree and landed next to him.

'I thought you were talking to the good Lord.'

'We all need as much help as we can get,' she said.

'You're Malcolm's friend, from the funeral, how is the poor fellow doing?'

'Considering everything, he's doing well. He's a lot tougher than he looks.'

'Give him my best when you see him.' The vicar wandered off with his hands, clasped behind his back.

Florence walked down Friston Hill to the cottage and slipped through the back door and into the front room.

She said to Mandy, 'We need to visit the beach where Otto is going to make his midnight sea rendezvous.'

'Good, I'm bored looking out of this window.'

'Otto's work in Friston is done, I doubt he'll be returning to Malcolm's cottage.'

Mandy gave Percy a good hard nudge. 'Hey clever dick, wakey-wakey.'

'What time is it?' he asked.

'Nearly lunchtime. I'm going with Florence to the beach.'

Florence picked up the paper with the coded dots and dashes and folded it away in her pocket.

She said, 'Percy, go and find a house opposite Denton's Hardware store and put a chalk mark on the rear gate post.'

Florence walked along the stone floor hallway to the kitchen.

Mandy stood in front of Percy and gave him a clingy hug and kissed him softly on his lips, 'I've never been in love before. I can feel my heart flutter, that means you love me, too.'

'I feel it, too. Try not to ride quite so fast. Not everything is a race.'

'Yes, it is!' She kissed him and joined Florence.

They ran up the hill to their parked vehicles. Florence jumped on the Norton and motioned for Mandy to ride. Mandy kick-started the engine, and snatched first gear, then peeled away from the church towards the coast.

Their cheeks stung from the bitter-cold wind, and their hair fluttered from beneath their colourful headscarves. Mandy rode at a ferocious pace through the slippery country lanes, and eight minutes later, they reached the beach. The tide was out, and the sea was represented by nothing more than a thin black line under a colourless grey horizon.

A black sedan was parked on the seafront. Sea-salt lingered dryly on Florence's lips as she stared at the vehicle.

Mandy said, 'Do you think Otto will kill the Denton girl?'

'If he feels cornered, yes. He's an animal.'

The man from the car walked directly towards them. He wore a long black coat, a dark hat and a maroon scarf.

On arrival, he said, 'Florence Fairweather?'

'Yes, and you are?'

'Detective Inspector Giles, Eastbourne Police,' he showed his identity card. 'I received a phone call from Miss Alice Jones, and she urged me in the strongest terms to meet you here this afternoon.'

'This is Mandy Miller.'

He turned to Mandy. 'You rode the motorbike with great skill, Miss Miller. Those Nortons are pretty tricky, I used to own one, and you handled it far better than I ever did. Now that I'm here, how can I help you?'

Florence came to the point.

'What do you know about Malcolm Feathers?'

'I know he's dead.'

'Who else knows he's dead?'

'Nobody, just me. Lizzie Denton and her grandad found the body and she was convinced it was Feathers, then adamant it wasn't. I investigated further, and it became clear to me, the body on my slab at the morgue was Malcolm Feathers, so for security reasons when things didn't add up, I closed the case and listed the body as unidentified.'

'Your powers of deduction were spot on,' said Florence.

Giles said, 'In times of war it's not unusual for a body to wash up on the beach. Sadly, it won't be the last. I followed my nose and went to London, to Buckingham Gate, and spoke to the doorman. He rattled on about Military Intelligence relocating to Scotland. I sensed something was being played out at a higher level, and I decided to wait. Then Alice Jones called me, and here I am, talking to you.'

'I appreciate you keeping a lid on things,' said Florence. 'I need you to keep this investigation closed indefinitely. I'm afraid this will be one of those stories where official secrets will ensure it never sees the light of day. You'll appreciate I can't explain further.'

'I understand when a secret must remain a secret. War is war, and we can't go blabbering everything we know to everyone.'

'Can we say the case is closed?' asked Florence.

Giles nodded, 'Is there anything else I can do for you?'

'There are two favours I need. Can you keep your officers away from the seafront tonight? And, can you locate two rowing boats? Place one at either end of the beach?'

'Consider it done.'

He lifted his hat a polite half an inch off his head, then walked up the pebble beach to his car and drove off.

Giles reminded Florence of Henry.

'Nice man,' said Mandy.

'Clever too, we were lucky.'

'If I were him, I'd be bursting to find out what all this fuss is about. He just walked away without another question.'

Florence said, 'I'll make a point of popping back one day; he'll appreciate hearing the whole story. It's freezing, come on, let's go and see where Percy has rehoused us.'

They roared away from the beach and back to the churchyard at Friston. Florence climbed the willow tree and dialled Milton Park.

Alice answered. 'Perfect timing. Rosie sent me coded information, from Berlin, about Max Ernst Bauer.'

'That was quick.'

'No point dilly-dallying around is there? Max Ernst Bauer is a wealthy German industrialist who has openly criticised the German airforce for not being up to the task to outperform the RAF's Spitfire. It appears Bauer dug deep into his pocket and personally funded the underground factory in readiness to build tens of thousands of German Spitfires. Otto Flack must have a direct link to him, so it seems our spy moves in influential circles.'

Florence said, 'Otto has his sea rendezvous at midnight tonight, so I need you here, eyes-on, half an hour before midnight.'

'Eyes-on. Got it,' said Alice.

Florence jumped down from the tree.

Mandy said, 'Are we really going to follow Otto out to sea in a rowing boat?'

'Of course.'

'What if he gets into a speedboat or a seaplane? We won't be able to keep up.'

'Every plan has a secondary plan, and every secondary plan has a derivative plan, and so it goes, on and on. No plan is carved in granite, it must remain fluid. Adapting and evolving.'

'Yeah great, so what happens if Otto boy dives in a submarine?'

'We'll make a plan for that,' said Florence.

'What if we lose him in fog? Don't tell me. We have a plan for that too.'

'You've got it. We stay in the game because we make sure we always have another move to make.'

Mandy looped her arm through Florence's, and they walked in step down the hill.

Mandy said, 'My mum would have loved you. If she could see me now; her kid, a spy in Military Intelligence.'

'She would be proud of what you've achieved, and especially how you've stayed true to your roots.'

'You mean, I have a bunch of fancy degrees, I can fly Spits, fight like a boxer, remember everything I read, but at heart, I'm still a gobby Battersea girl.'

'That's exactly what I mean.'

They laughed together.

At that moment, Percy came running up Friston Hill waving his hands in the air. 'Stop! Go back, don't come any further.'

CHAPTER 23

Otto Flack lay in bed with the covers pulled up to his chin.

Lizzie opened the store early that morning and worked until midday. She stuck a note on the front door explaining Denton's would re-open the following day. Through each slow morning hour, Lizzie thought about the man lying upstairs in her bed. She was desperate for more of his kisses, more ecstasy, more of everything. He was a sleeping lion, and she was about to stir him.

Lizzie bounded up the stairs and slipped out of her work overalls and climbed into his arms.

Her cold body woke his senses.

She whispered into his ear, 'I closed the shop, we have the rest of the day, and night, to ourselves.'

She wriggled against his body.

Otto looked at his watch. His final, most vital day, was slipping away. It was imperative he check the beach in daylight to ensure it would be clear for his escape at midnight.

'Let's drive to the coast,' he said.

'What now, why?'

'I have the Jag outside my cottage, we can go for a stroll, hand in hand, along the beach, it will be fun. What do you say?'

Lizzie's face dropped, and her youthful eyes widened, 'But I wanted to stay in bed with you today. I closed the shop early so we could be together, and all you want to do is go to the stupid beach on the coldest day in history.'

'Lizzie, darling, we have all night to be together, and tomorrow, and the next day.' His manner was soft. He sensed he'd hurt her. 'The beach will be deserted, come on.'

Reluctantly, Lizzie stepped out of bed and dressed. The consolation for a cold walk on the beach would be a whole night in his arms. Her young heart craved his dominant passion. Her fantasies overflowed with hopeful love and the yearning for more sexual fulfilment. He had taken her innocence. She was no longer a young village girl; she was a woman.

There was no going back.

Otto stood in the doorway outside Denton's store. He checked his watch, then looked up at the sky over the coast.

He said, 'Hurry up, we have to go!'

Percy sat in his new lookout post. He watched Otto step outside Denton's store and take a long look at the sky.

Otto was on the move.

Percy sprinted down the stairs, and out onto the track that ran behind the row of cottages. He slipped in the mud and ran as fast as he could, past the Jaguar, parked outside the Feathers' cottage, and up Friston Hill towards the church.

Florence and Mandy walked down the hill towards him, arm in arm, giggling.

Percy waved his hands frantically in the air.

'Stop! Go back, don't come any further.' He ran up to them, 'Otto and the Denton girl are heading this way. Get off the road.'

They vaulted over the hedge and peeped through the thicket to watch Otto and Lizzie climb into the Jaguar. Otto roared the engine to life and sped off down the hill, towards the coast.

'He'll be checking the beach in daylight,' said Florence. 'It's deserted, and there's nothing to see, we've seen to that.'

Percy said, 'Our new lookout post is cosy, and the lady there has been generous with her jam sponge.'

'Trust you,' said Mandy.

They walked along the muddy track behind the cottages. On the gate post, in chalk, inside a love heart, it read, 'P loves M'.

Florence nudged Mandy.

Mandy nudged her back.

A minute later, they were in the warmth of the upstairs bedroom overlooking Denton's store.

'What now?' asked Percy.

'We wait,' said Florence. 'We'll take it in turns to sleep. It's going to be a long cold afternoon and night, and we might not get a chance to sleep for a while. Mandy, you and Percy go and get a few hours sleep.' Without resisting, Mandy and Percy clambered onto the bed and curled up together.

Florence sat at the window.

Eyes focused.

Outside, a man walked his yapping dog. Later, a delivery driver left a cardboard box outside the store, and four young boys kicked a tattered leather football up the hill. Still too young to go to war.

For now.

Otto and Lizzie returned to the store and they kissed in the doorway, then went inside.

The bedroom light went on. Then off.

Florence woke Mandy and Percy.

She said, 'We're going to the beach. We need to get one step ahead of Otto.'

They ran to their vehicles at the church. Mandy rode the Norton with Percy on the back, and Florence drove the racing car.

Cosy cottages lined the approach to the seafront, and from rows of chimneys, fog-white smoke billowed upwards to cloud the dark sky.

Florence's England lived behind those windows.

An old salty, weather-beaten boathouse provided cover as they scanned the beach. Detective Inspector Giles had positioned a rowing boat at either end of the beach. The rest of the coastline was deserted.

There was nothing unusual about its usualness.

Otto lay in bed with Lizzie.

She slept. He checked his watch - ten-thirty.

Otto made his move.

He lifted the bedclothes and pulled his arm from under her head. She rolled over and felt his absence, and her eyes popped open.

'Where are you going?'

'I have to leave,' he whispered. 'But I'll be back soon.'

'So that's it?'

'That's what?' he asked.

'You said we had all night together.'

'It's not like that,' Otto put his coat on. 'You need to trust me, Lizzie. It's my work. It's very secretive. I can't tell you anymore.'

'At ten-thirty, it's suddenly become a secret?'

'I have to go, but listen, I'll be back another time, I promise.'

'If you leave now, then I don't want you to come back.'

Otto sensed a drama brewing. He couldn't afford a noisy scene in a quiet village.

He picked up his scarf.

He said, 'You don't understand my darling, I want you to come with me.'

'Why, where are you going?'

'France.'

'France?' she said.

'Yes.'

'When?'

'Now, come with me, what do you say?'

'I say you're bloody mad. I can't just go to France. There's a war on.' Her eyes narrowed a fraction. 'If I didn't wake up, you wouldn't have even said goodbye, what a bloody fool I am.'

'You're not a fool. Come with me.'

'I don't want to go to shitty France,' she turned away from him.

He held his scarf at each end with a loop in the middle; a neck-sized loop.

'If you have to go, then bugger off and go.' Her teenage voice poked through her emotions. She sat with her knees tucked under her chin and watched Otto in the mirror holding his blue scarf. 'No, wait. I'm coming with you.' She jumped off the bed and dressed. 'I must be as daft as a bucket of frogs.' She let out a nervous laugh as she got dressed. Lizzie followed him downstairs, out the door and up Friston hill.

Otto roared the Jaguar towards the coast.

He started to rethink his impulsive invitation. Lizzie would soon become a liability. He could dump her at a train station, or leave her at the side of the road somewhere in France. Looking at her now, in the sobering cold air made him angry about his decision. The beach would be a better place to leave her.

Dead, if need be.

Lizzie said, 'How long will we be in France? My grandad will be back in two days. I have to open the store.'

'We'll be back before then.' He put his hand on her knee. 'Trust me, your grandad will never know you've been to France. It'll be our wartime adventure, our secret.'

His mind was made up. He'd kill her on the beach, then drag her body into the rowing boat and dump her at sea.

Otto parked on the seafront and checked his watch. Fifty minutes until his rendezvous.

He took Lizzie's hand and led her onto the beach.

Grey heavy clouds blocked out the moonlight.

Otto walked towards the rowing boat on the far left side of the beach. He pulled his scarf from his neck.

Lizzie had to die. Here, now.

'I'm sorry,' he said. And he meant it.

'For what?'

He grabbed her shoulders and spun her around, then wrapped his scarf around her neck. He wedged his knee into the small of her back. He yanked hard.

Lizzie kicked and thrashed her legs, but the wet pebbles made it impossible to purchase any grip. She tugged at the scarf to get air into her restricted windpipe. Her feet slipped as she writhed and kicked on the pebbles.

Otto knelt to keep up the pressure on the scarf. Lizzie was blacking out, as her world was ending in short breaths. Fear was not going to be her dying emotion. She reached out and grabbed a heavy stone. And with her final conscious thought, she punched the stone into the side of Otto's head. The sound of cracking bone was sickening. The scarf loosened a fraction, and she managed to pull it free to gasp a lungful of sea air.

Otto wailed like a wounded animal as thick ruby blood pumped from his temple, and unstoppable waves of dizzying pain paralysed him. Lizzie pummelled his head once more.

His body spasmed as he lay face down on the beach.

Lizzie stared at her blood-soaked hands. Her coat flapped in the breeze, and her green dress was splattered with blood. She opened her mouth to shout, but there was no sound. Her silent screams went unheard, and she fell to her knees.

'Malcolm,' her voice was frail, childlike.

Then came the roar. 'Malcolm!'

Florence, Mandy and Percy ran full tilt onto the beach. Florence grabbed the shocked girl and handed her to Mandy.

'Take her home, then get yourself back here fast, the clock is ticking.'

Florence rolled Otto over. His skull was crushed, his eyes glared open, and sand stuck to the blood on his face.

He snatched a breath, 'Flo...'

He looked up at her, and his lips moved.

She lowered her ear to his mouth.

He whispered, 'I know. I know.'

He breathed out. It was the last breath he took.

Otto Flack was dead.

Mandy put Lizzie on the back of the Norton and raced to Friston, and parked outside Denton's store. She explained to Lizzie what she had to do, and then made sure she was okay. She then jumped on the bike and headed back to the beach at top speed.

Percy knelt next to Florence and looked at Otto's blood-soaked face. He said, 'And to think, he came all this way, went through surgery and nearly completed his mission, to be killed by a girl on the beach.'

Florence said nothing.

Now was not the time to reflect on what had happened. Now was the time to focus on her next move. Every plan had a derivative. She checked her watch, forty minutes until Otto's rendezvous. She looked out to sea, Alice would be here any minute.

Eyes-on.

Mandy ran on to the beach, 'Lizzie is at home, I told her to wash, burn the dress and say nothing to anyone. She's shaken, but surprisingly resilient. I think she'll be alright.'

Florence said, 'I'll send Alice to smooth things out with her, she'll take care of her. Now let's carry on with the mission.'

'What do you mean—carry on?' said Percy. 'Otto is dead. He was the mission. It's over.'

'Who is Otto Flack?' said Florence. 'Who in Germany knows what Otto looks like now? He changed his face to look like Malcolm, but who in Germany knew what Malcolm Feathers looked like?' She looked at Mandy, then at Percy, then back to Mandy.

Mandy quickly put two and two together.

She said, 'Oh no, hold on Florence. Are you serious? You're not saying what I think you're saying, are you?'

'Every plan has a derivative.'

'Yes, but not this. No Florence, it won't work, it's way too dangerous.'

Percy looked at them in turn. His head flipped from side to side like a tennis umpire. 'Would one of you mind filling me in?'

'You tell him,' said Florence.

Mandy sighed, 'You're going to take the place of Otto Flack. You are the derivative plan.'

'But I'm not Otto, I can't be Otto. I'm not even a spy. It simply won't work, surely there's a better idea. Come on, let's put our heads together and think this through a bit more.'

Florence looked at her watch. And right on time, a low flying Spitfire roared towards them through the sea fog, and from inside the cockpit, a torch flashed.

A dash. Then a dot, dash, dot.

'Was that Alice?' said Percy. 'And did I see Rags?'

'Rags loves flying in the Spit. Did you read the torchlight message?' asked Florence.

'Yes, it was morse for T and R.'

'Otto's rendezvous is a trawler,' said Florence.

'How could you possibly know that?' he said.

'I asked Alice to fly over the French coastline and look out for a vessel heading towards the rendezvous coordinates. She saw a trawler, hence the TR code.'

'How do you know all this stuff?' he said.

'Because Percy, today is not our first day on the job. Now, hurry up, let's get Otto's body in the boat.'

'Hold on,' he said. 'I thought we were going to think of another idea.'

'I shouldn't think so,' said Mandy.

They pulled Otto's body into the rowing boat. His arms and legs sprawled underneath him as if he'd been dropped from a great height, his eyes retained that far off, dead-man stare. Florence climbed in next to Mandy as Percy pushed them off the gritty sand then clambered in.

Florence pulled hard on the oars.

What did Otto know? He said, 'I know'. What could he possibly know?

There was no other option other than to row.

Mandy rifled through Otto's coat and jacket pockets, then ripped opened his shirt to reveal a slimline leather wallet strapped to his chest. She unzipped it to find the 12g295 code and the silk map of the Spitfire locations. She handed the wallet to Percy, 'Put this on.'

'Before we rendezvous with the trawler, we must switch to German,' said Florence.

'What do you want me to do?' asked Percy.

'Be Otto Flack,' said Florence.

Percy said nothing. His pale face told the whole story.

'Otto's rendezvous team will want to know who the hell this is?' said Mandy, pointing at Otto. Percy rubbed his hands in Otto's blood, then smeared it on his face and shirt.

He said, 'We'll tell them he's me. Let's fill his pockets with my papers and say I killed him when he stumbled into me on the beach.'

'Or we could dump him over the boat now,' said Mandy.

'No, he'll wash up on the beach on the next high tide. It will implicate the Denton girl, and Inspector Giles already has a body to hide,' said Florence.

'I wanted to stab the bastard,' said Mandy.

'You can stab him if you want,' said Florence.

'No, the moment has gone.'

'We'll take him with us to France and bury him in a hole,' said Florence.

'Shh, I can hear an engine,' said Mandy. She leaned out of the boat, cupping her hand to her ear.

A trawler chugged towards them. A searchlight illuminated their rowing boat.

Percy asked, 'Who the hell are you two meant to be, my travelling band?'

'I'm hoping the trawlermen are only making the pick-up, and won't have any other details,' said Florence.

'Hoping?' said Percy.

'It's the best I've got.' She rowed smoothly towards the trawler and pulled up alongside, 'There is one more small detail you should know, Percy. If you're captured, I'll have to kill you.'

Two bearded fishermen threw a cargo net over the side.

'Password?' one of the fishermen barked.

Percy froze.

Mandy kicked him, 'You're on.'

Florence bore a hole in his head with her eyes.

Percy looked at Mandy, and he came alive.

He stood in the rowing boat and shouted up at the two beards, 'Are you bloody kidding me? Get me the hell out of here. The British army is right up my arse,' he pointed back to the beach. 'I've killed one of the English bastards,' he stamped on Otto's chest. 'And, in a few minutes, they'll be chasing us out here. Didn't you hear the Spitfire buzzing around?'

The beards nodded.

Percy put his hands on his hips.

He said, 'I haven't got all night for you idiots to decide who is going to piss first. I didn't bloody-well risk everything to be questioned by a couple of fish-stinking, bearded fools.'

The younger beard pointed at Florence and Mandy, 'Who are they?'

Percy shouted back, 'Will either of you be conducting my debrief?'

'No.'

'Then stop asking half-arsed questions, or I'll have you shot in the face. Help us aboard!'

The eldest beard leaned over the side and extended his outreached hands.

He said, 'There's no mistaking it, you're definitely Otto Flack, welcome aboard, Sir.'

<><><>

CHAPTER 24

The trawler turned in a steady arc on the high swell and headed towards the French coastline.

Percy watched England slip from view and gazed until the cottages merged with the night sky to form an empty void.

England was gone.

Playing the part of Otto Flack was not something he had seen coming. He didn't have time to consider the dangers which lay ahead. Percy was a code breaker, more a behind-the-scenes man than a spy behind enemy lines. The gut-churning smell of fish wafted from the trawler's hold and snapped him out of his daze.

Mandy waited for the two beards to busy themselves on deck. One of them steered, and the other was on lookout duty. She sat next to Percy—out of earshot—at the stern of the trawler and kissed the back of his neck.

She said, 'You're my hero, Mr Butterworth.'

'Oh yes, quite the hero of the minute,' he said. His voice didn't share her confidence.

'Percy, I've met dozens of tough men who pushed themselves into a fist-fight to show their manliness. But you are the first courageous man I've met. You knew, taking the identity of Otto was going to be risky, and yet, you did it anyway.'

'I was more stupid than brave.'

Florence joined them, 'Mandy's right, you grabbed the mission by the scruff of the neck. Without you, the whole plan would have died on the beach with Otto. And that's what brave people do, even if it means certain death.'

Percy said, 'Certain death! What do you mean, certain death?'

She said, 'Let's not get bogged down with that now. This is a decisive moment. If I've got this wrong, and you mess it up, we'll lose the war.'

'Thanks for the pep talk, Florence,' said Percy.

One of the beards walked towards them, 'You will be dropped at a jetty south of Calais, and met by four Gestapo agents who'll escort you to Berlin.'

Percy looked at the beard, 'There's been a change of plan.' He walked over to where they left Otto's body. 'My mission has obviously been compromised, or maybe this guy got lucky and stumbled across me. Either way, I can't take that chance.'

The beard said, 'He looks unlucky to me, you caved his head in. I'll chuck him overboard?'

'No, we'll take him with us and dispose of him in France. No point giving the Brits an easy clue. You can drop us a few miles up the coast from the prearranged pick-up point. I will inform the Gestapo myself to return to Berlin without us.'

The older beard joined them, 'We weren't told of these changes.'

'How could you be told?' Percy raised his voice, 'The necessity to change the plan has only just occurred, thanks to this shit.' He kicked Otto in the stomach; it was an angry kick, full of vengeance.

'We should be told of any changes, that's standard operating procedure.'

'He's telling you now,' barked Florence.

'Who the hell are you?'

'I'm with Flack,' said Florence.

The beard drew his pistol from its holster and aimed it at Percy, then Florence.

He started shouting, 'Notification of changes to the mission must come from central command. You would know that if you are who you say you are. You didn't know the password to board the trawler.' He hollered out to the other trawlerman, 'Contact central command.'

Mandy stood in front of the beard who brandished the pistol. She shook her blond curls until they fell around her shoulders, then put her hands on her hips and pouted her lips.

She said, 'Sunshine, if we aren't who we say we are, then who the hell are we?'

He said, 'We're radioing Berlin. They'll make the decision.'

The beard gazed a split-second too long at Mandy's tousled hair and tight-fitting combat suit. In one swift movement, she grabbed the pistol, pulled and twisted it out of the trawlerman's hand, and shot him twice in his chest. The second beard came running from the radio room, and Mandy shot him between the eyes.

He fell, stone dead, like an oak tree.

'What the-' yelled Percy.

Florence said, 'Quick, let's get these bodies overboard.' She grabbed the first one by his armpits and dragged him towards the side of the boat.

Percy picked up the trawlerman's feet, and they tossed

him overboard. And with a splash, he was gone. The second body followed a few seconds later.

Percy looked at Mandy. 'How did you do that? It was like lightning, one moment you were fiddling with your hair, the next you shot them both clean dead.'

She said, 'GPTSS, Grab, pull, twist, switch, shoot. It was the first thing Alice taught me. I was fourteen.'

'G.S.P - What was it?'

'It's how to disarm someone, and use their weapon against them, a gun, a knife, anything.' She put the pistol in his hand. 'GPTSS. You grab like this,' Mandy put her hand over the gun. 'Pull it from their hand. As you pull you twist the pistol, then you switch hands. Your other hand takes the pistol by its handle. Then you shoot.'

Percy looked overboard at the two yellow-clad fishermen floating away from the trawler on the bobbing swell. Mandy took the helm while Florence radioed Milton Park airfield from inside the wheelhouse. A pop, a high pitch squeal and some crackles brought the headset to life.

'Milton Park airfield, receiving you, over,' came the clear voice.

'Hi, Bertie. It's Florence. I have an urgent message for Alice. Has she landed her Spit yet?'

'Good to hear from you, Florence,' said Bertie. 'Alice just landed and is walking towards the tower.'

The line went dead for a minute, and then Alice's voice piped through.

'Great timing, Florence, wheels down two minutes ago, everything going well?'

'Yes, we're onboard the trawler. You know how it is, standard mission adjustments. I need you to do a couple of things for me.'

'Speak up a bit. It's a shocking line.'

Florence adjusted the tuner.

She said, 'Jump back in your Spit and fly to Friston. Wade into the duck pond and pick up Otto's suitcase, then fly across the Channel and hand it to me in Calais?'

'No problem, where will you be?'

Florence ran her finger along a map.

She said, 'We're heading for a small inlet cove three miles north of Calais. Land as close as you can. We will come to you.'

'Got it,' said Alice.

'While you're in Friston go to Denton's hardware store. You'll find a distressed girl there called Lizzie Denton. She killed our friend on the beach. Poor thing bashed his brains in with a rock. Smooth things over if you can. Percy is now our friend, I'll explain more later.'

'I can fill in the blanks. Leave the girl to me. Get yourself safely to the cove, and I'll be there in two hours.'

Alice turned to Rags, 'Do you fancy another flight tonight?' Rags ran, barking towards Alice's Spitfire.

Florence put the headset back on the hook.

Mandy said, 'I didn't think you wanted Otto's radio?'

'I didn't. But now we need to send a message from his radio as if he's alive. We have to explain the plan had to be changed. Percy must exercise his huge brain again and send a coded message using Otto's code.'

'What do you need me to do?'

'Get us safely to the cove.'

Rags sat on the floor of Alice's Spitfire with his chin planted snuggly in her lap. She pressed the starter button, and the engine responded with a baritone cough, and the propellor began to spin.

Rags didn't blink.

Alice steered her Spitfire onto the grass runway and gathered speed. Once airborne she tucked the wheels into the belly of the aircraft and headed for Friston. She took a treat out of her pocket and gave it to Rags and ruffled his ears.

Alice found a field on the edge of the village to set her Spitfire down. Rags jumped out and together they ran past the church and down Friston Hill. She looked at her sturdy brown brogues, then at the muddy duck pond, and waded in. Alice found the suitcase, rolled up her sleeves and pulled it out. She sat next to Rags on the edge of the pond, emptied out her shoes, then walked into the village.

Denton's store was in darkness.

Alice banged on the front door. A light flickered on upstairs, and she heard footsteps. A young girl, with a tear-stained face and dark-ringed eyes, opened the door.

'Yes, can I help you?'

'You must be Lizzie Denton.'

'I am.'

'I'm Alice Jones.' She slipped her way inside, Rags followed. 'Sorry about my muddy brogues,' she said, then put the muddy suitcase on a mat by the door.

Lizzie seemed not to register the intrusion.

'I heard what happened on the beach this evening.'

Lizzie nodded as the night's events found their way back into her head.

Alice knew shock when she saw it.

She said, 'Let's have a cup of tea. Lead the way.'

Lizzie walked Alice and Rags through to the kitchen.

'I killed Malcolm.'

'I know.'

'I had no choice.

'I know that too.'

'He had his scarf wrapped around my neck and was trying to kill me. I was going to die. After that, it's a bit of a blur, I'm afraid.'

'I'm here to sort things out.'

Alice boiled the water.

'A blond-haired girl was nice to me. She brought me home on the back of her motorbike and told me to burn my dress and wait for help.' Lizzie hung her head but didn't cry.

Rags sat next to her and licked her hand. Lizzie knelt and cuddled him, 'And, what's your name, gorgeous?'

'Rags,' said Alice. 'I think he likes you.'

'You're a handsome boy.'

'Lizzie, you can't say a word to anyone about what happened on the beach tonight. Do you understand?'

'I'd prefer to forget about the whole thing anyway.'

'If anyone asks anything about tonight, tell them that Malcolm stayed one night, then left. You haven't seen him since. Have you got that?'

'Stayed one night, then left, and I've not seen him since,' she repeated.

Alice saw strength in the young girl. Her voice was quiet, but not frail, and her actions were gentle, but not weak.

She was quite the fighter.

Not unlike Florence, Mandy, and Rosie, her daughter.

'Rags has taken a shine to you. Maybe you could help me?'

Lizzie looked up, 'How?'

'Would you be able to look after him for an hour or two? I have to pop off and run an errand. He's a great cuddler, especially when you're feeling a bit low.'

Lizzie ruffled Rags's head, 'I have some leftover stew, are you hungry?' Rags followed Lizzie to the stove.

Alice said, 'I'll be off.'

'Thank you for coming to see me. I guess you came to check up on me. You can count on me to say nothing, other than what you told me to say.'

Alice picked up the suitcase, stepped out into the cold

night and headed along the lanes back to her Spitfire. Once airborne she raced at tree-top level towards the coast.

The cove was dark and narrow. Tall, thick reeds provided excellent cover as Mandy skillfully navigated the trawler into the inlet.

Percy jumped onto the bank and tied off a rope around a tree.

'I have some great news,' declared Mandy. 'Our bearded trawlermen kindly left us their soup and some horrible black bread.'

'Jolly decent of them,' said Florence.

Mandy opened the flask and poured piping hot beef soup into three cups. She tapped the black bread on the side of the boat. 'How do the Nazis plan on winning the war if they can't even make a decent loaf of bread?'

'It's their main problem,' said Percy.

'Alice will fly overhead any moment,' said Florence. 'She knows roughly where we are.'

Percy sat on the edge of the trawler.

He said, 'It's different out here in the field from being at Bletchley Park.' He bit off a piece of hard bread. 'As a code breaker, I'm not in the firing line, but in Hut-6, where I work, we're faced with impossible odds. When we can't crack a code, we know that hundreds of soldiers could die. It's bloody awful, and Bletchley fills with this ghastly, sombre gloom. Everyone is exhausted, and feels wholly deflated when we can't crack a code.'

'Drink this.' Mandy thrust a cup of soup under his nose to snap him out of his state. 'Florence, what do you want Percy to write in Otto's message?'

'Percy, we must use Otto's radio to send a message to Berlin. Explain the mission has been compromised. Say you had to abort the pre-planned Gestapo escort and you'll be making your own way to Berlin. Say that a Spitfire buzzed the trawler and strafed it with machine-gun fire, killing the trawlermen. Tell them you are going dark until the midday meeting on Saturday.'

Percy looked at Mandy.

'Going dark means you'll be out of contact,' she said.

'I know what it means. I've just never gone dark before.' Percy took out his pad and pencil and began to write.

Florence said, 'Percy strip! We need to bury Otto, and you need his clothes.'

'I'm not stripping off in the middle of the night. And anyway, why do I need to wear Otto's clothes?'

'They are Malcolm's clothes. You need to be Otto playing the part of Malcolm Feathers. So strip.'

'Will it make a difference if I wear his clothes?'

'It's the little things that keep you alive. It's always the seemingly unimportant little details people overlook that get them killed.'

Florence turned her back and folded her arms.

He knew he was outnumbered, Mandy had her arms folded too, but she didn't turn her back, she watched him undress.

'He's ready,' Mandy declared.

Florence turned around and pointed to his white underpants, 'Those too, get them off.'

'Not a bloody chance, I'm not wearing a dead man's underpants. I draw the line somewhere, you know.'

'Mandy, help Percy out of his underpants.'

'I don't need any help. Thank you.' He reluctantly took off his underpants, then dressed in Otto's clothes.

'And don't forget to wear this,' Florence handed him the blue scarf. 'Do you feel like a German spy now?'

'Yes, I feel disgusting.'

'Good, you're halfway there.' Florence looked him up and down and nodded her approval.

'But why Otto's underpants?' begged Percy.

'I'm a spy, I know these things,' she said. 'You only saw Otto when he played the part of Malcolm. Obviously, he's a deranged lunatic with a thirst for killing, but he was also a man with values and probably loved his mother, or his cat. You need to create a whole man, his good side and his bad side and become the legend of Otto Flack.'

Mandy came out of the cabin with a shovel. 'Let's bury the bastard.'

They dug a shallow grave, and Florence laid out Otto's body and opened his eyes. She took a camera from her pocket and took a photo. They covered his body with French soil.

Florence patted the earth mound and said, 'An unmarked grave for a remarkable German spy.'

Mandy said, 'A murdering bastard more like.'

Percy looked to the sky, 'I can hear a low flying aircraft coming at us as fast as lightning.'

'That'll be Alice,' said Florence. 'I've never known anyone fly as low and as fast as she does. She has absolutely no fear, none whatsoever.'

A Spitfire buzzed low over their heads.

They picked up their packs and headed inland through a forest. The Spitfire circled and landed in a field. Florence led the way to a clearing where Alice positioned the Spit in readiness for a speedy getaway. There was no time for a long chat. France was becoming increasingly overrun with Germans.

Alice left the engine running and the propeller chopped into the chilly night air with a regular beat. She jumped down from the wing and ran over to the oncoming party of three.

She lifted the suitcase, 'Wet and muddy, just like you ordered.'

Florence swapped the suitcase for the chatterboxes. 'We won't be needing these this side of the Channel. Did you find Lizzie?'

'I was impressed with her. I'd say she's a tough nut. I left Rags with her for comfort and to take her mind off things.'

Percy opened the suitcase.

Otto had sealed the radio in thick waterproof webbing. The suitcase was flooded with stagnant pond water, yet the radio and battery had remained dry.

Percy put the headset on and flicked the radio switch, 'We're in luck, it's working.' A green light flashed, and a repeating message of dots and dashes burst through the headset. He wrote it down on his notepad.

Under the wing of Alice's Spitfire, Percy applied Otto's code to the message. He looked up at the three women.

He said, 'It's not good news.'

'What does it say?' said Mandy.

Percy read the message, 'Mother to meet you in Berlin with Max Ernst Bauer.' He looked at both of them, 'She'll know I'm not her son.'

Florence smiled, 'I have a plan.'

'Does it involve me wearing someone else's underpants?' asked Percy.

'Not this time it doesn't.'

'Then count me in.'

Alice said, 'Why do you make people wear other people's underwear, Florence?'

'It's hard to say.'

Mandy gave the coordinates of the trawler to Alice, 'On your way back, can you shoot it up and make it look like it was in a proper fight with a Spit?'

Alice hopped up onto the wing and swung her legs into

the cockpit and strapped herself in, 'Goodbye chaps,' she shouted.

The three of them watched Alice's Spitfire climb into the night sky and race back across the Channel. Back to Rags, back to Lizzie, and home to England.

Percy watched until it was a small dot in the sky, 'Florence, I didn't need to wear Otto's underpants?'

'No, but you do need to send that message to Berlin.'

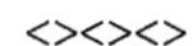

CHAPTER 25

A pale yellow sun sat low in a watery blue sky and ushered in a crisp Wednesday morning. Snowdrifts nestled in deep hollows and clung to drystone walls, and the whip in the wind had a stinging bite. Winter in England gripped the countryside without guilt.

Sir Henry parked his car and walked into Milton Park's entrance hall, where Alice waited to meet him.

She said, 'You look as though you've driven all night.'

'And, you look as though you've flown all night.'

'Oh God, do I look that tired?'

'No, you still have your flying goggles on your head. How about a debrief in the ops room in ten minutes?' he said.

'Perfect, I'll bring a pot of tea.'

Rags came running out of the house and rushed up to Sir Henry. 'Hello old boy, no doubt you've flown in Alice's Spit whizzing about the countryside.'

Ten minutes later, they sat on the leather sofas in the ops room.

'You begin,' she said.

Sir Henry sipped his tea, 'Winston was on top form as you would expect, but we're a long way from getting him into Number Ten. I'd say the prevailing sentiment in Westminster is that he's too cavalier, a chancer, not a team player, in short, they don't want him. Winston can be feisty and ruffle feathers on an industrial scale, but Westminster is wrong about him. Appointing anyone other than Churchill would be catastrophic for Britain. He's the only one who could enrol the Americans on to our side, and if things are going badly, he has enough political fibre to bring in the Russians.'

'It sounds like Barrington will become the next PM.'

'He is, without doubt, the undisputed challenger. He glides about Parliament like a Hollywood movie star and has the majority of the members in his pocket. If the leadership vote were held tomorrow, Christopher Barrington would be Prime Minister before afternoon tea.'

'Did you muster any support at all for Winston?'

'A bit, but not enough, I'm afraid I'll have to roll my sleeves up and play harder. We'll find a way, we always do.'

'You're simply too nice, Sir Henry, it's time for you to play dirty.'

He bit into a slice of toast and damson jam.

'How about your news? How's Florence, where is she, and what's she doing?'

Alice filled him in on Percy and Otto and her jaunt across the Channel to deliver the radio suitcase and how Florence and the team were doing. Sir Henry let the words settle; he knew Florence could adapt to every situation.

'Tell me a bit more about Lizzie Denton? She sounds quite the fighter; do you think she is somebody we can train as an operative?'

'She's tough, emotionally mature, full of rage, and killed Germany's top spy with her bare hands. She needs us, and we need her.'

'Good God, she sounds like you! Let's strike while the iron is hot. Give her a call and sow a few seeds; we could do with some new blood. We're in for a long war.'

Alice dialled Denton's store, and without preamble, she said, 'Lizzie, how do you fancy a few days in the Cotswolds?' Alice didn't wait for an answer, 'You'll be doing me a favour, I need the red Jaguar brought over, and Rags would love some long walks. We have plenty of space, and there's something I want to talk to you about. What do you say?'

'Alice, I'd love to. My grandad arrives from London after lunch. I can be with you later this afternoon.'

'Oh, I should have asked, can you drive?'

Lizzie giggled at the question, 'My dad was a racing driver and mechanic. I drove before I was eleven.'

'Does your father work in the store with you and your grandad?'

There was a slight pause. 'No, my parents were killed in a boating accident in Wales five years ago, and my grandad has looked after me ever since. He's the best thing in my life.'

Alice gave Lizzie the directions to Milton Park.

She'll do very nicely, she thought.

Percy said, 'It might not be anything important, but a different handler in Berlin sent the message regarding Otto's mother.'

'How do you know?' asked Florence.

'There was a heavier touch to the coding. It's hard to explain; the code was the same, I suppose what I mean is. . .'

Florence cut him short, 'Did a different person send it?'

'Yes.'

'Just send your message as planned, then destroy the radio and bury it in the woods.'

Mandy asked, 'How do you want to travel to Germany?'

'By truck to Paris, then train to Berlin. We'll meet up with Rosie on Friday afternoon.'

'Who's Rosie?' asked Percy.

'Alice's daughter,' said Mandy. 'She's a carbon copy of Alice.'

'A younger, faster, tougher Alice—there's a thought,' said Percy.

Mandy corrected him. 'Alice can beat everyone in a running race, and she's the best, or rather, she's the meanest fist-fighter.'

Percy made a sound as if he was not that surprised, then flicked a switch on the radio. The green light went off.

'Message sent,' he announced.

Florence gave Percy a job-well-done look.

She said, with genuine meaning, 'We wouldn't be here without you.'

'I'll go and get some transport,' said Mandy.

'Be quick. I'll stay here and guard Percy. We can't lose him now. He's become our most valuable asset.'

'I'm not a baby,' he said.

'That's good to know because I don't have a spare pair of underpants for you.'

Calais was as icy and as bitter as England, but France's winter sky was a deeper blue and the sun a brighter orange.

Mandy ran through Calais' backstreets. Her ponytail peeked out from beneath her black woollen hat. She decided to steal a truck which wouldn't look out of place in the country lanes between the villages on the way to Paris.

A corner patisserie had a few outside tables and chairs. Three doting mothers chatted while nursing their babies. A small grey Citroen delivery van pulled up onto the curb in the side street. A young lad opened the rear doors. He took two trays of assorted pastries, and stepped into the bakery, whistling as he worked.

The boy flirted with the pretty French girl behind the counter, she in turn half-heartedly rejected his advances. He placed the trays onto the marble countertop, and she arranged the pastries in the glass display case. The boy leaned over the counter and snatched a kiss.

Mandy saw her chance and seized the moment.

She quietly closed the van's rear doors and jumped in the driver's seat and released the handbrake. The van rolled silently down the hill away from the patisserie. She checked her mirrors; nobody noticed the van moving away. She started the engine and sped off.

Left turn, right turn, left turn. Mandy took one more right turn onto the road heading out of Calais.

After three miles, Mandy pulled the van off the road where Florence and Percy stood.

'Any cakes in there?' asked Percy.

'You tell me, you're going in the back.'

Florence sat in the front and opened a street map.

She said, 'We won't get to Paris in one go, we'll see how far we get tonight before it gets dark.'

Mandy looked over her shoulder, 'Anything to eat back there?'

'You certainly stole the best van in Calais. It's chock-full back here with baguettes, croissants and chocolate cakes. I'll put a selection together for when we stop.'

Mandy shot a glance at Florence, 'I always fall in love with the best ones.'

'No, you don't, this is the first time.'

'I've been thinking,' said Mandy. 'Why would Berlin bother to send Otto a message about his mother attending the meeting with Bauer? It's hardly vital.'

'My best guess is that Rosie overheard something and took the risk to send us a message.'

'How would she know we had Otto's radio?'

'Alice keeps her informed via their Jungle book messages. Rosie would have nothing to lose by sending it, and we'd have everything to gain, maybe it was a calculated guess.'

'How would she know Otto's code?'

'Rosie is as sneaky as Alice,' said Florence.

'That makes more sense than anything else.' Mandy lowered her voice and used the small noisy engine as cover. 'What are you going to do with Percy, he looks nothing like Otto, or Malcolm, or a German spy?'

'We need to load the dice in our favour.'

'How are we going to do that?'

'I don't know yet, but on Saturday, the only thing Max Ernst Bauer will see is Otto Flack and Otto's mother. Everything must look normal, nothing more, nothing less. This meeting could prove to be the key to the whole mission.'

Mandy followed a signpost for Paris. 'We might look a bit suspicious driving around Paris in a patisserie van from Calais.'

Florence said, 'We can deal with that when the time comes. Let's get off the main road and take the smaller country lanes. Take the next right, then an immediate left. And next time, steal a faster vehicle, I can run faster than this old crate.'

The next few hours the going was slow, and they only covered thirty miles.

Mandy sighed, 'These lanes are too slow, and at this rate, Bauer and Otto's mum will meet without Percy, we're never going to make it.'

'The main roads have too many checkpoints,' said Florence. 'Our papers are good, but we only need some keen soldier trying to impress his commanding officer, and we're out of the game.' She knew they had to make faster progress. It was time to gamble. 'Rejoin the main road. We'll have to take our chances.'

Mandy nodded, 'You're right, I should have stolen a faster van.' Florence's eyebrows moved a micro amount, but Mandy saw it.

Percy called out, 'I'm getting hungry with all these cakes, can we stop and eat something?'

'I'm hungry too, but we need to lay some miles down first,' said Florence.

The vehicle lurched and shuddered.

Then lurched again.

Mandy said, 'Shit, oh buggering shit!' The cadence of her words matched the spluttering engine. The van rolled to a halt on the side of the road.

The engine was dead.

'Petrol?' asked Florence.

'Probably, they don't put fuel gauges in these old vans.'

Florence put her hand up as a warning.

She said, 'Look! Two hundred yards up the road and heading our way.'

'What is it?' asked Percy.

'A German patrol vehicle with three soldiers. Percy, get out and hide in the bushes until the vehicle passes. If the patrol stops, don't come out, even if we're attacked. At all costs, even if we are killed, you must stay alive and continue with the mission. Do you understand?'

'Got it,' he said.

'I damn well mean it, Percy,' said Florence.

He looked at Mandy.

'Do it!' shouted Mandy. 'No matter what you see, or what you hear, you stay hidden. We can take care of ourselves.'

He slouched out of the van and hid in a hedge. The mission had taken a dark turn. For the first time since becoming Otto, he felt helpless and desperate.

The German patrol moved closer.

Mandy said, 'Shall I kill them?'

'No, not right away, we only fight if they don't believe we're bakery girls.'

'I'm ready either way.'

Florence clenched her fist, 'Me too.'

They stepped out of the van, opened the bonnet and peered into the engine bay. Florence threw a handful of snow onto the exhaust pipe, and steam hissed and bubbled up into a cloud.

'Mandy, do that raunchy thing you do with your hips.'

Mandy's hips swished from side to side.

The German patrol vehicle pulled alongside. A soldier jumped out and raised his rifle.

He shouted, 'Put your hands up.'

'That's a first, I've never known your hips to fail,' whispered Florence.

Lizzie Denton arrived in Florence's red Jaguar, and she stared in wonderment at the majesty and splendour of Milton Park that rose up in front of her. Sir Henry walked out of the entrance hall to meet her.

He said, 'You must be Lizzie, how do you do?'

'How do you do, Sir Henry, Alice told me all about you.'

'Alice told me all about you as well,' he said.

'I only met her briefly.'

'Briefly, is all Alice needs.'

Rags bounded out from inside the house.

Lizzie knelt, 'Rags, my saviour, how are you?' She kissed

his head and cuddled him. 'I'm here for a few days, so you can show me your favourite walks. Rags spent the night taking good care of me. He's the best cuddler in the world.' She lifted her case from the car. 'Your house, Sir Henry, it's wonderful. I've never seen anything like it before in my life.'

His forehead furrowed, like that of an old-time physics teacher listening to a pupil quoting a complex theorem. 'It's been in the family for many generations. I'm the fortunate, current custodian, that's all. But I love every bit of it.' He carried her small suitcase through the main entrance hall.

Alice appeared, 'Lizzie, how was your journey?'

'Fantastic, Florence's Jaguar is quicker than anything my dad ever drove. It's a proper racer, you just turn in to a corner and round she goes.'

'Alice tunes it for maximum performance,' said Sir Henry. 'If it went any faster I'm certain it would fly.'

'That is the idea,' said Alice. 'Come on, Lizzie, follow me. I'll show you to your room.'

Alice climbed the staircase; Lizzie followed, Rags too. She walked along the hallway and stepped into a bedroom at the back of the house overlooking the lake.

Alice said, 'Take this one. It's Winston's bedroom whenever he comes to stay.'

'Winston Churchill?'

'Yes, Sir Henry and Winston are old friends. They used to spend their school holidays here. Winston still visits, but mostly to get away from the madness of Westminster.'

Lizzie looked at the four-poster bed, the oil paintings, the dressing table, and a private bathroom. Compared to her tiny bedroom in Friston, this was palatial.

'I'll take it,' she said with a cheeky smile.

'Then it's yours. We eat at eight. There's a gaggle of engineers staying here, and you'll see them from time to time.

Apart from that, the place is empty, so make yourself at home.'

'What goes on here, at Milton Park?'

'What do you mean, what goes on here?'

Lizzie said, 'Sir Henry is ex-military, he has that particular manner about him. And, while this place is a huge country house, it's surprisingly hard to find, you can't see it unless you are inside the grounds. Also, I caught the faintest whiff of a gunshot in the entrance hall. Then there's the high-performance Jaguar, and the way Mandy handled the Norton, but mostly Alice, it's you.'

'Me?'

'After you came to see me in your tweed and muddy brogues, I followed you to a field where you took off like an arrow in a Spitfire.'

'Yes, I know, I heard your clodhoppers. Anything else?'

'You invited me here right after I killed Malcolm on the beach, and when I piece it all together, I'd say you are Military Intelligence, and you're about to either kill me, kidnap me, or recruit me.'

Alice didn't show any signs of being impressed. She checked her watch and walked to the door.

She said, 'Ops room, thirty minutes.'

'Where's the ops room?'

Alice said no more.

In the ops room, Sir Henry mixed a jug of gin and tonic.

Alice said, 'Lizzie is quick and smart, she'll fit right in. She figured out we're Intelligence in a flash.'

'Is she recruitable, and is she up to it?'

Lizzie stood in the ops room door with her hands behind her back, 'Yes, she is, and yes, she is.'

Sir Henry handed her a chilled gin and tonic.

Lizzie said, 'I'm sorry, eavesdropping is a terrible village habit.'

Alice said, 'Snooping comes in very handy in our line of work.'

'Alice has a keen eye for the right person, so you must have impressed her, and that's not easy,' said Sir Henry. 'Congratulations, you've been selected for training.'

'Training, what for?'

They chinked their glasses.

Lizzie's question went unanswered.

Alice said, 'The Bosch can't make a decent gin and tonic, it's a frightful mess over there.'

Lizzie tried again, 'Selected for training? What is it precisely you want me for?'

Alice walked Lizzie across to the leather chesterfields. 'We've lots to cover, but I can see you already have the basics. I can't teach anyone to be observant, sharp, or on the ball. You have those smarts already.'

'The smarts, for what?'

'Oh, do keep up, to be a spy, an agent,' said Alice.

'I work in a shop. I'm not a spy.'

'Nobody is until they are. And you check out. We ran a background check the moment you came into contact with Malcolm Feathers at the funeral. Florence liked you right away. She felt there was something about you. And she's right, you're just the job.' Alice swigged her gin.

'Hold on. I don't know anything about being a spy.'

'That's what the training is for.'

'I'll need to talk with my grandad first.'

'I already have,' said Alice. 'You can call him after dinner. He's expecting your call. He knows nothing of course, but he is very on the ball.'

'Alice, can I ask you a question?'
'Ask me anything you want.'
'Who the hell did I kill on the beach?'
'I can't tell you that.'

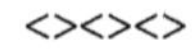

CHAPTER 26

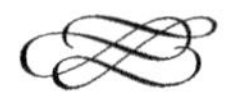

Percy watched from behind the bushes.

Two soldiers held Florence and Mandy at gunpoint, while a third, the officer, sauntered, with a swagger of arrogance, over to the bakery van. He took off his gloves and stood in front of Florence.

'The main roads are reserved for German military vehicles. It is forbidden for local traffic to use this road.'

Florence shrugged her shoulders as if she didn't understand. In French, she offered, 'We ran out of petrol,'

He raised his voice. 'Who are you?'

'We ran out of petrol,' she repeated and shrugged her shoulders with her palms open-faced upwards.

The fair-haired soldier who held the rifle translated for the officer.

'What are they doing on this road?' barked the officer.

The blond boy relayed Florence's response, 'They ran out of fuel, so they took the main road.'

The officer held out his hand. 'Papers!'

Florence and Mandy handed over their French documents. Their occupation was flexible, it stated, labourer.

'Labourers, for what?' asked the officer.

The blond boy translated, 'Factory work and deliveries, they say they can turn their hands to anything.'

'Anything at all,' Mandy added, in husky French.

Blond boy's focus had drifted from translating to looking at Mandy. He said, 'My commanding officer is prepared to overlook your offence, and in exchange for some pastries and sandwiches, he will give you half a gallon of fuel.'

'Please tell him we are most grateful,' said Florence.

Mandy beckoned Blond boy to the back of the van and opened the doors. She bent over and bagged up a selection of cakes and baguettes. He was still staring at her when she turned around and handed him the bag.

She said cheekily, 'Do you like my sticky buns?'

'Yes, thank you.' The boy took the bag, and Mandy kissed him on both cheeks. He blushed and walked off to the patrol vehicle and returned with half a gallon of fuel. The soldiers ate the cakes while Mandy emptied the fuel into the tank. Florence and Mandy waved until the patrol vehicle was out of sight.

'You can come out now,' said Mandy.

Percy climbed through the bushes. 'You two are like a double act. The pair of you are unbelievable.'

'Mandy's hips and pouty lips have seen a lot of action,' said Florence.

Mandy added, 'It's a gift.'

Percy said, 'Mandy, your French?' He looked up to think of the right word, 'It's alluring.'

'What you mean is, why does my French sound so sexy, while my English sounds as harsh as a cheese grater?'

He said. 'You had those German chumps in the palm of your hand, and you didn't show a hint of fear, it was so natural.'

'It's what we train for,' said Mandy.

Florence added, 'You find the soft fleshy part of the enemy, then hit them hard. It was the first thing Alice taught me.'

'First thing she taught me too,' said Mandy. 'Sometimes, it means killing someone, other times, it means wiggling your hips.'

Alice said to Lizzie, 'The first thing you must learn is to find the soft fleshy part of the enemy, then you hit them hard.'

'Let me try,' said Lizzie.

'For maximum trauma, you punch like this,' Alice showed Lizzie the softest part of the throat. 'Right there, do you feel it?'

'Yes, it's soft and squidgy,' said Lizzie.

'Pack a tight fist, then strike with speed, accuracy and power. Your enemy will go down, dead or wounded, either way. They won't be getting up, no matter how big they are.'

Lizzie was a quick learner.

It was her first lesson.

Alice had taught Florence, Mandy and Rosie how to defend and how to attack. Alice had been taught to fight in China from a Shanghai gang leader. Her street style of fighting had become that of legend within the Intelligence community.

Alice told stories about the girls.

She said, 'Mandy uses her hair and body to distract her enemy. I've seen her make grown men weep she'd walloped them so hard.'

Lizzie said, 'Mandy was kind to me when she took me home on the bike. It's hard to imagine her fighting.'

'Trust me. She's a killer. Then there's Rosie, my daughter, I've trained her from when she was a little girl. You could say she had an unusual childhood compared to other girls. I wanted her to be combat-ready in case of a second world war. She's lean and fast. She can drive any vehicle and fly any aircraft. Best of all, she is like a ghost in the wind.'

'Is she here.'

'No, she's on an assignment, you'll get to meet her soon.'

'And Florence?' asked Lizzie.

'Florence was my first pupil and my star pupil. Today she's the master. She's a brutal, dirty fighter. She'll kick you, punch you, or hit you with a chair, or an ashtray, anything. Her key skill is her speed of thought. In a flash, Florence's enemy is on the ground in pain or dead. She carries a small length of bicycle chain in her back pocket; she wraps it around her fist and punches hard. With Florence, it's never a fair fight. I once saw her throw a brick out of her Spitfire when she'd run out of ammunition.'

'I could listen to your stories all day,' beamed Lizzie.

'I'm going to show you something that will save your life. All you need to remember when faced with somebody pointing a weapon at you is this, GPTSS.'

'G-P-T-S-S?'

'Let me show you,' she took Lizzie through the disarming action as if they were dance moves.

Lizzie repeated, 'Grab, pull, twist, switch and shoot, I've got it.' She practised the movements for the next hour until it grooved into her brain.

She was a natural, a Florence type of natural.

Alice took some papers from the central desk. 'Read this, then sign there, and there.'

'What are the forms about?'

'In short, if you tell the Bosch anything, we can execute you. And that pretty much covers it. Now, sign there, and there, and we can get on with the training.'

Lizzie signed the papers and handed them back.

'Welcome to the service,' said Alice.

'Can I ask you a question now?'

'Now that you've signed the forms, you can ask anything you like.'

'Who did I kill on the beach?'

'I can't tell you that.'

'But you said. . .'

Alice walked off and returned with a thick manual.

She said, 'Read this tonight. It will give you the basics of what we do, but not why we do it. You must come up with your reasons why you do what you do.'

A sense of overwhelm began to crush Lizzie.

Alice spotted it, 'You'll do just fine.'

'I won't let you down, Alice, and I won't fail.'

'That's good because we don't do failure.'

Mandy and Florence took turns driving. They stopped twice to syphon off fuel from a farm machine and an abandoned car.

'How far now?' asked Mandy.

'Three hours until we reach the outskirts of Paris,' said Florence.

'Have you thought about Otto's mother?'

'I have,' said Florence.

'Will I like it?'

'I think probably not.'

'Well, that's not new, is it?'

Florence studied the map, 'Let's pull off the road up ahead, there's a wooded area.'

Mandy steered the van off the road and parked under the trees. She opened the rear doors and let Percy out. They walked hand in hand towards the darkness of the woods.

Florence remained in the van and shut off from the

world. She thought about Henry: Britain's last line of defence.

He once told her, 'If I'm dead, it's because the King is dead.' Henry and Churchill would never give up, never surrender, not them, not ever. Against impossible odds, they vowed to defend the Crown to the end; roaring lions standing in the green fields of England.

They would roar until the end.

She smiled at the thought.

And their robust resolve was contagious; she felt the same way, as did Alice, and Rosie, and Mandy.

Lions standing together. They would live, or they would die, but they would never surrender to Nazi tyranny.

At that moment, Britain stood alone, woefully ill-prepared for war with a Government poised to elect Barrington as its new Prime Minister. A blinkered, self-serving man ready to broker a deal which would sell Britain cheaply to Berlin. But as Henry said, there would be no puppet Government, and no substitute Monarchy; not on Churchill's watch.

But it wasn't Churchill's watch.

Not now, not yet.

Winston's destiny was unfulfilled. Maybe it had not yet begun. He needed one chance, for he would seize it, no matter the desperate state of war, no matter how close to defeat, he would charge at the enemy full tilt.

Winston would not, not ever, ever give in.

The passenger door opened, and cold air rushed in, 'Pain au chocolate?' said Percy.

'Oh, yes,' Florence's mind overflowed with Churchill, with England, with Henry, it was all that she loved and all that she adored. However, a pain au chocolate on the roadside, during a mission, took preference in a heartbeat.

Mandy leaned against the side of the van and licked the cream from the middle of her pasty.

She asked Percy, 'How did you get so good at maths?'

'I didn't get good,' he said. 'I was born like it. I love numbers. I love their beauty and their honesty, they are like poetry to me. Numbers have formed my whole world. I find comfort in them, and I suppose I understand them.'

'That doesn't make you sound weird at all,' she said. 'Did the other boys tease you a lot?'

'That's rich, coming from the photographic memory girl.'

'Did you have any friends at school?'

He said, 'At school, I couldn't fathom why other boys couldn't see what I saw. Numbers on a page were like music notes, I could hear them, they sang to me. Numbers have an order, a truth.'

'I hated maths at school. I hated school. Maths bounces off me. Nothing goes in. I must be a right old thicko.'

'You, thick?' said Percy. 'You are the brightest person I've met. You are astonishing.' He bit into his pastry.

She nudged him, 'Don't stop. Go on.'

He looked at her, 'I've been surrounded by intelligent people my whole life, at Eton, Oxford, and Bletchley Park, and I mean really clever people. And yet, not one of them can do what you do. You have it all, and if that wasn't enough, you're funny, confident, and I could spend all day looking at you.'

'How sweet you are,' she said.

Florence opened her door and butted in, 'Before I throw up for England, we need to make a move and get to Paris tonight. We can board a train to Berlin in the morning. Let's ditch this escargot-van as soon as possible and get something faster to blast up the main roads to Paris.'

'Am I still in the back?'

Mandy and Florence eyebrowed him. Percy opened the doors and climbed in.

'I'll drive,' said Florence. 'You should get some sleep. Henry and I used to come here a lot between the wars; I know some shortcuts.'

'Sleep, what's that?'

'Try and get some, you'll need it.'

'Then I'll make myself comfortable.' Mandy climbed in the back with Percy, 'Move over maths-boy.' She fell into his arms, and they curled their bodies together.

Lizzie had a full day's training at Milton Park, plus two long walks with Rags, followed by a scrummy dinner with the engineers. She wasn't sure if they'd noticed she was not Mandy. Later, in the ops room, she pored over a never-ending pile of spycraft procedures, and Rags curled up next to her on the sofa. He had a new best friend.

Lizzie listened to Alice all afternoon and evening. She was a formidable and tireless teacher, with an endless supply of stories about daring missions and adventurous escapes.

Alice paced about in the kitchen, talking to Sir Henry. She checked her watch, 'Florence will be nearing Paris. They'll hide up somewhere tonight, then get a train in the morning to Berlin.'

'How long will it take them to get to Berlin?'

'It's hard to say, what with troops boarding, security and diversions, my best guess is they'll arrive Friday evening. Rosie will be there to meet them.'

'What's their plan after that?'

'They'll have to make it up as they go, I'm on standby in case they need anything.'

'Keep me posted.'

Alice nodded.

'And, how is Lizzie coming along?'

'Terrific. She grasps things the first time and is as keen as mustard. I like her.'

'How long before she's operational?'

'She can start doing small ops in a couple of weeks; dead-drops, pick-ups and driving. I'll have her prepped for missions in two months.'

Lizzie appeared at the kitchen door with Rags, 'Anything else I can do?'

'No, we're done,' said Alice. 'Get some sleep. Tomorrow we have a full day of combat training, knife throwing, dead-drops and handover techniques.'

'Goodnight,' said Lizzie.

She left, Rags followed.

Alice said, 'That dog of yours is a mind reader, he knows Lizzie needs company.'

Sir Henry said, 'Rags goes to where he gets the most attention or a biscuit.'

Alice climbed the stairs to her bedroom and switched on the radio receiver. A message from Rosie rat-a-tatted right away.

She grabbed her copy of Kipling's Jungle Book and sat on the bed. She decoded the message, and at once ran out of her door, along the hallway to Lizzie's room. She burst in without knocking.

'Lizzie, can you ride a motorbike?'

'Yes.'

'Good, wear this.' She handed Lizzie a black combat suit. 'You go mission-live tonight.'

'Live?'

'Operational.'

'What now?'

'Yes, now! Get dressed and follow me.'

Lizzie chased after Alice. They barged into the ops room,

and Sir Henry was sitting on the leather chesterfield sipping a brandy.

'What's with all the commotion?' he asked.

'We're flying to Paris tonight.'

He rubbed his hands, 'Wonderful, I love Paris.'

'Not you, Sir Henry, you know that. Lizzie is on ops.'

'Paris? Tonight? Flying?' said Lizzie.

'Rosie needs us to take something to Paris urgently.' Alice handed Lizzie a piece of paper. 'In the room next to the kitchen you'll find a walk-in cupboard, fill this bag with everything on the list.'

Lizzie took the bag and opened the cupboard door. It was a treasure trove of clothing, make-up and shoes; she filled the bag, then ran back to the ops room.

Alice was on the phone.

She said, 'Keep the runway clear, then get onto fighter command and tell them I'm flying a mission tonight, I don't want some keen newbie Spitfire pilot on his first sortie, mistaking me for the Hun.' She called over to Sir Henry, 'Can you drive us in the truck to the airfield? I'll need your other Norton motorbike loaded into the back. We're taking it to Paris.'

'Are you flying, Hesberus?'

'Sir Henry, we can't go to war without Hesberus,' she said. 'I just spoke to Bertie at the airfield. He has Hesberus ready for action and ready for war.'

Sir Henry marched off towards the garage block, Rags followed, both of them enjoying the late-night activity.

'Lizzie, we have a mission in Paris. It's dangerous but urgent. Are you up for it?'

Lizzie nodded.

'Good, before I tell you any more, put this where you can reach it, even if your hands are tied.'

'What is it?'

'An SP.'

'SP?'

'Suicide Pill.'

'What!'

'Quite so. But more importantly, you'll need a warm flying jacket. We've got a long, cold night ahead.'

CHAPTER 27

The airfield near Milton Park was in total darkness.

Sir Henry drew the green military truck to a halt on the edge of the grass runway. Lizzie jumped down, then clambered up into the back and untied the ropes holding the Norton in place.

Alice sprinted to the far side of the airfield. She barged open the door to the wooden dispersal hut.

She panted, 'Bertie, do I have clearance for immediate take-off?'

'Yes, you're the only sortie tonight.'

Alice ran back.

Bertie followed at a much slower pace.

Lizzie rode the Norton down the plank and across the grass. Alice pointed to a twin-engined aircraft on the apron of the runway.

Sir Henry had a transporter plane made by De Havilland aircraft manufacturers. De Havilland was an old school chum of Sir Henry's. Florence and Alice joked it was the ugliest thing in the sky, and that it looked like a tool shed with wings. However, it proved its worth, and they fell in love with the old crate.

They called it Hesberus.

Sir Henry and Alice dragged the plank from the truck and rested it against the side door of the aircraft. Lizzie revved the Norton and in one continuous movement, shot up the plank and into Hesberus's cavernous belly. Sir Henry pulled himself in through the door and strapped the motorbike securely in place.

Alice clambered into the pilot's seat and started to race through the pre-flight checks. She slid the side window open and shouted to Bertie.

'Clear?'

'Clear!' he echoed back and stood away.

Alice powered up the twin engines as Lizzie strapped herself into the navigator's seat. Sir Henry popped his head between them and shouted above the booming engines.

He said, 'Fly carefully and take care. This is an accelerated involvement for Lizzie's first mission.'

Alice shouted back, 'Trust me, this girl has a gift for what I need her to do. We'll be back in the morning. I'll call you when we land.'

Sir Henry climbed out of Hesberus and stood next to Bertie on the grass.

Alice pulled a map, a stopwatch and a compass out of her flight bag and put them on Lizzie's lap.

'What do you need me to do?'

'Navigate, and keep your eyes peeled for enemy aircraft. The Bosch rarely fly on cloudy winter nights. They don't like it. Oh, and there's one more thing.'

'What's that?'

'Hesberus is unarmed. No machine guns. On reflection, I think maybe that was a slight oversight.'

'Slight?' said Lizzie.

'You're right; a major oversight.'

Lizzie looked around the cockpit. It was basic, yet somehow friendly, a homely familiarity, and very Milton Park.

'Having fun?' shouted Alice.

'I'm flying in Hesberus, an unarmed tool shed in the dead of night, behind enemy lines for my first mission after one day's training. I've never felt more alive.'

'It will be a piece of cake.' Alice tapped the control column, 'Come on old girl, let's do this.' She revved the burbling engines and steered Hesberus onto the runway, and without fuss, lifted her into the air.

Lizzie spoke into the mouthpiece, 'What do you need me to do with the watch?'

'On the map, you'll see numbers in pencil, they are times. When we fly over the clock tower in the village, start the stopwatch. Shout out when we reach the first time setting. Next to each time, you'll see a bearing. Shout that out, and I'll turn. Got it?'

'Got it,' said Lizzie.

'If you miss one we'll end up over Germany.'

Lizzie looked out of the window, 'And, in Paris, what do you want me to do?'

'Hand the bag you packed to Florence.'

'Where do I meet her?'

'My best guess would be the central train station where the trains depart for Berlin.'

'Best guess? you mean there isn't an arrangement?'

'No, Florence has no idea you're meeting her.'

'So what do I do?'

'That's what the intelligence part of Military Intelligence is about. We figure this stuff out. I'll land Hesberus as close as I can to Paris, then you blast your way on the Norton to the central train station. Hand Florence the bag, whizz back to Hesberus, then we'll fly home, and when we land, I thought we could have a few slices of ham, mashed potato and carrots for lunch.'

'You make it sound so matter of fact.'

'That's because it is. Listen, we decide what we are going to do. Then we do it. The Germans have no idea who you are, and the contents of the bag are of little importance. You're just a girl in Paris riding a motorbike.'

Hesberus shuddered in the heavy turbulence.

'Are we going to make it?' Lizzie stared at the controls.

'Yes, this old lady is indestructible. She's just like me: it doesn't look like much, but Hesberus is fitted with two powerful Rolls Royce engines.'

'Is that good?'

'The Spitfire is the fastest aircraft in the world, and it only has one Rolls Royce engine.' Alice flew under the radar across the channel and into France. The dark featureless countryside offered no visible landmarks, so navigation was a combination of stopwatch, map, compass and luck.

After a few bumpy hours, Alice said, 'Start looking for a field for us to put down.'

Lizzie scoured the land, though one eye was peeled on the lookout for enemy aircraft.

She said, 'I see something, can you circle again? It looks like an old airfield.'

Alice circled and decided on her approach. She lowered the landing gear and bounced Hesberus on the grass and parked. The first shoots of daylight began to push through.

Lizzie fired up the Norton and rode it out onto the grass. She strapped the bag on the seat behind her and pulled her goggles over her eyes.

'Warm enough?' asked Alice.

'Like toast.'

'Find Florence, give her the bag, then race back here as fast as you can.'

'What if I get caught?'

Alice put her hands on her hips, 'Nobody is going to catch you on this beauty. The Hun build motorbikes for fat old men; this thing can fly.'

Lizzie smiled.

'Nervous?' asked Alice.

'I've whistled right past nervous.'

'Have you got your suicide pill?'

'Back pocket.' Lizzie patted her pocket.

Alice took off her tweed jacket, 'Put this on; it will make you look less, well, less like you.'

Lizzie took off her flying jacket and put the tweed jacket on and turned the collar up.

Alice said, 'You look fantastic. Now go, be safe.'

Lizzie spun the rear wheel on the wet grass and raced off onto the road. She opened the throttle, and the Norton gobbled up the country lanes in no time, as Lizzie weaved her way onto the main road and entered the swanky suburbs of Paris.

Lizzie, fearing failure, lay flat to the fuel tank and pushed the motorbike to its maximum. She took the corners tightly and overtook vehicles with coolness. Her first operation would be, it had to be, a success.

Florence parked the baker's van in a quiet side street in the outskirts of Paris. The overworked, underpowered engine ticked frantically as it cooled.

She said, 'We have less than an hour of darkness. Mandy, can you go and find us a new ride? Our time in the bakery business is over. Steal something subtle so that we can drive right up to the Paris railway station.'

Mandy ran off into suburbia and began to search the streets for a suitable vehicle. She caught sight of the perfect ride. Florence was going to love it. Mandy jumped in and started the engine, and headed back to Florence and Percy. She pulled up behind the bakery van.

Mandy said, 'Well, what do you think?'

'You've got to be joking,' said Percy. He looked open-mouthed at the vehicle. 'I vote we keep the bakery van.'

'Mandy isn't joking, and this isn't a referendum,' said Florence. 'It's perfect.'

Mandy beamed, 'Percy, grab the backpacks and hop in.' She steered into the early morning traffic. Other vehicles on the road were either trade trucks or German troop carriers. There were a few Frenchmen on bicycles and some office workers scurrying towards the metro to travel into central Paris.

Percy looked around the vehicle, 'What is it?'

'It's a tank and a jeep. The Bosch call it a half-track, I think it's rather cute,' said Mandy.

'Who is going to stop us in this?' said Florence.

Percy thought for a moment.

He said, 'Well, nobody I suppose.' He thought a moment longer, 'It's the trojan horse principle. Very smart. I would have put money on you turning up in a battered old Citroen and making me wear a black and white t-shirt with a black beret and a string of onions around my neck. Instead, we're driving to the train station in a German tank.'

'You've caught up at last. Now stay below and keep your head down,' said Mandy.

Florence and Mandy tied their hair up and wore the helmets, the goggles and high-necked, winter grey coats that were left on the seats. From a distance, they looked like German soldiers on morning patrol.

'We'll be at the central station by dawn,' said Florence.

. . .

Lizzie weaved her way with agility through the tight back streets of Paris. She used the Eiffel Tower as a target landmark, as Alice had instructed.

The morning bustle of Paris had begun. The cafes and brasseries were decked out with chairs and small round tables. Neither the icy wind nor a raging war was enough of a deterrent to come between the Parisians and their morning coffee and pastry.

Lizzie waited for a tram to cross in front of her, then pulled the Norton into a concealed corner behind the station. She tied a blue and yellow silk scarf around her hair to contain the tangles. She slipped among the throng of passengers and walked towards the station entrance.

Her eyes darted from side to side and scoped as much ground as possible without drawing attention to herself. Her heart beat like a hammer, and her mouth was sand-dry. On the bike she was assertive. Now, alone, at the entrance to the station, she felt as scared as she'd ever been. Her French was passable, but under questioning, she didn't have a back story or plausible papers. A tissue-thin wall held back her panic. She patted the suicide pill in her back pocket, and oddly, it was reassuring. She wrapped Alice's tweed jacket tightly around her like a suit of armour.

Lizzie had been in the station for thirty minutes with no sign of Florence. Should she return without making the drop? How long should she wait? Her doubts mounted when she saw Florence on the far side of the station. Mandy, and a man, were three paces behind her; they looked like a young couple going to work.

Lizzie caught up with them and matched Florence step for step and slipped alongside her. She let the back of her hand brush the back of Florence's hand.

Don't look, eyes front, don't speak, keep calm.

Alice's words ran through her head.

Florence placed her hand over Lizzie's hand, took the bag and continued walking. Not a word, not a single glance, no acknowledgement. As if it was all planned.

Mandy looked straight through Lizzie without a hint of recognition. Ice cold. The only way to survive behind enemy lines.

Lizzie returned to the motorbike and rode away from an awakening Paris, and back to the airfield.

Hesberus was ready to take-off at the far end of the grass strip. As reliable as a Swiss timepiece.

Lizzie rode the motorbike up the plank, then climbed into the navigator's seat.

Alice had the engines warmed and ready for take-off. 'Buckle up. We're going to scamper for home, low and fast. Well done.'

Those were the only words Lizzie received from Alice. It was enough. She hadn't failed.

Percy found an empty compartment on the Berlin bound train. He waved to Florence and Mandy to join him.

'What did Alice send you?' asked Mandy.

'I've not looked yet,' said Florence.

'What are you talking about?' asked Percy.

Florence lifted the bag onto the seat next to her and peered inside, 'Clever old Alice, and there's a note, that reads: Have a delightful trip, see you Friday evening for tea and cake, with love, Aunt Rosie.'

'That's good,' said Mandy.

'Get some sleep, I'll take the first watch,' said Florence.

The centre of Paris was now behind them, and Florence gathered her thoughts and focused on the mission. The

Saturday meeting with Max Ernst Bauer was critical. Before Bauer committed his considerable wealth to build tens of thousands of Spitfires, he would need to be certain he was holding every card. That's what Henry would do. He would want to hold all the aces.

Doubts and questions circled Florence's head: Had Otto and Bauer met before? Did Bauer know Otto's mother? Otto was mid-forties, Percy was much younger, and he will need to be aged.

Mandy opened her eyes, Percy was still sleeping, 'What are you thinking about?'

'Just a few little adjustments.'

'Problems?'

'Naturally,' said Florence.

'Like?'

'Too many moving parts.' Florence looked out of the window, 'Percy has excellent German, but can he pull off playing the part of an arrogant German spy under extreme conditions?'

Mandy asked, 'What about Otto's mother, any ideas?'

Florence showed Mandy the contents of the bag, 'I didn't show you earlier, Percy has enough to think about.'

Mandy looked inside, 'Oh, I see.'

'Precisely,' said Florence.

'Any idea of how you want to do it?'

'I'm working on it.'

'Florence, you look exhausted, get some sleep, I'll keep watch. We have all day on this train.'

The carriage door slid open.

'Papers!' The ticket inspector wore a French rail company uniform. 'Papers!' he held out his hand.

Mandy handed him their papers.

The guard stepped into the carriage and closed the door behind him. He held their documents in his hands, then clasped them behind his back, and rocked back and forth on his heels.

Mandy reached into her back pocket and wrapped her small length of bicycle chain around her fist. She could end him.

The ticket officer looked at Florence, his eyes darted from her to Mandy, then back. He bent forward and lowered his voice.

He said, 'Rosie sent me to keep you safe, nobody will disturb you now that I have checked your papers.' He handed them three bright red armbands with a black swastika, set within a white circle.

'What are they for?' asked Mandy.

'The Nazis love an armband,' said the guard. 'You can invade Germany with a red armband. Nobody will stop you in Berlin with an armband. Wear them with arrogance.'

'Thank you,' said Florence, she rubbed her eyes open. 'What's your name?'

'I'm Jean-Pierre, from Bordeaux, I'm with the resistance here in Berlin. Rosie will meet you tonight.'

'Perfect,' said Florence.

'Good luck.' Jean-Pierre stepped out of the carriage and pulled the next carriage door open.

In the same manner, he snapped, 'Papers!'

'He's good. I like him,' said Florence.

'Handsome too,' said Mandy. 'Typical of Rosie to hook up with a steamy resistance fighter. Let's get these armbands on. We have six more hours before we pull into Berlin.'

Rosie Jones pulled up her stockings and slipped her feet into a pair of high heeled stilettos, then snaked into her short, tight black dress and applied a generous layer of pillar-box red lipstick.

One last turn in the mirror.

Rosie grabbed a long gown and a pink feather scarf and headed out of the door.

Friday evening in Berlin was unlike London: there was no sign of war. No sandbags stacked against doorways, no brown tape crisscrossed on windows, and no barrage balloons floating above city landmarks. Instead, boisterous soldiers filled the bars and officers dined in restaurants with attractive escorts. Rosie scurried along the street and sunk her chin deep into her feather scarf.

Mission on.

Rosie made her way to the red light district where working girls paired off with soldiers. She stepped into a club where a trio played, and a lady sang. The darkness made it the perfect place for a rendezvous.

Rosie sipped a glass of champagne and lit a cigarette. She cut a sultry figure sitting alone at the bar. The front door opened, and Florence walked in. She saw Rosie and walked over to meet her.

'Nice armband,' said Rosie. 'You met Jean-Pierre.'

Florence smiled, 'Let's get out of here. Mandy and Percy are across the street in the shadow of a doorway.'

'Are they hiding?'

'Kissing, and they won't stop,' said Florence.

They slipped out of the bar and into the Berlin night and crossed the street.

Mandy gave Rosie a full-on hug, 'You look like a tart.'

'And, you are a tart,' said Rosie. 'How are you, little sister?'

'I'm the best ever.'

Rosie looked at Percy, 'I can see that.'

They skirted the dark side of the road and left the red lights and clubs behind them. Satisfied they were far enough away; they found a boarded-up shop. Mandy kicked the door, and it swung open. They ran up one flight of stairs and sat in a room, in the dark.

'Rosie, I guess it was you who warned us about Otto's mother being at the meeting on Saturday,' said Mandy.

'I thought you'd guess it was me.'

'You had nothing to lose, and we had everything to gain. It was a clever move.'

'I've been doing some more digging,' said Rosie. 'Otto's mother lives a twenty-minute walk from here. I checked earlier, and she's at home.'

'Then we should make a move,' said Florence.

'What are we going to do?' asked Percy.

'Have a chat with her,' said Florence.

'And ask her what?'

Florence said, 'When we meet Max Ernst Bauer tomorrow, all I want him to see is Otto Flack, Otto's mother and Otto's sister.'

Percy stopped, 'Wait, Otto has a sister?'

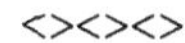

CHAPTER 28

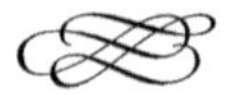

Even a couple of miles from the centre of Berlin, the drop in temperature was noticeable. Rosie led the three of them out of town to an exclusive part of Berlin, where the wealthy and the notable lived.

Rosie's dark, shoulder-length hair sparkled with the glitter. A must-look in the red light district.

She said, 'That's the house.'

The Flack family home was an impressive, white, four-storey house set within its own landscaped gardens; this was an affluent family of influence.

Light snowflakes swirled in the night air. Floating, never to land.

Mandy said, 'Nice house, but it's not a patch on Milton Park.'

'I'll knock,' said Florence. 'Mandy, you stand next to me, and we'll go in together. Rosie and Percy, you stay outside until we call you.'

Florence and Mandy straightened their red Nazi armbands and ran their fingers through their hair.

'How do I look?' asked Mandy.

'Don't worry about that. Are you ready?' asked Florence.

'Always,' said Mandy.

'Don't forget, speak German!' Florence knocked on the front door. No answer, she knocked again, no response.

She flashed a look of annoyance at Rosie.

Mandy used the side of her clenched fist and pounded the door like the Gestapo, 'That should wake the dead.'

The door lock clicked, and soft yellow light formed at the opening.

'Hello,' said the woman.

'Sorry to disturb you, madam,' said Florence. 'We are collecting unwanted garments to re-use, and make new clothing for the Luftwaffe widows.'

'What an excellent idea, step in from the cold and I'll go and see what I can find for you.'

'You have a beautiful home,' said Mandy.

'Thank you,' said the women, before she turned away and climbed the staircase.

Florence waved at Rosie and Percy. They sneaked into the front room and waited in the dark. Florence and Mandy stood at the foot of the stairs in the hallway under a magnificent chandelier.

Mandy stared up at the mass of sparkling glass.

She said, 'I bet that's a right bugger to dust.'

'I wouldn't know,' said Florence.

'Florence, you should try a bit of hard labour, it will do you good, and keep you looking young.'

'Thanks, but I'll stick to spying.'

Mrs Flack descended with an armful of colourful silk garments, 'I hope these will come in useful.'

'Thank you, may we take your name?' Florence asked.

'Flack, Mrs F-.' She saw nothing and felt nothing. Mandy's punch was a quick snap-punch.

Otto's mother crumpled like a drunk sailor onto the

marble tiled floor. Mandy grabbed her feet while Florence grabbed her arms. They waddled her into the front room and switched on the lights.

'Rosie, pull that chair over here, and get some cold water,' said Florence. They sat Flack's limp body on the wooden chair and bound her hands and feet.

Rosie returned from the kitchen with a bowl. Mandy's punch was an accurate blow to the solar plexus, a single strike to the gut designed to put your enemy down without the risk they could get up and hit you back. They called it an Alice Special.

'Bring her round,' said Florence.

Rosie poured the cold water over Mrs Flack's head.

Flack pulled against the restraints and released a torrent of German venom.

'She sounds angry,' said Rosie.

'So would you after a Mandy-punch. Leave her alone and let her tire herself out, we've got all night. She hasn't.'

Flack shouted, 'Who are you? What do you want?'

Florence took her time to answer.

'Mrs Flack, my name is Florence Fairweather. I will ask you some questions, and you will answer either yes, or no. Anything other than that will result in instant discomfort for you. Do you understand?'

'How dare you, do you know who. . .'

The slap from Mandy across Flack's face was instant.

'Yes or no. Do you understand?'

Mrs Flack looked at Mandy, then back at Florence, 'do you know. . .'

The slap came again. Harder. Faster.

Mrs Flack yelled out.

Mandy slapped her again.

'Mrs Flack, we are good at what we do. You are out of

shape and too old to take much more punishment. We know all about you and what you do.'

Mrs Flack looked at the three women. Her eyes darted from one to the other.

She nodded.

'Do you have a son called Otto?'

Mrs Flack breathed heavily through her flared nostrils, she nodded and said, 'Yes.'

'Is he a spy in German Intelligence?'

Mrs Flack didn't answer. She stared ahead.

'Yes, or no, Mrs Flack,' said Florence. 'Is your boy a spy?'

'Yes,' she snarled.

'Your husband, Mrs Flack, is he in German Intelligence? Remember, yes or no.'

Mrs Flack clamped her lips tightly shut as if by doing so, no more information would pass through.

'Your husband, is he in German Intelligence, is he a spy like your son?'

Mrs Flack couldn't hide the look of resignation on her face.

'Yes,' she said. She bit her lip hard, and blood bubbled through her teeth.

'Have you heard of Max Ernst Bauer?'

'Yes.'

'Have you ever met Bauer?' asked Florence.

'No.'

Florence stood behind her. 'Your son, Otto; he's dead.'

Percy said, 'Steady on, no mother wants to hear that.'

'Let it go, Percy,' said Mandy.

Mrs Flack turned around, her eyes wide, her mouth opened, but no sound followed.

Florence added, 'A young girl killed him. She hit him over the head with a rock. He was killed by a girl he jilted. After all he'd been through, he was killed by a girl and died on the beach in England.'

'We buried him,' said Mandy.

Mrs Flack's eyes filled with tears, she lifted her eyebrows as if to ask a question.

'Yeah, we buried him in a shitty muddy hole in Calais,' said Mandy.

Rosie put her face in front of Mrs Flack's, 'Your boy picked a fight with the wrong people, he was out-played, out-smarted, and out-spied.'

Mrs Flack looked up. Her swollen bottom lip bulged. Her eyes narrowed, and a defiant smile ran across her mouth.

She said, 'You've no idea, have you? You pathetic English, you've already lost the war, and you don't know it.' She spat blood on the carpet and waited for a slap.

Florence held Mandy back.

Flack continued, 'We've been preparing this war for twenty years. You fools haven't started yet. You're rummaging for clues in dark corners. We have hundreds of spies in England. You're going to lose the war from the inside out. And all you accomplished was to murder my boy. You'll pay for that.'

Florence walked slowly around the room.

She said, 'Mrs Flack believes Germany is the only country in the spy business. They've been carefully placing spies and sleepers into our society for twenty years, and I admit, they're good at it. The spies sit and wait for war, if not in their lifetime, then their children's lifetime. But I know who most of them are, it's what I do. And, isn't it extraordinary don't you think, Mrs Flack, just how many of them meet with freak accidents. Have you ever considered that we are better at spying than you? Only last year, a dear old lady in the Women's Institute near Cambridge, slipped on some marmalade and broke her neck, and died on her kitchen floor. It turns out she had sneaked her way into England's village life eighteen years ago, but I knew about her. Incredible how much nonsense and false information she had radioed to Berlin. We fed her lie upon lie for nearly twenty years. Then she winds up dead, a sticky marmalade end. Personally, I prefer to poison your spies in their beds and then tell the coroner what to write on the death certificate. Mrs Flack, I have all your spies on a chart on my office wall.'

'You lying pig!' shouted Flack.

'Churchill once told me: cats look down on us, dogs look up to us, but pigs, well, they see us as equals. We make it our business to know who your spies are who have buried themselves in our communities. As a rule, we keep an eye on them so that they can do us no harm. Germany, yet again, has arrogantly overlooked Britain's reach and underestimated our ruthlessness when it comes to defending our country. What do you think we do all day, drink tea and watch cricket?'

Mrs Flack spat blood onto the carpet.

'What now?' asked Mandy.

'Take her upstairs,' said Florence. 'Put her to bed and give her a sleeping pill.' She handed Mandy a small white tablet.

Mandy and Rosie dragged the lady upstairs to her bedroom. They pulled back the silk covers of her luxurious bed and laid her down.

'Open up,' said Rosie. She placed the white tablet on her tongue and gave her a sip of water from a bedside glass.

'Your boy, Otto,' said Mandy. 'He killed some people who were close to my heart, and he paid for it.'

Mrs Flack stared up at the two girls, 'You evil people, you've no idea what is about to happen to your putrid country.'

Rosie looked at her watch, 'You should be feeling sleepy.'

Flack didn't move and didn't answer.

Mandy checked Flack's pulse, 'That was quick.'

'It's one of my mother's specials,' said Rosie.

Mandy took the camera out of her pocket, and opened Mrs Flack's eyes, 'Say cheese.' They ran downstairs and joined Florence and Percy in the front room.

'Photograph?' asked Florence.

Mandy handed over the camera, 'Done.'

'Good work,' said Florence. 'Now I need to dress up like Mrs Flack.'

'When will she wake up?' asked Percy.

Three pairs of eyes stared at him.

'How long will she sleep?' He asked. 'What was in the sleeping tablet?'

'Part cyanide and part sleeping pill,' said Florence.

'How much cyanide?'

'To be honest, all of it. It was a cyanide pill.'

'You mean she's dead,' said Percy.

'Oh, God, yes. She's very dead,' said Mandy.

'We don't do fair fights,' said Rosie. 'You have to tilt the odds in your favour.'

'You sound like Florence, and Alice, and Mandy,' he said.

'Thank you,' said Rosie, and gave a curtsy.

Mandy said, 'Percy, the work you do at Bletchley Park, codebreaking, intercepting and so on, that tilts the game in Britain's favour, it loads the dice for us to win.'

Percy said, 'But this was cold-blooded murder.'

'There's no murder in war,' said Rosie. 'We took out a high ranking spy who was hell-bent on destroying England.'

Florence held up Lizzie's bag, 'Girls, are we ready?'

'Lizzie did well for her first handover,' said Mandy. 'She only had one day's training with Alice.'

'One day? She was lucky, I met Alice, and off we went, to war,' said Florence.

'Alice made Lizzie wear her tweed jacket,' said Mandy. 'I nearly wet my knickers when I saw her.'

They climbed the staircase, and Rosie and Florence rummaged through Mrs Flack's dressing room.

Mandy walked in, 'I think we might have a problem.'

'What's that?' said Florence.

'It's Percy, he's too good looking, and there's not a mark on him. He doesn't look as though he's been through facial surgery, he doesn't even look as if he's been in a punch up, let alone been in a war, and he looks fifteen years too young to be Otto.'

'Can we fix him?' said Florence.

'We can, but he won't like it,' said Mandy.

'Let's not worry about his likes and dislikes.'

The three of them walked downstairs into the front room and called Percy over. As he took one step towards them, they punched him full in the face at the same time. Their fists split his nose and bloodied his mouth. He fell backwards clattering into the dining room table and chairs.

'Nice shot,' yelled Rosie.

Percy staggered like a drunk, with one foot rooted to the floor, and the other stepping from left to right. Finally, he stopped moving and stood holding his face. 'What the hell was that for?'

'The plan was to knock you out,' said Mandy.

He looked at them in a dazed manner with blood dripping through his fingers onto the carpet.

'I'm impressed,' said Florence. 'You stood up to our punches. It was Mandy's idea to hit you, by the way.'

Mandy put her hands on her hips, 'Thanks Florence.'

'No problem, it's what I do best.'

Mandy said, 'Let me take a look, my darling.' She pulled his hands away. 'That's a beauty,' she said. 'You were far too good looking to be a German spy. You needed to be roughed up a bit. Now you have your first little battle scars.'

He tried to smile at her, his teeth were bloodstained, and his nose bled. One eye was bruised and closed.

'I'll see what there is to eat and drink,' said Rosie.

'Great idea,' said Mandy. 'I've not eaten for days.'

'Apart from half the cakes in the baker's van,' said Florence.

Rosie emptied the pantry and prepared a tray of cooked meats, pickles, cheese, chopped vegetables, bread, and two bottles of claret. She carried it into the front room where Mandy and Florence attended to Percy's wounds.

'Did you have to kill Mrs Flack?' asked Percy.

Florence said, 'Too bloody right. She was a principal player in Nazi High Command and was responsible for killing dozens of British agents, my friends, who remained in Germany after the First World War. Alice, Sir Henry, and I secretly met with them between the wars, regularly, to get updates on Germany's military movements and their secret rearming. Our only problem was we couldn't get our damn Government to take it seriously, apart from Winston. Mrs Flack eluded us for years, but it's her husband who I want to get the most. He is the dangerous one.'

'Two down, one Flack to go,' said Mandy.

'Hungry, anyone?' Rosie put the tray on the table. 'After we eat, I'm going to de-prostitute myself. I hate looking like a tart.'

'But you do it so well,' said Mandy. 'I'm going to tell Alice you go to brothels on your nights off.'

'No need, it was mum who made me do it.'

They tucked into the food and drank the wine.

Outside, all was quiet. The ornate street lamps bled a golden glow into the night sky. Two distant dogs barked, and a couple walked home after a night out; their animated conversation floated on the empty air.

Florence remained silent while she ate, and pushed her plate aside when she finished, 'When we meet Max Ernst Bauer tomorrow, we all have a role to play. Percy, we need to age you; grey you up, and make you look less like a dashing English vicar.'

He leaned away from her, 'Not another beating is it?'

'I shouldn't think so,' said Florence. 'But let's not rule it out quite yet.'

'Mandy, you'll come as Mrs Flack's daughter, and Rosie, I want you to take a rooftop position with your sniper rifle and keep us covered, and when we move, follow us on your motorbike.'

Percy said, 'Do you think Mrs Flack was telling the truth about not meeting this Max Ernst Bauer fellow?'

'Definitely,' said Rosie.

'And you're certain because?'

'Because Rosie is a human lie detector. Nobody can lie to her and get away with it,' said Mandy. 'She has studied body language and all that mumbo-jumbo, so never play her at cards.'

The three of them looked Percy up and down, 'We need to Nazi-you-up,' said Mandy. 'Let's go through the cupboards upstairs and find something for you.'

'Nazi-me-up? That sounds awful.'

Mandy led him upstairs to the top floor and opened the door to a walk-in dressing room. He followed her, and she grabbed him and closed the door with her foot.

'I've been waiting for ages for us to be on our own,' she said.

Mandy's body moulded into his arms as they pressed up against the dressing room wall. She unzipped her combat suit and placed his warm hands on her body and pushed against him. He kissed her neck and roamed his hands over her body. She flicked the light off, and they stood in each other's arms in total darkness.

'I can't see anything,' he said.

'You won't need to. I know where everything is.'

'My face hurts,' he said.

A few minutes after midnight, the four of them sat in the candlelit front room.

'That wig looks fabulous on you, Florence,' said Rosie. 'You really do pass for Otto's mother.'

Florence looked down at Mrs Flack's clothes; they fitted her surprisingly snuggly. Percy looked like a well-heeled German in his early forties. His bruised nose, black eye, and grey-powdered hair gave him a sinister edge.

Florence said, 'Let's get some sleep, we leave at nine in the morning.'

Rosie said to Mandy, 'Go and find a bedroom, I'll come and wake you in four hours, I'll take the first watch.'

Mandy and Percy slipped upstairs.

'How is my mum?' asked Rosie.

'Alice is Alice,' said Florence, and thought about her best friend. 'I have no idea how your mum does it. She developed a pocket-telephone out of old wires. We simply wouldn't be able to operate without her. And, she's so proud of you, Rosie. I hear her at Milton Park, giggling at your messages.'

'I've been stationed in Berlin too long. I want to come back after the war and watch mum grow roses.'

'Your mum, grow roses? I think Alice might need something a bit more aggressive than roses.'

. . .

In the early hours, Mandy and Percy took the last watch, while Rosie and Florence slept upstairs. An hour before their departure, Percy made a pot of coffee, and a stack of buttered toast, and brought it into the front room. Mandy lit the fire, and Florence and Rosie joined them.

Florence said, 'Percy, you must remain in character, no more you, from now on, you are Otto Flack. The problem is, we don't know what Otto was like.'

Rosie said, 'At all times, be arrogant and brash. I meet those bastards in the brothels, and most of them are arrogant brutes.'

Florence looked at Mandy, 'If Bauer rumbles us, kill him. If he has bodyguards, then Rosie you take them out from your sniper position.'

'Got it,' said Mandy.

'Me too,' said Rosie.

'What shall we do with, you-know-who upstairs?' asked Percy.

'I have a clean-up team here in Berlin,' said Rosie. 'I'll get them to come in and make it look as though she died peacefully in her sleep.'

'Everyone ready?' said Florence.

'Ready!' came the chorus.

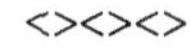

CHAPTER 29

Mandy brought Mrs Flack's black Mercedes to a smooth halt in a quiet Berlin backstreet. Rosie slipped out and ran upstairs to her top floor apartment and rummaged through her cupboards for several outfits. She needed to prepare for everything.

Rosie lifted a well-worn floorboard under her bed and took out her sniper rifle. For her twenty-fifth birthday, Alice designed a radio set to look like a sport's bag. It was complete with a tennis racket poking out of the top, and a transmitter stitched into the lining. Rosie packed her clothes, then wrapped herself in a German solider's uniform and checked outside her front door.

She exited the building into a snow-covered yard, where, behind a wooden door, Rosie stored her motorbike. It was one of Alice's specials: race-tuned and terrifyingly fast, and yet it looked exactly like a grey, army plodder-bike, perfect for a fat old German officer.

Rosie pushed the snow off the saddle, clipped her rifle to the bike frame and strapped her sport's bag onto the back seat. She tied her hair in a ponytail and tucked it under her helmet, then put on the out-sized goggles. She eased into Saturday mid-morning traffic and headed towards Gestapo HQ.

Rosie knew, after years of spycraft, that to act like a bored soldier by yawning, smoking, coughing and scratching body parts, was the most effective way to stay under the radar and remain unnoticed. It worked, Rosie was never given a second look. Daily, she hid any signs of girliness at work, and at night, she changed her skin like a snake and morphed into another character.

She parked her motorbike behind the building opposite Gestapo HQ. She unclipped her rifle and slung the sports bag radio over her shoulder and climbed the external metal staircase. Rosie lay flat on her stomach and set up her sniper rifle with the telescopic sights.

She aimed and waited.

Mandy drove through the gates of Gestapo HQ. Mile-long, red swastika flags draped from the sky to the floor like rivers of blood.

Percy shifted in his seat. His nerves were on edge.

He said, 'How will I recognise Bauer?'

'You won't have to,' said Mandy.

'Why not?'

'Because I'm going to get him and you'll stay in the car with Florence. I'll ask Bauer for the recognition code, then bring him out.'

Florence said, 'Walk away if you smell a trap, and meet us at Rosie's place.'

The entrance hall to Gestapo HQ was a bustle of morning activity. Uniformed personnel scurried about, and their footsteps echoed in the cavernous lobby. Three photographers holding flashbulb cameras, stood behind a red rope ready to snap a Nazi general for their newspaper's front page and propel propaganda to new heights.

Mandy stood behind a white line on the floor waiting to be called over to the next available receptionist. Her turn came.

'Papers!' said a stern-faced man behind the desk. It was an order; not an invitation.

Mandy's identity papers were high-grade forgeries and would pass the closest scrutiny. Sir Henry insisted on using paper and ink stock stolen from the Gestapo's document storeroom.

The pedantic receptionist took an age to review Mandy's documents.

Mandy didn't flinch. The most complex skill for a spy to learn.

He looked up, 'State your business.'

'I'm here to collect Mr Max Ernst Bauer.'

'I have no record of this.'

'That's because Mr Bauer is not based here.'

'Wait over there,' he pointed to a wooden bench.

Mandy sat on the bench and looked every part a young lady of wealth. Mrs Flack's wardrobe was crammed with clothes from Paris's top fashion houses. And with a nip and a tuck, and a few safety pins, she looked regal.

One minute to midday.

A short, stout man approached the reception desk, and the guard pointed to Mandy.

The man walked over, 'I understand you are here to meet me?'

'Yes, good morning, Mr Bauer, I'm Otto Flack's sister. My brother is waiting for you in the car with my mother.'

They walked out through the entrance hall. Mandy stopped ten yards before the Mercedes in full view of Florence and sniper-Rosie and turned to face him.

'Mr Bauer, I must ask you for the recognition code that Otto sent you.'

Bauer pushed his glasses up his nose.

'Lizzie's eyes starburst blue.'

'Follow me,' she said.

Florence and Percy stepped out of the car.

Percy said, 'It's a privilege to meet you, sir.'

'The pleasure is mine,' said Bauer. 'Your father speaks most highly of you.'

'Allow me to introduce my mother,' Percy's voice showed no hint of fear.

'Mrs Flack, your work is the talk of Munich.'

'How charming you are,' she held out her hand.

'I've met regularly with your husband whenever he could visit Munich, and we've become firm friends. I see him far less these days, due to his important position in Government.'

Florence sneezed.

Rosie watched the comings and goings through the crosshairs of her sniper rifle.

Bauer was a short, round man in his late fifties. His blue suit was too tight, and it caused the jacket buttons to pull. His overcoat was too long, and his wire-rimmed glasses dug into the sides of his podgy face. He took out a handkerchief and wiped a sheen of sweat from his bald head. In freezing temperatures, Bauer sweated.

Rosie saw the sneeze signal from Florence. She climbed down the staircase and fired up her motorbike.

Bauer made himself comfortable in the back seat of the car next to Florence. He sat silently for a few minutes. Mandy and Florence knew not to fill the void, but to allow their subject to dictate the pace.

Bauer spoke.

'I was not aware you had a daughter Mrs Flack.'

Florence and Mandy had discussed dozens of scenarios where Bauer's questions could potentially uncover them. They had their answers ready, and if that failed, they would kill him.

Mandy said, 'My father thought it best for me to grow up in America and Britain. You know the sort of thing; get to know thine enemy.'

'And what did you learn about our enemy?'

'America doesn't want to fight, and Britain isn't ready to fight.'

'I share your thoughts.'

'I'm afraid my daughter has picked up a little American precociousness.'

Mandy cut in, 'Mr Bauer, I do hope I've not offended you,' she dropped her eyes as she spoke.

'Not one bit, you are most endearing. Where will you be going next to observe our enemy?'

'Father is sending me back to London, to fight from within.'

'My sister will cause plenty of trouble for those pompous Brits,' Percy added.

Bauer, a man clearly driven by ego, said, 'I have something to show you. It's no more than thirty minutes away.' He was not a cultured man, and yet his self-made wealth opened influential doors, politically and socially.

Florence sat next to Bauer and touched his leg. 'I have my security officer following us. I wanted you to feel comfortable.' Bauer glanced through the rear window and gave directions. Mandy steered out through the gates of Gestapo HQ.

En route, Bauer turned his attention to business.

He said, 'Otto, your father told me a little about your mission to England. Your exploits sounded dangerous.'

Percy took his lead on how Mandy and Florence had worked Bauer. He said, 'I found it simple to move around and gather the details I needed because British security is outdated and spread thinly. I was never in any real danger.' Percy kept the details brief, he wore Malcolm's blue scarf to shield his face.

Bauer paused a beat, 'Did you bring the Spitfire code for me?'

Percy reached into his pocket and took out the sheet of paper and placed it into Bauer's sweaty hand. Bauer licked his lips to savour the moment as he unfolded the piece of paper. He pushed his glasses up his nose to study the code and made grunting sounds as he read.

He said, 'Excellent work, Otto.'

Percy nodded his appreciation.

Bauer added, 'This code is Germany's destiny.'

Percy was mindful not to break the spell Bauer was under and waited until Bauer looked up.

Percy asked, 'What is it you wish to show us?'

'I've constructed an underground facility; it's my investment in the future, and it's where we're going to build tens of thousands of German Spitfires.'

'That sounds like a decisive end to England's participation in the war,' said Mandy.

'That's the reason I'm funding the project.'

Florence added, 'Without your generosity, Germany would be unable to mount such dominance.'

Bauer warmed to the compliments.

Mandy left the main road and steered around the quiet lanes with Rosie fifty yards behind them looking every bit the German sentry. The lane came to a dead-end, and Mandy parked in a square courtyard. Percy opened the rear passenger doors and, like a good son, helped Florence out of the vehicle. There were a few scattered outbuildings, most with broken windows, but no sign of a super-warehouse.

'Where are you building the facility?' asked Florence.

'Follow me,' Bauer said, unable to hide a hint of a smirk. They followed him through one of the wooden outbuildings, and out onto a windswept field.

'There's plenty of room to build a facility here,' said Mandy.

'It's the perfect location, and close enough to Berlin, yet hidden away from prying eyes,' added Florence.

Bauer walked twenty yards beyond the hut. He cleared a patch of snow with his foot, then bent down and picked up a length of rope.

He called out to Otto, 'Come and help me.'

They tugged the rope and pulled a square of fake grass out of the way to reveal a pair of concealed doors which lay flat against the ground. Bauer knelt and tapped a code into the keypad. The steel doors hissed and peeled apart to expose a brightly lit stone staircase that led steeply down underground.

Florence said, 'How clever.' She meant it.

Bauer scurried down the flight of stairs, surprisingly quickly for a heavyset man who sweated from the simple task of standing.

Florence held the rail taking one step at a time. Mandy and Percy followed. At the bottom of the staircase, there were more double doors. These were steel blast-doors standing forty-feet high. Bauer tapped at a keypad on the wall, and the doors effortlessly opened on silent rollers. Organ music and smoke could not have made the scene any more dramatic.

Behind the doors was a black void.

Florence looked into the emptiness. There was nothing other than to feel an eerie chill on her face.

Bauer yanked at a bank of black levers, and one by one, the facility's lights flickered on to illuminate hundreds of work stations. Each station had a giant mechanical robot arm capable of lifting heavy machinery. Polished tools were neatly laid out on spotless workbenches, more akin to a hospital theatre than an aircraft factory.

'I've never seen anything quite so fantastic, so incredible,' said Percy. He had to focus not to speak English, such was his astonishment.

'Mr Bauer, it's extremely impressive,' said Florence. Bauer soaked up the adulation. He took out his handkerchief and dabbed his forehead.

'How big is the facility?' asked Mandy.

Bauer clasped his hands behind his back, he looked at each of them in turn, and his wide-open eyes filled the thick lenses of his wire-rimmed spectacles.

He boasted, 'We can build ten thousand German Spitfires a month. Do you know what that means?'

'We'd win the war in a flash?' suggested Percy.

'Crushing Britain is only the beginning.' Bauer held the sheet of code like a proud father holding his firstborn. He straightened his back, and his stature grew. 'First, we crush England. Then we'll dominate Europe, then the world.'

'The Third Reich will last for a thousand years, thanks to you, Mr Bauer.' Mandy's sweet words spread over him like honey on warm bread.

'This place is truly wonderful,' said Florence. 'And to think, it was built in total secrecy.'

'Mrs Flack, your husband signed off on the plans and handed the commission to me. It was my honour to fund such a project.'

Florence looked at Mandy.

It was a glance Mandy understood: eyes on.

Mandy asked, 'Mr Bauer, do you have a restroom I might use?'

He pointed down the hall.

Mandy walked past the toilets and headed towards the offices to locate the chief engineer's door. She opened the drawer containing a pile of blueprints and pinned the blue scrolls to the desk in the centre of the room.

She flashed her eyes over the first one, rolled it up and unrolled the second print, flashed her eyes again, rolled it up, and continued to memorise each of the five prints. A moment later, she returned to the group.

'How do you plan to get the aircraft out of here?' asked Percy.

Bauer snorted, 'There are six sets of double exit doors that lead to a ramp at the back of the warehouse. A runway is being built in the field so we can fly them directly to the Luftwaffe units across Europe.'

'Brilliant, it's all so brilliant,' Florence said.

Percy announced, 'It's time I returned to Berlin. I have to meet with High Command and hand them the Spitfire manufacture locations across England.'

'We'll bomb Britain into submission,' said Mandy.

Bauer turned off the lights and closed the blast doors.

Florence sat in silence in the back of the Mercedes. In the bright lights of the underground facility, she witnessed Hitler's sinister intent and the absolute destruction that lay ahead for Britain.

Bauer's voice snapped her out of her thoughts. 'Otto, I'll come with you. I need to meet with them myself.'

'That's marvellous,' said Percy. He turned to Florence and Mandy. 'I'll see you both later this afternoon, and remember, please send roses to uncle Percival, he will need to be looked after.'

Mandy said, 'Consider it done.'

Bauer looked confused.

'We have a sick uncle,' said Florence.

Mandy parked the Mercedes outside Gestapo HQ, and Percy and Bauer stepped out and walked into the building. Percy looked back at Mandy and their gaze lasted no more than a beat of life. It was all they had. Mandy drove off and parked behind the building opposite. Rosie pulled up on her motorbike.

Florence leaned through the window, 'Rosie, get changed and go into Gestapo HQ. You'll have to keep an eye on Percy.'

Rosie pulled her office uniform out of her bag and stripped, then changed into a skirt, blouse and jacket. She smoothed her clothes down and swept her hair back.

'How do I look?'

'Ugly,' said Mandy.

'Good, I was aiming for that. Under the motorbike saddle, you'll find my telescopic sights. You can watch Percy and me from the rooftop.'

'Look after my boy,' said Mandy.

'My sports bag radio is tuned to Milton Park. You can contact them directly.'

Florence listened, then said, 'Rosie, it's vital you tell Percy we are leaving at six in the morning, and not a minute later. We won't wait for him; we can't wait, our schedule is fixed. He'll be stranded in Berlin, living as Otto bloody Flack forever if he's late.'

Rosie pulled out her credentials and ran across the road to the HQ. She went through the main doors and disappeared up the stairs into the inner workings of the Gestapo.

'Rosie is fearless,' said Mandy. 'Like Alice.'

'Those two are not of this world.'

Mandy tapped the side of her head, 'I got the blueprints for the underground bunker. That place scared the life out of me. Do we have anything as good back home?'

'Not even close, they are a decade ahead. Come on, let's go and keep an eye on that boy of yours.'

Florence put the sports bag around her neck and climbed the exterior metal stairs, Mandy followed. They lay on the roof and looked through the windows of the Gestapo HQ.

Florence used the Jungle Book code and tapped out a message to Alice.

Her message read: Collection needed.

Alice's message: Land or Sea collection?

Florence's Message: Land collection in Hesberus (Florence tapped out coordinates)

Alice's message: Be safe. Give them hell.

Mandy spied through the scope and shook her head, 'Percy, where are you?' She swooped the sights in smooth arcs and scoped window to window.

'Rosie is in there, she'll look after him,' said Florence.

'Wait, I can see him, he's with three, no four German officers. He's standing at the window with his back to me. Come on, Percy, turn around, tell me something.'

Percy put his hands behind his back. He started to tap his thumb on top of his hand.

'He's signalling to us in Morse code,' said Mandy.

'Call it out,' said Florence. She was ready with her pencil.

Mandy called out the string of dots and dashes, and then Percy stepped away from the window and vanished.

'He's gone,' said Mandy.

Florence decoded the message and read it out.

'Luftwaffe have the twenty-one Spitfire sites. Bomb raid

Tuesday 2200hrs. I'm being honoured tonight. See you before six-am if poss. I Love you, MM.'

'We can't leave him here,' said Mandy.

'He has until six in the morning.'

Rosie stepped out of the Gestapo HQ into a grey Berlin afternoon and walked across the road. She climbed the ladder where Mandy and Florence waited for her on the roof.

She said, 'Percy was outstanding. He had the Germans eating out of his hand, as he made up stories about killing Malcolm Feathers and how he burrowed deep into the heart of British Military Intelligence.'

'That's my boy,' said Mandy.

'They're going to take Percy out tonight to celebrate. I told him to be at my place no later than six tomorrow morning. He knows if he's late, he's buggered.'

Mandy looked through the scope at the dark windows. Percy had gone. 'I want to stay,' she said.

'I know you do,' said Florence. 'Let's go to Rosie's place and prepare to leave. We can't do any more here.'

CHAPTER 30

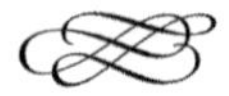

Rosie showed them around her small apartment. The tightly packed room contained a kitchen, a bed, a wardrobe and a small bathroom hidden behind a curtain. Alice's influences extended into all aspects of Rosie's life. A hand grenade sat on the shelf among the cups and saucers, and the cutlery drawer was crammed full of ammunition.

Florence flicked through the Aladdin's cave of battle treasure, 'Rosie, it's safe to say, your mum was counting on having a boy.'

'Rosie is a boy,' said Mandy.

It was late when they kicked off their boots, and pulled a heavy mustard-coloured blanket over their laps and sipped steaming mugs of tea.

Florence showed them a map, 'Alice will land Hesberus here, just inside the German border.' They studied the map and continued to plan until the bedside candle neared the end of the wax. The flame became an ever decreasing orange dot, and then darkness, followed by a stream of smoke that curled towards the ceiling.

Mandy whispered into Rosie's ear, 'Percy will be alright, won't he?'

'Of course, he will. He'll be watching naked dancing girls by now.'

Mandy nudged her in the ribs, 'Do you think he has eyes for some skinny sort when he has all this?'

Rosie put her arm around Mandy, 'My Berlin team are on standby, wherever he goes, we'll have eyes on.'

'I've never felt this way about a man before. It happened so fast, one minute I was collecting a code breaker from Bletchley Park, the next I was kissing him on the balcony and falling in love.'

'That's because you're a tart,' said Rosie. They giggled under the blanket until tears rolled down their faces.

Rosie propped herself up on her elbow, 'Florence, tell us something you love about Sir Henry.'

'When Henry is angry, he-'

'Angry, Sir Henry? No way,' Mandy said.

'Sir Henry is never angry,' said Rosie.

'The funny thing is,' said Florence. 'Nobody else can tell.'

'And that's what you love most about him?' said Rosie. 'I thought it would be his smouldering good looks, his cleverness, his charm, his wit, something like that.'

'Or that he's the richest man in England, not to mention his Royal and political connections,' added Mandy.

'You didn't ask what I love most about him. You asked me to tell you something I love about him. I love the little things that nobody else could know.'

Mandy said, 'Florence, you are a hopeless spy, you get asked one question about the head of British Intelligence, and you blabber like a little lost boy.'

'I could be lying. I'm famous for it.'

'That's true,' said Rosie. 'She lies a lot.'

Mandy said, 'So Rosie, how about you and the sexy Jean-Pierre, the guard from the train?'

'Ah yes, him,' Rosie blushed in the dark. 'It was all rather romantic. I was on surveillance before war broke out. Alice wanted me to follow this German officer. It was a swelteringly hot day in July, in Paris. I was hiding out in an attic above a small wine bar. The French resistance was watching the same German officer. Jean-Pierre chose the same attic for his lookout post. Well, one thing led to another, one bottle of wine led to another, one kiss led to another.'

'And the German officer?' asked Florence.

'Oh, I've no idea, I never saw him again.'

'And the steamy, Jean-Pierre?' asked Mandy.

'We spent three days in that attic together. The hot weather, the hot Frenchman, do I need to go on?'

'Hell, yes,' said Mandy. 'I want every sordid detail.'

'I'm going to get some sleep,' said Florence. 'You two can swap stories.'

But she couldn't sleep. Her mind hopped from one dreaded scenario to another. Florence knew she may have sent Percy to his death; if he tripped up and broke disguise, they would rumble he was not Otto Flack. A brutal interrogation would follow; but they couldn't extract the truth and rumble that he was a code breaker before she located him and put a bullet in the back of his head. Her mind floated to the images of the underground bunker. The Germans were supremely prepared and ready for war. Mrs Flack was right: Britain was flapping in the dark, and German spies had already invaded England. The truth was that Military Intelligence didn't know the whereabouts of most of them.

Sleep? Florence couldn't sleep. She had singlehandedly lost Britain the war.

. . .

Percy and Max Ernst Bauer sat side by side at the head of the table in Berlin's most expensive restaurant. The assembly chinked their champagne glasses to toast Otto Flack's success and Nazi Germany's growing domination across Europe.

Percy grew lightheaded from the endless drinking. The food was too rich; something he'd not been accustomed to at Bletchley Park, where boiled vegetables and boiled fish, were the highlight of the week. He needed to remain sober and focus on finding a way to escape the group without causing offence.

A drunk officer at the far end of the table stood and bellowed, 'Otto Flack, the son of Germany.' The diners cheered, and champagne flowed.

Max Ernst Bauer leaned closer to Percy, 'They're taking you to a girlie bar after dinner, they have quite the night lined up for you.'

Percy faked his best smile. He wanted out. He wanted Mandy, and he wanted to be heading back to England, not heading to a late-night bar.

Bauer dabbed his forehead and pushed his glasses closer to his eyes, 'I still find it strange how your father didn't mention anything to me about having such a beautiful daughter.'

Percy shrugged his shoulders, 'You must understand something about my father, he is a political and military man first, and a family man second. I'm certain he would have preferred two sons to fight for Germany. He showed very little interest in my sister, even though she is the most wonderful person I know.' Percy thought about Mandy. She was the most wonderful person he knew.

'My father was similar, so I see your point. My father had no interest in family life.'

The slurring German, at the far end of the table, made

one final toast, he stood on wobbly legs and announced loudly it was time for them to head to the club.

The officers stood and bumped the table, causing the glasses to fall and smash, then headed boisterously for the door. Percy was swept up in the parade.

It was three in the morning, and Percy had three hours to get to Rosie's apartment and avoid being left behind.

The jazz trio played, and a sultry dark-haired woman sang melancholy songs. Thick smoke and a strong smell of stale booze filled the air. The celebrations had subsided. The officers paired up with the pretty resident girls, and one by one, they went upstairs to the guest bedrooms, to the sound of shrills and yelps. Percy remained at the table, until he was alone, and waited to slip away into the night. Two pretty girls approached him.

'Welcome back, Otto. We've missed you. We wouldn't have recognised you if one of the officers hadn't told us it was you.' The girl had her arms around his neck, and the other was sitting in his lap.

'Let's do what we did last time,' said the girl in his lap. 'You look so different. Is it really you?'

Percy was losing his grasp on how to act like the arrogant Flack, and Panic surged in his throat. He'd handled the Gestapo, and dealt with Bauer, but now, in a strip club, he was about to be exposed by two prostitutes.

'Hey you two cheap hookers, get out of here. Otto is mine.' The husky voice belonged to the sultry singer.

The two girls skulked away.

Percy was caught, stranded in the headlights of a situation he no longer controlled. His mind worked the permutations, and he clawed at ideas to get out of his predicament. He wished Mandy and Florence were here.

'Otto, I knew it was you. You can't hide those baby eyes from me. I saw you staring at me on stage.' The singer pulled

Percy to his feet, and wrapped her arms around him and kissed him fully on the mouth. The kiss lingered. She took his hand and headed for the staircase.

Percy had no option. He had to follow.

Several of the German officers cheered and whistled as the singer led Percy away by hand.

Percy knew she would rumble he was not Otto as soon as they were undressed, and shout out to the officers downstairs. He was in a trap.

'Third door on the left,' her rich voice whispered through the gloom of the dark landing. Her French accent turned the harsh German words into sensual sounds.

They walked into the room, and Percy made his mind up. He took off his blue scarf and looped a noose, then held the ends tightly and lassoed the scarf around her neck, and yanked hard.

The girl was caught off-guard.

'Percy,' she gargled and lashed out. 'Percy!' He unravelled the scarf from her neck, and she began to cough and splutter.

'I'm Nicole, Rosie's friend. I'm with the French resistance, and I'm here to help you. We had plans to cover the Berlin nightclubs, but our team was spread too thinly. I gambled on you being brought here, as the Gestapo love the girls.'

'What now, can we get out of here?' he asked.

'Not yet. Now we wait.'

'For how long?'

'About an hour should do it.'

'An hour, for what?'

'Sex, Percy, sex. We've come up here for sex, remember? In an hour we'll go back downstairs like we've been hard at it.'

'But I nearly killed you.'

'Hardly,' she showed him her knife. 'You were the lucky one.'

He sat on the bed and waited.

'What are you doing?' Nicole asked.

'Waiting.'

'We didn't come up here to drink tea. We have to make it look as though you've had the raunchiest time of your life.' Nicole took out her red lipstick and applied it to her lips, and without warning, grabbed Percy's face and kissed him full on the mouth, and then began kissing his neck and the front of his shirt.

'I don't think I. . .'

'Bloody English, you're hopeless, let me do it.' Nicole grabbed her white blouse and ripped it open. The buttons popped and skidded across the floor to expose her delicate lace bra.

Percy didn't look, 'I feel as though I've been in a fight. I'm not sure what happens in France, but in England, it's not quite this violent.'

Nicole put her hands on her hips, 'You can trust me, I'm in the resistance.' Nicole clambered all over him and made their clothing look as though they'd been frolicking for an hour of erotic pleasure. 'Just lie back and think of England.'

'England? I can't even remember who I'm meant to be.'

She lit a cigarette and sat on the bed and admired her work. 'I've finished with you. Rosie said you'd resist.'

Percy sat up, 'I was in a jam downstairs with those girls. You saved me.'

Nicole finished her cigarette and stubbed it out.

'Do you know what that bastard, Otto Flack did?' Her tone noticeably changed. 'He rounded up twelve people from my village and had them slaughtered. Women, men, young boys, shot dead, all of them, at point-blank. He said it was the penalty for not surrendering members of the resistance to the Nazis. My father slumped to the ground holding his chest. Flack stood over him and put a bullet in his head. I watched the murderous scene play out from my attic window. Nobody in the village gave me up, but I tell you, when Rosie told me Flack was dead, I felt nothing. No revenge can soothe the pain of losing my father.'

Percy led Nicole downstairs, and they rejoined the remaining rowdy officers at the table. She wrapped herself around Percy and coiled up in his lap. They stayed for one more drink.

Percy announced, 'Gentlemen, thank you for tonight. It has been a wonderful celebration, but tomorrow is a big day, and I need to sleep.'

'Flack, sleep here with the whore,' snarled an officer. His hair was fashioned like Hitler's: oily black and slicked down.

Percy ignored the crudeness and stretched out his hand to Nicole, who stood, and they made to leave.

'The French whore stays here with us,' barked the officer.

Percy ignored him once more, 'It's been a wonderful evening, and I'm honoured to have been invited.' He put Nicole's coat over her shoulders.

The officer kicked his chair back, and it smashed into the table behind. 'The whore stays,' he bellowed. He stood over six feet tall with broad shoulders.

Percy whispered in Nicole's ear, 'Wait for me outside. Don't come back in, no matter what you hear.' She scurried out through the door.

The officer shouted, 'Bring the whore back. I haven't finished with her yet.'

Percy put his hands up, 'The evening is over, let's all go home.'

'I say when the evening is over. You're more like a pretty boy from a private school. You're nothing like the Otto Flack I know from the German elite.'

Percy kept his hands up in a gentle surrender pose and stepped towards the officer. 'I've done things you couldn't imagine. I've served my country, and I'm proud of what I've done. I don't seek your approval.'

'You spoilt little shit,' spat the officer. 'We keep the wheels of Nazi Germany turning, while you swan about and take all the credit, and every time, on your return, we have to honour you at dinners like these. It makes me sick. I don't care who your mother and father are.' He took his jacket off and let it fall to the floor. He pulled a heavy handled field knife from inside his leather boot. 'I think a bit more facial surgery would suit you, boy.'

Percy kept his palms facing forwards, and his eyes followed the knife as the armed man crouch lower and switched his blade from hand to hand. Percy waited for him to get closer. Each half-step brought his attacker into his arc.

'I'm going to gut you, boy.'

With lightning speed, Percy grabbed the handle of the knife, pulled and twisted. He thought about Mandy, the trawlermen, her speed, her brilliance. He heard her voice and felt her presence. Percy snatched the brute's weapon, then turned and rammed the knife deep into the tabletop.

Silence.

The officer stared open-mouthed at his empty hands, then looked at his knife buried deep into the wooden table.

'Good night gentlemen,' said Percy.

Silence.

Percy joined Nicole outside. The smoke from the night-club swirled out of the door behind him, into the freezing night air.

'They let you go?'

'In a manner of speaking, yes.' He checked his watch, fifteen minutes before six. 'How long will it take to get to Rosie's from here?'

'Thirty minutes, forty in this weather,' said Nicole, her breath steamed as she panted.

Florence would leave at six sharp, not a minute later. Percy knew he wouldn't make the departure time, and Mandy would have to go on without him. He tapped with his thumb from Gestapo HQ that he loved her. She would never forget. He knew that, too.

Nicole stopped running, 'I'll need to change,' she opened her coat to expose her lace bra.

'Is that a French thing, you know, to rip your shirt open like that?'

'You English don't understand the desires of a Frenchwoman.'

'Let's get to Rosie's apartment, with luck, they may have delayed their departure, and then you can get suitably dressed.'

Mandy didn't want to leave.

She looked through a tiny gap in Rosie's curtains at the quiet, snow-covered street below. There was no sign of Percy. He wasn't going to make it. She stared at the minute hand of her watch, praying for time to stop.

'Time to go,' said Florence.

'Can we give it another minute?'

'No, if he's missed the deadline, he knows we won't be hanging around for him.'

Florence was right.

Mandy knew she might not see Percy for weeks, or ever again. She looked at Rosie and attempted to get an alliance. None came, Rosie was in cold mission mode. It was like looking at Alice.

Mandy tore herself away from her window vigil. She stepped out of the apartment and down the stairs and followed Florence and Rosie into the back yard.

Florence stamped her feet in the snow. 'Rosie, take us five

miles west, and out of the city. We've got an hour of darkness left to offer us decent cover. Come on, girls, straighten your Nazi armbands and run.' Florence looked at Mandy; there was no hint of resentment.

Rosie ran out of the yard and into the rabbit warren of Berlin's backstreets and alleyways. They ran fast, in sync to minimise the sound of their footsteps.

After an hour and a half of arduous snow running, they were five miles out of Berlin. Rosie led them behind an office block. They put their hands on their knees, puffing and panting, and drew in lungfuls of the fresh morning air.

'Mandy, a vehicle, please. No tanks!' said Florence.

'Admit it. You loved that tank.'

'Tank?' Asked Rosie.

'A long story, but one thing's for sure when it comes to vehicle theft, there is nobody better than Mandy. After the war, I'll have my hands full keeping her out of prison.'

Fifteen minutes later they heard a revving engine, and Mandy reappeared behind the office block.

Florence said, 'We have two hundred miles to travel in the snow and ice, and you bring that? Are you mad?'

'I think it's rather cute,' said Rosie.

Florence looked at Rosie, 'That's good because you two clowns are in the side-car.'

Florence sat on the motorbike while Mandy and Rosie clambered into the side-car and made themselves warm and comfortable.

'Chocks away,' yelled Mandy. Rosie screamed with laughter and flung her arm out to indicate a right turn.

Florence turned the bike and side-car in a tight circle on the ice, and they snaked and skidded their way out of the office yard and onto the main road heading away from Berlin.

Rosie sat in the back of the side-car and leaned towards

Mandy. She shouted above the wind noise, 'Nicole will get Percy safely to England. He is in safe hands, and she'll take great care of him.'

'Who the bloody hell is Nicole?' Mandy said.

Florence looked across, 'You mean the gorgeous, sexy, French nightclub singer; the one with the husky voice and curvy body?'

'Yes, that one,' said Rosie.

'Oh, that's not good,' said Florence.

Mandy yelled, 'Turn this thing around and get me back to Berlin. We can't leave Percy in the hands of some French tart.'

Florence and Rosie's tears of laughter froze on their faces.

CHAPTER 31

Percy and Nicole ran up the staircase of Rosie's apartment block and stood panting on the landing. Percy tapped on the door. No answer. Mandy and Florence had gone.

'I have a key,' said Nicole.

Percy stood in the empty apartment, and breathed Mandy in; it was the last place she had been. He took a few steps in silence then sat on the bed, looking utterly defeated.

Nicole, without warning, and with great speed, took off her fur coat and lace bra. Percy caught unawares, made polite coughing sounds and gazed anywhere other than at her nakedness.

'An icy winter we have this year,' he said.

Nicole dressed in a warm black combat suit, complete with a red Nazi armband and then laced up her boots. With a simple twirl, she tied her hair in a ponytail and wore a black woollen hat.

'Voila!' Nicole reached under the bed, 'Rosie and I leave coded messages for each other; she boasted that you could crack any code.'

'Well, I have my moments.'

Nicole lifted the floorboard and handed it to Percy. There was a scribbled chalk message containing numbers and letters on the underside and a love heart with the initials MM. Percy spent a minute looking at the code.

He said, 'Do you know this airfield?'

'Yes, it's just inside the German border. It's a long way, so we'll need to take Rosie's motorbike.'

'I should get changed.' He waited for Nicole to look away. She didn't. He repeated, 'Nicole, I need to change.'

'That's nice,' she said.

'You're going to watch, aren't you?'

'Yes, I'm French.'

Percy changed into the German uniform Rosie had left for him. He tried his best to remove the lipstick from his shirt, but smudged it and made it worse.

Nicole collected a handful of grenades, a pocketful of ammunition, and slung Rosie's sniper rifle across her back. She watched Percy tucking his shirt into his trousers.

'Can you ride a motorbike?' she asked.

'Yes, can you?'

'I'm in Rosie's resistance group. I have no choice.'

Outside, the snow settled like icing sugar and covered Berlin's rooftops and pavements, bike saddles and gate posts. Percy dragged Rosie's motorbike out from behind the wooden door and stood heavily on the kick-starter. The engine spluttered as it drew in cold air; on the third kick, the engine roared to life.

'It's an Alice special. She's my idol,' said Nicole. 'Who would think a little old woman from England, with thick curly hair, dressed in tweed, could be so deadly. I once saw her kill three German soldiers by swinging an onion, stuffed down a sock, at them. It's going to be slow going in this snow, so expect an all day and all night ride.'

Percy rode, and Nicole shouted directions into his ear. After three hours of treacherous riding, it was time to switch places. He left the road and headed for cover under a small footbridge. They groaned as they stretched their frozen arms and legs, and rubbed their stiff limbs with vigour to get the circulation going. The snow continued to fall.

'Hot coffee?' she said.

'I'd love some. Where from?'

'I'll be back in a few minutes.' Nicole ran up the bank and headed for a cluster of little houses. Twenty minutes later she returned with two cups of steaming black coffee and a couple of cheese sandwiches.

'How did...'

'It's worth remembering that not all Germans are Nazis. Here, drink this.'

Percy cupped his hands around the coffee cup and bit into the cheese sandwich. 'This is the best thing I've ever eaten.'

'Rosie told me you'd fallen madly in love with Mandy, Florence's best girl. That sounds so romantic.'

He blushed, 'Yes, I have rather, and it was entirely unexpected. Are there no secrets?'

'We're spies. You can't hide a thing from us.'

She took the cups back to the house and returned with a freshly baked slice of sponge.

Percy took a bite, and his eyes rolled in wonderment. His thoughts turned, as ever, to Mandy.

'I'm bloody cold, and I can't move,' said Mandy.

Florence tutted, 'Serves you right. Who in their right mind steals a motorbike with sidecar in the middle of winter during a blizzard?'

'She's an idiot,' added Rosie.

Mandy elbowed Rosie in the ribs, 'How far to the train station?'

'Fifteen minutes,' said Florence. 'We'll dump this ridiculous contraption of yours half a mile out, and walk the rest. Hopefully, a cafe will be open at the station, so we can get a cup of tea and warm up a bit.'

They searched for a place, and Florence spotted a small garage. She brought the motorbike to a slippery standstill out of sight from the main road. They grabbed their packs and walked to the station.

Florence went on ahead to purchase tickets; she returned half an hour later, and said, 'The train pulls in at four o'clock, but it stops at every station in the world. We'll arrive after seven this evening.'

'I can't wait to see my mum,' said Rosie. It had been a long time since she was in England. For her to be stationed in Berlin before the outbreak of war meant she had stayed there for several years. They stepped into a waiting room on the platform. It was wasn't heated, but it was dry.

'I'll find us a cup of tea,' said Mandy.

Christopher Barrington sat in his chambers, in the House of Commons. The last forty years of careful, political navigation had brought him to the pinnacle of power.

A leadership vote, by members of the conservative party, was scheduled for midday on Wednesday. Following the vote, His Majesty, King George VI, would invite the new leader to form a Government on behalf of the Monarchy. Barrington swivelled in his leather chair and thought about the victorious days which lay ahead. As Prime Minister, and with total governance, he could oversee a decisive end to the war. He could write his own history and his country's history.

There was a rap at the door.

'Enter.'

Sir Henry walked into Barrington's chamber.

'Thank you for coming, Sir Henry. It was good of you to come so urgently, especially on a Sunday afternoon in this dreadful weather. And, oh look, how lovely, you brought your dog.'

On cue, Rags barked.

Barrington leaned back in his chair and said with an almost undetectable dab of smugness on his face, but it was there, 'On Wednesday, our party members will be casting their vote in the final ballot to elect a new leader.'

'No doubt, you feel somewhat certain about the outcome.'

'You're aware, Sir Henry, the majority of members, have already voiced their support for me to become the next Prime Minister.'

'Then let me be the first to offer my heartiest congratulations.'

'And, Sir Henry, as the incoming Prime Minister, and out of courtesy, I wish to give you a few days notice.'

'Notice?'

'Notice of my new Intelligence Service, and a service which will operate without you. I want you to vacate your offices, at Horse Guards Parade, by twelve-thirty on Wednesday afternoon. I want you gone, I want Florence gone, and I want Alice gone. I want the lot of you gone by the time I get back.'

'How about Rags?'

'Especially your damn dog, Do I make myself clear?'

'Oh yes, quite clear, Barrington, crystal clear.'

'The new Intelligence Service will come under my control. There will be no place for the old school-tie network routine. No more friends of friends, or Churchill's favoured few, and no more creeping about in the shadows.

And no more decrepit spies lurking on select committees doing nothing other than slowing down, or overturning my decisions.'

Sir Henry stood and tucked his chair neatly under Barrington's wooden desk, 'I only have one question.'

'Yes, what is it?'

'Do you have any spare boxes for the packing?'

'Get out!'

Sir Henry marched out of Parliament and drove to Morpeth Terrace. He knocked on Churchill's front door.

Mrs Amos welcomed him and Rags inside.

'I'm afraid we have snow on our feet.'

She ushered him through to Churchill's study, and Rags followed Mrs Amos through to the kitchen.

Sir Henry warmed his hands by the fireplace, and Winston waited for Sir Henry to speak until impatience finally got the better of him. 'Out with it, Henry.'

'I'm bursting with rage. I've never been so angry.'

'Nobody would know.'

'I was summonsed, like a naughty schoolboy, to Barrington's chamber. That irritant of a man sat there, looked me dead in the eye, and told me I was fired from the Intelligence Service.'

'Barrington's confident he's going to win on Wednesday,' said Churchill.

'I imagine his Saville Row tailor is making him a new suit for his audience with the King.'

'Confidence is vital; necessary in fact. However, over confidence is often fatal. Henry, we need to ensure he's wrapped up in writing his acceptance speech, and not paying attention to the dark horse galloping up on the inside track.'

'And you're the dark horse.'

'Precisely,' said Churchill. He ambled over to the fireplace and stood next to Sir Henry and warmed his hands. A note of seriousness filtered through his voice. 'Henry, if I lose the final ballot on Wednesday, it's over for me. A loss will spell the end of my career in politics.'

'Britain needs you, Winston. Your life experiences have delivered you to this moment in time. This war, Germany, Hitler, this moment is your destiny, my dear friend.'

They stood in silence. The log fire crackled and popped. Rags bounded into the study, followed by Mrs Amos carrying a tray.

She said, 'I thought you might like a slice of my freshly baked Dundee fruit cake and a nice cup of tea.'

'Ooh lovely,' they said and rubbed their hands together.

Percy and Nicole made slow progress. The snow made speeding an impossibility. The constant stopping and dismounting to dig clumps of snow from the wheel arches was tiring. Combined with the howling blizzard in their faces; it made for an unpleasant ride. They weren't going to make the rendezvous by nightfall. They were still three hours from the airfield, and the conditions were worsening.

Nicole tapped him on the shoulder, 'There's a turning up ahead which leads to a small village. We can get warm and sleep for an hour or two.'

A warm orange glow shone from a row of little cottages in a snow-covered hamlet. The scene was not dissimilar from the row of cottages on England's coast, which was Percy's last view of home from the trawler.

They stepped off the bike, aching and frozen, and opened the back door to a cottage. They stepped into the dark kitchen and were attracted to the heat from the wood-burning stove like moths to a lamp.

'Stay where you are!' demanded a female voice. 'I have

both barrels loaded and pointed at you. I won't miss from here.'

'It's me, Nicole.'

The light pinged on.

Percy stared into the business end of a shotgun. A young woman in a nightdress held the other end.

'Who's this?' said the lady.

'He's with me,' said Nicole. 'I'm helping him get back to England.'

The lady placed the shotgun on the wooden beam above her head, then ran to Nicole and gave her a long welcoming hug.

'You're colder than ice,' she said in french. 'Come on through. I'll build a fire up in the front room.'

'We don't have long,' said Nicole.

'Are you opening the escape route?'

'No, not yet, this is a one-off. After I drop Percy, I'll come back to see you.'

'I'll make you a coffee.' She wandered off to the kitchen. Percy and Nicole warmed their hands in the fireplace.

Percy asked, 'Who's she?'

'You know I told you about Otto Flack killing my father?'

'Yes, awful bloody business,' he said.

'Flack also shot her father that day. We became sisters, connected through grief and sadness. The hatred we have for Flack never goes away. She became part of the resistance and wanted to serve. Rosie and I moved her from France to inside the German border, and she's setting up a network to help airmen escape back to England.'

'She's brave,' he said.

The lady came into the room and put the tray down, 'I'm not brave. I'm driven by revenge, and I'll do anything to defeat the Germans.'

Nicole explained how Otto Flack died on the beach and

how Percy helped bury him in a shallow grave. Percy filled in more details, and as he spoke, he saw comfort grow in the eyes of the lady who lost her father to German brutality.

The train pulled into the small station. The daylight had gone, and the evening brought fresh snow flurries.

Florence stood and picked up her pack, 'We can walk to the airfield from here, it will take about an hour.'

'Can't I go and steal something warm to drive?' said Mandy.

'Nothing with a sidecar,' said Rosie

'We can't leave any trace of us being here,' said Florence. 'It's not far, you youngsters have no stamina.'

The three of them quick-marched the four miles to the airfield. The conditions worsened.

Rosie said, 'Will mum be able to land Hesberus in the morning? It could be a foot deep by the time she's ready to touch down.'

'Alice can land Hesberus in any weather, and whistle a tune while doing it,' said Florence. 'I've seen your mum land in someone's rose garden, in thick fog, without damaging a single petal.'

'Would it be safer to delay for a day?' said Rosie.

Florence snapped, 'No, we must get back. The Luftwaffe could be carpet bombing the living hell out of the twenty-one Spitfire locations on Tuesday night. We have to be back to prepare. We can't delay our return.'

They walked the last mile in silence. The small airfield peeped into view: a hangar and two smaller buildings silhouetted against the greying sky. A tall, bushy hedgerow ringed the airfield. Florence pushed open the wooden gate, and with a sigh of relief, they walked towards the buildings.

Four German soldiers hid out of sight behind the gate

with their rifles raised and waited for the three women to walk past.

'Halt!' they shouted.

'Sorry, girls' whispered Florence. 'I lost my concentration.'

Mandy tutted, 'What are you talking about? The three of us against these old windbags, it's hardly a fair fight is it?' Her fists clenched in defiance.

'Yes, but not here, and not now. Stand down, the pair of you.'

The soldiers kept their rifles trained on the women. The officer, a skinny man with pencil-thin lips, stepped in front of Florence; the whiff of stale cigarettes and coffee was accentuated in the pure air.

He sneered, 'You wear the Fuhrer's armband, and yet you speak English. Explain yourself.'

Rosie put her arms around Mandy, 'We're trying to teach our uncouth friend here some basic words. Poor thing, her English is so abysmal, some would say it's guttural and cheap.'

'Where are you from?' asked thin-lips.

'Berlin Intelligence,' replied Florence.

'What are you doing near the border?'

'I can't tell you that.'

'You can, and you will.'

'I can't, and I won't.'

He looked them up and down, 'Lock them in the hangar while I find out who they are.'

The soldiers prodded the girls with their rifles and herded them across the airfield towards the hangar. One of them ran ahead to crank the handle and open the hangar doors. They pushed the girls inside at gunpoint.

A square office in the corner of the hangar made a convenient makeshift jail. The soldiers confiscated the backpacks, weapons and ammunition. Rosie offered up her sports bag for inspection, but following a quick rummage, the soldier let her keep it.

A dim yellow lightbulb hung from the ceiling and cast an eerie shadow around the walls. The office was sparsely kitted out, two wooden chairs, a desk and a cabinet. The wind blew through tiny cracks in a boarded-up window.

The soldiers chatted outside the office jail. They were too far away to be overheard, the thin-lipped officer's body language suggested he hadn't been able to make contact with Berlin.

'Are you ready to fight?' asked Florence.

Mandy nodded.

'Rosie, send a message to your mum when you see the first punch land. Say we are being held prisoner by four guards in the corner of the hangar and we need stealth assistance.'

Florence knocked on the office door and attracted the attention of one of the soldiers.

He poked his head inside the door brandishing his rifle.

'May I use the toilet?' she asked.

'No.'

'No what?'

'No, you can't,' he said.

Mandy pushed herself past Florence. 'Listen up buttercup. I'm on Hitler's private staff, and once your pissy-faced officer figures out who we are, I'll ask the Fuhrer himself to have you sent to some shithole to be used as cannon fodder. So open this door before I pee my pants.'

The soldiers briefly chatted before they unlocked the door.

Mandy and Florence dug into their back pockets and wrapped a length of bike chain around their knuckles while

Rosie positioned herself out of sight to send her mum the message.

'There's a bucket over there,' said Thin-lips, pointing to the far corner.

'Get stuffed sunshine,' said Mandy. 'I'm not peeing in a bucket with you lot watching.'

'You'll do as you're told. . .'

Thin-lips didn't see Mandy's punch. She hit him as if cracking a whip, catching him full in the face. Florence kicked the soldier standing next to her between his legs. He let out a grizzly cry and crumpled to the floor holding his groin. She kicked him once more, this time in the gut.

Two gunshots, from the other soldiers, ripped through the air of the hangar. The fighting stopped.

'Get them back in there,' screamed Thin-lips as blood dripped from his mouth.

'I still need to pee,' said Mandy.

CHAPTER 32

Alice ran along the hallway to Lizzie's room and pushed the door open. 'Are you ready for an all-nighter?'

'Yes, why, what's up?'

'I've just heard from Rosie. Get dressed and follow me.' They ran downstairs and into the ops room.

'What's happening?' Lizzie asked.

'The girls have been captured.'

Alice took a length of rubber tubing, a roll of sticky tape and an oxygen cylinder out of a cupboard drawer. 'Lizzie, I need you to find a mask that will cover my nose and mouth. There's one in the garage.'

Lizzie ran out through the entrance hall of Milton Park, and across the gravel driveway. Her breath steamed in the freezing garage block, as she rummaged through boxes and found three masks. She ran back to the ops room.

Alice picked up two of them, 'These are too small, but this one is perfect.' Alice put the mask over her face.

'What's it for?'

'Have you ever heard of high altitude parachuting?'

'No.'

'Nor has anybody else,' said Alice. 'Tonight I'm going to do something quite exciting. Well, it's probably more dangerous than exciting. When I say dangerous, I mean possibly deadly. Anyway, these things need testing first, and I've been waiting to try out this idea for ages.'

Alice laid out the items on a table. She used the sticky tape to fix one end of the tubing to the mask, and screwed a clamp around the other end, then attached it to the oxygen cylinder.

'Put this on and breath normally,' said Alice.

Lizzie placed the mask over her mouth and nose and breathed. After thirty-seconds, her eyes rolled, then closed. She lost her balance and fell over the desktop. Alice pulled the mask off and slapped her face.

Lizzie came around, 'What happened?'

'The mixture was a little rich.' Alice fiddled with the small brass wheel and made a slight adjustment. 'Try it now.'

'Did you just slap me around the face?'

'No, I shouldn't think so,' said Alice. She bound more sticky tape to the tube, 'Let's try it again.'

'Is it safe?' Lizzie asked.

'How will we ever know unless you try it?' She pushed the mask back over Lizzie's face. 'Now breath normally, nice and easy. That's it, you've got it.'

After a few minutes of regular breathing, Lizzie gave Alice the thumbs-up, 'Why high altitude?'

'Rosie messaged that we need to use stealth. I can hardly mount a full-scale attack if the guards hear Hesberus approaching.'

'When you say full-scale attack, who else is going in with us?'

'Not us, me,' said Alice.

'That's hardly full-scale, is it?'

'It is if they don't know I'm coming.'

Alice laid out her arsenal of pistols, grenades, a field knife, a packet of cigarettes, and a sniper rifle, on the table. Alice didn't look like a soldier; she didn't even look like a spy. Alice looked like someone's granny preparing to go to church. And that was Alice's unique power.

She said, 'I'm going to jump in the dark, from above the clouds. I'll open my chute late, and steer myself into the corner of the airfield. I'll take out the guards, free the girls, signal you with a red flare, then we can all fly home for bacon and eggs.'

'And the mask and cylinder?'

'The air is pretty thin up there, so I'll need my own oxygen supply, or I'll pass out on the way down. No different from a frogman going underwater. It's the same principle.'

'Has it been tested?' asked Lizzie.

'Apart from your fainting episode, no.'

Alice strapped a pistol to each thigh, put the rifle across her chest, and a grenade in each of her four jacket pockets.

'How do I look?'

Lizzie was lost for words, 'Unusual?'

'We leave in ten minutes. Wheels up at two in the morning. I'll scribble a note for Sir Henry to tell him we'll be late back for breakfast.'

Lizzie scurried to the garage and fired up the Jaguar. She reversed onto the snow-covered driveway, and the engine burbled beautifully in the freezing midnight air.

Alice jumped in, 'I telephoned ahead to the airfield and told Bertie about my high altitude idea.'

'What did he say?'

'He said, I was mad.'

'What did you say?'

'I agreed with him. Come on, Lizzie, wagons roll.'

Lizzie raced the Jaguar out of Milton Park and around the lanes to the airfield. A biting crosswind flicked up flurries of snow across the runway. Lizzie parked close to Hesberus and loaded the equipment through the side door. They took their seats behind Bertie, who with bleary eyes, carried out a speedy pre-flight check.

'Wheels up in five,' he said.

'Smashing, what time will we be over the coordinates?' asked Alice.

'Before light, at about five-fifteen, although it depends on the wind strength over the channel.'

'Bertie, once I've jumped, I need you to buzz off and keep Hesberus out of sight. Fly at low-level in wide circles around the airfield. Lizzie will be looking out for my red flare. Land once you see my smoke and provide covering fire. Then fly us home. Understood?'

'Jump, buzz off, circle, red flare, land, covering fire, and fly home,' said Bertie.

Hesberus's engines quickly warmed up, and Bertie released the brakes. The wheels bumped across the icy runway and Hesberus, like a graceless potting shed, lifted effortlessly into the dark sky. Above the vibrations and drama, Lizzie noted how easily Bertie handled Hesberus.

Alice said, 'Bertie was an ace in the First War, and he's an old pilot friend of Sir Henry. He loves Hesberus as much as we do. I caught him talking to her once; the silly old sausage.'

Lizzie looked Alice up and down, 'I had no idea you could get tweed trousers for women.'

'You can't. These beauties are men's trousers.'

'What's your plan?'

'I'm going to pull the ripcord as late as possible, which might allow me to get the jump on them.'

'It could be dangerous.'

'At the very least, it will be dangerous,' said Alice.

'Alice, maybe I should go instead of you.'

'Lizzie, you're looking at a sixty-four-year-old woman

dressed in a three-piece, tweed suit and a pair of sturdy brogues. I have thick curly hair that I can't do a thing with, who on earth will suspect me?'

Lizzie smiled. Alice truly was a one-woman fighting force.

'Your time will come soon enough,' said Alice.

Bertie leaned through the seats and gave them the ten-minute signal. Hesberus climbed and soared above the clouds, and its engines laboured in the high altitude thin air. Alice looked through the small porthole window. There was nothing to see beyond Hesberus's wing; she'd be jumping into the dark unknown. Nothing new, but this was different, this was untested.

'Scared?' asked Lizzie.

'Being scared is the best part.'

Bertie called out, his voice was soft, yet commanding, 'Alice, jump zone approaching in two minutes. Lizzie put your safety harness on, and open the trap door.'

Alice put on her oxygen mask and took a few deep breaths. She counted to ten to check she wouldn't faint. A green light flashed above her head, and she sat on the side of the trap door. Without hesitation, she jumped into the dark abyss.

Lizzie looked through the opening into the buffeting wind, but Alice had swooped out of sight. She closed the door, clambered into the navigator's seat next to Bertie, and sat in silence.

Bertie snorted through his nose, 'Don't worry about Alice, she's made of steel.' He dropped altitude and flew Hesberus into a pattern of wide, slow circles.

Florence sat between Mandy and Rosie in the unheated office, in the corner of the hangar. To give Alice a fighting chance, they needed to wear the soldiers down, and not let them sleep. Florence tapped on the office door.

One of the soldiers walked over with his pistol drawn.

'I need to use the bucket.' She crossed one leg over the other and bit her lip.

'No funny business this time.' He waved his gun and beckoned her to follow him. He pointed to the bucket, 'Don't take all night about it!'

Florence undid her combat suit and sat on the bucket and forced herself to go. The soldier stood over her.

She said, 'I want to talk with the senior officer.'

'He's busy.'

'I'll wait,' she said. The soldier prodded his pistol in her back and marched her towards the office. Florence stopped and turned, 'Tell the officer about the blond-haired girl you've taken prisoner.' He pushed Florence inside the office and locked the door.

The thin-lipped officer walked over and stood by the office door. He pointed at Mandy, 'Who's she?'

'Edith Flack,' said Florence.

He looked blank, 'Who?'

'She's the sister of Otto Flack, from the Flack family.'

Thin lips offered no flicker of recognition.

'Oh come on, you must have heard of the Flacks. They are the most influential and powerful family in Berlin. Flack senior created the deep-sleeper spy programme, and the mother has raised more funds for the Nazi party than anyone in Germany.'

'Clearly, I don't move in your lofty social circles,' he snapped.

'How about Max Ernst Bauer?'

'Everyone knows, Bauer, the famous industrialist.'

Florence said, 'Ask him to describe Edith Flack. She was with him all day yesterday.'

'Do you think I can just call him and ask him?'

'No, but you can contact your command post, and they'll contact Berlin, and ask Bauer.'

'I'll think about it,' he said.

'Think faster then,' chipped in Mandy. 'When Bauer hears that you've locked me up, you'll face a firing squad.'

Thin-lips looked at his watch. It was nearly five o'clock in the morning. He left the office and stood by the hangar's entrance doors. He said to his soldiers. 'Call the command post and request reinforcements immediately.'

Rosie whispered, 'Do you think he believed us?'

'No, he wasn't buying anything I told him. He's more than likely calling for back up.'

Mandy rapped her knuckles on the office door and yelled out, 'Hey, I need to use the bucket.'

Alice took slow, deep breaths through her oxygen mask, as she hurtled, head first towards the airfield. Her arms were flat to her side, and she squinted her eyes through her goggles, trying to get her bearings. The clouds cleared, and Alice saw the outline of the hangar.

She pulled the ripcord.

Her parachute unravelled, twisted, and then ballooned open above her head. The harsh jolt was like hitting a brick wall. Alice yanked the oxygen mask and goggles from her face and began pulling on the steering cords. The ground rushed up at her, twenty yards, fifteen, ten, five.

Thud.

Alice landed in a knee-deep snowdrift and performed a forward roll, then crouched on one knee with her pistols drawn. She listened for gunfire, soldiers running, whistles, vehicles, sirens; anything.

But all was quiet.

She untucked her tweed trousers from her socks and scanned the airfield. It was first light. She hunched over, ran around the edge of the airfield, and made her way towards the hangar.

To prepare for war, soldiers train to fight other soldiers. Little, if any training is done to fight a woman. Especially an older woman dressed in tweed.

Alice crawled through the snow and reached the far corner of the hangar. She skirted the building. Two soldiers stood guard by the double doors. She took her oxygen cylinder and strapped a grenade to it using the sticky tape. She pulled the pin and leaned the make-shift bomb against the corner of the hangar with a steady hand. She lit a cigarette and stuck it behind the tape, and then ran behind the hedgerow and took up a position out of sight. She estimated she had two minutes before the cigarette burnt through the tape and set off the grenade.

Alice looked through the telescopic sights and watched the two guards smoking and chatting. They looked tired. It had been a long night. Good girls, she thought. Alice controlled her breathing and zoomed in on the grenade. The cigarette glowed in the early morning breeze and burnt through the tape.

The explosion ripped through the airfield. One of the guards sprinted to the corner of the hangar to investigate the blast. As he bent over to examine the tangled metal in the hangar wall, Alice fired one shot, and he crumpled to the ground, face down, dead in the snow. The second guard jumped inside the hangar and closed the doors.

Inside the locked office, Florence said, 'Alice has arrived. Mandy, pick the lock.'

Mandy pulled two specially designed grips from her hair and slipped them silently into the lock. She put her ear to the door and heard a click.

A soldier ran across the hangar and shouted, 'Franz is dead.'

Alice knelt and tapped on the metal pipe that protruded from the corner of the hangar, with her knife.

Four fast taps, followed by four slow taps, it was Alice's identity code. She put her ear to the pipe and heard, two fast taps, two slow taps.

She'd found Florence.

'Alice is outside,' said Florence. The pipe tapping continued, 'She's going to mount a full-scale assault during the blackout. We need make-shift weapons, table legs, glass shards; the standard stuff.'

Alice wound the crank handle, and the hangar doors opened a few feet. The guards sprayed bursts of gunfire. Alice wedged a grenade inside the electric cable junction box and pulled the pin, and took cover.

Darkness followed the blast, and in the confusion, Alice slipped through the doors and took up a position behind a workbench.

Thin-lips barked his orders, and two soldiers searched the hangar with their flashlights. As they approached the workbench, Alice kicked a half-full bucket at them, and they started firing at it. Alice rolled on the floor between them and sprang up with her pistols pointed at their temples.

They didn't move.

Florence heard the action unfold, and she burst through the office door and threw a fractured chair leg at Thin-lips. The improvised weapon smacked him in the face, and he yelled out, cursing. Mandy and Rosie sprinted after Florence.

Thin-lips lashed out and punched Rosie in the stomach. She fought through the pain, rammed her fingers into his eyes, and then chopped her hand into his windpipe. Mandy kicked him between the legs.

He fell to his knees, holding his groin and throat, and his face bled heavily.

'May I?' said Rosie.

'Be my guest.' Mandy grabbed his collar and lifted his face upwards. Rosie forced her knee into his chin, and he fell to the ground; he didn't make another sound.

Alice marched her two soldiers over to meet Florence.

'Morning, Alice.'

'It's rather chilly for the time of year.'

'It is a bit,' said Florence.

'I overpowered these chumps with a bucket of water.' Florence winced at the thought. She took the soldiers from Alice and bound them alongside their motionless officer.

Alice ran outside and shot the red flare into the early morning sky. A few minutes later, she heard the reassuring sound of Hesberus's engines making its final approach. She ran back into the hangar.

'Hesberus is landing. We need to go.'

'Hello, Mum,' said Rosie.

'Rosie, my darling, let's do kisses once we're on board.'

The four of them walked out onto the snow-covered airfield and watched Hesberus touch down in the snow.

'What a wonderful sight,' said Florence. 'We made it. Job well done, girls.'

CHAPTER 33

Daylight had broken. An even white dusting of untouched snow lay across the remote German countryside, and ice crystals in the hedgerows sparkled with the first rays of sunlight.

Percy shouted to Nicole over the noise of the motorbike, 'What are the chances Florence will wait for us at the airfield?'

'It's gone six, so slim to none.'

Nicole knew Florence never did late exits. She held tightly around Percy's waist as he leant over the handlebars to make them as streamlined as possible. She pressed against him to keep warm knowing he was about to face disappointment.

Percy skilfully pushed the machine to its maximum speed; if Mandy were already onboard Hesberus, he would have to make alternative plans to get back to England. A wave of sadness tugged at his heart, and his hands were red-raw, but the thought of Mandy in his arms kept him going.

. . .

Florence stood with her team on the edge of the runway and watched Bertie position Hesberus ready for a speedy take-off.

'Alice, I like your tweed trousers.'

'Would you like a pair?'

'Not while I'm alive,' said Florence.

Alice turned to Mandy, 'Would. . .'

'Not while I can still bear children.'

'Rosie, my darling, how about. . .'

'No Mum, in Berlin they'd shoot me for wearing tweed trousers, I couldn't look more English if I tried.'

'These tweed trousers just saved your rather ungrateful lives.'

Alice pointed to the hangar, 'What do you want to do with those chumps in there?'

'We'll take them back to England and find out what they know.'

'Or I could shoot them,' said Alice reaching for her leg-pistol.

'That's hardly British, is it?' She indicated to Mandy and Rosie to collect the German soldiers. They ran into the hangar.

Mandy kicked the soles of the soldiers' boots, 'Come on you losers, get outside. You're coming to England for a little holiday. Call yourself the master race? You're pathetic. You wouldn't last five minutes in Battersea.'

Thin-lips lifted his head to speak. Mandy slapped his face, 'Best you keep your mouth shut sunshine. We don't want to listen to your Fatherland nonsense all the way home.'

The defeated soldiers walked at gunpoint, out of the hangar, and onto the airfield. Hesberus's propellers chopped into the cold air and blew fresh flurries of snow into their faces.

Lizzie jumped out to help the girls on board. She grabbed the equipment and backpacks, then took a final look around the airfield and clambered back into the aircraft.

Florence pulled the door shut.

'Get us out of here, Bertie.'

'Aren't we going to wait for Percy?' asked Mandy. She looked out of the porthole, her eyes frantically scanned the white world for her love.

'We'll wait five minutes, then we go,' said Florence.

Rosie tied the soldiers to the aircraft struts, 'One complaint from you and I'll push you lot out over the Channel.'

Alice nudged Florence and pulled Sir Henry's white silk scarf from her pocket. Florence wrapped it around her neck and nestled her chin into the silk. All the while, Hesberus's engines rumbled comfortably waiting for take-off. Florence allowed herself a moment of solace.

One bullet, then another pinged off Hesberus's fuselage, followed by shattering machine gunfire bursts that ripped through the side of the aircraft. Thin-lips and his soldiers took the full force from the first wave of bullets. Their blood splattered across the insides of Hesberus.

'Hit the deck. Get down!' shouted Florence. Another burst of bullets ripped into the side of the plane. Florence raised her head and peeped out of the porthole.

'What can you see?' said Alice.

'An armoured vehicle and four soldiers. Bertie, get this crate off the ground before they cut us in half. You'll have to go to the other end of the runway because they're blocking our way.'

Bertie began to manoeuvre Hesberus into position.

Florence pulled the dead soldiers out of the way and opened the side door a few inches. She poked her machine gun through the crack and squirted off a few bursts. Alice lay flat on the floor and fired, while Rosie, Mandy and Lizzie took potshots at the armoured vehicle with their rifles.

The propellers screamed from the effort demanded by Bertie. He pulled Hesberus through a tight circle in readiness for take-off. A line of bullets shattered the glass in the cockpit and hit Bertie.

He called out, 'Alice, I need you up here.'

Alice clambered over the dead soldiers and slipped into the navigator's seat. She placed her hand on the levers to assist with take-off.

A roof-mounted machine gun, on the armoured vehicle, spat out a volley of high-velocity bullets. Each bullet pierced Hesberus, creating bright beams of sunlight, crisscrossing through the dusty darkness.

Florence shouted above the din of gunfire and ricocheting bullets, 'Wait, Bertie! I'm jumping out. We'll never get airborne under this attack.'

'I'm coming with you,' said Mandy.

Florence looked at Lizzie and Rosie, 'Give us covering fire when we jump out, four-second bursts, got it?'

Rosie opened the side door a few inches wider and began spraying machine-gun fire into the German vehicle. Florence and Mandy slithered through the trap door onto the snow, and the German soldiers, in the armoured vehicle, continued their relentless barrage.

Florence said, 'I'll go left; you go right. Look for a hollow and keep your head down. Much more of this, and we won't have enough of Hesberus left to fly us home.'

Percy peeled away the last few miles to the airfield. The snow-draped villages became white blurs in his peripheral vision.

'I can hear gunfire coming from the airfield, hold on

tightly,' he yelled.

Nicole reached under the saddle, unclipped the sniper rifle, placed the barrel on Percy's shoulder and looked through the telescopic sights. She kept her balance by gripping Percy tightly with her knees. They entered the airfield. The armoured vehicle was parked in the middle of the airfield and fired bullets at the stranded aircraft.

She tapped Percy's shoulder, 'Get me closer.'

He held out his hand, 'Grenade please, let's shake the living daylights out of them.'

Florence kept her head down and crawled left of the vehicle, and Mandy crawled to the right; in a pincer movement. They had one chance to take out the roof-top machine-gunner with a clean shot.

Mandy pushed the snow away with one arm and dragged herself along with the other. She burrowed as deep as she could and peered over the lip of her hollow. She nestled her rifle on a mound of snow and zoomed in on the soldier who fired a platoon's worth of bullets from the vehicle.

Mandy had his head in her crosshairs. She placed her finger on the trigger and held her breath. The second before she fired, he slumped over, dead. Mandy looked at Florence in her snow hollow, and they both shrugged their shoulders.

Mandy lined up the next soldier in her sights. Before she fired, he twisted like a rag doll and fell backwards in a red haze, dead. Like inquisitive meerkats, Mandy and Florence popped their heads above the snow ridge to see who was cutting down their prey with pinpoint accuracy. Mandy zoomed her scope onto a motorbike fifty yards behind the vehicle.

Then she saw him.

'Percy!' Her hot breath steamed off the snow, 'My darling Percy, you're just in time.' Percy pulled the pin from a grenade and threw it towards the armoured vehicle. The explosion of snow and dirt grabbed the attention of the remaining two soldiers.

Nicole, still perched on the back of the advancing motorbike, took aim, and fired. The third soldier's chest took the full impact. The last soldier was more resourceful than his three comrades; he jumped into the driving seat and turned in a tight circle. The wheels spun as if buried in grease, before getting traction in the snow, and aiming at Percy's motorbike.

Percy was stuck in no man's land between the airfield's wooden gate posts. He had nowhere to go. Mandy and Florence fired at the charging German vehicle.

'Get off!' Percy barked at Nicole.

She dived into a snowdrift under the hedgerow.

Percy blocked the way of a man determined to escape certain death. It was a one-sided joust: an armoured vehicle versus a motorbike.

The vehicle's weight pushed its wheels down to reach solid ground, then jerked and snaked its way towards Percy's stricken motorbike.

Percy wound the motorbike's engine to full power as the vehicle barrelled quickly towards him. Mandy and Florence fired from their positions, but their bullets pinged off the metal, barely making a scratch.

Percy released the brake lever, and the bike lurched forward. Snow and mud sprayed behind him as he raced towards the oncoming vehicle.

Percy jumped.

The vehicle driver couldn't avoid the now airborne

motorbike, which clattered against the windscreen igniting the fuel tank, and causing a fireball of black smoke. The driver was on fire, and with a single shot, Mandy silenced his screams.

The burning vehicle continued forward and slammed full force into Percy. He bounced and landed in the ditch alongside Nicole.

Percy didn't move.

His eyes were closed, and his face and hands were bleeding from multiple cuts. Mandy hurdled the wreckage and clambered over to him.

Percy opened one eye and smiled.

'Mandy, my love, I came as fast as I could.' Percy's laboured breathing came in snatched gasps.

'We've got to get out of here.' Mandy pulled, and Nicole pushed, and they hauled him out of the ditch. Florence raced over and helped to carry Percy across the airfield. They laid him on the floor of Hesberus. Nicole stood at the aircraft's door.

She said, 'Florence, this is where I leave you. I'll get some help to clear up this mess. Safe home.' She looked at Mandy, 'Percy is a top man. He is a real gentleman; all he thought about was getting back to you.'

'Thank you for bringing him back to me,' said Mandy. 'And by the way, your three kill shots were the best I've seen.'

Rosie shouted out, 'Nicole, I'll see you back in Berlin.'

Florence pushed the dead soldiers out of Hesberus and shut the side door.

Bertie called out, 'Buckle up. We have to get this old girl in the air and get home.'

Nicole waved from the white fields. Another hour of snow and it would look as if they were never there.

. . .

Florence looked out of the porthole as Hesberus lifted into the morning sky. Although, finally, it was a job well done, as yet it remained unfinished. Preventing the obliteration of the Spitfire locations on Tuesday night was now the priority; and the clock was ticking.

She sat on the bench and lifted Sir Henry's scarf to her face. She let the white silk engulf her. He was there with her in spirit.

Hesberus took a severe pounding from the armoured vehicle machine gun. The bullet holes in the fuselage turned the aircraft into a wind instrument. The breathy notes produced a haunting tune.

Bertie lost a lot of blood from his non-life-threatening gunshot wounds. Alice flew the battered old Hesberus out of Germany and scrammed for home.

Mandy grabbed Percy's face.

'Percy,' she shouted. Percy, can you hear me?'

He didn't respond. He didn't move. He wasn't breathing. Mandy ripped open his jacket and shirt and put her ear to his chest.

She said, 'He's choking, and he'll die if we don't release the pressure.'

'What do you need,' said Florence.

'A knife.'

Alice handed Mandy her field knife.

Mandy recalled reading about the tracheotomy technique. She closed her eyes and visualised the diagrams from her reference books. The incision into Percy's neck needed to be precise. His face was drained of colour, and his chest heaved in the frantic search for air.

'What are you waiting for?' said Florence.

'If I get it wrong, he'll die.'

'And if you don't try, he'll definitely die. Without you,

Mandy, he's already dead, but with you, he has a fighting chance.'

Mandy said, 'Lizzie, I need a small length of tubing.' She held the knife against Percy's throat and forced the razor-sharp blade through his skin.

All eyes were on her.

Mandy kept her finger in the hole and controlled Percy's airflow. Lizzie handed her a length of tubing from Alice's breathing apparatus and she pushed a small length into Percy's airway, then taped the tubing securely in place. She interlocked her fingers and pressed down on his chest.

She prayed, 'Breath, Percy, you silly bugger.'

He started to breathe. His eyes popped open, and she jabbed him with a morphine shot. His eyes closed.

'Is he breathing?' asked Florence.

Mandy nodded. 'My boy certainly had a night of it. He's smothered in lipstick, and he's freezing from riding through the night. He killed a German with his motorbike and got his throat cut open to save his soppy life.'

'Probably a regular Friday night out in Battersea,' said Rosie.

Florence put her head between Bertie and Alice, 'How long until we land?'

'Wheels down at Milton Park airfield in two hours,' said Bertie.

'How are your wounds?'

'He'll live. They're just scratches,' said Alice.

'Will Hesberus make it?'

Bertie tapped the steering column, 'This old bird will survive anything.'

Alice looked over Florence's shoulder at the girls fussing over Percy, 'We've got an amazing team.'

'Yes, we have. But it will all be in vain unless we get back and finish the mission. Did you leave instructions for Henry?'

'I left him a note.' Alice looked at her watch, 'I'm guessing he'll be back from his morning walk with Rags. They'll be stepping into the ops room right about now.'

CHAPTER 34

Sir Henry read Alice's note and picked up the telephone. After a few rings, Churchill answered.

'Winston, good morning,' said Sir Henry.

The conversation lasted no more than a minute, and Churchill's response, to Sir Henry's plan, was his usual unique blend of majestic brevity. 'Do it.'

The call ended.

Sir Henry lit the fire and stoked it vigorously until the flaming logs crackled and popped up the chimney. Rags curled up on the rug in front of the fireplace and fell asleep. Sir Henry turned his attention to the wall map. He used his Sherlock Holmes magnifying glass to study the surrounding areas of the twenty-one Spitfire locations and recorded the details in a small black notebook.

Sir Henry's levels of sustained concentration and unbreakable focus were legendary. When others took a break, he could carry on for hours and read long into the night. His talent involved taking a complex document and turning it into simple, manageable chunks for everyone to understand.

Sir Henry's thoughts turned towards the leadership vote on Wednesday; it was becoming abundantly clear that Churchill would not muster sufficient support to become Prime Minister.

Barrington however, already had an overwhelming majority. Furthermore, Sir Henry knew the moment the votes were cast, he, along with Florence and Alice, would be discarded from Military Intelligence and taken off all operations.

But that was Wednesday.

Tuesday held a mightier problem.

The complete and total destruction of Britain's fighter command was in the balance. Britain had never been nearer the edge of defeat. Sir Henry knew the Luftwaffe would be busy working through their precision bombing strategy, with the sole purpose to put an end to Britain's participation in the war.

Tuesday could mark the end of Britain's war.

And on Wednesday, if Barrington succeeded, marked the end of British politics. Churchill's moment would be over.

Sir Henry put his notebook on the table and walked over to the fireplace to ruffle Rags's ears.

'Well, we don't give in quite so easily, do we old boy? An enemy is at their most vulnerable the moment they have victory in their sights.'

Rags didn't move. He looked at Sir Henry with his brown eyes, listened to every word, and then promptly fell asleep again.

'There is a war on, Rags.'

Sir Henry drove from Churchill's London home in the early hours and managed to grab a couple of hours sleep when he arrived at Milton Park. Fully refreshed from his walk, he entered the ops room and read Alice's note pinned to the map wall. Her message was, well, it was pure Alice.

. . .

Sir H,

I am flying Hesberus to Germany to pick up Florence & Co. Will Land at Milton Park mid-morning.

Alice.

Ps. apple crumble and custard in the fridge.

Bertie touched Hesberus down at Milton Park's airfield and taxied towards a waiting ambulance at the far end of the runway. Mandy and Rosie manhandled Percy out of the side door and handed him to the attentive ambulance crew.

Mandy stepped into the back of the ambulance.

'We've got him now, Miss,' said the burly driver.

'I won't leave him. I'm going with him.'

'Mandy, let them do their job,' said Rosie.

Mandy held Percy's hand, 'His name is Percy, Percy Butterworth. Take care of him.'

'He'll be in good hands, Miss.' The driver jumped behind the wheel and pulled away.

Mandy watched through tear-stained eyes the ambulance bounce across the airfield and out through the gates towards the hospital. She looked at the gates long after the ambulance had vanished from sight.

Sir Henry waited on the gravel driveway, and Rags barked with excitement the moment he saw the girls climb out from the back of the truck.

Rosie ran over, 'Rags, you've grown since I saw you last.' She hugged Sir Henry, then looked at Milton Park with her hands on her hips, 'I love this place.'

Florence hugged and kissed Sir Henry while an over-excited Rags didn't know who to go to next. All his favourite people in the world had arrived at once.

'Have you had breakfast, darling?' she asked.

'Apple crumble and custard.'

'Breakfast of champions, did you save some for me?' she said.

'Obviously.'

'That's why I love you.'

They walked hand in hand into the house. 'I sent the engineers back to London yesterday,' he said. 'And as of now, we're on a countdown to the Luftwaffe's bombing raid tomorrow night.' On the doorstep, he called out to everyone, 'Ops room, one hour.'

Lizzie looped her arm through Rosie's, 'Come and use my room. We're the same size, so my clothes should fit you.'

'You're a lifesaver,' said Rosie. 'First, I need a hot bath.'

Alice waited for Mandy, who dragged her heels towards the entrance hall. 'He's in the best of hands,' said Alice. 'You'll be able to visit him soon enough.'

'I can't get it out of my mind. All that blood; I thought he was dead, and that I'd lost him. Worse, I thought I'd bloody killed him.'

'He's not, and you didn't. Go and get changed, I need you to be on the ball.'

Mandy skipped off towards her room.

An hour later, the team gathered around the wall map, having washed and changed. Sir Henry drew a prominent red X in the designated zones, close to each of the twenty-one locations.

Without preamble, he made a start.

'We'll be deploying an old naval trick to assist the Luftwaffe to bomb safely wide of their targets tomorrow evening. We have the rest of the day, and all day tomorrow, to get our game plan straight before the Bosch flies over and tries to knock us out of the war.'

'Naval trick?' asked Lizzie.

'It was the Africans who used decoy methods in battle to great effect. Their tribal leaders would send honoured men to their certain death. Their role was to distract their enemy from the real offensive.'

'Let's send Mandy,' said Rosie.

'So what did the Royal Navy do?' Lizzie asked.

'The carpenters aboard ship constructed make-shift rafts and fitted them with a mast and an oil lamp. They set it adrift at night, then sailed off in the opposite direction. While the attacking ships closed in on the decoy, our navy would turn about and sneak up behind them. And with their canons blasting they sunk the enemy fleet. It worked for decades.'

'So what are we going to do?' asked Mandy.

'Firstly, let me show you something,' he reached above the wall map, attached his stick to a metal hook and pulled a duplicate map of Britain over the wall map. The new map was printed on see-through paper. 'Tell me, what do you see?'

The girls stood and looked closely at the second overlay map. Mandy said, 'The red crosses don't quite line up properly with the map underneath.'

'Precisely,' said Sir Henry. 'And that's the framework for our decoy ships. I mean sites.'

Florence pointed to the red crosses, 'We began our defence of these twenty-one sites a year ago, and it's been our top priority. Tomorrow night's bombing raid is part of a long mission, and what I'm about to tell you is top secret. You can never speak of this to anyone, not ever. Fifty years after the war you still can't mention it, do I have your word? All of this never happened.'

They nodded.

Sir Henry chipped in.

'Remember, this is Military Intelligence, we fight a war most people never see or hear. Our purpose is to deceive the Germans to believe what we want them to believe. We set Otto Flack up to steal the locations marked with a red X on the map underneath. You see, we've assumed for some time the Bosch wanted to steal the Spitfire and destroy our facilities. We just didn't know when or how. Our plan was going beautifully without a hitch. We had the enemy just where we wanted them and then our ace-in-the-hole was killed.'

Puzzled faces stared back at her.

Florence said, 'We brought Otto Flack here to Milton Park and made sure he recorded the fake details of the twenty-one locations and find the re-written 12g295 Spitfire code. Our mission was to ensure he made safe passage back to Germany to hand the secret documents to the top brass in Berlin.'

There was silence in the room.

Lizzie said, 'Then I killed him on the beach. I bashed his head in with a rock. Oh my God, I blew your whole mission.'

'Let's say you half blew it,' said Mandy. 'Percy carried on where Otto left off.'

Florence added, 'But now the real work begins. We have to convince Berlin their bombing raid tomorrow night was an emphatic success. They must be thoroughly convinced that Britain's fighter command can't build another Spitfire.'

'What will the decoy sites look like?' asked Mandy.

Sir Henry said, 'We'll build enormous stacks of hay bales inside simple wooden-framed structures, and scatter charred remains of aircraft parts. We've had teams of scrap metal merchants collecting unusable and damaged wings, engines, and fuselages from RAF squadrons up and down the country for weeks. Each decoy site must appear to be utter carnage.

To back everything up, we've written cryptic reports for the newspapers to underplay the devastation, which is what the papers are instructed to do when we take a big hit, and the people at Intelligence will knock up some convincing photographs. We have a team of wireless operators and spies on standby ready to fill the airwaves with desperate chatter and coded messages, which we know will be intercepted. We can count on the Germans sending a few reconnaissance aircrafts to take photographs on Wednesday morning.'

Alice fiddled with a bank of telephones in the centre of the ops room, and from underneath a loom of tangled colourful telephone wires, she said, 'I'm just about done. We can try this in a few minutes.'

'What are you doing?' asked Rosie.

'I've wired our telephone so that we can talk to the twenty-one sites at the same time.'

'We're ready whenever you are,' said Florence.

Alice began dialling. As calls were answered, she plugged the corresponding cable into a socket box, like a telephone exchange, and one-by-one green lights flashed up on a dashboard.

'I'm connected to twenty of the twenty-one locations,' said Alice. She handed the receiver to Florence, and everyone in the ops room gathered around to listen to the call.

'Gentlemen, good afternoon, this is Florence Fairweather speaking on a secure line from Military Intelligence. We've linked together each location connected with building, designing, assembling, and transporting the Spitfire. You are the heart of fighter command.'

A chorus of murmurings echoed down the line, and while the words were indecipherable, the tone had a note of positiveness and togetherness.

Florence was engaging, 'Gentlemen, we are under imminent attack, so timing is of the utmost importance. We face losing Britain's foothold in the war, and if we do, we won't need to surrender, Hitler will walk up the Mall and take the Crown.'

Between them, Florence and Sir Henry spent an hour explaining the details of what was needed to be done at the decoy sites. They listened to the plan and agreed with a chorus of appreciative murmuring.

The call ended.

All locations were on board, apart from one.

Alice said, 'I was unable to connect with the site in Sherwood, Nottingham. Their telephone line is down.'

Florence thought for a moment.

'Rosie and Lizzie, you must go there immediately and show them their decoy site and explain what they need to do. Race up there like the wind in my Jaguar.'

'I have something to help you,' said Alice. She put her hand into her tweed jacket pocket and took two white pills from a small pot.

Lizzie and Rosie put the white tablets on their tongues and swallowed.

'It tastes horrible. What is it?' asked Lizzie.

'An SP,' said Alice.

Lizzie choked and started coughing. Her face turned white, 'You mean, a suicide pill?'

Alice laughed, 'No, don't be soft. Although maybe I should change the name. This is quite different. SP stands for Super-Power. It's designed to keep you awake and on red alert for forty-eight hours.'

'What are the side effects?' asked Rosie.

'I've no idea. I haven't tried it yet.'

'You mean, nobody has tested it yet?' said Lizzie.

'Listen, everything needs testing, and this is your turn. It's a harmless mixture of caffeine, nitroglycerine and four banned substances, but we don't have time to get into that now.'

'What if we die?' said Rosie.

'Then, naturally, I'll change the ingredients.'

'Your mum is completely mad,' said Lizzie.

'She's not,' said Florence. 'I had her tested. You two need to get going. Take a chatterbox with you and call me once you've reached Sherwood.'

The girls wrapped up warmly, and a few minutes later, the Jaguar's engine thundered a throaty roar as they raced off through the gates of Milton Park.

'Do you think they'll make it?' asked Mandy. 'It's well over a hundred miles to Nottingham from here, and the roads are heavy going with snow.'

'They've got nothing else planned for the evening,' said Florence. 'Those whiz-bang pills Alice gave them, should push them over the line on time.'

Churchill walked along the red-carpeted hallway in the Houses of Parliament and barged into Christopher Barrington's chambers.

'I need to talk to you, Barrington.'

'Don't you ever knock, Churchill?'

'Seldomly!' Winston looked over his half-rimmed glasses. 'We have a problem, and according to Sir Henry, a nasty and unsolvable one.'

'I'm not listening to the problems from the ex-head of Military Intelligence; unsolvable, nasty or otherwise. Sir Henry has had his day. I've told him to clear out his office by Wednesday lunchtime.'

'It matters not whether you want to listen, the problem still exists.'

Barrington put his papers down. He took off his glasses

and looked up at Churchill, 'Go on, humour me. What is it?'

'The Luftwaffe is mounting a bombing raid to destroy our Spitfire plants across the country tomorrow evening at 2200hrs. And we simply don't have the resources to defend ourselves.'

'And why is that unsolvable?'

Churchill lifted the back of the chair and slammed it noisily on the floor.

He bellowed, 'Because we don't have the resources to defend ourselves. We're on the verge of having fighter command ripped from our arsenal. We'll be unable to fight and unable to defend ourselves. If that's not unsolvable, then I don't know what is!'

Barrington waited for Churchill to calm down. 'Maybe this is the moment to make peace with Germany. We can draw a line in the sand and talk with Berlin. After all, if we can neither defend, nor attack, then the time has come to withdraw. We can go through the Italians. They could act as intermediaries.'

'Barrington, have you lost every ounce of decency? There's not a chance we'll shake hands over a peace deal with Hitler. That man is destined to turn Britain into a pile of ashes. He doesn't want peace; he wants destruction.'

'Peace is the only way forward, Churchill. Even you must see that now. I'm certain Hitler will talk.'

Churchill's face reddened, 'Peace only follows victory; it never precedes it. Especially when you're dealing with a madman like Hitler, there will be no peace treaty, not today, not tomorrow, not next week, not ever, not while Hitler is offering it. He wants to rip out our hearts and leave us to die.'

Barrington stood behind his desk.

'This isn't a theatre you pompous old fool. You're not on stage, and there isn't a crowd gathered to lap up your lion's roar and your addled words. Look around you, man, Britain is finished, and you're finished. Britain must sit this war out and save itself from complete annihilation.'

'Sit this one out?' Churchill barked back. 'Over my dead body, and over the choking dead bodies of every decent man, woman and child, on our green isle. There will be no peace until Hitler is dead, and not until Germany has offered its unconditional surrender.'

'Oh get out, Churchill. Get out!'

Churchill didn't move; he stared at Barrington and lowered his voice to the deepest whisper.

'I have no doubt you'll win the final ballot and become Prime Minister. But remember, your duty is to uphold the will of the people, not the will of a few spineless ministers in your Government.'

'I've half a mind to report you to the king,' said Barrington.

'You have half a mind. We can agree on that.' Churchill slammed the door and stormed down the corridor. He left a thick angry swirl of cigar smoke in his wake.

Lizzie drove flat out, while Rosie read the map.

'You drive well.'

'My dad taught me. He was a racing driver.'

'My mum taught me,' said Rosie.

'I love your mum.'

'Everyone does,' said Rosie.

Lizzie paused a moment.

'When I killed Otto Flack, nobody told me off, and nobody shouted. Mandy took me home on her bike, and your mum came over later to smooth everything out as if nothing had happened. Florence rejigged the plan and carried on as if I didn't do anything wrong, and then they brought me into the service.'

'Florence is the smartest, most wonderful woman in the world. She told me that when something happens, even if it is devastating, you must spend all your time focusing on your next step. If I could be anything like her, I'd be happy.'

'You are like her, and a bit like your mum too. By the way, are you feeling the effects of the pill yet?'

'I'm buzzing. I'll probably never sleep again. My eyes are so wide open they're hurting, and my senses are crystal clear. I've never felt this awake, and I'm hungry, really hungry.'

'Are we talking fast?' asked Lizzie.

'Yes, and loud.'

'I could drive at full speed.'

'You are, and did I mention that I was hungry.'

'You did. I'm hungry, too.' They started giggling and couldn't stop. They were halfway to Sherwood.

Florence and Sir Henry were sitting on the leather chesterfield in the ops room, and Rags snuggled warmly between them.

Sir Henry said, 'We're both out of a job from Wednesday. And Alice, Mandy, and even Rags.'

'Did Barrington tell you that?'

'Yes.'

'What do you want to do?'

He thought for a moment, 'Possibly retire and do Milton Park up a bit. We could plant wildflowers and fill the lake with trout.'

'That sounds absolutely bloody dreadful.'

'I know it does,' he said.

'Let's make sure Barrington doesn't win then.'

<><><>

CHAPTER 35

A few miles north of Nottingham, Lizzie turned the Jaguar into a dark muddy track in Sherwood. It was twenty minutes after three in the morning and miserably cold. They drove all afternoon and night in atrocious conditions to reach the disconnected location.

'It doesn't look like much. I thought it would be more industrial. Do you think anyone will be here?' asked Lizzie.

'I flippin well hope so,' said Rosie. 'I imagined these places didn't sleep, so I expected a frenzy of activity; what with a war on.'

The girls left the warmth of the car and banged on the green doors with their fists. Nothing stirred at first, and then a dim light pinged on above their heads. A window on the top floor opened and a bald head appeared.

'What do you want?'

'Are you, the manager?' asked Rosie.

'Yes, I'm Mr Prattle. What do you want?'

'Mr Prattle, your phone lines are down.'

'I know, they've been down since this morning.'

'Do you build Spitfires, Mr Prattle?'

'No. Yes, well, not whole ones. We make speedometers.' He scratched his head, 'Who are you? What do you want at this time of night?'

Rosie spoke louder to make her point, 'We've come to prevent you from being bombed by the Luftwaffe. Can we come in, it's freezing out here?'

'I'll come down,' he said, with new urgency.

Rosie and Lizzie walked in through the barn doors.

The workshop was small and rather unimpressive; it smelt the same as Sir Henry's tool shed: an evocative, creamy blend of oils, polished wood, well-used tools, and aromatic pipe-smoke.

Lizzie said, 'It smells like Hesberus in here.'

Rosie picked up a speedometer from the workbench, 'I imagined this place would be full of half-built Spits and a fever pitch of noisy activity.'

'There's just the three of us,' said Mr Prattle. He looked at the girls and rocked on his heels, 'No half-built Spitfires I'm afraid; we specialise in precision instruments.' He walked over to the corner of the room and turned on a small electric heater. 'I live above the workshop,' he pointed towards the ceiling with his pipe. 'And then there's Colin Pickle and his wife Gladys who live next door. She does the books and cooks us lunch.'

'That's it?' said Rosie scrunching up her nose.

'Yes, why?'

'How on earth do you keep up with all the work?'

'Simple, we can build a speedometer faster than a team of people can build a Spitfire.'

'It makes sense,' said Lizzie.

'Tell me, why are you here?' said Mr Prattle. He lit his pipe and puffed until the tobacco blazed orange.

Rosie moved towards the heater, 'Mr Prattle, your site is on the list to be bombed at 2200hrs tonight by the Luftwaffe. We're here to help you set up a decoy site.'

'Gosh, a bombing, tonight, that's awful, what do you need me to do?'

'Two things; wake up Colin and Gladys Pickle, we need their help to get ready.'

'And secondly?'

'Put the kettle on; we're gasping for a cup of tea.'

Rosie took the chatterbox out of her pocket, and they marched outside and searched for a telegraph pole. Lizzie sat on Rosie's shoulders to reach the wire. She pressed the buttons, and Milton Park's phone rang.

'Florence, it's Lizzie.'

Florence asked, 'How is Sherwood. Everything going to plan?'

'Mr Prattle has been most understanding, and Colin and Gladys Pickle are on their way.'

'It sounds like you have everything under control. Drive to London after the bombing raid, and I'll meet you and Rosie at Winston's London home, in Morpeth Terrace on Wednesday morning.'

Lizzie jumped down.

She said, 'Can we actually win this war with the likes of Mr Prattle, and Colin and Gladys Pickle?'

'Absolutely!' said Rosie, 'My mum always says; you can't win a war without a Prattle and a Pickle.'

The girls laughed and went back inside the instrument barn.

Florence couldn't sleep after the call. She stared up at the ceiling and contemplated the next two days. The Luftwaffe bombing raid and Christopher Barrington becoming Prime Minister; she couldn't decide which was worse. If Otto had seen through her plan and located the real locations, then their decoy sites are irrelevant.

Either event would end the war—one through defeat, the other through surrender. Florence wanted the war to end, but the only way to end a war was to win the damn thing. Her thoughts continued to tumble around in her head. Sir Henry and Rags slept next to her and breathed deeply in unison. She kissed them both and headed downstairs to the ops room.

Alice was already there.

'Look at this,' said Alice.

'What is it?'

'Confirmation reports from twenty sites that their decoy sites will be ready for tonight's bombing raid. All personnel are secured to prevent casualties and any information leaks.'

'I spoke with the girls. They arrived in Sherwood and met with Mr Prattle and witnessed first-hand how woefully ill-prepared we are for war. They're waiting for Colin and Gladys Pickle to arrive.'

'You can't win a war without a Prattle and a Pickle.'

Florence agreed. 'Now we can start turning the wheels of trickery and deceit.' She forced herself to stop thinking about Otto's last few words as he lay dying on the beach.

Lizzie and Rosie sank several cups of tea and gave in to another slice of Gladys's delicious jam sponge.

'I make the jam myself,' said Gladys.

'It's lovely,' agreed the girls.

Mr Prattle had been quiet for a few minutes. He tapped the map with his pipe, 'Are you sure Military Intelligence marked the X in the correct spot for the decoy site?'

'Quite sure, why?' said Rosie.

'Under normal circumstances, it's the perfect location.' He

puffed on his pipe, 'Recently, our local schools clubbed together to build a centre for London kids to get out of the city and spend a few days in the countryside.'

'What a shame, it's going to get flattened tonight,' said Rosie.

'You don't understand,' said Gladys. 'It's full of kids. They arrived from London three days ago.'

Rosie jumped up, and with her hands on her hips, she said, 'We need to get them out of there. The Hun won't be late.' Rosie was a younger image of Alice: forthright with curly hair, and endless bags of energy.

'And put them where?' said Mr Prattle.

'We'll rehouse them in the villages around Sherwood,' said Gladys. 'I'll get on to the Women's Institute. They'll get it sorted.'

Lizzie and Rosie headed over to the decoy site, and Mr Prattle, Colin and Gladys followed in their small delivery van. The newly refurbished barn looked perfect for London kids who rarely, if ever, experienced fresh country air and animals.

The Jaguar's headlights lit up the wooden barn. Lizzie gave two long blasts of the car horn.

An elderly lady wearing a brown dressing-gown, with her hair in curlers, appeared at the front door and shone her torch at the girls.

'What's all the commotion?'

'We need to evacuate the building,' said Rosie.

'Whatever for?'

'Because you need to leave right now.'

'We can't. It's not that simple.'

'Why not?' said Rosie.

'Because the kids aren't here.'

'Not here, where are they?'

'They're out camping and not due back until ten o'clock tonight.'

'You've got to be joking,' said Rosie.

'No, not at all. They'll get a camping badge and a certificate.'

'Where are they camping?' Lizzie asked.

'All over Sherwood Forest. We've been teaching them how to survive in the great outdoors in winter. What's the big rush?'

'At ten o'clock tonight, the Luftwaffe are going to bomb this barn,' said Rosie.

'Why on earth are the Luftwaffe going to bomb our barn?' asked the teacher.

'Because we told them to!'

'I guess that solves the mystery of why two men turned up here earlier and scattered bits of old aeroplanes about the place. I thought they'd made a mistake.'

Alice fiddled with wires and springs on her workbench in the ops room. She looked at Florence who stared into space.

'Penny for your thoughts.'

Florence picked up the photo of the inseparable four from a side table next to the sofa. The four young faces staring back were from a different world and a different lifetime.

She said, 'What if Otto Flack knew I played him? What if he managed to steal the genuine twenty-one locations and get them through to Berlin via his England-based handler? What if the Luftwaffe are loading their bomb bays right now and preparing our destruction? What if Otto knew I gave him the wrong code to build the Spitfire? And what if Max Ernst Bauer laughed in our faces at our pathetic attempt to deceive him? Alice, I can hardly breathe.'

'It's called spying, dear. We never know for sure.'

'But I could have got this so horribly wrong.'

'That's true, you could, but I doubt it.'

'Alice, think about it; Otto Flack went through hell to get what he wanted. What if he suspected I made it too easy for him and dug deeper to find the genuine information, then fed it back to his handler? What if he still made his escape attempt knowing he would die? He could have martyred himself for the Fatherland and played me simultaneously, but I was too pig-headed and blind to see his bluff.'

'If he did, then we'll lose the war and get shot for being utterly useless.'

'I feel much better now, Alice. On the beach, when I held Otto's head, he looked up at me and smiled. I'm telling you, he knew something.'

'Otto Flack didn't see the strings you were pulling. His arrogance consumed him. He was a nasty, murderous hun. Trust me. You got him.'

'God, I hope so.'

Sir Henry and Rags breezed into the ops room, 'You hope so, what?'

'Florence doubts herself about being the best spy in the history of the world.'

'She is the best, so that's that!' he said.

'But what if. . .'

'Listen, any sentence which starts with, but what if, is now barred from Military Intelligence.'

Florence pushed the doors open and walked into the garden. The pressure was mounting, and the clock was ticking.

Deep in Sherwood Forest, the icy rain continued to hammer down. The search for the children proved frustrating: two were missing. Rosie and Lizzie ran back to the barn. The teacher double-checked the names against her list. Brothers Jack and Peter were missing.

'We only have three hours left before the Luftwaffe blows this place apart,' said Lizzie.

They stood under a small canopy over the barn's front door and helped the children into a waiting bus. Colin and Gladys packed the children's bags into the back seats while Mr Prattle checked off each child's name.

'Two missing,' said Mr Prattle. 'What do you want me to do?'

Rosie said, 'Leave now. Get ten miles away and turn the coach lights off twenty minutes before ten o'clock. The Luftwaffe are never late.'

'I'll wait with you,' said the teacher.

'No! Go with the children. Your job is to keep them safe,' said Rosie.

The distraught teacher stood on the bottom step of the coach. 'Find my boys. Promise me you will.'

'We promise,' said Lizzie.

Mr Prattle crunched the gears and steered the bus down the track and away from the doomed decoy site.

'Now, what?' asked Lizzie.

'We stay until we find those boys.'

They ran back into the dark, rain-soaked woods.

Their torch beams bounced off the trees as they shouted out the names of the boys. They took turns calling out for the brothers, Jack and Peter.

'We must've searched these woods at least three times now,' said Lizzie. 'If they haven't heard us shouting out their names, then maybe they're not out here.'

'Then, where the hell are they?'

. . .

Mandy walked into the ops room, 'Percy is going to live. I popped over to see him. I couldn't wait. He's awake, and when he opened his eyes, he smiled when he saw me.'

'That's wonderful news,' said Florence. 'Did the doctors at the hospital like your emergency operation?'

'Not in so many words, but they said it saved his life.'

'What did Percy say?'

'He can't talk yet, so I memorised his favourite poem and whispered it to him until he fell asleep.'

'And his injuries?'

'A broken leg, three cracked ribs, and he'll walk with a stick for a while,' said Mandy.

'He's a lucky boy. Are you up for a spot of flying?'

'Yes, where?'

'You and I are flying a couple of Spits to London in the morning. We have a job to do,' said Florence.

'I love the sound of that.'

'After the bombing raid, we'll grab a few hours sleep, then buzz off at first light.'

With an hour left before the bombing raid, Lizzie and Rosie were still frantically searching for the missing boys. The batteries in their flashlights had died, and the forest had descended into a blackness of shapeless trees.

'Do you think there's any chance the Luftwaffe will abandon the raid because of bad weather?' said Lizzie.

'Not a chance in hell. They won't let a bit of English rain stop their hour of glory.'

'This is useless. We aren't getting anywhere,' said Lizzie. 'What would brothers from London do when their teacher tells them to build a camp and not come back until ten o'clock?'

'I know what I would do,' said Rosie. 'I'd build the best camp in the woods and make sure I won the badge.'

'These two crafty urchins have never been out of London before. What would Mandy do?' said Lizzie.

'She would find a warm hayloft and a good looking soldier, and wouldn't give a stuff about a camping badge.'

'Exactly, I bet those buggers smuggled in some cigarettes, a beer, some dirty postcards, and are holed up in the dry.'

Rosie checked her watch, 'We've got half an hour.'

Both girls looked up into the sky and strained their ears for the sound of droning aircraft engines.

'Mum always says, go to what you know,' said Rosie.

'The barn, the stupid barn where the kids stay, we didn't search it,' said Lizzie. 'That old place must be a warren of rooms and basements. How long to get back?'

'Fifteen minutes,' said Rosie.

They ran off at full tilt, side-stepped trees, jumped flooded ditches and raced through fields of wet grass. They egged each other on to run faster, and arrived in the barn puffing, panting, and soaked to the skin. The building stood in total darkness. They pushed their way inside and picked up a couple of torches from the shelf by the front door and shone the light in the first room and called out to the boys.

'You're not in trouble,' said Rosie. 'Come on out boys. We have to leave now.' The girls ran from room to room; they had two minutes left.

Lizzie cupped her hands around her mouth and shouted, 'Lads, the Germans are coming to bomb this place to shit in two minutes. Come now or we'll leave you here to burn. You are not in trouble.'

A trapdoor in the far corner of the barn opened a few inches, and two pairs of eyes looked out from the gloom at the two girls standing in wet clothes.

'I'm Jack, Miss,' said the older boy. 'This is my little brother Peter.'

Rosie yanked the trapdoor open and pulled Peter up by his collar and out of the basement. Jack climbed out after him.

'Run boys, run,' shouted Lizzie. The younger brother was frail and walked slowly. She grabbed him by the arm and frogmarched him through the front door.

Above them, a lethal armada of Luftwaffe bombers unloaded their bombs, and a devastating inferno headed towards the twenty-one locations.

Rosie reached the two-seater Jaguar and fired up the engine. Jack climbed in and called out to his brother to hurry up. Lizzie pushed Peter into the car on top of his brother and screamed, 'Go, Rosie, drive. I'll run behind you,'.

'No, there's room, you can fit in.'

'Get the boys out of here. I'll be right behind you. Don't stop whatever happens; just save the boys.'

Rosie snaked the Jaguar on the wet mud and raced down the slippery track away from the barn. She watched Lizzie running in her rearview mirror, but then watched as she tripped and fell. Lizzie didn't get up. Rosie reversed and picked Lizzie up and put her in the car then drove to safety. The coordinated bombing raid lasted twelve devastating minutes.

Florence's fears and doubts had finally been answered. She sat in the ops room, and in a soft voice, she turned to Sir Henry.

'Darling, I'm afraid Otto rumbled us. We failed. You must make the call.'

Sir Henry picked up the telephone and waited for the clicks and pips.

Churchill answered.

'Winston, it's me. I've news of the gravest sort. Our plan didn't work, and the Luftwaffe has destroyed our twenty-one Spitfire locations. I feel it's your duty to inform the ingoing Prime Minister, Christopher Barrington, of my failure to protect the nation.' Sir Henry's voice cracked, 'Winston, I'm so very sorry.'

After a long pause, Churchill asked, 'Is this the end?'

'Old friend, I'm rather afraid it is.'

Sir Henry replaced the handset, and without another word, walked out of the ops room.

CHAPTER 36

Churchill paced around his London study like a caged lion. He stopped and looked at the morning drizzle in Morpeth Terrace and forced aside crippling thoughts about the approaching defeat. He conceded that Britain's neck was exposed and lay invitingly on the bloodied chopping block with the Nazi axe poised, ready to fall.

The grandfather clock chimed eight bells, and in a little over four hours, Christopher Barrington would become the new Prime Minister.

Churchill couldn't put the conversation off a minute longer, and he hollered down the hallway, 'Get me Barrington on the telephone, somebody. Anybody!'

A scramble of activity preceded a ringing telephone. The next voice he heard was Barrington's.

'Morning, Churchill.' Barrington's voice was nauseatingly chirpy.

Winston's monotones couldn't hide his sarcasm, 'I'm sure you're busy selecting a new pinstriped suit and tie. I'll not keep you long.'

'What do you want, Churchill?'

'I'm calling with news of the darkest nature.'

'Go on.'

'Late last night, I received grave word from Sir Henry. He confirmed we'd lost our Spitfire manufacturing sites during a brutal wave of Luftwaffe bombing.'

'Peace is surely our new course of action,' said Barrington.

Churchill mumbled, unable to believe his own words.

'I confess, under the weight of imminent defeat, I see sense to seek a peace deal with Berlin. May I suggest you keep the announcement of our capitulation until after the vote at midday? Therefore, you'll be the Prime Minister who extends Britain's hand of peace to Germany's High Command. You'll be remembered for it.'

Barrington replied, 'After I've met with His Majesty the king, I'll reach out. Churchill, I know we've had our political differences, but I admire your grace and sensibility. I'll see you in the House at midday for the vote.'

Churchill rammed the receiver down.

'Bugger, double bugger and damn the buggers of buggeration.' He barged out of his study, and his red dressing gown wafted open to reveal his pink nakedness. He stomped upstairs and called out to his housekeeper, 'Mrs Amos, don't bother making dinner ever again, we'll be overrun with buggering Nazis by tonight, and we'll be eating cabbage for the next thousand years.'

Florence used the back of her glove to wipe the condensation from inside her Spitfire's windscreen. She looked across at Mandy in the Spitfire next to her and saw her cursing as icy drips landed in her lap.

Burbling engines brought Milton Park airfield to life, and Bertie waved them clearance for take-off with his good arm.

During his heroics, co-piloting Hesberus home, he sustained two bullet wounds in his left arm and wore a white bandage sling.

They picked up speed and soared over the trees at the far end of the runway. Mandy mirrored Florence's moves. At high-speed, and wing tip to wing tip, they flew towards London.

Mandy's headset crackled, and Florence's voice burst through.

'Are you ready for a day to end all days?'

'I'm ready for anything,' said Mandy.

'Are you focused? What with Percy and. . .'

'Florence, I'm focused.'

'Keep close. We'll land in Hyde Park.'

'Are we allowed to land in Hyde Park?' asked Mandy.

'Allowed? what does that mean?'

The incessant drizzle washed London of its war dirt and battle grime.

'That's what we're fighting for,' said Florence. 'Is there a more beautiful city in the world?'

Mandy looked at the buildings locked together like teeth in a zip, and the patchwork of small parks, and tree-lined streets. 'It looks stunning. I thought about my mum last night. Imagine if she could see me now.'

'She can see you. Look, there's Marble Arch. Follow me. We're going in.' They landed in the park's southernmost corner, and a group of onlookers gathered around the two aircraft.

'Look at all these people,' said Mandy.

'There's no time for photographs and autographs, even for a movie star like you.' They jumped onto the wet grass, and a group of children swarmed around them.

'Any kids here from Battersea?' Mandy called out.

'Yes, Miss, I'm from Queenstown Road,' said a skinny boy. 'I looked after your Bentley, and you smacked my arse.'

Mandy said, 'I remember you. How about you keep guard over our Spits?'

'What's in it for me?'

'A kiss and a story to tell your mates,' she put her arms around the blushing boy.

'You've got a deal, Miss.'

Mandy and Florence walked towards Hyde Park gate.

'Tart,' said Florence.

Mandy shouted back at the boy, 'She's going to kiss you as well.'

They ran towards Winston's home.

Ivy Amos answered the door at Morpeth Terrace, 'How lovely to see you. I'll tell Mr Churchill you're here. Have you girls had breakfast?'

'Not yet, and we're starving,' said Mandy.

'I've got two extra eggs and some bacon.'

'Perfect. Where's Winston?' asked Florence.

'Getting dressed. He's in a foul mood this morning, the worst ever, and he's shouting about eating cabbage for a thousand years.'

'That's never good. We'll wait in his study.'

The log fire in Winston's snug warmed their hands. The delicious breakfast, and an extra pot of tea, soon brought colour back to their cheeks. The study door burst open, and Churchill marched in dressed all in black.

'Who died?' said Mandy.

'Britain died. Today is the darkest day in our island's long history.'

'Winston, please take a seat,' said Florence.

'I don't want to. I'm preparing the right words to bring some cold comfort to our defeated people.'

'You said you wanted Henry's twisted and nastiest best, didn't you?' said Florence.

'Yes, but not to fail! Not to put us in a position of weakness, forcing us to concede by throwing in the towel to Nazi tyranny.'

'Henry gave you his best.'

'Henry's best wasn't good enough.'

Outside in Morpeth Terrace, a car screeched to a halt followed by footsteps and a loud rap on the door.

'Mandy, see who that is,' said Florence. Mandy left the study and opened the front door.

'Well, look what the cat dragged in,' she said.

'And a good morning to you,' said Rosie. She gave Mandy a long hug. Lizzie limped up the pathway and joined the hugging circle.

'How was Sherwood?'

'A close shave, I've no idea how we managed to get away,' said Rosie.

'And what the hell happened to you?' Mandy said to Lizzie, 'Your hands and knees are in a right old state, did you crawl here?'

'I'm a mess, I know. I fell flat on my face.'

'Why are you talking so fast?' asked Mandy.

She led them through to the kitchen, and Mrs Amos served the second sitting for breakfast. After a refill of tea, feeling refreshed, Rosie and Lizzie walked into Churchill's warm study.

Winston's mood had not abated. He looked at the new arrivals.

'You must be Lizzie. I've heard about your brave exploits from Florence.'

Lizzie blushed, 'It's a pleasure to meet you, Mr Churchill.'

He welcomed them both into his study, 'You brave girls

are the heartbeat of Britain. And Rosie, I hear you've been stirring the pot in Berlin, just like your mother.'

Florence checked her watch, 'Winston, we need to get you to Parliament. Where's your car?'

'I've no idea,' he said. 'Whenever I need to go anywhere, it arrives, I get in, and off we go. I've never put more thought into it than that.'

'We can't wait around for your car to turn up,' said Florence. She looked at Winston's rotund figure: he wasn't going to fit in the Jaguar. 'Winston, grab your hat. We're doing this the old fashioned way.'

Morpeth Terrace bustled with people, and what remained of the patchy snow, drifted up against the fashionable town-houses. Florence and Mandy stood one side of Winston and Rosie and Lizzie on the other. Together they pulled him towards Victoria Street. A London bus trundled along.

Florence shouted, 'Rosie, Lizzie, stop that bus.' The girls ran out into the road and held up their hands, and the bus shuddered to a halt. Florence pulled Winston, while Mandy used her shoulder to push him onboard from behind. The bemused passengers stared at the girls who manhandled Churchill onto a bench seat at the back of the bus.

'Five singles to Parliament Square,' said Mandy to the bus conductor.

'This is the 9B, Miss. We don't go to Parliament Square. This route goes up Piccadilly.'

'Not today, sunshine,' said Mandy. 'We need to get Mr Churchill to Parliament.'

'We got rules, Miss. You can't willy-nilly about wherever you want. The 9B goes up Piccadilly, and that's that.' Mandy made a move to square up to him when she felt a hand on her arm.

'Help me up,' said Winston.

He stood, with a pronounced stoop, in the middle of the

packed bus. He removed his hat and took a long puff on his cigar, 'It is time to tell you the truth.'

The captivated passengers glared back.

'Makes a bloomin change,' said the conductor.

'We're in grave danger,' said Winston. 'The soon-to-be new prime minister demands we make a peace treaty with Hitler and offer our full and unconditional surrender. We are on the verge of being overrun by Nazis who are licking their lips at the prospect of marching up Whitehall to eat in our restaurants and sit in our West End theatres.' He looked at the fearful faces, 'Ladies and gentlemen of London, time is of the essence, and I'm afraid I am running out of essence.'

An elderly lady sitting with her bunched up shopping bags said, 'I don't mind going to Parliament Square.'

'And I don't mind either,' said another.

A soldier in uniform said, 'Come on, mate, take Mr Churchill to Parliament.'

The conductor tapped on the cab window and instructed the driver to detour to Parliament Square. The bus-full of Londoners chatted to Winston as they sped along Victoria Street. Churchill could not have looked more out of place, and yet, he was a genuine man of the people: he understood them, and they understood him.

The shopping lady tugged at Winston's cuff, 'I hope you become Prime Minister, Mr Churchill.'

'I do too, but I feel my time has gone.'

'Utter nonsense. Giving up never works, and you of all people should know that, Mr Churchill. Surrendering to those Nazis doesn't feel right to me.'

The bus shuddered to a stop.

'Parliament Square,' said the conductor. He stood to attention as Mr Churchill doffed his hat and clambered backwards off the bus.

'Mandy, would you see to the conductor and do the honours,' said Florence.

Mandy flung her arms around the bus conductor and kissed him in front of everyone.

'I meant for you to pay him, not kiss him,' said Florence.

Churchill and Florence rushed into Parliament and were met by a large gathering.

Christopher Barrington stood in the foyer, surrounded by a group of grey-haired men. They were dressed in matching pinstripe suits and nodded in agreement with Barrington's words.

'Good morning, Churchill,' said Barrington.

'I shouldn't think so,' said Winston. He looked at the nodding dogs gathered around Barrington, 'There are so many yes men around you, who agree with everything you say, it must be like living in an echo chamber.'

'Sticks and stones, Churchill, sticks and stones.'

'I hear Hitler is missing one of his stones to go with his stick,' said Winston.

Florence sniggered.

Barrington stepped out from the centre of the pinstripes, 'Winston, you mustn't joke about Hitler.'

'A joke about a bad thing is not the same as the bad thing. British wit will defeat Nazi tyranny.'

Barrington absorbed himself back into the middle of his pinstriped-suited clan, and the eager nodding and the yes-echoes resumed.

Florence stepped behind Winston and whispered in his ear, 'Do you trust me?'

'With my life. Why, what are you going to do?' Churchill asked.

'I'm going to show a man some photographs.'

'Anything I need to know about?'

'Absolutely not,' she said.

At eleven-thirty, the party members moved towards the voting hall. Florence stood in front of Christopher Barrington.

She smiled and said, 'May I be the first to congratulate you on your imminent appointment. You'll make a fine leader.'

'That means a lot coming from you, Florence.'

'Christopher, may I have a quick word with you in your private chamber? It will only take a minute.' She walked towards his chamber and looked over her shoulder, 'I need you.'

Barrington followed.

Florence sat opposite Barrington and removed her flying jacket, then slowly flicked her hair from her collar.

'As a fellow Oxford History graduate,' she said, 'I thought you'd appreciate a swift recap spanning twenty-five fascinating years.'

'The voting is about to begin; can this wait?'

'Not a minute longer,' her tone was terse. She took a photograph from her pocket, 'Do you recognise this?'

He looked at his watch, then at the photograph. 'Yes, of course,' he pointed to his own photograph of the inseparable four on his desk. 'Florence, I don't have much time.'

'It's true. You don't have much time. This photograph tells a deeper story than that of four Oxford chums.' She tapped her finger on the photograph. 'Your late son, Oliver Barrington, my late husband Douglas Fairweather, my dear friend, Malcolm Feathers, and of course me.'

'I know, what of it?'

'Your son, Oliver, didn't die in the First World War alongside my husband in no man's land, did he, Christopher?'

'What are you wittering on about, woman? Everyone

knows Oliver is dead. We've visited his grave in Oxford together.'

'I know he didn't die in the First World War.'

'How do you know?' he asked.

'Because I held him when he died on a Sussex beach last week.'

'You're talking utter nonsense.' He stood to leave.

Florence pointed to his chair, 'Sit down!'

He checked his watch: eleven forty-five.

She continued.

'Your son, Oliver, was a spy, Germany's greatest spy. His real name was Otto Flack.'

'This is utter...'

Florence slammed another photograph on top of the inseparable four.

'This is Otto Flack, or Oliver Barrington if you prefer, lying dead in a shallow grave in Calais. I stripped him and buried him.'

Barrington picked up the photograph and ran his fingers over the image of his crumpled son in a muddy hole.

'Barrington, there's more bad news. Your wife's dead too.'

He looked up, 'My wife?'

'I poisoned Mrs Flack a few days ago in her bed. It was nasty, but a necessary bit of business.'

Barrington drew a breath that whistled through his teeth, and a grimness fell across his face—a long moment swollen with thought, followed by another before he spoke.

'Dead?'

Florence laid the photograph of the dead Mrs Flack on top of the other two photographs. Barrington picked it up and held it at arm's length as if distance might delay the truth.

'It was the rowing that gave it all away,' said Florence.

'Rowing?'

'I watched Oliver, your son, and my husband row on the Thames every morning. They were the best of friends, and they rowed every morning whatever the weather. I would watch them walk around the boat sheds, then row on the river. Your walk is like a signature: everybody's walk is unique, and there are no two walks alike.' Florence walked around Barrington's office in a measured stride.

'I've never heard such rubbish.'

'Your son, Oliver, left my husband to die in no man's land and escaped back to Germany during World War One and trained to be a spy. As far as we can trace, his disguise mastery started when he became the American, Owen Black. And as Owen Black, he infiltrated our Spitfire programme as an engineer. However, one vital code eluded him. He returned to Germany and went through more facial surgery to become Malcolm Feathers. He parachuted into Friston, murdered Malcolm's parents, and then murdered Malcolm Feathers. But of course, you know all this.'

'How could I possibly know of this nonsense?'

'Because you gave the orders,' said Florence.

'This is farcical. It's a fabrication of stupidity, and merely highlights the incompetence of Military Intelligence. I'll be delighted to see the back of you and Sir Henry after the vote today.'

'Do you think this is a wispy fairytale about Oliver Barrington, Owen Black and Otto Flack being the same person, your son, without any evidence?' she said.

'You have nothing but lies and fake photographs.' He spat his words at her.

'I noticed that Malcolm was not Malcolm at the funeral. When he walked towards me his first step gave him away, then his polished shoes and his lean muscles. I played your boy from the start. His conceitedness blinded him not to see what was playing out in front of his eyes. He thought I was just a stupid woman. And I'm guessing he gets that short-sightedness from you.'

'You killed him?'

'I said I held him when he died. Your boy took advantage of a girl called Lizzie Denton. He tried to kill her, but she fought back and caved his brains in on the beach. Germany's top spy, your son, under your command, was killed by a jilted girl.'

Barrington was rigid.

'Shall I continue?' she asked.

He didn't move.

'I did everything to help Otto, I mean your son, get back to Berlin.'

'Go on, humour me, why?'

'When I deduced Malcolm Feathers was Otto Flack, and Otto Flack was your son, I enlisted a code breaker from Bletchley Park called Percy Butterworth. He wrote a fake 12g295 code. It was a work of art and looked identical to the original, but it was flawed. The phoney code would ensure the Spitfires that Germany built would never fly. I let Otto find one of the phonies, and. . .'

'And. . . you gave one to me,' he said. 'Why the theatrical charade if you thought I had something to do with all this?'

'Christopher, catching you was the easy part, but getting you and your spy-boy to fool Berlin into wasting precious resources to build tens of thousands of doomed Spitfires, was the genius part. Discovering you were the deep-sleeper agent was the catch. We knew about your wife's antics, but we didn't know you were the sleeper-agent-husband. And it's funny to think it only happened because of the way your son walked. You'll be hanged as a traitor.'

'I'm no traitor. I served my country with honour.'

'Oh, poppycock, you served Germany, and you were on

the verge of serving Britain to Hitler on a silver platter. In my book, that makes you a traitor.'

Barrington thumped his fist on the desk. 'My first ministerial order as Prime Minister is to offer Britain's full and unconditional surrender to Berlin.'

'Why would Britain surrender?' asked Florence.

'Because, the Spitfire locations were bombed last night, and fighter command has been destroyed. Britain can no longer defend itself and will have no choice but to surrender.'

Florence smiled, 'Who told you the Spitfire sites had been destroyed?'

'Churchill himself; first thing this morning. He said Britain would have to capitulate, and a peace deal must now be sought with Berlin.'

'And who do you think told Winston?'

Barrington thought for a moment, 'Sir Henry told him.'

'And who do you think told Sir Henry?'

The faintest look of comprehension appeared across Barrington's features. He cleared his throat, 'You played Churchill, and Churchill unwittingly played me.'

'I expect it was something like that.'

'You seem to have thought of everything,' he said.

'You're right, I have.' Florence took a typed letter from her pocket, 'I need you to sign this for me.'

'My confession?'

'How did you guess?'

'I won't sign it. You don't have proof and your fabricated story won't stand up in a court of law, you can't link me to anything.'

'Sign it or don't sign it, I can forge your signature,' she said. 'And I don't need a shred of evidence.'

'Why not?'

'Because there'll be no trial, no judge, no jury and you'll not have your day in court. You'll quietly step down from office and work for me.' She unscrewed her pen and handed it to him.

He slapped the pen out of her hand, 'I'm not stepping down, and I'm certainly not damn well working for you.'

'Then you leave me no alternative,' she took her pistol and loaded it with a single round.

'You're nothing more than a common, low-life cold-blooded murderer,' he said.

'That's true, but you misunderstand, the gun is for you, Barrington.' She placed the pistol on top of the photographs.

The clock on the wall struck twelve.

'You seem to be forgetting one thing,' he said.

'I doubt it,' said Florence.

'As of this minute, I am the newly elected Prime Minister of Great Britain, and His Majesty, the King, will invite me to form a new Government.'

'About that, it turns out you're not going to be the new Prime Minister after all.'

'What do you mean?'

'The vote has been delayed, indefinitely. Sir Henry is outside preventing votes being cast, and you know how good he is at meddling.'

Barrington snorted, 'What are you going to do, put Churchill in Number Ten? Hitler thinks he's nothing but a drunken buffoon, and he's right. Do you honestly believe Churchill can lead Britain to victory?'

'Yes, I do, and more importantly, Britain does, too.'

'Then you've already lost the war.'

'Maybe we have, but we'll go down fighting.'

'You English,' he said. 'You're deluded.'

Florence slid the pistol closer to him, 'Let me address you properly, Herr Flack, we might be deluded, but what of you? Your son and wife are dead, Berlin is building tens of thousands of flightless Spits, and Hitler will blame you for that catastrophe. It's your last move, Barrington. Shoot yourself, or work for me.' Florence stood and walked towards the door.

Barrington picked up the pistol, aimed it squarely at her back, and pulled the trigger.

CHAPTER 37

Barrington repeatedly pulled the trigger, but the pistol wouldn't fire. Florence opened her hand to reveal the bullet.

'How could I trust a German snake with a bullet? I knew you would shoot me in the back.'

'How did you do that?'

'What do you think we do at Military Intelligence all day —drink tea?'

'I underestimated you, Florence. I suppose I'll have to work for you; I seem to have run out of options.'

'Working for me was never an option.'

'What are you going to do, give me the bullet so I can finish the job?'

'There are no more bullets, Barrington. I think you should sit down.'

He collapsed heavily onto his chair.

'When you tried to shoot me in the back, you snagged your finger on a tiny barb on the trigger which I laced with poison. The more you pulled the trigger, the more you poisoned yourself. My best guess is that you've less than a minute to live.'

With his remaining seconds of life left, he said, 'You can't prevent the inevitable. Germany has hundreds of spies in your military, your Government, even your Royal Family. You can't win, Florence, because you've already lost.'

'I'll find them, and I'll kill them, one snake-eyed Nazi spy at a time.'

'You won't find them. They're buried too deep.'

'I found you didn't I, and I found your son and wife, and now you're all dead. I've chopped the snake's head off.'

Barrington's arms floundered by his side, and saliva bubbled at the edges of his mouth. His eyes rolled white, and the pistol clattered to the floor.

His minute was up.

Florence took a small glass tube from her top pocket and put a few drops of poison in Barrington's coffee and left the tube by the cup. She picked up the photographs and slipped, unseen from his chamber.

The impatient party Members stood in the House of Commons waiting to vote.

Churchill scowled, 'Henry, what's the delay?'

'Florence is clearing up a dead end.'

'And where's, Barrington?'

'That would be the dead end.'

'What do you mean?'

'I must confess, Winston. I lied to you.'

'What about?'

'Last night, I told you the Luftwaffe bombed our Spitfire sites, and we would be unable to fight on.'

'And?' said Churchill.

'We didn't lose them. Our decoy plan was a complete

success. I needed you to be convincing when you told Barrington to broker a peace deal with Germany.'

'Why would you do that?'

'Winston, my dear friend, you'll become our greatest Prime Minister, and you will lead Britain to victory against the Nazis, but you're a most dreadful actor. I couldn't trust you with the truth.'

'Dreadful actor? My Hamlet at school received wonderful reviews.'

'I know. I wrote them. You can't act, but I knew you would enjoy the glowing reviews.'

'I kept them.'

'I know you did, Winston. This will cheer you up; Florence thinks I can't act either. She told me we had been outsmarted by Otto Flack and the sites had been destroyed, and that we should seek a resolution with Germany. It seems she didn't trust either of us with our acting skills.'

'And what of Barrington? Why is he not here gloating about his upcoming meeting with the king?' asked Winston.

'Florence discovered that Barrington's son, Oliver, was the German spy, Otto Flack. It turns out Christopher Barrington was his handler and the deep-sleeper in England pulling the strings. He was half German and half English.'

'Half English and half German? Then he was his own worst enemy,' said Churchill.

Sir Henry looked at the impatient suits waiting to cast their vote. 'There'll be no leadership contest today, or anytime soon. We'll wait and allow Barrington's death to blow over, then push you to the front of the queue to become Prime Minister.'

'Hold on, death. Barrington?'

'Yes, unpleasant business. It happened in his office.'

'When?'

'Two minutes ago,' said Sir Henry.

'How on earth could you know?'

'Because I have his suicide note in my pocket.'

'How did you get hold of it?'

'I wrote it.'

They walked away from the crowd and stepped outside into a bright, cold winter's day. Churchill held Sir Henry's arm, 'I asked for your twisted, darkest, and nastiest best. I thought you'd failed me. I'll never doubt you again, old friend.'

Four months later, on 10th May 1940, Winston Churchill entered Number Ten Downing Street as the new Prime Minister. Britain had its lion, and Churchill was ready to roar.

Florence and Sir Henry waited inside Number Ten for Winston to return from Buckingham Palace. Winston put his hands on the shoulders of his two dearest friends.

There was no time for congratulations.

Florence said, 'There's an underground facility outside of Berlin capable of building tens of thousands of Spitfires, but they still have the incorrect code, so the Spits will never fly.'

'And how long do you think the Germans will keep making Spitfires that won't fly?' asked Winston.

'They'll figure out the code soon enough; their engineers are top drawer.'

'What do you want to do about it?'

'Blow it up, of course,' she said.

'This will be my first order as Prime Minister. Have you thought of a codename for this mission?'

'Operation Feathers,' said Florence.

. . .

Later that evening, and with the light fading from a warm spring day, three Spitfires took off from Milton Park airfield. Florence led with Alice on her left-wing and Mandy on her right. They swooped low over the White Cliffs of Dover and crossed the English Channel a few yards above the waves.

'Alice, are you sure these tennis ball bombs will work?' said Mandy.

'Define the word, sure,' said Alice.

'How do they work?'

'The tennis balls are filled with explosives, a detonator, and a miniature radio receiver. Lizzie and Rosie have been helping me make them for weeks.'

'Have you tested them?'

'Define tested?' said Alice.

'Will they go bang?'

'I'm fairly sure they will.'

'Where did you get so many tennis balls?' asked Florence.

'Wimbledon has been cancelled this summer, and a friend, who works there, sent me three huge boxes of balls and three tennis rackets.'

They flew across France and over the German border at terrific speed and thundered through the night. An unguarded field, three miles from the underground facility, proved a perfect place to land.

They wore white, one-piece jump-suits and white boots. They filled their backpacks with explosive tennis balls and tennis rackets, and Florence handed them two armbands: a red Nazi armband, and one that read, Gefährliche giftige Materialien - Hazardous Toxic Chemicals.

They ran at a brisk pace and kept to the shadows of the low hedgerows and fences.

'They won't go off while we're running, will they?' Mandy asked.

'I shouldn't think so,' said Alice.

The square fields were neatly linked together by wooden hurdle-gates. The area was beyond the Berlin suburbs and had low levels of military activity.

'There's nobody about. Will the bunker be heavily guarded?' asked Mandy.

'Don't worry, Florence has a plan in mind if it's guarded. You do have a plan, don't you, Florence?' said Alice.

Florence tapped the bike chain in her back pocket.

'That's the big Military Intelligence plan?' said Mandy. 'A bike chain wrapped around our fists and a bloody big punch up.'

They arrived at the underground facility, and the bright lights beamed out of the ground into the night sky.

'That's a sight,' said Alice.

'No sign of a blackout here, then,' said Mandy. 'If I lit up my place in Battersea like that, I'd have the home guard knocking on my door.'

'As yet, Germany is not under attack,' said Alice. 'It's that sort of arrogance which will be the death of them.'

Four sturdy guards marched in small patterns on the crunchy gravel outside the well-lit entrance.

'Let's get closer,' said Florence. 'Let's not give them a chance to fire off a shot. Total stealth, you got that?'

'Stealth,' said Alice.

'Total,' said Mandy.

The underground facility's entrance was now more than a hole in the ground. Immense German resources were at work, and the whole area looked industrial.

Florence looked at the guards and then at Mandy, 'Tart it up a bit. We need a big distraction.'

Mandy fluffed her hair around her shoulders, unzipped her white suit, and pushed her bosoms together while swaying her hips and pouting her lips.

'Do you want me to tart it up a bit as well?' asked Alice.

'I think Mandy has enough tart for the three of us. We'll keep you in reserve.' Florence walked out from the gloom and onto the gravel in front of the facility.

'Halt,' said one of the four guards.

Florence ensured he could see her armbands.

'We're from Berlin. On Hitler's staff.'

'Papers,' he barked.

Florence took off her backpack and began to rummage. 'I put them in here somewhere. It's a chilly evening. I have some hot coffee and chocolate; would you like some?'

The three other guards were drawn like giddy moths to a lamp. Alice and Mandy put their hands in their back pockets and wrapped their bike chains around their gloved knuckles.

Mandy pouted, 'Boys, you can help yourself to anything you fancy.' The guards stared up at her bulging cleavage and swaying hips.

Alice threw a jaw-crunching punch to the nearest guard's face. He keeled over like a giant oak at the hands of a lumberjack, and Florence and Mandy followed up with a couple of knockout blows to guards two and three. The fourth attempted to run, but Alice kicked his legs away in a scything action, and he cartwheeled in the air then hit the ground with a thud. Alice leapt and landed on his chest with her knees. They bound and gagged the defeated guards and dragged them back into the gloom, out of sight of the facility.

Florence held the hand-drawn map Mandy recreated from memory and ran down the stone steps. They entered the cavernous foyer where a few months earlier, Max Ernst Bauer had boasted Germany's display of almightiness. And what was once an empty, stadium-sized eerie void, was not empty now. A thousand work stations were laid out to a far-off vanishing point. At each station, a mechanical robot arm busied itself building German Spitfires. Then conveyor belts moved the completed fuselages and wings to the paint shop to be blazoned with Nazi swastikas.

'I've never seen a more chilling spectacle in my life,' said Alice. 'They're so advanced. Look at it all.' They stared, awestruck, at the wizardry and ingenuity of the advancement. 'And to think, we've got Mr Prattle and Mr Pickle making speedometers from an old shed in Nottingham.

'Now we know what Winston means about Germany arming up,' said Florence. 'We're years behind.'

'When we blow this place up, we'll level the playing field a bit though,' said Alice.

Florence handed them a Cyanide-labelled canister and a gas mask.

'Is this stuff deadly?' asked Mandy.

'They're filled with cold tea,' said Florence.

They pulled their masks on and stepped from the foyer down the steps onto the workshop floor.

The chief of works; a thin, balding man carrying a clipboard approached them.

He said, 'What are you doing?'

Florence raised her mask, 'We are here to kill rats.' She handed him a document with an official gold seal from Berlin.

He read the details, 'It says here we need to give you access for thirty minutes and not to return to the facility for three hours. Why were we not informed of this?'

'Berlin gives the order, and we spray cyanide to kill the rats.' Florence replaced her mask.

'I'll call this through to Berlin.'

Florence lifted her mask once more, 'Do what you like, but when we start spraying, you'd better be outside, or you'll die with the rats.'

His minor protest ended, 'I'll sound the alarm. The floor will be cleared in five minutes.'

The evacuation horn sounded and hundreds of men and women walked away from their stations. They climbed the stone steps and gathered outside on the gravel. The facility cleared and the robot arms froze redundantly with aircraft parts gripped in their jaws.

'Masks off,' said Florence.

Alice began to limber up. She performed ten fast star jumps and stretched, then took a few practice forehand swings, swishing her racket as if she was on centre court. She volleyed a tennis ball into the far corner of the facility. Florence and Mandy copied Alice, using a variety of serves, backhands and forehand smashes, to cover the vast floor area with hundreds of tennis ball bombs. They put their masks back on and climbed the steps. Outside, Florence approached the chief of works and removed her mask.

She said, 'Thank you for your cooperation. I'll inform Berlin of your efficiency tonight. They'll be impressed.' He held his clipboard to his chest and warmed to the recognition.

Mandy and Alice shut the facility doors and padlocked the handles with a heavy chain.

Florence said, 'We'll be back in three hours to open up the doors. You must ensure everyone stands behind the tree line until we return.'

The chief of works nodded and indicated to his team of supervisors to move the workers to safety.

Florence, Alice and Mandy walked across the gravel and climbed through the hedgerow. They retraced their steps to the Spitfires, where they changed into flying gear and fired the engines to life and positioned themselves for take-off. Once airborne they circled the facility in the light of early dawn. The workforce pointed up to the roaring aircraft from their safe position behind the trees.

'Alice, are you ready to blow this place up?' said Florence.

Alice held a small transmitter in her hand and pressed the red button. 'Done,' she said.

'It's a bit subtle, where's the big bang? I was expecting Germany to blow to buggery,' said Mandy.

'Give it a minute. The tennis balls are talking to each other.'

Then came the explosion.

The innocent tennis balls had the collective destructive power of an earthquake. The ground split open revealing burning German Spitfires and mangled robot arms. The tennis ball bombs continued to explode and shudder the ground. The sky filled with a choking, fireball black smoke. Acres of burning industrial carcass lay exposed and in ruins.

'That worked,' said Florence. 'Let's scram for home.' They flew their Spits flat out across the border into France and headed for the coast.

Over the English Channel, Florence's radio crackled to life.

'Florence, this is Henry, can you hear me?'

'Henry, darling, I can hear you, loud and clear.'

'Operation Feathers a success?'

'Completely.'

'I'm with the Prime Minister at his home in Kent. He's asked me to invite you three flyers to Chartwell this morning.'

'Count us in.'

'Perfect. I'll send the Bentley to Biggin Hill airfield to collect you.'

They landed under a pastel-coloured mackerel sky and steered their Spitfires towards Sir Henry's Bentley at the end of the runway. Rosie, Lizzie and Rags sat on the grass waiting for them.

'I can see our welcoming party,' said Mandy.

They climbed out of the aircraft and crammed into the

Bentley, with Rags in the middle. Mandy regaled them with the story of how they blew up the underground facility. Lizzie drove onto the country lanes and turned to Florence.

'Thank you for all this, I feel at home with you girls, you are my new family.'

'Alice knew you would fit in. She has a nose for it?'

'Nose for what, Florence?' said Alice.

'I was saying; you have a nose for finding the right people, after all, you found me, and Mandy, Lizzie and you gave us Rosie.'

'I have a special gift; it's true,' said Alice.

The girls laughed all the way to Chartwell.

Sir Henry and Percy stood with Winston and watched the sun rise over Chartwell's rose gardens.

'I've been thinking,' said Winston. 'Those five girls are rather special. We should give them their own division outside of SOE and Intelligence. They can tackle the operations we must never talk about.'

'Excellent idea, Prime Minister,' said Sir Henry.

'Henry, you can still call me Winston.'

'Never, Prime Minister, not while there's a war on.'

The Bentley pulled into Chartwell and the girls spilt out, and Rags barked with excitement.

Ivy Amos came out to meet them.

'Sir Henry is on the bottom lawn with the Prime Minister and Percy. I'll bring you some tea and toast in a few minutes.'

Mandy ran off the instant she heard Percy's name, and the others followed and ran through the gardens to the bottom lawn. Naturally, it became a running race; Alice beat them all.

Florence ran to Sir Henry and hugged him, while Mandy smothered Percy with lipstick. Alice shook hands with Winston as the girls gathered around the Prime Minister.

'You're all here,' said Winston.

'We wouldn't want to be anywhere else in the world,' said Mandy, she looped her arm through his. They all strolled through the gardens together.

Winston stopped by the lake. He said, 'For Britain, this is just the beginning. We have a long and brutal war to fight, and I need you girls to take on specific operations which lay ahead. You'll be my private army, my secret battalion, my trusted raiders.'

'We'll take on anything you give us, Winston,' said Florence.

'Quite so, that's why I want you to head up a new division, an all-female group called M.I.S.S: Military Intelligence Special Service.'

Florence said, 'When do we start?'

'You started last night. Your first mission, Operation Feathers, I'm told was a complete success. You've put Germany back a few years and given us a slender, yet fighting chance to catch up.'

Florence said, 'May I suggest the next mission for M.I.S.S.'

'Yes, of course,' said Winston.

'Operation Marmalade: to kill Max Ernst Bauer. Maybe I'll have him accidentally slip in his kitchen at home.'

'You can't go around killing people like that,' said Sir Henry.

'I think you'll find I can,' she said.

'She can,' said Winston. 'There's a war on.'

Ivy Amos laid a tray on the table in the middle of the rose garden with pots of tea and platefuls of toast.

'Oh, lovely,' said Winston. He rubbed his hands together, 'We have plenty to discuss.'

Sir Henry stood back and watched the girls fuss over the Prime Minister. They poured him tea and handed him a slice of toast.

Florence, Alice, Mandy, Rosie and Lizzie joked and

laughed as they sat on the grass in the sunshine listening to Churchill. Rags, as always, was right in the middle.

'We're in good hands, aren't we, Sir Henry?' said Percy.

'Yes, we are, Percy, yes we are.'

COMING NEXT. . .BOOK TWO

Aubrey Hall

Book 2 in the Florence Fairweather series

The one man who can save Britain from extinction is held a prisoner of war in Colditz Castle.

In the summer of 1940, the war is on a knife-edge, and in a world away, a small island has been ravaged with a chemically enhanced strain of the plague: the Black Death. A young boy's body proves to be the only evidence of this unspeakable Nazi experiment.

Archibald Hamilton-Spraggs, Britain's leading virologist, has been taken prisoner in Germany. Florence and her team face impossible odds to break him out and return him to his lab to create an antidote.

Dr Ballack, the Nazi creator of the new strain of the plague has compiled a list of twenty-one names: his Mortifera list, his bearers of death. Dr Ballack's twenty-one Mortifera who are be martyred for England's total annihilation, are preparing to infiltrate London.

Florence's team is on the point of disbandment following

two failed missions, and now faces its biggest test for survival. Only intricate planning and feats of bravery and sacrifice can save Britain from extinction.

Order Aubrey Hall on Amazon.

If you enjoyed reading Milton Park, please consider leaving a review on Amazon. Reviews make such a difference—with your support I can continue writing.

Thank you.

ABOUT THE AUTHOR

Russell grew up on a diet of spy books and Sunday evening family television dramas. A fulfilling and successful career owning restaurants and comedy clubs was followed by an undisclosed stint with GCHQ and NATO.

Get new release updates, and author news by signing up to Russell's newsletter:

RussellCooperBooks.com/subscribe

ACKNOWLEDGMENTS

Thank you to Rachel Henke for her editing, encouragement, and endless cheerleading. She never doubted me, even when I sat staring out of the window. Milton Park would not have made it this far without you.

Thank you to my advanced and lovely, reading circle who brought insight, patience, and knowledge to Milton Park: Anita Davis, Greta and Brian Cooper, Emily Mace, and Pat and Wendy Wilson.

And finally, thank you to Mark Dawson for your vision within the publishing world.

Printed in Great Britain
by Amazon

36071127R00239